GOODBYE TO THE SUN

GOODBYE TO THE SUN

WIND TIDE BOOK I

JONATHAN NEVAIR

Copyright © 2022 by Jonathan Nevair

All rights reserved.

No part of this book may be reproduced in any form or by any electronic or mechanical means, including information storage and retrieval systems, without written permission from the author, except for the use of brief quotations in a book review.

This is a work of fiction. All of the characters, organizations, and events portrayed are products of the author's imagination. Any resemblance to actual persons, living or dead, or actual events is purely coincidental.

Cover art by Zishan Liu

Cover design by Tarzian Book Design

Editing: Susan Floyd, Jonathan Oliver, and Mandy Russell

Published by Cantinool Books

For those who confront the beast, win or lose.

AUTHOR'S NOTE

This novel is inspired by the Greek tragedy, *Antigone*, written by the 5th century BCE dramatist, Sophocles. It is neither an adaptation nor a retelling of the original play. Rather, *Goodbye to the Sun* distills the themes, plot, and characters present in *Antigone* and transports them to a far-future space opera to be born anew. There's no need to be familiar with the Greek play before reading this book.

If you are acquainted with the story of *Antigone* you may happen upon some easter eggs along the way, but you might also end up following literary footprints that disappear in the sand. Either way, I hope this book offers a new set of tracks worth following. Where they lead, only the reader's imagination can tell.

ONE

Personal Narrative (language: Neo-Contex)
Signed: Razor
Found: Cell #7, Targite City Prison
Dated: 3101, Third Span

When people ask me about Keen Draden, I always lie.
     The truth is, I never really knew Keen. He wasn't the kind of person who let you in. There was always a wall. You knew he was pushing against it, trying desperately to break through. In the end, it crumbled around him and bared his soul. And yet, that still doesn't tell you anything about him.

I was angry when we first met. Part of it was a youthful stampede, galloping over anything in my way. But it was also the result of an oppressive world. I was molded from the struggle of hard rock, dry sand, and grit. The desert wind blew through my blood. From an expanse of dunes, I learned to speak arid words.

We were all that way, those of us raised on Kol 2 and not lucky enough to live in the Fins. Out in the sands, life wasn't about tariffs, trade, and eco-tech competition. It was about scrapping and surviving.

We, however, had something that no one could take away: a reason to endure. Our culture, our land, and our subsistence had been stolen from us. And because of that, we sought revenge. The bullseye of my vengeance was Keen Draden.

It's a complicated and costly endeavor, seeking retribution. When I think back on those who didn't make it through our struggle, I'm reminded of the way the credits roll at the end of a beautiful tragedy. The nostalgic music makes it all seem worth it, as if everything was meant to happen. That every life lost was given so that the way things ended made up for it. Maybe that was the case on Kol 2.

But the tide of tragedy wanes. Pity grows tired. Those of us who survived convince ourselves that justice is the expected consequence of sacrifice. That loss is what it takes to receive something worth the suffering and grief.

I don't like to remember Keen that way and I know he wouldn't like others to either. As I said, it's complicated. Keen would have preferred to leave it before the finale when the threads of our lives and those we fought were still tangled in a balled mess.

Maybe that's the best way to describe Keen. His life was in perpetual stasis, mired in the third act. He'd tell you it was bogged down in the middle of Act II, but that would be another lie.

The third act. Just before the end. His wall had crumbled but that gave him the strength to finally accept himself and do what was right even if it was too late to turn the tide.

Keen is gone and I endure, my cold plate of revenge served long ago. This is my story, and therefore his as well, remembered by the one who despised him, resented him, and sought to destroy him.

And I did.

I'll never forgive myself, though I desperately want to. That would be enough for Keen.

TWO

Keen Draden wasn't one for welcoming parties. The feigned hospitality and diplomatic bootlicking did nothing for his overinflated ego. His self-importance was already spilling over the rim onto his exterior. It showed in his ostentatious attire and the casual arrogance with which he chose his words. At this point in his career, a welcoming party only delayed the road to more important (and not, coincidentally, self-indulgent) occupational rewards. Skip the formalities and get straight to business. That had been his motto for over two decades.

The irony of the personal credo wasn't lost on him. The part of the job he hated *was* the job. He was a Notos Ambassador, charged with negotiating energy trade between star systems. There was no avoiding the endless parade of gestural formalities, greeting lines, and obsequious groveling at every stop throughout the Sagittarius Arm.

Today would be no exception. The planetary delegation on Kol 2 were extraordinary hosts. Despite their vicious business acumen and strained relations with other colonies, the lone inhabitants of the Altiron system had a knack for diplomatic flattery. Isolated by over 40 light-years from their nearest neighbors, they were apt to be gracious with guests, especially an official visit from a member of the Sag-Arm

Council. Whether Keen liked it or not, he was heading for an overblown ceremonious arrival.

"Brace for atmospheric re-orientation, Ambassador," a voice announced over the intercom.

Keen picked up on the subtle singsong speech unique to Kol 2's inhabitants. So, the shuttle pilot bringing him out of orbit was local. That was good. It meant familiarity with the planet's turbulent flying conditions.

The pilot's roll of the "r" on "Ambassador" in neo-Contex, the official language of the Sagittarius Arm, lingered in a way unfamiliar to his ears. He'd only heard the formal diction of delegates who'd made the trip to speak at Council Headquarters on Ceron. The diplomats who represented Kol 2 in Garassit, Ceron's capital and the political nexus of the interstellar Garassian empire, spoke with less inflection. Perhaps it was a dialect or reflected a less official, vernacular mode of speech.

He tightened the chest straps against his portly belly. A crease appeared on his ambassadorial robe where the belts rested. Ring-laden fingers gripped the white fabric, pulling it taut in an attempt to erase the fold. It refused to settle.

"For the sake of..."

Keen huffed and gave up, releasing his grip. The wrinkle wasn't worth his time. These backwater zealots were too crude a culture to notice or care. The whole visit was nothing more than a time-consuming performance to please the Council and once again allow a failed diplomatic effort to serve as evidence to justify all-out war.

He pressed the refill button on the armrest, watching as chilled quicksilver bubbled into the cocktail tube from the interior beverage system.

There was a time when my trips mattered.

Keen slammed back the elixir and glanced out the portal as the transfer pod banked into Kol 2's rushing winds. The shuttle's internal stabilizers absorbed the brunt of the turbulence. Little more than a mild vibration ran through his corpulent body in the fluid-shelled passenger seat. He'd been expecting worse.

Carpati technology's finally making a name for itself. About time, considering the investments we've made.

A few miles distant, the wind-shielded landing tarmac on the edge of Targite, Kol 2's capital city, edged into view. Straight ahead to the horizon was nothing but blue-grey arid and barren wasteland. Kol 2's cloudless, rose-hued atmosphere met the rolling dunes in a rich color juxtaposition like an evaporated sea at permanent sunset.

The shuttle completed its turn and five long, sleek buildings intruded on the emptiness out the portal. Their geometrically precise forms ran along the planet's sands like stealthy aquatic creatures breaking an ocean's surface. Inside each, a hidden cornucopia of biodiversity and affluent human culture countered the harsh outside realities of the isolated planet.

Soothed by the quicksilver, Keen's attention shifted from Kol 2's uncouth exterior to thoughts of upcoming delights at Targite's sheltered oasis. He edged up in his seat, eyes following the slender, mirrored structures as they ran into the distance. The legendary Fins. Miles back at their terminuses, colossal circular capture tubes curved upward and forward to face the barrage of raging air during the Wind Tides, channeling the wayward currents to power the city.

Even though Targite was considered a rival energy manufacturer, he couldn't help but admire their innovative and pioneering enviro-synchronization. Without Targitian ingenuity in the early years before the Patent War, eco-technology would still be centuries behind its current innovations. There would be no Third Revival. No Hamut Alliance. No resurrection from the ashes of the last galactic civilization in the Sag Arm. And no Consulate to give him employ.

The vibration ceased as the pod completed its arc into the headwind. Mild turbulence gave way to a subtle sensation of deceleration as the craft fought against the tenacious jet stream. Out of the portal, beyond Targite's five blade-like city ridges, lay nothing save empty ripples of blue-grey dunes.

Kol 2's waterless ocean. Let's hope you don't ruin my visit.

Keen knew accepting the Targitian invitation of an on-site inspection of turbine-capacitors was risky. It wasn't the harsh conditions or wind amidst the planet's vast and largely uninhabited landscape that worried him. It was the Motes.

Council Security assured him the Targitians had driven the rogue nomads back into the Rock Hills enough times that their raids were now few and far between. Their weapon technology was nothing more than a mash-up of flotsam and jetsam from their scavenger lifestyle and no match for the sophistication of Sag-Arm defense systems. Between their crude arsenal and hit-and-run tactics, the Motes were nothing more than anachronistic sand pirates.

Specks of dust refusing to give in to the inevitable... They'll sober to the world or die fighting against it.

Keen didn't care either way. The time of resistance to eco-tech monopolies ended over two decades ago. *His* resistance, along with everyone else who'd fought in the Patent War, had passed as well. Like a rogue wave on a placid sea, that momentary revolutionary fervor rolled out to crash on some other's distant shore.

But it hadn't swept everything away. Like barnacles clinging to submerged timbers, decisions hold fast for decades. By now, in 3049, the tide of war had ebbed long enough for fate to resurface.

Keen's hand went to the milky green medallion on his chest, circling its metallic trim. The fallout of his choice lay hidden inside the jewel's interior chamber.

"Would you like a headshielder, Ambassador?" Stao, Keen's AI assistant, appeared in the aisle holding a transparent circular capsule. The bipedal droid blinked and smiled with its usual overly polite deference. Keen did his best to restrain his annoyance. The AI's demeanor was a hint of the social game to come.

"No, Stao. I've got Eye-Dusters." He held up the two pressure-suction lenses, peering through the parallel slits at the humanoid's face. "Plus, I want to get a taste of Kol 2's wind."

Why? I've no idea... lost youth rising through stubborn waters perhaps.

Keen gazed out the portal. A trail of dust caught his eye, far off to the North. A smile pushed his heavy cheeks upward.

To be back in my youthful glory, a Talon Caster in my hand and nothing but a drink waiting at the end of each day. Before it all went wrong...

"That's a Windcutter, Ambassador," Stao said, leaning down and peering out the portal.

"Mmm," Keen grunted. He was looking forward to stillness, not speed on their arrival. He'd been in hyperspace for a week and on this pod for almost two hours. He expected the upcoming landing to be the roughest part of the flight. His back hurt and though he knew he should move around more, all he wanted was to move less.

Keen hit the refill for more quicksilver and ran a hand through his long, brown curly locks. With dramatic flair, he re-positioned the two cascading manes onto his chest, so they lay equally between his Ambassadorial medallion. The pendant, worn by all Notos diplomats, echoed the green hue of his eyes. His thumb and index finger, a deep olive, arced over his elegant mustache before gliding down his black and gray goatee, fingering the ruby pendant tied at its base.

These backwater wind-eaters better have a decent sense-chamber in-suite. And an impressive stock of ferments, considering the amount of tariff blood they've squeezed out of half the Sag-Arm.

The diplomatic visit to Targite originally on his schedule for Council politics was now a professional layover *en route* to a more important and personal destination. One he dreaded but needed to reach, at least since his conscience made an appearance and broke up the party. Keen had wrangled that beast before. He knew how to break through its guard and send it reeling back into the bottomless depth whence it came. It wasn't last call yet.

If he did his job today, he'd be fine. Get out to a turbine field, look around on-site and make enough of a show pushing to inspect the internal mechanisms (which he and the Council knew the Targitians would refuse), and return to their capital. One obligatory evening inside the city making his way through the diplomatic niceties of a dinner reception and then on to the Nushaba system. He'd wrap up his private matter and be back on the Cruiser for the long ride home to Ceron and the comforts of his residence in the Garassian capital. Guilt-free and ready to resume the party.

The Council would have what it needed to wage war. Keen didn't agree, but he didn't care. This was his last run. He'd retire rich. *Very* rich.

Keen knocked back the quicksilver and returned to the view out the portal. The Windcutter in the distance tacked left to ride the wind's edge, zigzagging its way to the horizon.

"Speed is approximately 162 mph," Stao said. "If it stays on its present course it will reach the closest turbine field in a half day's travel time."

"We're not going on one of those, are we Stao?"

"No, Ambassador. Council Security negotiated... excuse me, *demanded* that the Targitians take you in a Dustcarrier Transport with four Windcutter escorts."

"Good. You're coming too, I hope?" Keen stroked his goatee, still gazing out the portal.

The transport will remind them of my importance.

"If you like, Ambassador. I know that..."

The Windcutter tacked right, its trail of dust mushrooming as it came about in the wind. Keen's eyes squinted as he picked up movement at the horizon.

He leaned closer to the portal. A series of black dots spread into view, moving towards the Windcutter.

They look like mites.

Stao hadn't finished his sentence.

"You know what?" Keen asked. He squinted to focus on the distant specks on the horizon.

Stao didn't respond.

Not mites...

"Stao, are those..."

"Motes," a voice said. It was the same quirky accent he'd heard earlier over the com.

Keen turned. The AI droid was down on its knees, the hair of its head gripped in the hand of a tall person with spiky red hair. Onyx skin and the telltale green and yellow Targite pilot uniform left no doubt that they were from Kol 2.

Keen looked at Stao. The droid's face held a lifeless stare that indicated deactivation.

The pilot raised their other hand and Keen found himself staring down the barrel of a blaster. Red Dunemarks on obsidian knuckles stretched as they tightened their grip. His stomach dropped.

Mote.

"Actually, Ambassador," the pilot said giving him a mocking smile, "you won't be going on that Dustcarrier." Ice blue eyes shot to the empty cocktail tube. "Good, you've had some quicksilver." Their hand released Stao, who crumbled to the floor. They pressed the button, refilling his drink, keeping the blaster aimed at him. "Have another," the pilot said. "You'll need it."

"SO, is this to be abduction and ransom or are you intending to trade me?" Keen pushed his pawn forward on the board. Despite the blaster muzzle pressed against his temple while the Mote locked him into the seat with wrist and ankle bracelets, he wanted the first rhetorical move.

The pilot eyed him and fastened the second ankle to the Carpati seat unit.

It was feigned annoyance. Well performed but still not good enough to be convincing.

"Who's flying by the way?"

The Mote ignored him, rose, and stepped back into the aisle.

Here it comes. The "here's the deal" and what you are and aren't going to do.

"Ok Ambassador, here's the deal."

Keen chuckled at his rhetorical foresight. His ears caught the same unfamiliar pronunciation of "Ambassador" that he had heard earlier. Now he knew why. It *was* a regional dialect; Contex spoken with a Mote accent.

"Are you paying attention?" the Mote asked.

He looked out the portal.

"Hey," they grabbed his curly locks and tugged him in their direction.

"Ouch!" He glared at them. "Mind the hair."

"Listen up, Ambassador. We're going to lay this pod down behind that line of Dustcarriers." A firm hand pivoted his head back towards the portal.

More specks emerged over the horizon. The earlier ones at the head of the regiment had overtaken the Windcutter. Whatever or whoever was heading towards the Turbine Field was either dead or in a predicament similar to his own. The specks raced over the dunes in a triangular pattern, employing standard battalion formation. That meant someone out there or back at the Mote home base had served in the Patent War and was familiar with open planet engagement.

"Once we're down, you're going to get on the com and contact Targite Lead Council."

"Why, exactly?" Keen glanced at the cocktail tube, wishing he could down more quicksilver to steel his nerves. His finger glided in a gentle circle over the fill button. He could push it, but he couldn't drink in the braces unless he asked for help. Better not to, it would bolster his weakness in the predicament. And if the Mote refused, he'd be eyeing chilled quicksilver with a watering mouth. Not his idea of a good time. Worse would be a hot landing with it spilling all over his white robe.

No, this would be a semi-sober negotiation with amateur rebels. His gall would grow from frustration.

So far Keen wasn't impressed. He'd been in their shoes. You needed to load the deck and make sure you held an unbeatable hand to take on a larger, more formidable opponent like the Targitians. The Motes were about to learn a hard truth.

"We're cashing in on your diplomatic value," the imposter pilot said.

"Oh yes? For what in return?"

"You'll know when I tell you." The Mote released his head, rough enough so humiliation and domination were intrinsic in the gesture, and walked back to the cockpit. "And it's 'pilot-té.' You'd think a diplomat would've asked by now."

Keen had been so caught up in the dangerous situation that he neglected to address the Mote. Even in a hostage situation, considering his profession, his neglect bordered on egregious disrespect. It might even come back to bite him later on.

As the pilot, she'd gained access to his chosen self-expression via the pod's flight log when she infiltrated the crew. Normally, individuals declared their gender to one another at first meeting through culturally ubiquitous suffixes attached to their spoken names, through hand signing, or if in a service industry, via a visible icon on a uniform. If someone's gender identity shifted between social interactions, the process was repeated so that they would be addressed and received appropriately. Otherwise, once declared the suffix, hand sign, or icon wasn't re-introduced unless forgotten or if someone accidentally (or intentionally, as did happen in cases of insult) misgendered an individual. If that happened, or if substantial time passed between social encounters, it was re-introduced as a courtesy to ensure respectful and appropriate discourse.

Keen knew the present situation was unorthodox. There was no social precedent and the Mote wasn't likely to offer her name in case he got away. As a Notos ambassador whose occupation centered on formal language and cultural etiquette, and with the conversation getting rigorous, the Mote was right. Social responsibility fell on him to ask.

So much for the first rhetorical move.

The Mote raised her chin and glared at him with ice blue eyes before turning to enter the cockpit. Something about the way she gestured read as performative. That, and the physical bullying. The excessiveness told Keen that this wasn't their usual tactic; it was forced and contrived. The Motes big move against Targite was part bluff, with too much hope resting on a large return for the high-risk play. He decided to risk pushing back to make up lost ground.

"You've got one problem, Mote," Keen said.

She turned halfway through the cockpit door.

He eyed her with performative drama, pushing back. Outwardly he exuded arrogance and defiance, but internally he operated with diplomatic engines running full-steam.

There it was: a flicker of hesitation on her face. It kindled a fire of doubt to his eyes as hot as the spiky hair rising from her head. The Motes didn't spend much time gambling out in the blue dunes.

"You're not holding any cards," he said.

"You mean because you're more interested in your second stop in the Nushaba system?"

Keen's confidence left him, and his eyes went wide.

The Mote smiled and slipped the blaster into her thigh holster. She reached into a pocket of her flight suit and pulled out a gold bounty cube, a smug expression on her face.

So, I'm for sale.

"Well played," he said, buying time. He'd been sold out to a bunch of pathetic rebels?

Keen had been through a buyback once in the past when he was in his diplomatic prime. That time he'd almost been exposed in a corrupt side deal that would've jeopardized his job. It cost him more to retrieve the cube than the profit of the entire ruse. But now? He never expected it a second time so late in his career.

"You want the cube? Get all our prisoners in Targite released."

"Easy," Keen waved a hand. Was that it? Pathetic.

"And we get two seats on the Council."

"In Garassit? Mote representation as part of the Kol 2 delegation?"

She nodded. "Sitting next to the Targitians. Full veto power for anything planet-based."

Keen laughed and shook his head. "You'll never get it. They won't take that deal. I'm not worth it, Mote. Plus, you aren't even in the energy business."

"Then they get the cube, Ambassador. And war, at the fault of diplomatic corruption. I'm sure the Targitians know how to exploit evidence of the clandestine funding you plan on streaming to Heroon. A traitor to your government, supporting anti-monopoly rebels to keep Garassit from squashing a threat to their control of a territorial planet? And Heroon, no less. The core of the rotten apple for the entire history of corruption and abuse of power in the Third Span. Seems like an easy way to rally half the Sag-Arm against Garassia. Not to mention a charge of high treason. You'll be executed under orders from your own fellow Council members, including your parent if I'm not mistaken."

The Mote's got it wrong, this isn't political.

Under the circumstances, Keen couldn't deny it. If he did, he'd be outing a personal scandal far worse and with greater reach and job-related ramifications. He should have known better than to trust his private information to an inter-system banker with ties to the underworld. The only option now was to play the game and negotiate his way to a feasible political offer that would get him out of this mess.

"So, I get the Targitians to open their confinement cells," Keen countered, "and release your rebel kin. How about I set up an exploratory committee to consider reviewing Kol 2 representation on the Council?"

"No deal. We trade you back and you leave with no way to follow up."

"Would you accept an agreement through a third party?"

"On the Council?"

The Mote knew her diplomatic law book, he'd give her that.

"Best scenario, yes. A non-Targitian supplied star system. If not, I get you an invitation and safe passage to plead your case in person."

She fingered the gold cube. Keen watched her long onyx fingers roll the small data box around in her hand. Red Dunemarks swirled like ripples across still water.

"And I get that," Keen eyed the bounty cube since he couldn't point a finger.

Which buys me enough time to get to Heroon. After that, let them come for me.

The Mote put the small square back in her pocket and opened the cockpit door. "Not good enough. We'll take our chances on the value of your treachery instead." She walked through and closed the door.

The pod bucked as the autopilot disengaged. Keen's hold over the situation collapsed. "This day is getting better and better." It didn't make sense. No one is this desperate.

The pod dove at a hard angle. Stao's lifeless body shot up to the ceiling. Keen clenched the armrests and gritted his teeth. Quicksilver rose into his throat.

What's she doing?

The pod shook and rattled, cutting a diagonal path through the raging winds. The Carpati gel-capsule was way past its absorption range. Keen's stomach swirled like rough sea against a rocky shoreline. The quicksilver belched up into his mouth, burning his esophagus.

"A Hamut's ass, what're you doing?" he yelled.

The craft cut across a lesser current, responding to the shift in air temperature by surging upward. Stao slammed to the floor. The quicksilver came back up for an encore.

"Blah!" Keen spewed opaque grey liquor and chunky bits of his breakfast all over his white robe. He wretched after the initial hurl, dry heaving and drooling saliva onto his Ambassadorial medallion.

"Arghh!" He pulled and kicked at the wrist braces and ankle locks. "Fucking Carpati technology!"

The pod leveled off.

He worked to find his center, gazing at the blue horizon line out the portal.

They dove again, banking the other way.

Keen's head whipped around. Stao flew up and across the neighboring seats. The droid stared at him, plastered against the wall, eyes open yet lifeless.

Keen spat post-vomit mouth juice and sneered at the mess that was now his outfit. Perfect. He laughed, dribbling a long strand of saliva.

"What do you think, Stao?" he asked, acquiescing to his state of helplessness and humiliation. "Will the Targitians take my robe for the latest trend in Garassit?"

The pod shot upward. Stao collapsed into the seats across the aisle.

"Hey, Mote!" Keen barked at the cockpit door, fighting the gees. "Check out my new look. It's the latest fashion…"

The pod swirled in a double roll and banked hard right, cutting off his sarcastic banter. A green flash through the portal illuminated the interior as a stream of laser bolts passed to port.

"What the…?"

The pod nosedived.

Why would the Motes be firing?

The craft leveled off and the cockpit door flew open.

"What's going on?" he demanded.

The Mote hurried over and unlatched him.

Something's wrong.

"I need you in the cockpit."

"What?"

She heaved him up and shoved him towards the door.

"Who's shooting at us?"

The Mote pushed him down into the co-pilot seat.

"Here." She withdrew his safety buckle for him and got back into the pilot's chair.

Keen pulled the belt over his vomit-drenched robe. It squished as he tightened it fast. "For the sake of the Arm…"

The Mote hit the thrusters as another burst of green lasers sprang up from defense lines on the edge of Targite's city boundary.

"That's Targite fire." Keen leaned forward over the dashboard to view the ground attack.

She banked down and left to avoid it.

He tracked back towards the horizon. A full-on battle raged on the planet surface between the Mote forces and the defense lines of the city.

"We're almost locked on the air targeting system," a male voice similar in accent to the pilot's but filled with urgency reported over the com. "Get past our line."

"On it," she responded and maneuvered against another barrage.

Keen watched the Mote work the virtual grid. She was a cool customer. A damn good pilot in the chaos. For that he was thankful.

She leaned over him, reaching for a set of controls, and winced as her arm smeared the vomit on his chest.

"You encouraged me to drink more," he said in his defense.

A single stick with finger grips popped up on the dashboard in front of him.

"I need you on this," she nodded at the handle and pulled out a set of glasses from an overhead compartment. "Put these on – use the internal crosshairs. Look and lock with the trigger. The system will stay tracked. Hit the thumb button and it'll fire. Got it?"

"You want me to fire on the Targitians?"

"You want to live?" she said, working the pod's controls to maneuver in the heavy winds while dodging enemy lasers shots.

"Don't care that much, either way, Mote."

Keen folded his arms on his chest and immediately regretted it.

Vomit seeped into his sleeves. It took all his diplomatic skills to keep his expression obstinate.

The Mote glanced over. He shot her a defiant look. Winning this one was no contest.

She was struggling with the controls, losing her concentration in the firefight.

"You know what I want," he said.

Her nostrils flared. She tightened her grip on the yoke, slamming the pod to port. Keen's arms went wide, gripping the dashboard instinctually. He quickly re-folded them.

She reached in her pocket and slammed the gold cube into his stomach, splattering bits of vomit all over the dashboard. "Typical politician."

Keen took the cube and dropped it into a slit in his robe.

"Good enough, Ambassador?"

"That'll do, thank you."

Laser fire whizzed past the pod. Keen peered through the eye-guidance lenses. Another set of fighters launched from the shielded landing tarmac at the north end of the city. He locked on one and fired, taking it out before the craft rose more than a few hundred feet off the ground.

"Not bad," she said sending them into an evasive roll and pitch, working a path towards the safety of the Mote defenses.

"Not my first shit storm, Mote."

She glared at him. Keen interpreted it as equal parts contempt and surprise.

"I don't get this. They should be trying to protect me," he said while struggling to take out another fighter. The remaining Targitian attack pods rose out of their low altitude launch zone and fired their thrusters up to full. Now they'd be more crafty and evasive.

"Don't care that much, either way, Ambassador," she said.

"Who... you?"

"The Targitians. It only took them about a minute to decide after I sent them the hostage demands."

She was right. How easily the life of an Ambassador is cast aside for the greater politic shouldn't have surprised him.

Keen locked on another fighter and took out its wing, sending it hurtling towards the surface of Kol 2.

"Seems they took this as an opportunity to get rid of two enemies," she said.

"I'm not the enemy, I'm an Ambassador. They're business rivals." That was stretching the truth, but that's what he did for a living. It came naturally, even under pressure.

So, the Targitians intended to make him a casualty of a Mote ambush? It was a clever ruse. A Council Ambassador taken out by anti-monopoly rebels, and the bloodline of the High Council Chair, no less. That would put a serious dent in the Council's war agenda and give the Targitians the excuse needed to get past the Diasporic Clause. At minimum, it would delay any political action by the Garassian Council and give the Targitians the ability to take care of their Mote problem once and for all.

And where did this leave him?

A large explosion at the edge of the city raised a blazing smoke plume.

"Air defenses out," the voice from earlier yelled over the com. "Should have a lane if we can hold off those fighters. Get back here, this thing is blown. They're sending counters. We have to..."

The Mote speaking from the ground assault never got to finish the sentence. Five streams of orange flame ripped through the Mote line of Dustcarriers like a massive beast swiping a claw across flesh. It devastated the arrow formation of the rebel force.

The Mote's blue eyes went wide in horror. "Hoti!" Her face erupted in desperation. "No!"

Green lasers passed close to the cockpit window.

"To starboard, watch out!" Keen lunged for the controls.

The back half of the pod whiplashed as the laser struck. He slammed against the side of the seat. Warning lights flashed and alarms sounded. The Mote snapped back and worked the controls. The pod bucked and started losing power.

"We're hit! I have to get us below the Wind Tide or..."

"Or what?"

"We'll tear apart." She struggled with what was left of the pod's flight system. Electrical smoke wafted into the cockpit.

Keen watched the altimeter run down. The pod jounced and let out a mechanical belch. All the dashboard lights flickered then went out. An eerie quiet intruded the cockpit.

"No power," she said, her voice stuttering against the turbulence of the Wind Tide's current. "Switching to flaps." The Mote reached down and pulled out the foot pedals and tucked her feet inside the toe slips. She wiped the sweat dripping from her forehead and gripped the hand controls.

"We're screwed, aren't we?" Keen asked.

"Been screwed my whole life. This is only new to you."

Her icy eyes shone with cold fire; they burned cooler than when she'd first restrained him yet were more intense with anger. Or was it fear? Keen opened his mouth to respond but found himself at a loss for words. That was a first.

He took off the glasses, hands rattling from the jet stream, and watched as they passed the five blazing fire lines where the Mote ambush had been demolished. Ahead was nothing but blue sand.

"I'm going to ride the bottom edge of the current as long as I can to give us some distance," she said. "In case we make it."

"Make it where?"

"The dunes."

Keen's eyes went to the Mote's hands wrapped around the pod's controls. The red Dunemark letters on her onyx knuckles, the telltale signature of the Motes, took on a potent mystery.

"What do they say?"

"Huh?" The Mote's head didn't turn.

"The Dunemarks on your hands."

"Fuck off," she said jerking her legs back and forth, working to stabilize the injured craft.

Keen counted the letters in his head. It fit, but that would be too ironic.

"No, seriously. What do they say?"

The turbulence halted.

"We're under the wind current," she said. "That's as far as I could get us."

Keen scanned the dune landscape in all directions. "How long to the nearest Turbine Field?"

"You're on your own if we make it."

"What about holding me ransom?"

"You're worthless now, Ambassador." A smirk edged onto her face, like a card player placing an unbeatable hand down on a gambling table in front of a large pot. "Welcome to *my* world."

She was right. They were screwed. He had to admire her honesty in the face of it. It was more than he could muster and that stung.

Even if they did survive the crash, where would that leave him? The Targitians would send a crew out but after what went down wouldn't they kill him? Maybe he'd make it and she wouldn't. He might be able to bargain with the Targitians. If the Mote was badly injured he could finish the job before then. What did he owe her? He was in this situation because of what she did. Heck, she *deserved* it.

It had been over twenty-five years since he'd killed someone. Could he still do it?

And what do those Dunemarks say?

"We're going down, hold on," she said.

The blue sands neared. Altiron's orb of white light shone in the rose-tinted sky.

Keen's robe was a hot mess. How perfect. This was exactly the way he should be at the end.

"Brace for impact," she said.

The words seeped into his ears like honey rolling from a jar. Time slowed and stretched, his mind graciously opening space for a final mortal reflection.

So, this was it. His hand went to the medallion on his chest, clasping it with regret. Out of the cockpit window, a high dune ridge loomed.

"Rise Kol 2," the Mote whispered.

THREE

We made it. How could we not with me behind the controls? But we went down hard.

This wasn't the end for Keen. Not yet. We're just getting started, the two of us. But this was where it all shifted. His life ended then and there in that pod. I mean his life of lies. Don't get me wrong; he kept on lying both to himself and others, including me. It took a lot longer for that to stop. But it was the bookend for the personal lying, the one eating away at him. Ironic, isn't it? By throwing death in his face I gave him the means to move past it. For years, I was resentful. Today, I'm grateful to have done it.

As for me, I was busy flying. Doing what I could to survive long enough to come to terms with the loss of my younger sibling and all the others who burned in the fire of battle. I was the last person to hear Hoti-ti's voice over the com as the flames consumed him. Amidst the chaos in those final seconds, I sensed a shift in the seat next to me. Keen and I were thrown together in the grip of death. That does something to you. Whether you want it to or not, it strips away the bullshit. All the lines in the sand that separated us were washed smooth by the passing wave of imminent demise. The truth is, I was scared, and I thought he was too. Maybe he was. That far into the act, what would be the point?

What I'm not afraid to admit now is that I needed to feel connected. And even though Keen was part of the machine responsible for the suffering and death of my people, I was thankful he was in the seat next to me. I had the upper hand then, as I reminded him on more than one occasion. I looked good going down in that stolen flight suit. He was a vomit-drenched, ostentatious mess.

As for what happened next, Keen was full of surprises. Not the kind you would hope for or expect.

When I came to, I found Keen dismantling the quicksilver tank in what was left of the aft section of the pod. Something in his eyes when I stumbled back through the wreckage told me it wasn't because he was thirsty. He couldn't have been thinking straight because my blaster was still on my hip. I remember that conversation like it was yesterday. That was the beginning of Keen and me.

FOUR

"**D**rink up."

Keen swung around, startled by the voice.

Shit.

Something in the way the Mote eyed him told him she knew he was scheming. He'd woken in the cockpit and debated whether to kill her, decided he would, but then hesitated.

He'd lost his old nerve. A couple shots of quicksilver would put him right back in the fighting spirit, back in his Legion reds. The merciless and violent fury of his youth would bubble to the surface (and give his conscience a swift kick on the way up for good measure) and make easy prey of the Mote.

She raised the blaster and aimed it at him. His upper hand crashed and burned, joining the rest of the surrounding debris.

Stayed too long at the bar… story of my life.

"Go ahead, Mote." Keen cut the line on the quicksilver tubing system against the edge of the tank and let it stream into his mouth. He plopped down onto the blue sand, legs splayed wide, leaning against the wreckage of the pod shell. Quicksilver ran down his throat. Some dribbled down his chin to his robe, mixing with vomit and blood where he'd been cut open in the crash.

"You're a pathetic mess," she said.

"Thank you." Keen pinched the tube between his lips and spread his arms wide in a gesture of mock appreciation.

The Mote walked away.

"What do you want?" He spoke the words out of the corner of his mouth, between sips on the tube.

She halted and turned to face him. "From you? Nothing. You can't offer me or my people anything now."

"Then shoot me."

The Mote's grip tightened on the blaster. She aimed it at his face. The Dunemarks stretched, pulling on the taught onyx skin of her knuckles.

She wasn't going to do it. He still had enough of his Legion days left in him to sense it, even through the haze of the quicksilver. What his diplomatic mind couldn't unravel was why. She hadn't lost any nerve that was for sure. His mouth pulled on the tube, sucking in more liquid, taunting her.

"What do you want?" he repeated.

"I told you, Dreck. Nothing."

"What's a Dreck?"

She didn't answer.

"Not from me. You're a Mote. What do you *want*?"

"If you can't figure out what we want, you don't deserve to know."

"Oh, I think I do know," Keen said. "But I'll take my chances and wait for the Targitians. I'm pretty sure I can buy my way out of this and get off this sandpit of a planet. My next stop is Heroon."

As much as I dread it.

The Mote shook her head. "You're wrong on that one, Ambassador. The Wind Tide will be here by nightfall. The Targitians won't risk coming out until after it passes. By then you and this whole wreckage will be buried deep in the dust."

Keen stopped sucking on the tube. He hadn't considered the Tides.

"You'll suffocate in the winds before your body disappears, blanketed by the blowing sands. The Targitians don't dig up the dead, either. Never have. It's against their beliefs. They'll make sure you've kicked it with an overhead flyby scan and then come after my people. After today, they'll do their best to wipe us out for good."

"That's on you, not me," Keen said. "I didn't ask to be abducted. You screwed that up."

The tank of quicksilver next to him exploded.

"No! Why?"

The Mote holstered the blaster and walked away through the wreckage.

Time to play the ace.

"Who's your tactician?"

She stopped.

"Arrow formation," Keen said. "Open planetary engagement. It would've worked but you sent the first wave too soon and without a flank for diversion. Couldn't draw off enough fire to get the second round in deep enough. That's a death wish. Let me guess, someone's local pride overrode your Patent War veteran on that one?"

The Mote spun around. Keen read surprise at his astute critique of military strategy on her face.

"You're going to need more than a rebel ground force if you want to take down Targite."

"So, this is a negotiation?"

"That's my job, Mote." Keen sipped the tube, smirking and forgetting it now led to nothing but dead air. His gloating halted as he glanced at the smoking, ruined tank next to him.

"I desire to reach Heroon," he said, spitting the tube onto the blue sand between his legs. "Get me there and I can put you in touch with the right people who can provide you with what you need to give the Targitians a run for their money."

"Your 'desire'? Why?"

"It's personal."

She shook her head. "Not good enough."

"Then leave me to the Tide… or shoot me."

The Mote fingered the blaster holstered on her thigh.

Can't even the sand spirits on this forsaken planet have mercy on me?

"Look, Mote… if you were able to reach my business associate at the Ortor jump hub and infiltrate an Interstellar Cruiser, and hijack a transfer pod undetected, I'm sure you can get me off the planet."

It was time to push. The money was gone from his hands, either to bribe the Targitians if by some miracle they attempted to get out here before the Tide, or to fund a rebel mercenary resistance in return for safe passage off this godforsaken planet. He could skimp on the latter and still have enough left from his years of double-dealing to do what he needed to once he reached Heroon.

"A larger militia running flank diversions and air support to allow infiltration of the main systems. That's what you lacked today. I can't speak to holding the city or for how long. That's beyond our terms and not my problem."

The Mote's spiky red hair was like a vibrant fire rising from her scalp. Keen sensed that inside, deep within a subconscious cave, the origin of her anger and fury was sourced.

"Let me guess," she said. "This is a convenient way for Garassit to take care of a business rival? And get you out of a charge of treason?"

"I *am* an ambassador." Keen splayed his arms wide, mockingly. Even if the plan was a partial lie, the fact that it would offer the potential, at minimum, for civil war on Kol 2, and at best a new regime in need of guidance and trade agreements couldn't make for a better smokescreen. "Safe passage off Kol 2," he said. "Do we have a deal?"

The Mote walked off through the wreckage.

Let's kindle that fire.

"Rise Kol 2," Keen muttered.

A laser shot hit the sand between his legs. Blue dust sprayed his robe and face, covering him in blue-grey powder. The Mote's steel-blue eyes burned in fury down the barrel of the blaster.

He spat sand from his mouth.

"If you ever repeat those words, they'll be your last." She strode towards him and pushed the blaster against his forehead. "Understand?"

Impressive. Well disciplined. Coolheaded yet vicious.

Keen raised his hands in a defensive gesture.

"You understand? Answer me!" She pushed the muzzle tighter against his forehead.

His head tilted back, and their eyes met. Twenty-five years ago, he would've rolled the dice and gone for her legs with a seated scissor kick, hoping for a takedown and disarm. Today? He didn't have the will or the energy.

"Yes, I understand."

The Mote holstered the blaster and walked away.

"Does that mean we have a deal?" he asked.

"You want to wait for the Wind Tide to kill you, be my guest." The Mote splayed her arms wide, mocking his earlier gesture as she strode away. She rounded a corner at the broken pod's shell and disappeared from view.

"I'll take that as a yes," he whispered to himself.

Even with a belly full of quicksilver, the rush of the confrontation was surging to his extremities. He had to admit, this was more exciting than two decades of extravagance and luxury.

"Quite the day."

His hands searched inside his robe pocket. His fingers touched the precise edges of the gold cube. Below it, deeper down, the rounded forms of The Eye-Dusters pressed into his thigh. He pulled them out. Not broken. Keen gazed around the wreckage. Stao's bust and one arm lay a short way off on the blue sand, wires and synthetic muscle jaggedly torn where the droid had been ripped apart. If not for the lower half of the AI's body lying nearby, they would have appeared to be buried to the neck.

"Well, Stao, this is farewell," Keen said, rising gingerly. He stabilized his balance with a hand on the wall of the wreckage, unsure if it was the crash or the last of the quicksilver making him dizzy.

He pushed the two Eye-Dusters onto his face and walked out into the rosy sunlight.

The Mote was gathering her things.

"What's your name?"

The Mote strode by him and snatched up a gear bag. She hoisted it over her shoulder and made towards the first dune leading away from the wreckage.

"Razor-té," she said without turning, adding the gender suffix as insult for his earlier ignorance.

"No, I mean your actual name," he said to her back. "You must've been given a proper name?"

"Must have," she said, still walking.

Keen cocked his head, confused about being made a victim of sarcasm.

"This is going to be fun," he said, loud enough that her ears would catch it. She made no indication she'd heard.

Smoke plumed from the wreckage of the shuttle pod. Debris lay scattered about the blue sand. Razor was walking at a clip, halfway up the first dune.

"Hey, will you slow down?" Keen started off, holding his robe at the waist and hurrying to keep up. "Just wait a moment, will you?" He scurried up the slope, struggling with the heat and his out-of-shape condition.

"So, you don't know it?" he added, panting.

"Know what?" She kept walking.

"Your real name."

"Must not." She stopped at the crest of the first dune. Backlit by Altiron's intense light against the cloudless red sky, she appeared statuesque.

"Do they call you Razor because of your sharp wit?" Amused, he struggled with the last few steps to the top. His feet sank into the sand, sending portions of the soft ridge cascading down behind him. He raised his head to the view. Blue dunes and red sky ran to the horizon.

"No," she said and walked down the other side.

So much for the sociability of Motes.

"So why then?" he yelled down at her.

She ignored him, taking easy wide strides, slide-stepping down the dune.

"Hello? Are we having a conversation here?" Keen waited at the top, expecting her to stop. "People *answer* when an ambassador questions them."

Razor rotated to face him as she made her way up the next ridge, walking backward. "You don't want to know, *Ambassador*," she yelled back. "Trust me."

"Trust you," Keen grumbled and made his way down the dune. He clambered up the next rise, pawing at the blue sand as he lumbered upward. Sweat ran down his face. He was struggling for the first time in a *long* time. Ironically, it reminded him of his early days, that Talon Caster in his hand.

Be careful what you wish for, old fool...

Keen struggled with the last few steps to the dune's crest.

"Two hours and we can shelter at that spot." Razor pointed to a distant bluff, the first piece of solid rock to enter their view. "If we hustle, we'll make it before the next Wind Tide."

He shielded his Eye-Dusters with his hand and gazed at the outcropping. It swayed in a blurry mirage.

"I have a name, you know," he said.

She cracked a wry smile. "Do you now? I thought you preferred titles?"

"You don't know me," Keen said, lowering his hand and staring out over the blue-grey dunes. "Any more than I know you."

"You're right." She shoved a canteen into his belly.

He winced and eyed her.

"Let's keep it that way," she said and gave him a quick 'fuck you' smile.

Keen was too thirsty to be insulted. He took a long pull of water. Out of the corner of his eye, he caught her examining his exposed forearm where the robe slipped back.

Her smirk vanished, replaced by surprise.

"As I said," he handed back the canteen. "You don't know me." He wiped his face with a stained sleeve and stepped down the next dune.

FIVE

I remember when Keen drank from the canteen that day. The Delta Sagittarii Legion tattoo on his arm told me two things. One was that I needed to be careful and not underestimate him. He'd been a killer. Lucky for me, something had stayed his hand when he first came to in the cockpit after we crashed in the dunes. Whatever it was, it drew him away and confirmed my suspicion of what he was up to, raiding the quicksilver tank in the wreckage. Looking back now, encouraging him to drink before the botched abduction might have been a bad idea. I got lucky on that one, considering what followed on later occasions when Keen was under the influence. How ironic that by blasting the quicksilver tank I'd saved his life, and possibly mine.

Second, the insignia of the DS Legion on his arm made my hatred blossom. It should have caused us to understand one another, to find common ground as allies. Instead, it spoke of corruption. Keen wasn't just a cog in the post-Patent War machine. He was a hypocritical, two-faced traitor. A flipper. Whatever momentary empathy I felt in the cockpit as we plunged towards the dunes vanished. I began stacking bricks up in the wall between us. But this wasn't Keen's wall. It was mine. I shut out what I didn't want to see, what I couldn't stand to have in my field of vision.

My moral compass was well oiled in those days, it functioned without fail. The needle, a laser, burning through anything in its path. On the straight and narrow, that was me. The twin suns Delta Sagittarii might be the centaur's hand in the constellation that holds the bow steady, to 'aim true' (that was the DS Legion slogan), but mine was the single bright star Nunki, the arrow's vane. *That* didn't bend or falter.

I anticipated the satisfaction of watching an ambassador from Garassia get fed to the wolves. My Mote brethren in the Rock Hills, especially Crest-ti, would not take the particulars of Keen's situation lightly. Crest was a stickler for details. All humans, he'd said more than once at a trial, are judged not by what they do for others, but what they've done to themselves.

Keen was a traitor, a greedy and selfish bastard who sold out his fellow legionnaires and waved away the cause of shared justice for a life of comfort and decadence. What he'd gained for himself came at the expense and exploitation of entire worlds. Not just Kol 2. Eleven other star systems in the Sag-Arm were at the mercy of the patents, all suffering and dying for nothing more than the pleasures and comforts of those on the Garassian Council, their benefactors, and their partners throughout the Sag Arm. Under the Alliance enforced by the Hamut space pirates, rewards trickled down the line and outward from Ceron to all who swallowed their morality to join in the ruse. Keen was at the top of that pyramid, reaping the harvest sowed by others.

Most hated by me were my local oppressors, the Targitians. Those spiritual zealots used nothing more than a bogus prophecy to justify their strict control and prudent distribution of the highest, advanced form of energy known to human civilization.

Let Keen get a taste of what it's like to live on a planet where you can't generate your own cells outside the Fins. Let him learn of the other star systems where planets held untapped energy while enviro-synchronization technology was secure in the hands of heartless, imperialist monopolies. Where you have to buy energy through submission and servitude. Where resistance is futile, with Hamuts patrolling and enforcing the patents. Defiance meant only one thing: extinction.

Unless you were a Mote.

Our refusal may not have caused our eradication but what

happened to us was a subtle and injurious tragedy. The Targitians were too wrapped up in their convoluted dogma to realize their unique brand of spiritual tolerance was craftily at work as perhaps the most deviant form of hegemony in the Sag-Arm. Their religious practice was a compassionate blade that loved you as it cut your heart open. We became outcasts on our own world, a desperate and diasporic resistance, the last holdout against the end.

Keen was supposed to be our bargaining chip to change that, but it failed. That was my fault and that of Crest and the others who planned the assault. By the time Keen and I crashed in the dunes, it didn't matter who was to blame. The damage was done.

My plan after our attack debacle was to make an example of Keen. Let him take a bite of my life and taste the struggle. And it would hurt because we'd hurt, and Keen had been responsible for his part in what became the suffering world in which my people lived. He was nothing more than a typical piece of Garassit shit to me.

No, that isn't quite fair. That's the old Razor speaking, snaking its way back from the grave where that dream lies buried, blown under by Kol 2's indifferent sands. That Razor wanted justice served and sought payback. Life was simpler back then, a simple matter of sides. I wanted to bear witness to the reaping of what was sowed. That was the truth *then*, but it isn't the truth now. That truth was a lost idealist promise, a vision of a much different world and a different future.

How ironic you are, truth. You're a shapeshifter who swindles knowledge. But I'm wise to you.

Disrobed and laid bare before me, I must acknowledge the truth in those two little fingers clasping a feather (that was the DS insignia branded onto all legionnaires); they complicated everything.

Keen had fought for the cause, our cause, my cause. What had sent him to the Patent War? And Heroon at that... where things were rough, to say the least. Only those who volunteered got shipped out to that swamp-infested rat nest where the fighting was toughest and most desperate. The DS are legend incarnate, the ones the Patent Force grunts used in tales to inspire loyalty, discipline, and the code of honor. The ones my elders called forth in the Rock Hills amidst flickering firelight in the deep hours of the night to keep morale up in the face of Targitian hegemony.

Keen survived the Legion life. By what means, valor and luck? It was hard to believe. Had he already become an immoral and narcissistic snake, weaseling his way through that mess of a war? Or did an earlier Keen exist that fell, cut by a blade that loved him?

Despite my misgivings, the new wall I was fashioning didn't shield me then or in the time that followed. It was like trying to breathe in the face of the Wind Tide by putting your back to its current. Two lives changed out in the vast blue dunes that day; one for the better and one for the worse. That's why I said it was the start of Keen and me.

It was the day I began lying to myself.

SIX

"There's wind," Keen said, stumbling in the growing dark. A current pushed gently against his back, billowing his sweat-soaked robe. The voice of Kol 2 whispered, fluttering the white fabric in the silent desert evening. He'd noticed it at the top of the last sand ridge. It was only a wafting breeze, no more than a whisper. Between the fall and rise of the next dune, it rose to a soft but constant nudging on his backside. The air was almost polite, a welcomed interruption in the otherwise dry and hot barren twilight.

Unless he'd gotten their directional bearing mixed up, something didn't make sense. The Wind Tides blew towards Targite across the open dunes, not away from it. It should be at his face.

The bluff was close. Altiron fell below the horizon and the glowing remains of a rose sunset dissolved into darkness. In all directions, the vast desert spread like a night sea. Stars dappled the crepuscular sky. Their glimmer grew denser as Keen arced his head up and back, away from the fading light. He recognized the Perseus constellation, observable from most solar systems in the Sag-Arm, and the Pistol Star. It glittered to his right, low to the horizon, its size and orange twinkle unmistakable. Keen tracked left, about halfway up from where the sand met sky. 700 light-years away, orbiting snugly around Nushaba, was Heroon.

Beyond the visible stellar curtain lay the great unknown. Keen's ancestors were on those vessels, drifting on a galactic current in uncharted space. A fleet of ships, its passengers in cryostasis, held the promise of answers to questions posed by curious, long-dead innovators. The exploratory armada was the Second Span's last principal feat before civilization in the Arm collapsed into ruin and near extinction. Now, with the Third Span in full bloom, a stable society had returned and demonstrated the potential of species endurance. If life, human or otherwise, existed elsewhere in the galaxy perhaps the armada would find it.

Keen knew the odds. The chances of encountering anyone in the vast emptiness and returning eons hence to a still-living world were as small as the significance of humanity to the scale of the cosmos itself.

He lowered his head back to the liminal landscape of rolling dunes. Razor was a shadowy silhouette, standing on the last rise before the looming rock outcropping.

Keen trudged up the slope.

"There's wind," he repeated when he reached her.

"It's the drawback. The front will be here soon. Keep moving."

"Give me a minute." He bent over panting, his hands on his knees.

"We stop, we die. The fissure is on the far side of the bluff." She moved on without waiting for him.

"Sake of the Arm," he said, gasping for breath. "I'm too tired."

Keen dropped to the sand, legs resting on the downward side of the dune, and wiped his face with a sleeve. Ahead, in the twilight, the bluff's jagged outline loomed. A second, higher ledge appeared behind it, blocking out the last glow of Altiron's sunset. The rock structure was more extensive than he'd first realized. Something about that didn't make sense unless he'd been fooled earlier in the daylight by a heat mirage.

The drawback breeze faltered. Keen's robe fluttered about, intruding on the desert silence. The hair tingled on the back of his neck. If he'd been on Heroon with its dense undergrowth, he would've sworn an unseen presence was about. His head swung around, seeking a source for the anxiety. In all directions lay nothing but dunes in the night.

His robe slammed back, pushing hard against the front of his body. The wind reversed. Like a fast-moving object colliding with a wall it jolted him back to attention. A distant rumbling filled his ears.

Tide wave.

He was up and scrambling down the last dune, his mind processing the reality before him. What was he thinking? That second 'ledge' wasn't rock. Tide waves were the signature feature of the winds on Kol 2. One led each tidal cycle, drawing Kolgite dust from the drawback up into the air, forming a swell that rose high up into the atmosphere until the gathered particles of sand pulled it down through gravity and it broke, crashing in a gale of unimaginable strength.

The wave's force had never been measured. No equipment could yet withstand its titanic might. Targite was located just beyond the breakpoint, with an added measure of distance for insurance. The city was safe from its devastating impact but close enough to the danger zone to harvest the most powerful gusts of each Wind Tide that followed in its wake.

Keen might not have cared about living all that much, but his instincts defied him before the sublime terror. He made flight in haste and was down the last dune and crossing the open ground to the bluff. Razor's faint silhouette rounded the bend on the rock's far side. The gusts blowing towards him intensified and grew hot.

He remembered why his brain made him run. A front wave wasn't just wind. It was heat, far beyond what a human body could withstand. No one knew which way you died when consumed in the turbulent swell. Either way, he wasn't interested in finding out.

The approaching storm roared. A shrill whining grew to a near deafening pitch. His Eye-Dusters shielded his eyes against the blowing sand but if he didn't move fast, he would lose his bearing in the growing darkness. The bluff's corner was ahead.

He ran faster than he realized, the looming terror rising inside his chest. His mind flashed back to Heroon, a memory of fleeing an ambush that killed most of his platoon. The mental recall sent a high-voltage charge through his unfit and underworked limbs. Survival mode kicked in, pushing his body to its limit. Would it be enough? It wasn't on Heroon. Even with that surge of combat adrenaline on the tropical planet, he hadn't escaped his attackers. That was where it all went wrong in his life.

Not this time. He was either going to make it or this was going to be the end.

He rounded the corner and a wall of wind slammed him into the side of the rock face. His head and elbow crashed against jagged stone. Clinking metal echoed through the swirling gale. He was down on the ground, disoriented from the blow to his head. Razor's voice was calling, but he couldn't comprehend what she was saying.

Move, Draden. Or die. Your choice.

His hand went to the medallion around his neck. It touched only skin.

Razor's screams whirled around him like a conjured spirit. Where was the pendant? Without it, nothing was left. There was no reason to live.

Sand pelted the rock face and spat back, barraging him into blindness. He groped his hands in wide arcs, the Eye-Dusters useless in the intensity of the sandstorm.

A hand grabbed his robe, pulling him.

"No!" He screamed over the howling gale, resisting. His palm made a wide arc across the ground. It crossed nothing but rock and sand.

A second hand wrapped around his neck, long fingers holding him tight. Keen's mind knew those hands. Red Dunemarks on onyx knuckles.

Razor dragged him away. He fought her, seeking blindly across the ground.

Her strength overpowered him, and he slid away amidst the violence of the surging winds. A gust pushed open a seam in the circling river of sand. Razor's red hair appeared against the bluff wall. Beyond her fiery spikes was nothing but darkness, the sky and stars shut out by a blanket of blue dust and wind. The backdraft was almost too strong to resist as the swell curved into a barrel overhead.

"Get up," she screamed.

Keen slid across the ground, kicking his heels to dig in and get to his feet. He slipped and braced himself with a palm. It hit metal. The medallion! His hand closed on it.

"It's over us," Razor yelled. Keen was up and groping in sand-swirling darkness, his injured arm dragging its fingers against the rock face as they hurried forward.

"Inside," she said, as the horror revealed its full terror. Orange and red static electricity sparked against the cliffs as the heat arrived, the flashes illuminating a narrow entrance and the doom enveloping them overhead. Razor shoved him into the pitch void.

He tumbled over hard rock and down an abyss. And couldn't have been happier about it.

Keen rolled onto the sand at the bottom of a cavern. Razor crashed into his backside.

He recovered and threw off the Eye-Dusters. The hand that clasped the medallion was empty.

"Where is it?" His head went side to side, searching, as his eyes adjusted to the dark. The walls of the cave shuddered and small rocks and dust fell from above.

"Cover your head!" Razor yelled over the roar above them.

The cavern grumbled, resisting the fury passing overhead.

Keen's eyes caught a glint of gold in the dark. He lunged and snatched the chain as a rock fell, narrowly avoiding smashing the medallion. He wrapped his hands around his head, kneeling into a ball in his portly frame.

"How long until it passes?"

As if in answer, the cavern settled. A steady howl, like a battalion of ghosts, sang above them. The regimental chorus echoed down the narrow passageway they'd fallen through. The wave passed. Now followed the Tide.

Keen lowered his arms from his head and collapsed onto his back. His labored breathing bounced off the walls, competing with the Tide's howling outside the protection of the small cavern. He leaned his head to the side and glanced over at Razor. She sat, panting in the near darkness, arms hugging her knees.

"Are we safe?"

She didn't respond. Her rapid exhalations echoed off the cavern walls.

"Are you hurt?"

The Mote rose, ignoring him.

Her shadowy form unslung the gear bag from her back and reached inside. She rotated to face him, her eyes like twin stars glimmering in an otherwise pitch night sky. Still, she didn't respond.

He didn't know what else to say. Or do. Luckily, the darkness of the cave hid the shame on his face. He felt like a useless burden.

Razor withdrew a thick metallic ring and waved it through the air. It flickered into life, illuminating the interior. A bare cavern some fifty feet wide in a rough circle surrounded them. On the far wall, the same Dunemarks on Razor's knuckles glowed on the rock face. The precision of the carved letters was pronounced against the otherwise jagged and unpredictable stone surface.

A dark recess adjacent to the Dunemarks led to another passage running down deeper into the bluff's internal structure.

Razor's face was covered in sweaty blue dust. In the luminous light cast by the glow ring, perspiration dripped down in slow and haunting lamentations, streaking her head and neck.

"What is that?" She nodded at his hand. Her words bounced off the rock ceiling, echoing against the Tide's ghoulish howl.

"Nothing."

She walked to him, her blue eyes wide and intense. "You lie."

He glared at up her. "It's none of your business."

"It's my business when you choose a piece of jewelry over your life when my life is also on the line."

He fumbled up into a seated position, struggling with his injured arm. With a trembling hand, he shoved the pendant into his robe pocket. "It's an ambassadorial medallion. Without it, I'm no one."

"Then guard it well. You're only here because you're *someone*. You're an ambassador with strings to pull. We have a deal."

"Yeah, I know." Keen collapsed back onto the ground and closed his eyes, listening to the Tide raging above them. The bluff's hollowed interior embraced them like a sheltering womb. All the terror of the outside world was so close, yet kept at bay by a giant petrified body, a natural rock formation whose belly rested under the sands.

Keen raised his good arm, hand extended. "Give me some water."

"You had your share and more already."

He opened his eyes and watched her walk away, the light ring grasped in her hand. She used it to guide her way to the opposite side where the darkened opening led further down into the subterranean shelter.

At least he would get to sleep tonight. The sandy floor was as welcoming as the bed that had most likely been made for him back in Targite.

"Don't get comfortable," she said from the far side of the cavern. "We're not staying."

———

"HOW DEEP DOES THIS GO?" Keen asked.

They'd been descending a series of narrow passageways for fifteen minutes. Taking tentative steps with each foot, he did his best to follow the light cast by Razor's ring in front of him.

"Deep."

"Sociability of the Motes," Keen muttered.

Razor swiveled, her eyes on fire.

"What?" He splayed his arms.

She turned back around and kept moving.

"We're almost to the bottom," she said and stopped.

Keen bumped into her backside.

"Sorry."

Razor ignored him and raised the glow ring. A large underground gallery, the far end beyond sight with their available light, opened before them. Stalactites and stalagmites in tiered layers of blue, gray, and black formed a pillared subterranean forest. Keen had never been in such a place.

"This is…"

"Was," Razor corrected him.

"Huh?"

"This was once part of the ecosystem connected to the surface of our planet. Long ago."

Keen looked around. "You mean in geological time?"

"Geoengineering time," she said and started off, navigating through the cave's labyrinth.

"How long ago was this?" Keen made his way behind her, watching his footing.

"Long."

"I should've known that's what you'd say."

Shallow pools of water between the stone columns lay in stillness as they made their way across the underground chamber. The Wind Tide's faint roar grew more distant with each step. Every few seconds a drip echoed off the ceiling.

"I've been thinking, Mote." Keen's voice bounced through the cavern. "The Wind Tides are on a 54-hour cycle, right?" His words fell on deaf ears. Razor wasn't engaging. She kept walking through the gallery in silence.

No matter. He was musing out loud, watching where he stepped to make sure he didn't slip as they made their way across the slimy rock floor.

"The Kol 2 day cycle is 26 hours. That means that we have just over two days before your people can expect Targitian retaliation. And if we can't go anywhere until the Tide passes then two questions arise."

She kept walking, with no indication of interest or that she was listening.

"First," Keen said, a bit louder for emphasis, "why are we making for the Mote settlement if we won't arrive before the Targitians? And more importantly for the present, where are we going if we can't leave the bluff until the Tide passes?"

Keen bumped into Razor.

"Oh," he said, surprised at the sight of an underground river passing by in elegant silence. A small dugout lay on its side on the embankment.

Razor's face held the same look as when she had welcomed him to her world when the pod was going down.

"I'm impressed, Mote."

"I have a name. Use it or you're staying behind."

Keen rolled his eyes. He was putting together a sense of Mote dialectics. Sarcasm was big. So was parody. The memory of words spoken between individuals was important to them.

"Understood."

Razor raised an eyebrow.

"Really? Right now?"

"You like sleeping on cave floors? Or would you rather be lulled to sleep by a lazy river?"

If he got to sleep, he'd grovel.

"I understand, Razor… Thank you."

Was he mistaken, or did the earlier shame and guilt lessen?

It's only a power play on her part.

They dragged the dugout down to the water. Keen struggled with his injured arm. His elbow was damaged. The pain made him want quicksilver, lots of it.

"What I wouldn't give for a shot of the ol' 'silver. Back on Heroon, I used to…"

Razor halted and looked up from her bent-over position, prepping the back end of the boat.

"You used to what?"

"Nothing." He shifted the bow over to the river's edge to ready their departure.

"Legion days, Keen?"

It was the first time she'd spoken his first name.

Keen got into the dugout, avoiding her question. Razor steadied the craft from the shore and hopped in, shoving off.

She wasn't pressing him for an answer. He opted to let it drift off down the graceful stream. Shifting about, Keen tried to get into a comfortable prone position in the long and slender boat. It rocked back and forth, splashing in the otherwise placid current.

"Stop moving like a boulder or you'll flip us over," she said, working the rudder.

Keen settled on his back, head at the bow, and watched the rock ceiling drift by overhead. Lying down was wonderful. Razor was right. The subterranean river was a lullaby.

He closed his eyes and listened to the gentle ripples from the boat bounce off the cavern walls. "How far does this go?"

He waited, expecting the typical Mote response, "Far."

Razor didn't answer. A long silence followed. Keen drifted away from this unpredictable, yet strange and enticing adventure of a day. Deep in Kol 2's underground womb, the river's current rocking its gentle lullaby, the layers of woe shed themselves from his weary soul.

After several minutes, the question forgotten in semi-sleep, Razor finally answered.

"No one knows," she whispered.

SEVEN

Keen did care about something. That medallion was more important than his life. And mine. Outside the caverns with the Tide wave cresting over us, I met the person underneath the arrogant robe. I believed he would help me and my people so long as that pendant was around his neck and his business on Heroon remained unfinished.

Later I would learn just how wrong I was.

I remember toying with him in the cavern. Each small jab was a pinprick giving me a burst of satisfaction, feeding my stamina, and will to continue. I needed to avoid thinking about where I was, who I'd lost, and who I still had to rescue from the prison cells under the Fins.

My name game was a part of that as well. I was testing how far gone Keen was, how much or how little pride and confidence he had left. Where was the Legion soldier? That lost identity flashed into life as he struggled against me outside the cavern, seeking his precious metallic lifeline in the swirling darkness. But it fled when we sheltered inside. In relative safety, it retreated somewhere deep within him. One more piece of the puzzle emerged from that event: Keen wasn't a lost cause.

A part of me also tried to convince myself that he was an ally.

Maybe I'd gotten him wrong and he still could care about others. I wanted him to. I needed him to, so I could justify taking him with me. It wasn't enough to have a deal in my pocket. I wanted a Legion soldier on our side. We deserved the same moral high ground and respect. We earned a right to the same justice.

My mind couldn't comprehend that he'd turned from the cause. Friendly fire, whether tangible or moral, wasn't allowable for a former Legion ranker so it didn't figure among the possibilities. And so, I kept us moving. My more sensible half, the Mote in me, knew that the sooner I could get us to the destination the sooner I'd be safe.

I was dangerous. He was dangerous, albeit wounded. Lucky for me, his was the kind of trauma that didn't target others for blame and resentment. That was my way.

I'll admit this now: as a parent, I missed my children and something about Keen in that state drew out my nurturing instincts. With my two little ones far away and oppressed, in conditions I couldn't bring myself to ponder for fear of collapse, my center was hollow. I was in charge of Keen. He didn't stand a chance without me. It was pathetic. He tried to hide it in the darkness of the cave when we tumbled down, escaping the Tide. But it peeked through on his face in the shadows. I knew where we had to go, how to get there, and what to do. He followed because he needed to get somewhere.

And so, when Keen fell asleep in that dugout as we glided underground on the hidden waters of Kol 2, I let go of my anger and my need to be in control. The veneer peeled back. I was alone for the first time since before this all started. No more armored words. Even the dark river around me failed to reflect my face. I thought of Hoti, my younger sibling, never again to be a part of my life. And my children, taken from me over two years ago. Would they return or were they too absent forever? Were they even…?

Do you know what it feels like to move closer to home yet farther from love? I was an estranged parent, deep underground, drifting in the quiet of a rock womb towards a lost destination. Awake and alone, gliding on still waters, I wept.

EIGHT

Keen woke to voices. He propped himself up on his good elbow.

Razor sat steering at the back of the boat. The Mote's eyes hung tired, their blue ice melting.

"How long was I out?" Keen made a pathetic attempt to reach the canteen past his legs. She kicked it towards him.

The glow ring on the floor of the dugout shone around them as they glided downstream. The river had widened since he'd fallen asleep, as had the size of the cavern. A narrow, sandy shore lined both sides.

"A few hours," Razor said.

He heard voices, blended in pleasant harmonies.

"Is that music?"

"For the dead." Razor raised a hand to her lips, rotating it in a small circle. A tremor twitched her cheek. "They're names," she said. "Of everyone who didn't come back yesterday." The muscles of her jaw flexed. She gritted her teeth, holding back what Keen assumed would have been an angry outburst.

"This isn't over. Remember, you're an ambassador who's going to make good on your word. Otherwise, you're no one."

Again, the Mote recitation of past words spoken.

The Mote refuge drew closer and with it, renewed confidence and determination in his companion.

"A boat!"

A child with shoulder-length red hair emerged from behind a boulder and bolted downstream. The youth waved a light ring to life and kept pace with them, glancing at Keen as they ran.

"Two people!" The voice echoed ahead into the darkness, towards the singing voices.

Keen rose to his knees and twisted around to face the bow. Shadows danced on an arched ceiling over a wide bend, cast from an adjacent gallery. The boat drifted closer and the chamber came into view. Scattered about an open cavern, a series of glowing blue pools shone their cool light across the stone. A small crowd halted their communal ritual at the closest pool. They made their way to a jetty carved from the riverbank. As the dugout neared, the group parted. A slender elderly figure and a stocky middle-aged person made their way forward to receive them.

Negotiation time. Put on your diplomatic hat, Draden.

Keen turned back towards the stern. He did his best to tidy up despite his filthy and defiled robe, reaching over the side of the boat and moistening his hand to neaten his long hair.

"Don't do that," Razor warned.

"I'm an ambassador," he said, running damp hands through both lengths of curling locks. "I'll be damned if I arrive without…"

Keen glanced at the ends of his hair resting on his chest. It was now salt and pepper, brown hair turning gray before his eyes.

"What the…?"

Razor smirked.

"My hair. I look…"

"Like you're old."

"Shit!" He rubbed at his hair with his robe, trying to dry it off.

Razor kicked him on the shin.

"Ouch!"

"Do *not* use that language here," she whispered in an earnest warning. "It will not be tolerated on the River Hidden."

"Alright, I understand."

"This is sacred space. We're deep in the caverns. You must be respectful. I'm giving you diplomatic information, Keen. And don't forget that you need to present a convincing case. Otherwise, we'll kill you."

"We?"

"That's right, 'we'. You and I spent a day together to get here, but it changes nothing. I want something you have, and you want something I can provide. If you can't deliver, you're on the short side of the deal. You're not holding any cards."

Mote wordplay tally goes up by one.

Razor nodded, indicating he should turn around. Keen swiveled to face the bow. A tall figure waited at the jetty. It looked like Razor's double, but angrier. Keen didn't like welcoming parties and this was one he preferred to skip. Behind the mirror image of his traveling companion stood the two Motes who had separated from the crowd to greet them.

"Nuntu ashemto," Razor's double said and placed a hand to their lips, making a small circle like the one Razor had performed minutes earlier.

"Nuntu ekteso," Razor answered from behind him in the dugout.

The language was unfamiliar. Keen guessed by the phonetics that it was an indigenous form of speech. Judging by the phrase's tone and its accompanying gesture, he assumed it served as condolence rather than greeting.

Razor steered them to a stop parallel to the dock. Her twin helped tie up the dugout.

"Well, she's back," the elderly one said, stepping up to the rock's edge with feeble legs.

Keen noted their use of Razor's pronoun. *So, they know each other.*

"At least we still have the hostage. This wasn't a complete loss." Alike to Razor in skin tone and hair color, long woven strands ran to their waist. Face and physique couldn't hide the obvious: the end of their life cycle neared. Eye sockets lay in deep hollows, casting shadows over aged, blue cataracts. Gaunt legs held up a withered frame. "Older than I expected," they added, glancing at Keen's grey hair.

"I'm no one's hostage, Mote," Keen said, and rolled up onto the dock. The move was anything but graceful.

He hadn't been engaged, and therefore did not benefit from social custom regarding gender self-expression. Unsure of how to respond without potential insult, he'd have to stick to detached, gender-neutral address to avoid misgendering. To do so as an Ambassador was to perform a major disrespect in Sag-Arm civilization, and unless quickly corrected, could cause an irreparable social rift. Accidents happened in vernacular culture all the time and were excused when quickly pointed out and corrected. But Ambassadors, especially one of Keen's status, were employed to represent and speak for others, to negotiate difficult cultural tensions and reach amenable compromises or solutions. It was their job to speak and address others correctly. A mistake on his part would be almost unheard of, even in the remote dunes of Kol 2, and taken as derogatory.

Keen had no idea if the Motes followed the customs practiced by their counterparts, the Targitians, and others in the Arm, or if they'd chosen to revise or rewrite cultural codes to fit their intrinsic life experience in the remote desert. As soon as one of the Motes addressed him, if it was not offered as part of a formal introduction or via hand signing, he'd be sure to inquire out of respect. He didn't want to repeat what happened with Razor in the pod.

He could hand-sign his own preference so they could address him appropriately, but something told him to wait until the formal exchange during introductions.

"I'm here to broker a deal," he said. His feet weren't ready to support him after so much time prone, so he sat up and tucked his knees. "And I'm younger than I look. No thanks to this..." he remembered Razor's warning about language and chose to avoid adjectives, "water."

"Razor," the middle-aged Mote said, approaching them. "Tell us what happened."

One eye inspected Razor. The other was missing, leaving the socket vacant and exposed. Keen studied the face. It was burned as if a flaming claw swiped it in malice. The side without the eye looked like wet paint. Undulating strokes of pink and tawny flesh contrasted with the obsidian of the uninjured skin. A bald crown stood in stark opposition to a dappling of tight curly white scruff on the jaw at the edge of the injury's reach.

This all paled compared to the burn. That scar extended from the face down the neck, continuing onto the broad chest below a loose shirt. Was this the Patent War veteran? Or had the Mote surfed a Tide Wave close enough to be seared by its scalding edge?

"Yes, what did happen Razor?" the older one said.

Keen's diplomatic mind registered the sarcasm, adding it to his rough summary of Mote dynamics.

"What Crest told you would happen," Razor snapped, eyeing her elder with a vengeance as she disembarked.

"How dare you!" the aged Mote said.

"You've killed us. All of us!" Razor lunged.

Her twin got to her before she reached them, restraining her blind fury.

"You've led us to ruin!" Razor screamed, fighting against her doppelgänger. The "ruin" bounced down the river, ricocheting from the walls of the subterranean refuge.

"Enough!" The one-eyed Mote stepped forward. "This is Ambassador Draden, I presume?" The words directed to Razor.

She nodded.

The Mote reached out a hand. Unsure, Keen took it. A strong arm heaved him up to his feet.

"Everyone back to the glow pools," the one-eyed leader said to the Motes gathered around them. The crowd receded to the series of circular basins in the gallery. The shallow waters glowed with a strange, blue radiant light; it filled the subterranean chamber with an eerie mood of reverence.

Keen looked downriver. The steadfast current cut through the cavern and disappeared around a darkened corner. So, this was the Mote refuge, a secret outpost underneath the arid surface of Kol 2. It was no wonder the Targitians couldn't find them. How far had they traveled? The river was swift, and he'd slept for several hours. Targite could be a hundred miles away.

Only the two lead Motes, Keen, Razor, and her doppelgänger remained dockside.

"I am Crest-ti," he said, declaring his gender alike to Keen. "And this is Urtani-ta-té." Crest gestured to the old Mote. "We are the Two Eyes."

Keen wasn't sure if the last word referred to 'I's or 'Eyes.' Either way, he understood. And from Crest's manner of introduction, it sounded like the Motes followed Arm-wide custom regarding gender or they used it knowing he would be unfamiliar with an indigenous alternative.

"Ambassador Draden-ti," Keen said, introducing himself with his suffix. After neglecting to declare earlier during the abduction with Razor, or ask for hers when she didn't offer it, he didn't want to repeat the offense.

Keen made a note of the self-expressions of both Crest and Urtani in case a longer conversation or debate ensued. Urtani's declaration as gender-fluid, by using "ta," meant she might choose to shift her pronouns at any time.

Keen's eyes went from Urtani to Crest and around the cavern. It was all so natural and ubiquitous now in the Arm, learned in one's earliest years and performed as instinctually as nodding "yes" or shaking a head "no." Whether in a densely populated urban metropolis on a planet at the center of the Arm, or a secluded star system on a lone world such as Kol 2, persistent respect for gender self-expression amongst humanity endured. He was standing underground, in a remote area within an isolated diasporic community. That long history of advocacy and expansion of personal rights flourished and allowed him to treat with others so culturally different from himself with equity and respect for diversity.

Despite the ongoing political conflicts and cultural hegemony in the Arm perpetuating cultural oppression, ecological abuses, and other social injustices, it was easy to forget the autonomy and respect gender had achieved. It wasn't always the case. But for over a millennium now, since the mid-Second Span, humans had conquered a longstanding prejudice and come to understand that one's gender self-expression (and sexuality, for that matter) was a right of all, not a privilege of the few. A tremendous ethical victory, but sadly one that did not send change rippling out through other politicized aspects of Sag-Arm civilization. That evidence was around him; both the Motes and the terraformed planet demonstrated the persistence of human and ecological inequalities and oppression.

"I need to talk to you." It was Razor, her words meant for Crest. She'd recovered and was standing next to her twin.

Keen had no doubt any longer. Those two were definitely siblings. Two Razors… this was getting better and better.

"Crest, things have turned in a way we didn't predict or expect," she said.

"Indeed," Urtani interjected.

No love lost between the two of them.

Crest held a hand up to halt the exchange before it rekindled the earlier spark. So, they were equals, or he outranked her. Either way, they were both going to decide Keen's fate.

"Come," Crest said to all of them, "we will speak at the Throat Pool."

KEEN SAT at a small pool with Razor's twin. She'd been introduced as Gushet-té. If he thought Razor was terse, Gushet made her seem like a chatterbox.

He now understood the source of light in the cavern. Bioluminescent plants, submerged in the shallow pools, emitted an azure glow.

On the edge of a large basin in the corner of the gallery – the one they called the Throat Pool – Razor, Crest, and Urtani spoke in hushed voices. Incomprehensible whispers echoed through the cavern from their private conversation.

Something nudged Keen's arm. Gushet was holding out a canteen. He accepted and took a swig.

"Woohoo!"

The Motes huddled across the glow pool went silent. Keen held up a hand. "Apologies, my good Motes. Just expressing my surprise at your gracious hospitality."

He took another large gulp.

"And here I was thinking you were like your sibling," he told Gushet. It was fierce stuff this liquor, and he liked it.

She snatched the canteen and took a long pull without so much as a flinch.

"My twin should've killed you," she said, wiping her mouth.

Keen wasn't sure how to take the comment. Was she serious?

"More juice for me." Gushet bared her teeth in a sinister, yet oddly ingratiating, smile before taking another long draw and handing the canteen back.

"Definitely not like your sibling," he said.

The other Motes around their pool cast him hesitant glances. They'd distanced themselves as if he had a disease.

In a way, I do. It's just not something you can catch.

Why Razor's sibling hadn't left him alone was lost on him. He guessed the 'Eyes' had assigned her to him. Something told him she'd keep him in line without much effort, even under the influence of this 'Mote juice.'

"They didn't have the right formation. Crest told them that for weeks. If they'd gone in all at once…"

"You know that doesn't work, Yiksi. It's been tested and failed."

The Motes on the opposite side of the pool were arguing in hushed voices.

"This was the right strategy. Urtani knew what she was doing. It was the ones on the ground… Hoti's cluster, they let us down."

Keen chuckled, the sound bouncing off the still water.

"Something to add, Dreck?" A surly Mote at the center of the group eyed him. They were roughly Keen's age, fit with shoulder-length curly red hair and arms covered in Dunemarks. They had 'the look.' Keen, like all former soldiers, could recognize it right away. They were a veteran and had seen a good deal of action in their time.

"Nope," Keen took another shot of the fiery liquid and winced as he swallowed.

This Mote elixir was different than quicksilver. Like a slow-burning fuse. Something told him it was soon to ignite. He wasn't sure if that was good or bad. Then again, it didn't matter. He just wanted more of it.

He took another shot.

"Easy, dreck." Gushet snatched the canteen from him. "Too much for your first time."

"In your dreams, Mote. I can drink with the best of them."

She shook her head, a smirk of anticipation on her face.

"What's a Dreck?" Keen asked.

"You. Anyone who's not one of us. You're all Drecks."

He had to admit, the Motes were one serious diplomatic challenge. Theirs was a diasporic culture stuck in the remote underground deserts of an isolated planet. Having to learn about their customs and language was proving difficult. So many contradictions, sharp turns, complex and unexpected roadblocks to communication.

But they were strong, fierce, and alive. Their culture and the strength of its bond within their hearts was palpable. The Motes reminded him of the Legion, holding fast to the value of every day. Could it be that this was a better life than his? It stirred a memory of his years in the service. That was when he genuinely appreciated life. The next sunrise was worth more than all the money in the Arm. In the following two decades, its exchange rate had plummeted to near worthlessness. And what had he become? An Ambassador. It offered him everything he needed; everything he wanted. He was supposed to change the world through diplomacy, bringing equity and fairness through the star systems in the Sag-Arm. When did that vision crumble into decadence?

No, this wasn't his fault. It wasn't even the Council's responsibility. This was always the way humanity leaned. The Targitians alone did this to their people.

Still, you're part of the system that's screwed them.

That system meant he had benefited from privileges built on the backs of others, even the Motes. Life flowed with ease for those lucky enough to live on planets wielding patent monopolies because other systems ran the rapids. Calm and order existed at the expense of another's chaos, that much he'd learned as an ambassador. And he hadn't done a damn thing about it since he'd been in the Legion. Out of sight, out of mind. Now, it was within sight. He was damned if he was going to deny it.

"You're right about that, Gushet," he said. "I am a Dreck."

Her glacial eyes flickered with surprise. It was the same expression Razor had when she'd seen his forearm in the dunes.

"Now give me back that canteen, before I show you what a Legion soldier can do."

"Hah!" Gushet laughed. The Motes on the far side of the glow pool halted their banter.

"My sibling is going to be angry with me, Dreck. But you're amusing me, and I need that after what's happened since the last Tide. So here, drink." She handed him the canteen.

Keen took another shot. The fuse growing even shorter.

That Mote... the 'soldier' across the pool.

His eyes narrowed as he watched them speak.

They've got some nerve. I'll bet they're more talk than action.

"You there," he addressed the surly Mote ungendered since they'd done the same to him earlier. "What makes you so cocky, anyway? You're still sitting over there because I'm in a generous mood." He was feeling good, *really* good. And he'd be damned if any of these Motes (except Gushet, she could stay and drink with him) would get away with mocking him. He'd outrank them in the Legion. *That* was certain, especially that mouthy one.

The Mote's eyes grew wide. They went to rise.

"Down, Keltek-tõ," Gushet said, waving a hand and introducing the Mote's gender for Keen's benefit. "He's in the juice. I have him."

"Have me? You couldn't..." Keen went to stand and got dizzy. He swayed.

"Ouch!" He opened his eyes to find that he was lying on his side, his face against cold, hard rock.

"Alright, Dreck, let's go."

It was Gushet speaking. Sweet Gushet.

"Did you hit me?"

"No, Dreck. If I did you wouldn't be talking."

"Did I fall?"

"He can't even stand," a voice across the pool said.

"A Legion soldier," Keen slurred in warning, struggling to get up. "You're going to regret it."

His arms went up behind him even though he hadn't lifted them. The glow pool receded, his legs splayed out in front of him. No, wait... behind him. That surly Mote was making a hand gesture at him.

"I'm backward," he slurred. The gallery ceiling ran past like a moving picture. Stao's face materialized and hovered before him, shaking in disapproval.

"Don't give me any crap, Stao," Keen said. "You never got to meet Stao," he said to Gushet, aware now that she was dragging him by the arms. "That droid was... hey, why are we stopping?"

"What happened?" a voice said.

"I know it's you because you sound annoyed," Keen said. "Not like your twin... sweet Gushet."

"You juiced him?"

"A little, who knew the Dreck was so weak."

"Who are you calling weak?" Keen slurred. "My platoon never..."

"Be quiet, Keen."

"You didn't want to know about that, Razor wit... and by the way, you're not funny. You didn't want to know, or you would've asked. No one asked. No one knows. I have to find her all by myself. It's your fault!"

"Enough!"

Keen felt a slap across his face.

"Argh!!!" He bucked and resisted, kicking his legs and pulling his arms. It was no use. Gushet had him tight.

"He needs to sleep. Let's take him to the Reach. Here, sibling, let me help you."

NINE

Strong again. When my sibling appeared on the dock my feeling of emptiness abated. It was anguishing for her to stay behind during the assault, but we needed her in case I didn't make it back. As it turned out, I returned. And it was I who needed her to be waiting, more than my brethren. Without her, I may not have had the strength to fight Urtani's accusations.

Crest was an honorable and sensible leader. Unlike his namesake, his temperament ran smooth and steady like the River Hidden. He listened to my justifications and understood why I did what I did after we crashed. My decisions were practical under the circumstances and based on our culture's beliefs. It was the latter that made the difference for Urtani. The Eye couldn't challenge our ethics. She knew I did right.

I should have known better than to leave my sibling with Keen. Witnessing him in the juice, I realized how alike they were. Both hubristic and faulted to a fault yet determined to exist in a state of perpetual tragedy. Gushet had lost her life partner and young child. She suffered again when the Targitians took her nephews, *my* children, because of a foolish error on the part of Urtani. Now all she had was a sibling and her people. Nothing more except the juice. I learned more about Keen in those few minutes as we dragged him to the Reach than

I did during the journey from the crash site. He was angry. Resentful. Mad at the world and suffering from a deep longing. Just like Gushet.

I did something that, later, I would never admit to anyone when we got him to the cave. My sibling headed back to the others. I rolled Keen into a prone position near a low fire to leave him for the night. I pushed him onto his side to be sure he could breathe safely until the juice wore off. A twinkle of metal caught my eye from the edge of his robe. It was the medallion.

My hand reached for it and slid it out far enough to observe the milky green stone at its center. As I ran my finger over its convex surface it slipped out of the pocket onto the rock floor, ringing a small echo through the cave. Keen grunted but didn't wake. The pendant opened when it fell, the mechanism triggered by the impact.

Why did I look inside? I would be lying if I didn't want to satisfy personal curiosity. It was me he'd fought outside the bluff in a desperate attempt to recover his talisman. Its value was palpable through the effort and resistance he used to protect it. But I also needed to collect what knowledge I could to ensure we survived. At that point, I'd do almost anything for what was left of my people. We had to put ourselves in the best position possible. That meant knowing why his journey to Heroon was so important.

So yes, I opened the medallion. And learned that Keen had a child.

TEN

"Do you have to leave? Can't you stay the night?"

Keen's eyes took in the features of her face: full lips and yellow eyes that sparkled like Nushaba's radiance at high noon. The supple russet skin of her cheeks glowed with an internal light. Why did she have to be so beautiful? It made everything worse. Not only having to leave but everything, the whole situation: two people and two worlds at war.

"Yes, I must."

He ran his hand through her deep violet hair and kissed her. Outside the small elevated hut, the lush plant life and animals of Heroon watched in silence in the night's wee hours; a thousand eyes and ears bearing witness to all they'd said and done. Their tryst was a secret to all humans except one other. If they were discovered by anyone else, he'd be court-martialed and sent home in disgrace. And she, she would… he didn't want to think about that.

Of course, his sibling could be trusted. Reardon had known for at least a month before the two spoke of it. Keen felt his sibling's eyes on him on the daily patrols through the small town in the suburbs of the capital. At first, Reardon had ordered him along from up the street. Keen could tell by his tone that Reardon assumed he was stuck dealing with a pesky local. But after a week Keen knew his sibling had read through the performance. Another seven days and Reardon confronted him. Today, only a few hours earlier, his sibling had laid down an ultimatum.

"Keen, this is the last time. I can't cover for you anymore. You need to end this. Nothing good can come of it. If our parent were to find out..."

"It's the last time," Keen whispered outside the barracks. "After tonight, we have two weeks and then we're on leave. Tomorrow I'm meeting a courier. It'll all be arranged. All I need to do is take her to the drop point on the first day of R&R. She'll get off Heroon to Ceron. After we win and ship home, I'll talk to him."

"And if we don't win?"

Keen had heard this a hundred times. Why was everyone always on at him about not considering all possible outcomes? Their platoon sergeant, the tactician instructor, even his parent nagged him about it when he gave them basic lessons in diplomacy. Why did they waste their time with conclusions that weren't going to happen?

"Reardon, do you really believe we'll lose?"

His sibling's eyebrows rose the way they always did when Keen was right, but the idea was dangerous. He'd made the expression hundreds of times as kids when they'd carried out a range of pranks, capers, and tomfoolery.

"I didn't think so," Keen said, victorious. "Listen, I know you hate evening mess duty. So, you go out on patrol tonight for me, and I'll cover your morning shift tomorrow *and* I'll take mess at dinner. Deal?"

"You're serious about bringing a Heroonese partner home to him? To marry? I know they're not the enemy technically, but they're enemy-by-association."

"It's not their fault they live under a Hamut government."

"That we happen to be at war with."

"It's not her war."

Reardon shook his head. "You never cease to figure out ways to disappoint our parents."

"I have to do something to make him pay attention to me, right?" Keen's mouth rose into a jocular grin.

Reardon laughed. "Alright, but this is the last time." He looked around to make sure no one else was listening or watching. "Be safe."

Was he? In the still night air, the view of the rainforest through the open-sided structure was a camouflaged composition of gray, silver, and black in Ran's waning moonlight. What was hiding in the shadows about his future? He'd find out soon enough. He'd stayed too long, and it was time to get back. Reardon and the others would return from night patrol within the hour.

"I have to go," he said.

She clasped his hand, placing each of her fingers between his as if to deepen their bond.

"You'll come back when?"

"Two weeks. As soon as we finish this next op, I'll be back to take you to the courier. Be ready to leave."

He kissed her hand. "Then you'll be waiting for me when I get back."

"On Ceron?"

"On Ceron," he said and kissed her on the lips. She nestled close to him, the warm and humid air of Heroon leaving a skein of moisture that warmed as their bodies met.

He guided her hand around him, so it rested on his backside. His hand went to her neck, pulling her in, their eyes only inches from one another. Her breath smelled of a faint, alluring musk.

He smiled and kissed her again.

She withdrew her hand from behind him and stroked his cheek.

Something nudged his back. He turned. Nothing.

"You alright?" she whispered.

"Yes."

He kissed her. "Sorry, I have to go."

There it was again. He peeked over his shoulder. Nothing.

"What is it, Keenie?"

"Something is nudging me."

A small object pushed into his side.

"What is that?" He swatted at his backside without turning around.

"Dreck" a voice said, faint and far off.

Keen's mind paused, stunned by the incongruity of the word in this setting. He checked his surroundings, gazing out over the open platform to Heroon's dramatic skyscape. The night sky was clear and full of stars, but the towering shadows of storm clouds gathered at the horizon. Soon the nightly rains would drench the tropical rainforest.

"Dreck."

Another nudge.

"Stop it!"

Keen's arm flailed out around his body. It latched hold of something. Heroon vanished, replaced by a blurry scene of waning darkness with fluttering light. His left hand came into focus, splayed out in front of him, palm facing up. Why was it miles away? The world was sideways. He made out the edges of roughly hewn rock and a small round ring casting a beam of soft blue onto the remains of a smoldering fire. Proper perspective returned, and so did the realities of his physical condition.

His stomach was like a turbine in zero gee. His head pounded. He felt like a swollen corpse.

Mote juice.

"Dreck."

Keen rolled over, still holding on to what he now saw was a long, elegantly carved stick. The close-cropped red haircut and eyes of a child, no more than five, stood out against the darkened background. The Mote youngster had been poking him.

Keen gave the staff a hard shove, sending the kid a few steps. He rolled back over, wanting nothing to do with the child.

The Mote juice had taken a toll. He was damned if this stuff wasn't filled with some sort of outer planet impurities. He felt terrible from head to foot.

"Bring me some water," he grumbled, closing his eyes and hoping to go back to sleep.

"Razor says to get up," the voice said behind him.

"Later kid. Get me some water first."

The child nudged him again.

In a flash, Keen flipped over and tore the staff from the child's hand. He was on his knees, the stick at the young Mote's throat.

The child's eyes filled with cold fright and they dashed out of the cave.

"Wait, kid." It was no use. The Mote was out of sight. Wailing echoed down the tunnel.

"Didn't mean it," Keen whispered and threw the stick aside. He got to his feet, dusting off his robe. His head swirled.

He felt like crap.

"Suck it up, Draden," he said. And he did. He'd become an expert at it.

"DO YOU FEAR IT?"

Keen turned from the painted scene on the rock wall. Gushet stood at the entrance to the subterranean gallery, a glow ring in her hand. The radiance silhouetted her against the surrounding darkness. If she hadn't spoken in her distinct and gruff manner, he would've been certain it was Razor.

He'd taken one of the tunnels out of the cavern where he'd slept at random, realizing the child he'd scared off was supposed to lead him through the underground maze to Razor. Guided by the light of a glow ring left by whoever brought him to the room after too much drink, he'd wandered along a narrow, winding corridor. The subterranean path ended with a set of steps carved into the rock that ascended into a long open gallery. Its ceiling was littered with short stalactites hanging above a central glow pool about fifty feet across. Calcium salt deposits formed a cornucopia of sedimentary icicles that reflected from the still water, casting motionless shadows back up like an inverted forest at twilight. It reminded him of Heroon from the air during their pre-dawn raids. Something about that vista calmed him on the mornings he headed off into war, settling his nerves before the drop into the rainforest. Heroon's dense canopy hid the lurking reality at ground level. Each time he dropped through, unavoidable human conflict and trauma returned in all its screaming terror.

Here, light years away, deep under Kol 2's surface, the mood of that memorable vista persevered. Despite the historical narrative on the walls before him, the tranquil state spoke with the calm assurance of a time beyond the parameters of human presence and impact in the cosmos. Sheltered in this underground realm, even light-speed technology paled against the gnawing persistence of Kol 2's geological duration.

Gushet strode solemnly toward him, making her way along the narrow walkway around the pool. Carved patterns chiseled into the rock floor came to life as she approached. It was clear that the Motes had leveled the shoreline of stalagmites to allow for a circular path around the watery basin.

"I'll take your silence as a 'yes'," she said, stopping next to him and raising her glow ring to reveal more of the painted narrative. Her words bounced off the still water, echoing from the cavern's opposite wall.

"What is it I fear, exactly?"

"What you see before you."

"And that is?"

"The past. And the future." She held her glow ring up in front of him. "Feeling good today?" A smirk of victory crossed her face.

"That stuff is poison," Keen said, dismissing her dig. His insides festered like a curdled stew. He couldn't deny it. That Mote juice was a special kind of hurt.

"I thought a tough Legion soldier could take his drink?"

Keen scoffed. Had Razor told her? Or had he said something foolish under the spell of that firebrew? He examined the chronicle before him: a lush planet of bountiful flora and fauna painted by an expert, ancient hand. Motes, evident by their red hair and skin tone, collected an abundant harvest amidst fields and forests. All the elements of life appeared in harmony as if a symphony played in the key signature of the planet's ecosystem. Keen raised his arm with the glow ring higher, still sore from the crash against the rock. A sky with the same rose tint as that of Kol 2 hung over the terrestrial landscape.

"Yes," Gushet said, "despite your disbelief that is my planet."

"This is Kol 2?"

"As it once was. And will be again." Gushet pulled a canteen from her side, took a swig, and offered it to Keen.

He put up a hand. "Too early for me. I admit defeat this time."

"It's only water, Legion Dreck," she said and handed it to him. "Come." She walked past him, tracking her glow ring along the painted wall. Keen followed her a quarter of the way around the pool.

"Do you know the origin of the Targitians?" She halted, her blue eyes taking in the familiar narrative.

"They broke away, causing civil war," he said. "And sided with the rising geoengineers scouting for planets to eco-shape."

Gushet listened but did not take her gaze from the painting. Against the azure light of the pool and the glow ring, her short, spiky red hair took on an eerie glow.

Keen's eyes traveled up the rock face. A distinct boundary between a lush former world and the arid landscape of Kol 2's present climate was rendered in front of them. It read like the pause between movements in the planet's historical symphony. What lay on the threshold was far from silent. Two fleets of crude and brutish eco-synch vehicles, their massive steel and carbon-shielded shells a distinct marker of Second Span Sag-Arm civilization, ran into the distance. They chewed their way through the greenery and settlements, razing everything in their path with no quarter given. In their wake 'Kol 2' was born, its distinctive blue sands and swirling winds a familiar reminder of the world hundreds of feet over their heads.

"They abandoned us like heartless parents," Gushet whispered and turned to him. Her eyes burned like molten ice.

Keen's insides winced at the accusatory tone. She couldn't know about his child. Unless... had he been that 'in the juice?'

Kol 2's history was familiar to all diplomats. Isolated in the Sag-Arm, the early eco-surveyors offered a promise of abundant wealth and political connections to the indigenous population if they accepted a trade agreement to allow the planet to be geo-engineered. Kol 2's unique tilt and orbital cycle, combined with its atmospheric conditions and copious aquifers, held the potential for unheard of geo-engineered wind power. All that was needed was to convert the current ecosystem and increase the temperature by a mere 8 degrees.

The offer tore the population apart. Half welcomed the opportunity to join the growing trade network and reap the promised benefits, which included entry into political influence within the Sag Arm. Travel off-world, imported goods and services, and diplomatic perks were all dangled as temptations. The other portion of the population resisted, desiring nothing more than to remain independent and continue to preserve their well-formed intrinsic culture.

The two factions split, and confrontation led to all-out civil war. Those siding with the trade partners received outside military support and won a quick victory. Unwilling to wipe out their kin, they spared their former allies. Guided by a charismatic and eccentric leader, Har Targite, the victorious faction developed a theocracy based on a syncretism combining longstanding indigenous beliefs with foreign influence associated with early Sag Arm mythology. Their main inspiration: the worship of a wind force known as Helleuan.

Armed with a new dogma, Har and her supporters secured the future acceptance of their new government into the Sag Arm community while relieving their citizens of guilt from turning on their own kind. Soon the population accepted the transformation as prophecy. The rise of Helleuan on Kol 2 was foretold, a portent of their triumphant dominance as leading innovators in enviro-synchronization. They would now drive and rule a new epoch of Sag Arm civilization.

Thus were founded the Targitians.

Those who lost retreated to the far reaches of the now arid and wind-driven planet to live a nomadic lifestyle, becoming expert at surviving the Wind Tides, disappearing into the vast and empty landscape of a reformed Kol 2. They became the Motes.

The Targitians pronounced that mercy and surrender, as Helleuan demonstrated through the rise and fall of the Tides, was a necessary and respected cycle of the transfigured planet. The pre-Tide backdraft was a reminder to give to receive, and during the ebbs of the Wind Tide the Targitians made offerings to Helleuan within the Fins.

With the backing of the Apex, the elite spiritual triumvirate, Har Targite enacted the Diasporic Clause as a demonstration of their theosophy in practice. So long as the Motes didn't threaten the Fins, they were shown mercy and allowed to remain among the sands. The Targitians tolerated the occasional raids on their energy cell pickups out in the desert at the Turbine Fields. But if any act of aggression to their city were made, such mercy would transform into violence and their brethren eradicated with the fury and might of a Helleuan Tide wave.

It took only half a century to transition Kol 2 from a lush ecosystem to an arid, wind-borne desert planet. By the time the first generation of Targitians were at retirement age, Kol 2 was bringing in more accounts than they could fill. That's when the Targitians surprised their business partner light-years away in the Sag Arm. They improved the efficiency of their turbines and manufactured a new, concentrated form of energy for export, taking control of their innovation and relinquishing their need for the earlier patented technology that helped shape them into a competitor.

They understood enviro-synchronization better than anyone in the Arm. They'd lived for millennia in natural harmony with their planetary ecosystem and exploited it with great effect, harnessing the full potential of their new world of wind.

"Why did they do it?" Keen asked.

"Do what?"

"Turn on you? On the Motes?"

A fierce intensity returned to her eyes.

"Did I say something wrong?" Keen asked.

"The Targitians are Motes too," Gushet said. "They assume they're something else, with a false sense of superiority… like you."

What was the trigger for such anger? It shot forth so unexpectedly during his conversations with Razor and the others. The Mote fuse was short, like their drink.

"But they leave you alone, out here in the desert," he said.

Gushet shook her head with an air of disgust.

"What?"

"And that's acceptable, Mr. Ambassador? To be left alone, without resources?"

Keen didn't know what to say. He opened his mouth, but no words came to him.

"And what about when we become so desperate that we're forced to conduct a raid? When we have no choice but to turn to theft and ambush to provide food and energy for our children?"

Keen sensed an intensity surfacing on her features in the luminous blue light.

"You know where Razor's two young children are, Keen?" Her eyes burned brightly in the glow ring's illumination. "They're in prison under the Fins, brutally taken when the Hamuts decided to 'teach us a lesson' because the Targitians were too lenient. My sibling's partner died alongside mine trying to protect them. And my children..." Gushet turned away.

Keen stared at the back of her head, the tight red hair shaved close to the skin.

"You can't understand," she said, tracing her hand over the mural. Her long Dunemarked fingers followed the edges of a glowing triangle.

"What is that?" Keen asked.

"False prophecy. The justification for everything the traitors of our planet do and don't do."

"Is it meant to be a god?"

"Hardly," she said. "It's the symbol for the Apex."

"I thought they were oracles worshipped by the Targitians?"

"They are, for those who live and grow up on foreign worlds listening to stories of another culture from far away, imposing their skewed perspectives and misperceptions. Humans love mystery." Gushet held the glow ring up between their faces. Her eyes became fierce. "The Apex are mere mortals, driven by a dogmatic belief system that cloaks nothing more than heartless greed. Their followers consume it with wide-eyed pleasure, living in privilege at the expense of their brethren for over a thousand years." She directed her gaze to the strict triangular symbol on the rock wall, "The Apex are an infection running through the blood of my people."

Keen wasn't sure what to make of Gushet's explanation. Wasn't this myth, a way of opting and explaining unforeseen tragedy and human exploitation? The Targitians who addressed the Council in Garassit were pious, but they were pragmatic business rivals who spoke in economic terms and negotiated as politicians.

"And don't confine your perspective to humans, either. It's arrogant to forget what the Motes always remember." She directed the light of the glow ring back to the earlier section of the mural, depicting a pre-shaping fecund ecosystem. "The amount of animal and plant life lost is beyond measure. No words are capable of expressing that lament."

Gushet raised two fingers to her lips and rotated them, mimicking the gesture he'd seen both she and Razor perform at the dock on his arrival.

"Come." She grabbed the sleeve of his robe and pulled him onward, around the pool. They stopped at the end of the narrative cycle.

Keen held up his glow ring. The same lush planet at the beginning of the mural had returned.

Disappointed, he said, "I thought this was the future. It's only the past repeating itself." He considered the Motes as having a chance to envision something innovative and redemptive in the finale of the narrative.

Gushet grabbed the sleeve of his robe and led him back about twenty paces.

"Look closer," she instructed.

Keen scrutinized the mural. A catastrophic collapse of the planet's surface dropped tectonic plates down into the subterranean aquifers. Water swelled up and over the planet. Gushet pulled him a few feet further along the wall. The water spread and the abundant vegetation grew. The Wind Tides that swirled in sinuous linear marks across the rose sky in earlier sections of the painting diminished and eventually disappeared.

The whites of Gushet's eyes glowed with intensity against her onyx skin.

"But how?"

She pulled him past the lush finale to the epilogue at the end of the cycle.

Keen recognized the Apex by their black hooded robes. A large group carrying weapons led them from the ruins of the Fins. Above the broken and battered city, the familiar Dunemarks he'd seen on Razor's knuckles ran as a banner in the sky.

"It's simple," she said.

He turned to Gushet and fell back a step. Her two arms stuck straight out towards him, the fists pressed together so the red Dunemarks on her knuckles read as one linear phrase.

"Rise Kol 2," she said.

"ABOUT TIME," Razor said. "Did you get lost?"

"You could say that." Keen sauntered through the entrance to the underground chamber.

"And?"

"Your twin found me."

Razor's eyes narrowed.

"I got a private tour on the way. Don't worry," he waved a hand in the air, "No Mote juice was involved."

She and Crest stood at a circular flat-topped rock table, their attention fixed on a holofeed projecting a grainy and glitching image at its center.

"Loi was supposed to take you to the baths," Razor said, "so you could wash up and get into something…" she paused, looking him up and down, "clean and civilized."

Keen glanced at his robe. She was right. Clean and civilized he did not look. Strangely, he'd gotten used to it. His exterior appearance matched his interior reality. The union invited relief through cathartic acceptance, with no more pathetic attempts to maintain a pretense of dignity to outside eyes. At some point, he needed to reset and snap out of it, and once more 'appear' to have his life together.

"I'll take you down after we finish here," she said.

"What is this place?" An array of mashed-up nav-tech and com-stations filled the cavern. Small bumps, the remains of sanded-off stems of stalactites and stalagmites, dappled the floor and ceiling.

"Remote Command Center," Crest said, motioning Keen forward with his one eye. He handed him a canteen.

Keen nodded and accepted the water, taking a long swig.

"We need you to see this," Razor said, gesturing at the holofeed.

"One of our scouts took this yesterday about 40 rises from the Fins on the last ebb," Crest said. The Mote motioned for him to hand back the container.

Keen watched as three cloaked figures stood on the landing tarmac at Targite, black hooded robes hiding their faces in shadow. A pod approached and landed, fighting the last traces of the Wind Tide. The craft was outfitted with an unusual amount of defense systems.

"That's not a K2 pod," Keen said.

"No, it came in from a mid-lev cruiser, an interstellar Twin Needle with origin encrypted, holding orbit outside the exo-line," Razor said.

Two AI droids, super militia models with human sim-anatomy, exited the craft and secured the tarmac. Judging by their refits and combat burns, they'd seen heavy action. A pit grew in Keen's stomach. He didn't like where this was heading.

My parent? Not with that escort. Plus, he couldn't get here this soon…

A figure stepped out of the pod and descended the steps. Crest and Razor's eyes were on Keen, waiting for his reaction.

His jaw dropped to the floor. "The Targitians know I made it… out of the crash," he said.

"What makes you say that?" Crest asked.

Keen pointed a ringed finger at the fuzzy, glitching holofeed. "That's an old friend."

Razor picked up on his sarcasm. "What do they do?"

"They kill."

"Bounty hunter," Crest said. Something about the tone of his voice indicated this wasn't the first time he'd dealt with one.

"Not your standard freelancer," Keen said. "They're in a class all their own."

"Former Legion?' Razor asked.

Keen shook his head. "I wish."

"Hamut?"

Keen nodded.

Crest flashed him a concerned one-eyed glance. "You knew them?"

Keen's hand went to his mid-section, gliding over the bumpy deposits that spoke of past rib fractures. The scar from the exit wound on his left bicep pulled at his eyes. "They almost killed me." He pushed away the incoming flashes of the ten days he'd spent under Hamut 'care.'

"Then they know you," Crest said, raising an eyebrow.

"All too well. Not only that…"

"What?" Razor asked, leaning in to watch the bounty hunter.

"They're relentless," Keen added, deferring to neutral address for the killer. Twenty years had passed since his last 'interaction' with the Hamut and that warranted a return to neutral terminology. "This complicates things."

He followed Razor's gaze to his old nemesis. The mercenary still wore the same silver flex-armor. It shone in the rosy light of Altiron. The plates gleamed against the red undersuit that bore the typical colors of the Hamut warrior class. Their skin was the color of ice, gritty and hatched with scars. Bright orange eyes set against high and tight black hair made for a terrifying aura, the border of shaved hair edging the lower rim of the sleek personalized skullcap with sighting and data systems. They were assassin incarnate, bred to intimidate, maraud and kill.

The Targite escort exchanged a brief word with the bounty hunter before the group moved off towards the gate. The Hamut strode next to the three Targitians. Keen watched their feet. Each step was a micro-beat ahead of the trio escorting them off the tarmac. *Always at the ready.* Not that these spiritual leaders would dare turn on them, but if they did, the bounty hunter would be in a position to counter from a solid base with the time-lead before they committed to hand-to-hand tactics.

They're still a monster.

Keen's heart skipped a beat as he digested this new twist on his reality.

Where were they a year ago when he didn't care? He would've welcomed the bounty hunter's arrival anywhere in the middle of his wasted life. Now that he had a purpose, and somewhere to get to, another roadblock stood in his way.

Reap what you sow, Draden.

He watched as the Hamut craned their neck towards the scope. Orange eyes burned as fiercely as they had a quarter-century ago.

They'd used age boosters and looked as good as they had back in the shit on Heroon. Their outer appearance was more polished, but Keen knew that was all surface. Inside they were still as much the soldier they'd been back then. Something told him they were even better. They held themselves differently. The years gave them wisdom and prudence. Keen read his war history and combat philosophy, both in the Legion and afterward in his ambassadorial training. The best thing a warrior can ask for is wisdom; once you have the skill and the will, surviving long enough to accrue wisdom and prudence is what breaks the glass ceiling into the realm of the great and legendary.

I do know how to pick them.

"What's their name?" Crest asked.

"Huh?" Keen came back to the com-room from his internal reflection.

"Name," Razor repeated. "What is it?"

The killer turned to face the capture lens far off in the distant dunes. A small smile broke on their face.

Sake of the Arm... they know we're watching.

His eyes went to Razor.

"Kartilia Petari-ta-té. At least she'd presented herself that way in the war. Our intel said she was 'ta-ti' when off-the-clock." Was she ever off-the-clock? He couldn't imagine her not being a full-time killer. Keen looked from one Mote to the other. "She might be presenting differently for all I know."

"She's still 'ta-té' professionally, at least for this visit with the Targitians," Razor said.

"How do you know?" Keen asked.

"She just hand-signed it to them." Razor nodded at the holo.

"Petari," Crest said, "That's a Hamut name if I've ever heard one."

Keen nodded. "She goes by another name professionally."

"What name?" Razor asked.

Keen raised an eyebrow. Crest's one eye narrowed with concern.

"Pox."

ELEVEN

Pox. The mere thought of her shudders my bones. Keen's nemesis was no simple villainous rival. She was sheer terror incarnate. A reminder that evil didn't just blossom along political lines or through fierce competition for interstellar power. It also worked freelance.

Not much time remained after the Tide abated. We had to move now or nothing would be left to fight for. The Targitians didn't know our location, but they had a general idea. Free of their need to adhere to the Diasporic Clause, their dogma was thrown off their shoulders with the arrogance of a prince disrobing in the presence of servants. It was only a matter of days before they narrowed their search and located the subterranean refuge. To stand and fight against the larger force, one with so-called 'justice' on their side, was futile. We were sure to be wiped out, lost forever in the sands of imperialist expansion and colonial domination. Yet, what was the alternative? To run and hide? How many times can one cower before conceited power and not become weakened into submission? A time comes when everyone must take a stand.

Despite Urtani's resistance, my remaining brethren sided with Crest. We would do just that: cower one last time. If it worked, it'd be a feint to draw them in before we pounced. We'd appear to be a small, insignificant threat, on the run desperate to survive against a growing world of 'progress.' But if Crest and I returned with a sizable force we might lure them in enough to blow over them like an unscheduled Tide Wave.

If the effort failed, we'd join those who'd fallen under colonial circumstances in the Sag-Arm. Our history would be written by Others. We'd be spoken of as 'primitives,' preserved in the annals not as ourselves, but as fabrications molded through a distorted lens of power.

It was decided at the pools. Crest had tragedy on his side. Everyone has lost loved ones on our failed raid on Targite city. Trust came to Crest not through victory, but failure and defeat.

The plan was set. Our remaining people would ride the River Hidden with hopes that the Lore told truth. How long a journey it was, and where the shelter of the Ancients stood, was now a fated answer for those drifting underground to silent and unknown subterranean shores. Urtani would lead them. Crest, my sibling Gushet and I, along with Keen and a small squad led by Keltek-tō, would make for the closest Turbine Field.

The decision would cause a rift between our people. Loved ones would be left behind. Crest's companion, Tinu-ti, would stay to care for their young child. I would put light-years between myself and my children. Keltek too, was leaving a life partner. What would this cut, this void of distance between us need to heal? Outside medicine? Stitches? Time?

It was a roll of the dice, but it was the only way we'd get off the planet and on to Heroon. If successful, it meant trusting that a desperate ambassador would make good on his word.

Something Crest said at the Throat Pool the first night I returned lingered in my head, and I couldn't shake it loose.

"He's not the person you think he is, Razor."

"He can help us, Crest. Even if he's only doing it for his benefit."

Crest shook his head, his one eye closed.

"Don't be fooled," he said. "He suffers greatly. It shows like a desert flower at Tide's coming."

"And what of it? The Dreck should, considering what part he's played in *our* suffering."

Crest knelt and ran his hand over the still, glowing blue water. Faint ripples spread across the surface. The small waves widened as they crossed the pool and broke on the far side, their delicate splashes echoing off the cavern's ceiling and walls.

How right he was.

TWELVE

Keen sat in the steaming water of the thermal pool, overcome with bliss. Arms outstretched on the rock rim and head resting on the curving ledge, he savored the vapors that rose hot through his nostrils, their scent vegetative and fresh. Condensation clung like morning dew to his long brown spiraling hair and gray-dusted goatee. The subterranean spring had no visible bottom. His legs and toes shone clear, like driftwood dangling underwater. Below his feet was nothing but a cerulean cylinder, illuminated by the bioluminescent algae clinging to the undersides of the chasm.

Even without anything to drink at this ungodly early hour, getting out of his ruined ambassadorial robe and clean off the stench of quicksilver, vomit, and sweat was enough to bring a smile to his weary face. The vacation from maintaining a dishonest exterior was over.

The stillness and silence of Kol 2's subterranean realm was a shield from the eyes of the outside world. While tragic, the underground Mote refuge offered respite from surface realities. He came to relish the occasional drips of water and far-off voices that echoed through chiseled corridors. The isolation from social encounters and political performance lowered his guard.

But he had the itch. A combination of claustrophobia and self-conscious anxiety gnawed at him. Lurking in the shadows of his psyche, it whispered that the shelter of the underground womb was soon to end. It'd be a welcome relief to breathe desert air again. But it came with a price; the return to a sobering reality and all the bullshit that went with it. Well, hopefully not too sober.

He dried off and dressed in the blue fatigues that lay folded by the side of the basin. The ensemble was combat issue, with camouflage to match the hues of Kol 2's shifting dunes. The top billowed around his portly frame, at least a size too large. The old Mote who'd handed him the outfit before Gushet led him to the pool said the pants should fit, but they were too tight. He'd never had enough downtime to realize how much he'd changed over the last two decades. How much control had he relinquished to apathy and ignorance and how much of it was an unavoidable part of his professional life? All ambassadors engaged in indulgence. It was constant. You traveled from system to system and everyone wanted to flatter and ingratiate you. That meant excess, of all kinds. It was how you got things done in the political arena. The fact that he'd been doing this for over two decades and hadn't dropped dead of a heart attack was a victory in itself. Several others younger than him hadn't made it half as long. Twenty-plus years as an ambassador was something to be proud of back in Garassia.

He sat on the carved bench along the cavern wall and pulled out the medallion from under his top. It dangled on its chain, spinning as it unwound. He swung it back and forth, contemplating it like a patient entering hypnosis. Was this the only reason he had to live? Was it worth going through all this trouble to get to Heroon? He grabbed the moving pendant and ran his thumb over the milky green stone. Condalite, so revered in the Sag-Arm. Unique to the planet Ceron and of talismanic status, it turned heads and opened doors. Keen thought it lackluster, like a cloudy pool of algae. Why condalite and not tirex or pelaster? At least those shimmered and gleamed. Condalite's opaque and understated presence had to be some trite political metaphor that he was supposed to be aware of as a Council representative; one more thing to disappoint his parent.

Keen triggered the mechanism and opened the pendant's central chamber, taking out the small projection chip. Deep inside his chest, near the claustrophobia and self-consciousness, desire and nostalgia emerged from the shadows, holding hands. He hadn't read the letter since... when was the last time? Before the pod flight with Razor, while he was still on board the jump ship. The night before he arrived on Kol 2. His eyes had danced over the words while lying in bed.

He palmed the chip and flipped on the projection. The letter materialized in the air in the script that Scarpa-té loved; the one she always used when writing to him. Even the flowing, yet confident style of her unique font hurt. The nickname left little doubt she'd penned the missive, despite everything that had happened.

DEAREST KEENIE,

I'VE THOUGHT *for years about writing this letter to you. Every time I convinced myself to do it, something stayed my hand. Now, time is short and repressed desire has given way to a desperate necessity. Know this: I'm here, Keenie. I survived despite everything that happened. How I managed is too long a tale for this letter, but you can learn more about that if things work out as I hope they will.*

Why you didn't come back for me I'll never know but whatever the reason, I forgive you. War is at fault. Not you, not me, not anyone else. War. Ugly, selfish, and distrusting, it made for nothing but ruin.

But though you left me on Heroon, a part of you remained behind. You and I defied the shackles of war and a piece of beauty rose from the ashes. We created a life amidst death. You have a child, Keenie. I've named her Reynaria, after one of my parents (she is Reynaria-té at the time of this letter - she chose her gender early, at the age of nine). Through her, I fought off the lingering disease of war that otherwise would've taken me. From that small, sprouting stem has grown a strong and confident adult. She has your spirit of justice and unbending morality to fight for those who deserve fairness and equitable treatment. But she has my wits. It is an inspiring and frightening combination we've gifted her. I admire her valiant drive to accomplish anything she sets her mind to, but she has a temper - one that clouds her judgment and puts her in danger. In short, Reynaria is very much like us in our youth.

Why have I chosen now to write to you? I am falling into sleep, Keenie, like I used to do in your arms in the wee hours of humid tropical nights. But this time I will not wake. My body is failing me. The illness was sudden and soon I depart for eternal rest. If I didn't contact you now, you'd never know about Reynaria. In fact, by the time you read this, I will already be gone.

I have asked nothing of you these long years, but she needs you. Reynaria's taken charge of a cause that is worrisome and full of peril (are you surprised? She is, after all, our child. Did we not play that most dangerous game?). Come to Heroon and get to know your child. Make her not resent and hate you as she now does. I have tried to make her understand what happened between us was complicated. I fear for her future both politically and financially in these trying times.

Reynaria walks with a proud stick and has not yet loved another. She doesn't know how it pushes the table clean of all else. You must make her understand that the cause she fights for on Heroon is beyond the pale of justice.

How do I end a letter such as this? So many questions linger between us, unanswered. Only one burdens me still. In my heart, I believe that you absconded for a reason. I only wish I knew why.

HOLD ONTO MY MEMORY, Keenie. Never let it go.

-Scarpa-té

KEEN REACHED out his fingers to the hovering letters of Scarpa's name. Watering eyes of shame and guilt blurred the words and ached his soul. But the day he didn't show up to take her away proved even more painful. He had no choice but to stay away and remain silent. Even the dreams were too much to bear. Only drink and the distractions of luxury kept it all at bay. But it lurked; it paced like a caged animal.

He'd always held close to the reassurance that he could reach out if he wanted, someday. Scarpa was always going to live longer than him. How could they take her first? And yet now, on Heroon, a part of her endured, embodied in a child.

He'd go, for Scarpa. He owed her that.

Footsteps in the antechamber broke his silent lamentation. He shut the projection and locked it away in the medallion, slipping it around his neck underneath the fatigues.

Keltek entered the baths, holding a glow ring. They looked as pleased as Keen when their eyes met.

"It's time," they said.

KEEN TREKKED OVER THE DUNES, snaking his way with the Motes in single file. Dressed in hooded fatigues matching the blue sands, they were a solemn procession in Kol 2's pre-dawn glow. Body-warmed breath steamed in the lingering night air as they marched up and down crests of dry waves.

He was cold despite the miles they'd walked, and creaky. Why was it that your body reminded you it was deteriorating first thing in the morning? Nature, or the gods (if they existed, which he doubted), got it backward. End of the day exhaustion was a much better time for it. You could crash into a plush bed, belly full of food and ferments, knowing the worthy reward of recovery followed amidst slumber. Why not have death tap your shoulder then to remind you of the inevitable, when you could clasp its bony finger in drowsy acceptance? The reminder of mortality built into the process of waking up the body screwed up the start to the day.

Life had a way with irony. It was how he'd gotten here, in the vast and arid wastelands of a rival planet, about to participate in a task more suited to his youth than his fatigued maturity. His body would remind him again tomorrow morning… if he lived that long.

Razor's tall and lean frame at the front of the line bobbed in and out of view over Crest's head. Keen glanced back. Steam pulsed from under Gushet's hood as she pulled up the rear. To his left, Altiron hid below the horizon. In the crepuscular pre-dawn light, he made out portions of Keltek's team far off to the north. The distant Motes rose and fell between the dunes like shadowy fingers emerging and re-submerging into the sands.

Crest's pep-talk to both ambush parties as they ate a crude meal before the trek to the Turbine Field returned. The short speech had struck him, and he couldn't shake it off.

"This isn't only about a deal now," the Mote leader told the group. Crest's one eye, illuminated by the glow ring in the dark cavern, cast an earnest stare from face to face. "This is about the survival of our people. We'll need to be stronger than we've been. Every one of us." Crest shot Keen a hard look that dropped a weight of guilt into his belly. It lingered even now as he trudged over the dunes.

But this wasn't on him. He wasn't beholden to the Motes or their cause. They'd kidnapped him and put themselves in this mess. If helping them meant helping himself he'd do it, but not at the cost of his well-being or reputation. And speaking of expense, he had to get the Council to buy in so it would be on their tab. He needed his savings for the task on Heroon. Use what funds remained to relieve the burden of guilt and accountability laid on him from his dubious past.

That was the plan. Once he was off this arid rock of a planet, he'd contact his parent (reluctantly) and bear the usual lecturing about disappointment and failure. And being bailed out, again. He'd take it per standard parental parley and get the Council to support the Mote rebellion.

Despite the circumstances, it was a great deal. If he made it off Kol 2 alive they'd have an excuse to set up the Motes as a front for a kleptocracy. First, he had to foot the bill for the bounty cube and negotiate a price to get to Heroon. When he'd brought that up to Razor as they prepared the final assault strategy last night all he got back was, "Once we're off the planet we'll discuss that." Something in the way she said it made him aware that the odds were low enough that it wasn't worth wasting words on it before the raid.

Razor raised a hand, signaling them to halt below the ridge of a dune. She dropped down into a crawl and made for the rim. Crest motioned for Keen to move with him to her right. He'd been instructed to stay by Crest's side through the entire operation. Despite his best diplomatic efforts at persuasive Mote-style rhetoric, he'd failed to convince them to give him a weapon. Gushet was the only one who sided with him. He knew why and appreciated it. Once you'd gone through the bonding of a drinking session it changed a relationship, even with someone you hardly knew. It was like opposite ends of a swinging pendulum. One side was revelry and the other was life-risking circumstance. For soldiers, each one was bound to the other. But Gushet wasn't in charge and neither was he, so no weapon.

Gushet shifted to the far side and the team crawled up to the ridge in unison. Keen moved instinctively, climbing his way prone up the dune, the years of Legion training rising to the surface. With the soft sand of the dunes, his portly belly wasn't getting in his way. And, he was dressed the part in Mote fatigues.

Look at you, Draden, it's like you're moving backward in time.

"There," Razor nodded past Crest to Keen, indicating he should look ahead.

A mile out, gleaming in the first rosy rays of Altiron, lines of massive propellers sat on thick posts forming an arbitrary pattern in the empty desert.

He'd made it to the Turbine Field, only not the way he'd planned. How ironic this whole trip was turning out.

Keen's eyes tracked from one turbine to the next. The structures formed a series of curvilinear patterns across the blue dunes. He couldn't grasp any perceivable coherence to the layout and design.

The turbines might be low and stout, but their scale was tremendous. He had to hand it to the Targitians. They knew their eco-technology. No wonder they'd blocked the Council's ability to wield a full-scale monopoly.

"Why that formation?" he asked Crest. The Mote handed him a monoscope. Through the zoom lens, the control station on the near side of the Turbines came into focus. Protected by a curving bubble-shaped wind wall and buffered by the ferocity of the winds from the Turbines, it remained tiny and insignificant in comparison.

"No one knows," Crest said. "We've never been able to figure it out. Look past the Field, to the right."

Keen aimed the scope to the east. The blue dunes dissipated into a long open plain of parched desert dust.

"That's the break zone, where sets of Tide Waves crash each cycle." Keen handed the lens back.

"Keltek's team is in position." It was Gushet at the far side of their line, peering through a scope. "They're ready when we are."

"You've got the lead on this, Razor," Crest said. She nodded and gave Keen a cold stare.

"What?"

"You have your medallion?"

What is that supposed to mean? "Yes, Razor. I do." Underneath the fatigues, the pendant pushed into his chest against the sand.

"Don't lose it this time."

"You stay with me," Crest said to him. "Got it?"

"I can hold my own. Just get me off this planet in one piece."

"You stay with him, Keen," Razor repeated.

"I know!" Keen whispered. "I stay with Crest."

"Keltek's team will hit the station as soon as the Dustcarrier is packed up with cells and ready to return to the Fins," she said. "Their team will take out the Carrier cutter per our standard cell raids. The Carrier always stays back far enough from the station to harness the last of the low tide current on departure. Remember we only have about an hour before the next Tide." The Mote nodded to the west.

Keen picked up a faint cerulean wave rising like a mirage on the horizon.

"They load fast so they can get back in time," Razor said. "It'll play like business as usual to the Targitian guards; a typical Mote raid, so the focus will be on the cells in the Carrier. With this small of a force they won't expect us to go for the pod in the port. Got it?"

Keen nodded.

"No matter what happens don't divert," Razor added. "Make for the backside of the station with Crest. We need that aircraft if we're going to get into low orbit for the rendezvous."

"Another pod flight with you, Razor. How could I resist?" Keen smiled his best 'fuck you' smile.

Gushet leaned forward and eyed him. "This time there'll be juice on board, gray hair. None of your diluted quicksilver." She smiled an expletive at him.

He had to admit, hers was far better and more effective. And damn the water on this planet for the reverse makeover. One thing was certain. He was going to drink all of that filthy stuff once they were in the air.

Keen lay silent watching the Targitian carrier arrive and load. After several minutes, Gushet put away the scope and nodded to the others.

"Alright, give Keltek the signal," Razor said.

Her sibling pulled out a small Beam Bouncer and set the coordinates.

"Hit it," Razor said.

Gushet shot the invisible wavelength. It reached Keltek's homing device and bounced back a confirmation.

"Go!" Razor said.

Keen was up and running. Down the sands. Up the sands. Down the sands. Up the sands. With each ridge, the Turbines and the station came closer. It was hot. He hadn't noticed it while they lay stationary on the shaded side of the dune but Altiron was up over the horizon and the temperature had risen. Sweat tightened the creases of his pants and sleeves.

This was the worst part of an ambush. Until you reached the target and the element of surprise gave you the upper hand you were vulnerable and at the mercy of chance.

Heroon flashed into his mind. He was running at speed through the dense greenery of the rainforest. Red and blue laser shots whizzed by him. His feet strode in earnest through the mud. Large purple leaves and violet stems slapped and smacked his body. The screams of the fallen, and the falling, rang through his ears. Sparks exploded around him. Larger reports hit his platoon making for the attack zone, sending dirt, branches, and body parts into the air. The Legion ambush wasn't an ambush. It was a reverse slaughter.

"Get down!" his platoon leader screamed.

Keen dove to the ground and blue sand splattered his face.

"Move it, Dreck. Come on," Crest said and tugged him back up. "We're almost there."

Keen stumbled forward, relieved to be in the open on an ambush on Kol 2, with rebels he didn't support and not back in that memory of horror on Heroon.

"Look," Crest pointed as he ran. "Keltek's team's engaging. And there go the station guards after them."

That was good, at least. No one was going to pick them off. Until he made it to the building, he was like a target prop on those shooting games in jump port casinos, popping up and down, in and out of sight, with each dune crest. But in this case, the prize wasn't a small AI toy. And you couldn't push the reset button.

Keen reached the station and put his back to the wall, squatting next to Crest and panting. Razor and Gushet disappeared around the corner. Crest edged up and peeked with his one eye through a porthole.

"Clear. This way." He started in the direction of Razor and Gushet.

Keen followed, staying low. Crest reached the corner and turned.

"Remember, when I..."

An explosion ripped through the early morning silence. Crest was blown into the chaos. Everything from the edge of the building where he stood and onward was consumed in the detonation. Like a magician throwing a plume of red smoke the Mote vanished. The world shrunk in Keen's vision and closed its eyes.

The first sensation to return was hands on his face. Information came from both surfaces; the hands were his own. In a world of darkness, fingers stretched apart and the rosy light of Altiron shot streaks of pain through his head. He rolled to the side and observed his body dumbly.

What...

The explosion returned as a silent image, the Mote's body vanishing into a plume of flame and smoke.

Keen's brain rebooted. His eyes did a visual scan.

Legs. Arms. No blood.

With trembling arms, he pushed up to a seated position. The world swayed like a boat in rough seas. High-pitched sounds entered his ears but everything in the middle and low decibel range was muffled. A dark shadow cast his legs in shadow.

Razor stood, blue dust and crimson speckling her onyx skin. She spoke in jumbled language, pointing to her left.

"Can't hear you," Keen said from the ground.

Dunemarked hands gripped his chest and pulled him up. She shoved him away from the direction of the explosion. After a few steps, he glanced back. She ducked around the corner and was gone.

Get to the pod.

Keen stumbled towards the backside of the station.

What happened? Were they set up or did the Targitians know where they'd emerge? He took a minute before going further to pinch his nostrils, blowing air out his ears. The middle and lower ranges returned. And so did the sound of blaster fire.

He ran around the corner, and into the arms of Pox.

"Draden," the Hamut said, eyes glowing vivid orange, hand around his neck. The bounty hunter threw him to the ground. He hit hard. The same gritty surface of the holding cell and torture chamber on Heroon dug into his cheek. The same malicious enemy stood over him. Fear clutched him.

"Been what, twenty-five years?" she said and thrust a boot into his gut.

He yelped and cowered. Reality blurred between worlds of memory and the present. Masked faces eyed him from behind identity shields in the hot and humid torture cell on Heroon. Pox worked him for information, relishing the physical abuse.

"No, please. No more," he begged, holding his hands up from the ground in the hangar.

"No more? What are you talking about Draden?" The same fire burned in her orange eyes as in the cell on Heroon. "I haven't even started yet. The Targitians don't even need your body. So, I get to have some fun with you." She kicked him again and his kidney exploded in searing pain.

"Please… please." He shielded his face.

"Let's go." The Hamut grabbed one of Keen's arms and dragged him across the platform bordering the tarmac.

Bursts of green flashes erupted from across the interior. The bounty hunter released her grip on his arm and returned fire. Keen rolled over and caught a glimpse of Razor and Gushet engaging Pox and the two AI droids from the far side of the station.

Blasters fired in both directions.

"Keen go!"

It was Razor. He turned towards her voice. She and Gushet worked a double attack from two sides behind cargo containers, forcing Pox and the droids to find cover. The bounty hunter and her AI stooges made it to a nearby control system and hunkered down, returning fire.

Keen closed his eyes tight to shut out the battle.

"Keen." A voice, confident and supportive, spoke in his ear.

It can't be.

"Keen."

He opened his eyes. His sibling hovered over him, the purple foliage of Heroon's dense canopy around his head. Smoke and the smell of burnt flesh mixed with cries of terror.

"Rise sibling. Aim true." Reardon reached out his arm. Keen took it and he pulled him up.

"We're Legion. To the end." Reardon bumped his fist to Keen's chest.

To the end.

"This isn't your time. Not yet."

Keen shook off the secondary world before his eyes. He made for the station's corner where he'd been nabbed by Pox and rounded it. Five long strides and he was back where the first explosion started the chaos. Through the lingering smoke, Crest appeared. He lay, gasping for air, legs gone below the knees. Keen ran over and kneeled. He knew what to do. Crest's blaster was still on his waist. And there was a combat knife sheathed on his chest.

"Hold on, Crest."

Keen rested the angled blade against one of the open wounds and fired. The shot nicked Crest's appendage and flew off into the air. The Mote screamed and passed out. Keen repeated it on the second leg, cauterizing the raw flesh.

He dragged him to safety along the station wall. That was when he noticed it. No more blasters and no more explosions, only a haunting silence.

He chanced a peek around the corner. The Dustcarrier was in pieces, blown to bits. It'd been a plant, full of explosives and set in waiting for their arrival. Most of Keltek's team lay scattered around the vehicle, victims of the initial blast. The rest sat lined up on their knees, hands on their heads. Two Targitian station guards had their blasters on them. The Hamut strode toward the line of captured Motes.

"It's over, Draden," Pox shouted. "Your twins are pinned down. The AI droids have them in Y formation. You remember that one, I know. That's how we took down your platoon."

"Damn," Keen whispered. The Motes were trapped. They were all going to Targite, even Razor and Gushet unless they chose death.

Forget the Motes. Forget this planet. And screw that Hamut demon.

He went to rise and make for the pod.

"Let's have some fun, Draden." Pox yelled. "How many will it take?"

He stopped.

"You remember this one, don't you Draden?"

Oh no. He pivoted and peered around the corner. The bounty hunter drew the signature weapon from its scabbard on her hip, waving it arrogantly in the air.

The Spineblade. Pox's personalized pain-giver. A laser-blade with serrated charges glitching the circuitry to cause an otherwise keen blade to fight the very material it cut. The more physical strength used to slide it through its victim the more intense the pain it inflicted.

Keen collapsed down the side of the wall, pressing his hands into his face to squeeze out the world. This place. This situation. This bounty hunter. This weapon. He couldn't do it.

"No. No. No. No." He rocked forward and backward and squeezed tighter until tears pushed out of the corners of his eyes.

His chest heaved up and down but there was no air. He was wheezing and the edge of total meltdown.

"I'm going to enjoy this," Pox said.

"You can't do this!" he screamed.

"Oh, so you are still ticking," the Hamut shouted back. "I was worried you'd gone soft on me. What's my motto, Draden? Tell your two friends, the ones pinned down."

A Mote screamed in agony. Keen knew by the sound that Pox severed a limb.

"No quarter!" the bounty hunter yelled out. Another scream. Keen knew another limb fell.

I can't. I can't. I can't.

Fear took him. He ran for the pod.

"You're taking too long, Draden." Pox's voiced chased him through the desert air like an invisible wasp intent on stinging its prey. "Let's cut a throat."

He rounded the corner to the hangar and slipped, falling flat on his face. Hard rock tiles smashed his cheek. The medallion tore into his chest, ripping him with pain.

Scarpa's voice ran through him.

Spirit of justice and unbending morality to fight for those...

Another scream.

Keenie, please.

An alarm rang in his soul. It had been set two decades earlier. His eyes opened. Reardon was back, standing over him.

"Reardon?"

"Rise sibling. Aim true." Reardon reached out his arm. Keen took it.

"We're Legion. To the end."

To the end.

Reardon and the tropical rainforest of Heroon vanished. Keen stood alone in the hangar. A shaking hand reached under his fatigues and pulled out the medallion. His eyes stared at the milky stone. He gripped it tight.

For you, Scarpa.

He knew what to do. Crates of energy cells stacked and ready for loading sat on the side of the hangar closest to the others. They would do the job, but it meant what remained of Keltek's team making the ultimate sacrifice. If it worked there was still a chance. The Motes might get the dignity they deserved and become more than subaltern outcasts and victims of unjust execution.

Keen crossed the hanger. His trembling hands ripped open a box. He fought the shaking and worked a series of connections using the available wiring. The cells were like anvils. He could carry and throw three, at most. He hoped it was enough to do the job, and that they would reach far enough to get the result he wanted.

Screams from Pox's victims continued to haunt his ears.

Hands cradling three energy cells, Keen lumbered to the corner where Razor and Gushet were trapped by the Hamut's droids. Bewildered expressions crossed their faces from their trapped position near the smoldering Carrier when they saw Keen.

He signaled for them to hunker down and cover up their mouths and noses.

"You're farther gone than I thought, Draden," Pox yelled, admonishing him.

No Pox, I've just come back.

He hurled the energy cells, one after another, into the air and ducked behind the wall. The explosions hit in three reports. They were more noxious smoke than combustible force, but Razor and Gushet got the cover they needed to get to him and make for the pod.

Pox, and the remaining members of Keltek's squad, would be lucky to get away before they were overcome with noxious fumes. And once those cells fully leaked out, it would be a good five minutes before anyone could pass through without collapsing and retching. Or worse, lapsing into a seizure. Razor appeared through the fumes dragging a wounded Gushet, both shielding their mouths and noses.

"Where's Crest?" Razor asked, coughing and laying down Gushet.

"Around the corner. He's lost his legs. I cauterized them as best I could."

Razor was off to retrieve him.

Gushet nodded to Keen from where she reclined. He reciprocated.

"I'm sorry I couldn't do more," he said.

"This was a setup," she said, panting. "Anything salvaged is a win now."

His eyes went to her side. She was hit. By the amount of blood coming through her fatigues, it looked serious. Razor returned with Crest and lay him down a few feet back.

"Get out of here while you can," Gushet said and coughed. "Take Crest and make for the pod. I'll buy you the time you need."

"No, sibling. I won't leave you." Razor bent down and grabbed her sleeve to pull her up.

"You must," Gushet pulled her arm free of her sibling's grip. "Hoti and I were always protecting you. But you don't need us anymore."

Keen sensed the same bond in their exchange that he'd known with Reardon.

"Save your children, sibling," Gushet said. "Save our people while we still can." Her onyx skin softened around her blue eyes. "I was wrong and you were right."

The reference was lost on Keen, but it was clear that a long-held argument between them had been put to rest.

Razor's cheeks trembled. It was the same steady twitching, edging on collapse, he'd seen in the longboat.

Gushet smiled and placed a bloody hand on her twin's cheek.

"I was always fierce, sibling. Like the rushing heat of the Tide Wave. But you're the slow burn of the desert sun on the sand."

A distant roar passed over the Turbine Field. The sweat on Keen's exposed skin warmed as if hit with intense sunlight.

"This is to be my end. Not yours." Gushet put two fingers to her lips and made a circle. Razor reciprocated.

The wounded Mote pulled out her canteen. She took a long swig, chugging as much down as she could muster. Yellow liquid dribbled out the sides of her mouth and down onto her fatigues. Gushet spat out the last of what she couldn't swallow. Dark red blood mixed with the viscous golden elixir.

The Mote smiled through blood-stained teeth and tossed the canteen at Keen.

"The rest is for you, Dreck." She wiped her lips of blood and Mote juice. "If you can finish all of it." She gave him a drinker's grin.

Gushet held up her fists to Razor. "Rise Kol 2." She grunted an obscenity to work through the pain of the wound in her side and rose. "Now, I'm going to fuck this Hamut bitch up." She drew two curved daggers from an X-strap across her chest. Their blades held a red sheen along the edge as if they'd already tasted blood. "I've been waiting to use these." She grinned and walked through the wafting smoke.

"Goodbye, sibling," Razor whispered.

It was now or never. "Come on," he said to Razor, tugging on her arm.

He'd been here before with his sibling and understood the need for haste.

"Razor, we have to go now." He tugged her again.

She pulled away from him defiantly without turning.

He had to be cold. The Legion solider in him knew it was the only way to not be defeated by your heart in the heat of battle. Mourning had to wait until later when you too were still alive.

The Mote stared into the smoke.

"Razor."

She pivoted, two ice blue suns glaring at him. "Help me with Crest," she said and made for her wounded colleague.

The two heaved the Mote leader up and ran in a fireman's carry. Crest was still unconscious. Keen inspected the stumps that were once his legs. The cauterized wounds were holding, but he'd been exposed a long time before Keen got to him. The Mote's breathing was shallow. His skin, normally obsidian, looked as if it'd been dusted with ground gray dust.

Keen had seen this too many times on Heroon. Without proper medical attention, the odds were slim.

The pod neared. A battle cry rang out behind them. Gushet's voice echoed off the roof of the open hangar. The shrieking call in the Mote language was terrifying, and he loved it. Pox was in for a surprise.

He and Razor placed Crest in the back of the pod and hurried into the cockpit.

"Same as last time," Razor said and started up the ship. "Take out any ground fire, although I don't think that'll be a problem."

"Got it." Keen took out the visor from the overhead compartment and fastened it over his eyes.

A warning alarm sounded.

"What's that?"

"Tide Wave alert. That's the problem."

A dark shadow cut off the light of Altiron out the leeward side of the port. Mid-day turned into night. Blue dust swirled into the air. Razor shut off the alert tone. The pitter-patter of sand pelted the cockpit window. Small pieces of unsecured equipment inside the hangar rolled around and hit the walls.

"Backdraft," Keen said.

"Time to fly." Razor throttled up the engines and they surged out of the port. The pod bucked in the turbulent air. Heat lightning flashed, illuminating smoldering vehicles and destruction around the station. Keen caught a glimpse of Pox and Gushet in fierce hand-to-hand combat through the smoke.

"Are we going to clear it?" He glanced back at the approaching wave. It was bigger than the last one outside the bluff.

"I hope so," Razor said, fighting to keep them steady against the backdraft.

"What about Targite patrol in orbit?"

"Worry about the wave, the patrol's the least of our problems."

Keen didn't like the ongoing secret of their off-planet travel arrangements but with the Tide Wave barreling down on them Razor was right. No point in giving a damn. Melting into the dashboard or being tossed into that ungodly fury wasn't an appealing end to this day or his life. He preferred to be heavily drunk either way.

His hand went to the canteen, stroking it reassuringly. As much as he wasn't one to be invested in others, he had to admit he liked Gushet's company, especially sharing the juice. She went out in a blaze and he'd honor her by finishing this filthy stuff if they made it out of this predicament.

"We're gaining," Razor said, and ran a hand over her spiky hair to clear her face of sweat. "Four minutes at terminal velocity and we'll be ahead of it and can go exo."

Keen reached for his chest, fingering the medallion through his fatigues.

"And if it breaks first?"

She smirked and opened her mouth to speak. Keen cut her off with a raised finger.

"Allow me." He prepared to demonstrate a newfound mastery of Mote rhetoric. "*I'm* screwed. Because you've been…"

Another alert went off.

"Damn!" Razor flipped several switches.

"What is it?"

"Company"

"What?" The radar screen showed a red blip: another pod behind them.

Pox.

"How the...?"

"Turbo boosters. Custom job," Razor said, working the controls. "Saw them on the holofeed when she landed at the Fins."

Crest moaned from the passenger section behind them.

"Hang on, Crest." Razor banked hard to port, cutting across the backdraft parallel to the wave.

"Are you crazy? Turn back straight, we're losing distance."

"I've got an idea."

Keen watched Razor's eyes bounce from the Doppler radar to the pod window. What was she thinking? They were only about a third of the way up the swell. Electromagnetic flashes illuminated the titanic monstrosity to their left. It barreled over them.

"Sake of the Arm!" Keen didn't believe it could get any darker, but as the wave of wind-driven sand curled over them shadow became solid pitch, like a subterranean cavern with no light. A half-mile or so ahead a small illuminated circle remained where the barrel was open to the morning sky.

A green flash passed close to starboard.

"She's firing at us?"

The ship bucked about in the unstable interior.

"Almost at the break point," Razor said, ignoring the threat from Pox. Her eyes bounced from the radar to the narrow corridor of light ahead.

They were shooting the tube of the swell. The small exit was nearing.

"It's crashing!" Keen said as the barrel hit the planet surface to their right with immense force and noise. The pod was thrown up and inward. Razor worked to stabilize the craft, avoiding contact with the interior wall of wind.

"That crazed Hamut is still behind us," Keen said.

"Not for long."

"Will she bug out?"

"She can't now."

"What?"

"She can't get out back there," Razor said. "But she can pass us with her boosters."

More green fire whizzed by as she worked the controls and dodged the shots.

"Nice flying," Keen said.

They were gaining on the hole of light ahead, but it was shrinking.

"I think we can make it if she doesn't get us," Razor said.

Pox fired a series of laser rounds. Keen tracked them on the radar. In the narrow tube, they couldn't avoid taking a hit.

She's got us. Hamut slime…

"Hold on." Razor banked the pod to port, towards the inner Tide Wave wall.

"What are you doing?"

"It's the only way," Razor said.

Keen was at his limit. "Screw this! No way."

He clenched the dashboard. Razor released her hands from the controls with disturbing ease, as if relinquishing to an unknown force.

She's killing us. Why? We were so close.

Razor's eyes widened as the titanic blanket approached. She turned to Keen and raised her fists.

"Rise Kol 2," she whispered.

The pod levitated as if unseen, benevolent palms lifted it in a soft caress. They rose in front of the wind wall inside the crashing swell. Razor reached for the hand bars on the ceiling. The ship inverted as the current took it, following the barreling wave. Keen's body pulled on the harnesses in the seat as they went upside down. He braced himself with his hands on the bars over his seat.

"So much for getting back to Heroon." He pried the canteen from under his harness with one hand and opened it, letting Mote juice spill under gravity into his mouth. He leaned his head back as they came down the crashing side of the barrel to continue swallowing Mote juice.

Pox's pod whizzed past them on turbo boosters, making for the narrow opening to escape the sublime chasm.

"Fuck that," Razor said, "and fuck this Hamut bitch." She hit the thrusters and pulled back hard on the controls. They shot up, spiraling in the massive surge of current, pushed by the blowout of wind through the pinhole opening. The tube closed under the full break of the Tide Wave. They emerged behind Pox's pod.

"Now Keen. For Gushet,"

Keen fired on Pox's craft as they whizzed by into the open atmosphere. A burst of orange flame erupted as the vessel took a hit to one of its boosters. The wounded ship wobbled, losing altitude, a trail of golden sparks at its tail.

"Nice shooting," Razor said and slammed the burners to full, aiming the pod through Kol 2's rosy atmosphere, towards space.

Keen snickered at the mess of Mote juice all over his fatigues. Ironic? Yes, but the second time was a charm. They were on their way to Heroon after all.

THIRTEEN

First, they took my sibling Hoti and now my dear twin, Gushet. It was as if an infection was moving through my heart, forcing me to cut out portions to stave off further suffering. Hoti's death I could bear. He was always daring himself to the limit. And he was proud. Our younger sibling carried the soul of our people in his warrior's heart. He was out for justice and heroics, no matter the cost. Hoti was always going over the edge to make his presence known. Such is the way with those born last in a family, cast in shadow. I was prepared for him to take one step too far.

But Gushet's sacrifice cut me to the core. Deep down I knew that I'd never recover. You'd have to be a twin to understand. You're two bodies but one soul, spirit split, walking the world while a part of you lives outside yourself. She was older, if only by two minutes, but it showed in everything we did. My sibling was my shield from the harshness of the world, always making sure she stood between me and whatever might harm me. Now I was exposed, alone, and unprotected.

My twin went out in a blaze. Of course, she did. She was Gushet. She was more alive confronting imminent death than she'd been for almost a decade. It was good to have her back, even if only for one last display of fiery heat.

Keen's actions aren't something I can speak to with any accuracy. We were separated for most of the raid, at least until he got my sibling and me out of that jam and we made it with Crest into the pod. He could've left us, but he didn't. Somewhere along the way, he made a choice. It was a hard one. He had to take lives to save lives.

What I saw when Keen hurled the cells to create a diversion wasn't an ambassador. It was a Legion soldier. But through the cracks, an inner light shone: a broken person. Sadly, it was only a glimmer of how shattered he was.

I flew that pod inside the Tide Wave as I'd never flown before. I remember it feeling easy. When I let go of the controls, I wasn't sure my plan was going to work. Either way, it was a win. If the wave took all three of us, it'd be the grain of sand to start the dune slide that was the end of my people. As it happened, I was on the verge of recognizing my full potential as a pilot and trusting my understanding of the language of the wind.

I took a chance without forethought from somewhere within my gut. Keen assumed I'd turned on him when I released my hands. His reaction to what he perceived as my giving up, or giving in, did not affect me. I didn't care. I just did it. Gushet gifted me that when she walked through the smoke. She was holding on to the missing piece of my constitution for safekeeping. As my protector, she'd needed it. But it would've been selfish to take it with her into the flames. She was always giving to me, my older sibling. Never taking. Even to the end.

I miss Gushet every day, without fail. But a part of our divided spirit came back to me that day and it saved me. It saved Keen and Crest, and because of it, we were able to continue. That, and if I'm honest, some fine flying on my part that even drew out a compliment from Keen. I timed the thrusters at the bottom of the roll just right too. Got him good with the Mote juice.

How to sum up that day for the ages? An ambush turned into a disaster. That's how I'd record it. When the years pass and the story of that decisive incident in the narrative of our people and Kol 2 is retold, should we persevere, it will be tallied on the side of success. The sweat, blood, and tears of those who took part will vanish like smoke rising to the sky. No one will feel the tear of the fabric of life between two beloved twins. No one will know the personal regrets of Keltek and their team as they lived their last seconds of lucidity before the blade ran across their living flesh. No one will suffer a Patent war veteran's trauma under fire. These will all vanish like vapor in the desert night. The history of the state, of our culture, will endure. On that prodigious (and pretentious) scale the operation was a victory, for even with our heavy losses we were now out of the atmosphere and on our way to the rendezvous for the jump to Heroon.

FOURTEEN

"That's our ship." Razor pulled back on the pod's throttle. Ahead, a frigate hugged the arc of Kol 2. From space, the planet was deep blue. Cloudless and trimmed with a tinge of rose at the atmospheric line, it held a solemnity that hid the strife of ruin they'd left below on the surface.

"That's old school," Keen said, taking a swig of juice from the canteen. He recognized the hull type and heavy body: a weapon and transport runner from the days of the Patent War. It was a refit job. The upgrades to the defense and shield systems were subtle but state-of-the-art. Burn scars and patch repairs spoke of substantial action over the years.

"Go easy on that," Razor said. "Until we're on board and settled I need your head on straight."

"I thought you had this worked out?"

"Just lay off. And we have to get Crest help as soon as we dock."

Keen put the cap on the canteen.

Gushet… such a shame.

He was working on what was left of the juice for her (and himself) after what he'd been through in the ambush, not only for the explosion and the frenzy of the combat but Pox's arms around his neck and her leg in his side. Her contact tainted his body. He needed to scrub himself raw and remove her lingering presence.

His fingers touched his side gingerly. He winced. Every inhalation hurt. A hand ran over his ribs, inspecting them. None were broken, but he knew they would bruise. The side of his face that had slammed into the gritty floor was red hot. He'd feel all of it tomorrow morning and look like a washed-up boxer for a week.

Pox. The Hamut was a heartless killer for hire. She slaughtered Keltek's team and got off on it. Gushet would want him to pour all the juice down his throat without the mercy of social expectations. But he knew better than to push back or resist Razor's request. Losing your twin? He could barely cope with the death of Reardon. Like Gushet, Reardon was his senior, always looking out for him. But they weren't bonded in the same way she and Gushet were. Twins were different. He knew that. Still, nothing hurt like the loss of a sibling, not even what happened in the aftermath of Reardon's death on Heroon.

"Draden."

It was Crest, his first word since they'd put him on board when they fled the Turbine Field.

"Hang on, we're almost there," Razor said and glanced back as she configured the pod's docking algorithm. "Keen check on him."

Keen unbuckled and went back to the ailing rebel leader. "Hold on, Crest. Keep fighting, we're almost to the ship."

The Mote's one eye was shut. "Draden," he grunted, lapsing in and out of consciousness.

"I'm here, hang on," Keen glanced back towards the cockpit. The landing bay appeared through the ship's front window. "Razor, how long?"

"Five minutes."

Keen examined the field dressings where he'd burned the Mote's flesh shut. Only a few small trickles of blood leaked from the wounds, but Crest's face was heavy with sweat and ghostly pale.

The Mote raised a hand. "Juice me."

"We'll dock in a few minutes and then we can give you something for the pain."

Crest's ravaged face quivered, resisting Keen's denial.

"Gushet..."

He knows what happened.

"One soldier to another," Crest whispered.

Keen reached for the canteen on his hip.

"How's he doing?" Razor asked from the cockpit.

"Hanging on." Keen opened the cap and lay the rim of the canister on Crest's lips, pouring a small stream of yellow liquid down his throat.

The Mote coughed it down between gasps. He came alive and reached for Keen's sleeve. His grip tightened like a vice around Keen's bicep. The pungent smell of Mote juice wafted from Crest's mouth as he rasped out laboring breaths.

"I was wrong about you, Draden."

"What?"

Crest's eye opened wide.

"Wrong... I... tell Tinu... he and my child, that I will always .... "

His grip slacked, easing the pain on Keen's muscle. Crest's eye closed and his arm slumped down to the floor. The Mote's fingers settled like a deflated balloon.

"Crest?" Keen put his head on the Mote's chest. Nothing. Their bodies bounced as the pod came to rest in the docking bay.

"Down," Razor said and emerged from the cockpit. "Let's get him to sickbay."

Keen met her eyes and shook his head.

Razor pushed him out of the way. "Crest!" She tried to revive him, her hands pumping his chest. "Crest!"

Keen had been in her shoes. He'd done this many times in the war, often to friends he'd known from Garassia before they joined up and got themselves killed on Heroon. He knew how long to wait before you interfered. You had to give the grieving time to try, even when hope was lost. Too soon and you'd leave them with the belief they could have still saved the fallen. Too long and you risked them taking too much blame for what had happened. It was a small window. When it opened, you had to pull them away. They'd hate you when you did it and it'd never be something they'd realize had to happen. You did it because that had been you, or could be you, and you wanted the same even though when and if it did occur you didn't want to be pulled away either.

Keen watched Razor's face and waited. It shifted.

"Razor, it's over." He grabbed her arm.

"Get off of me!" She kept pumping.

"Razor, he's gone." He reached out again to pull her off Crest.

"No." She released his grip with less animosity, still pushing on the Mote's chest.

"Hey." Keen didn't go for her arm. He kept it to words. "Razor."

"What did he say?" She paused.

"What?"

"What did he say to you? I heard you two talking." The windows of her eyes buckled from an internal fury.

"Answer me!"

"He wanted juice. For your sibling."

"Juice?"

Keen nodded.

"Stupid drunks!" The strap around his shoulder snapped as the canteen was snatched out of his hands. Razor hurled it away. It clanged against the back wall, splashing yellow streaks of Mote juice across the surface.

"Get out of my way." She shoved her arm at Keen, knocking him over, and stormed out of the pod.

Well, that went about as expected.

He sighed over Crest's lifeless body.

"I'm sorry, Crest," he said. This moment had been a premonitory conclusion in Keen's mind since planning the raid. Something about the way Crest acted that morning when he spoke to the group struck him as prescient. It was as if he was passing on a reminder and relinquishing leadership like he knew this was going to happen.

Footsteps clanged on the stairs to the pod, coming back up. Keen didn't turn. He stared at the abstract pattern of tragedy dripping down the back wall.

"Well, would you look at that? Same as when I left you. All a mess with a spilled drink."

That voice. It can't be.

Keen turned.

Jati-tō.

Other than some crow's feet around the edges of their sleek and narrow green eyes and the new hairstyle, they hadn't changed in two decades. Skin the color of dried wheat covered a face carved with forceful strokes of hammer and chisel, with sweeping cheekbones and chin like fortress walls.

Built like a Legion tank, Jati stood a head taller than Keen. Heavily muscled, with broad shoulders and legs that could pull a fallen soldier for miles, Jati didn't walk around things. They walked through them. You either moved out of their way or got run over.

"Damn, Draden. You've aged badly," Jati shook their head. They nodded at Keen's long hair. "Going grey already? You need to learn to glide, my friend. You're heading to an early grave."

Curse that Mote water. Is this ever going to fade?

Keen made a mental note to ask Razor about it in private.

"I barely recognized you under that mess on your head and chin," Jati quipped.

"Yeah, well that's an interesting style you've got going on."

"Latest trend in the outer Arm, Draden." Jati ran their hands through the close-shaven hair on the sides of their head, careful to avoid the wavy lavender mohawk on top that trailed down the back to the nape of their thick neck. "Surprised you don't recognize it, being the famed Arm-traveler and all." They stepped forward and reached out a hand, smiling.

Keen was hurled to his feet as if he were a feather. Jati wrapped their arms around him, squeezing him affectionately. "How are you, soldier? What's it been, twenty-plus years?"

Keen winced in pain, resisting their embrace. "Easy, Jati." They released their grip and smacked him on the shoulder as he rubbed his ribs. "Twenty-five years," Keen said. Had it been that long? With Jati in the flesh in front of him, it felt like only yesterday that they said farewell as Keen was taken to the psychiatric rehab unit off-planet. Jati had gripped his hand and told him they'd see each other soon. Guess a quarter-century was soon.

"Still getting into trouble?" Jati threw a jab at Keen's ribs, stopping just shy of hitting him.

Keen flinched, which produced a barreling laugh from his old comrade.

"You could say that, although this wasn't my doing. Jati, what're you doing here?"

"Protecting my investment."

"You're working with the Motes?"

Jati shook their head. "I don't work with anyone, Draden. I'm freelance. Welcome aboard my ship, the *Carmora*."

"What investment?" Crest's lifeless body rested at peace next to him. It couldn't be the Motes. And where had Razor gone?

"Do you have it or does she? Because one of you owes me."

"Have what?"

Jati made as if holding a small object in their palm.

The cube.

Keen watched the smirk grow on Jati's face. Their flax-colored skin, weathered from years of hard living, creased into a tight set of folds. Green eyes sparkled with satisfaction.

"So, you have it?" Jati said. "Good. I was hoping you might at least be capable of that, old tot. Hand it over."

Keen pulled out the cube and placed it into Jati's open hand.

"I don't understand."

"That's alright, kid. You never had too much going on up there." Jati knocked on Keen's head with their knuckles.

"Ouch. Cut that crap, Jati." Keen shoved their arm away.

Jati laughed and smacked Keen on the shoulder again. One or two more times and he was going to have another bruise to add to the ones he'd already got.

"What about the ransom money for the cube?"

"What about it? You're here now so let's call it even. I owe you some winnings from that last game of Jinta anyway. With twenty-five years of inflation, it's a wash. Just be glad the Motes had me in orbit on retainer as a last resort option."

"I don't understand."

"Like I said," Jati went for his head with the knuckles again but Keen's hand was up before they could get to him. Jati backed off to explain. "I brokered some weapons for the Motes to fight the good fight on Kol 2. When I caught wind of the target for their little abduction and ransom scheme, I decided it was worth it to cube you. Got in touch with an old pal who works dark-ops and dirt… you know, a ghost trader. Turns out some fresh financials on you are floating around, so I took out a life insurance policy on you in case their plan failed. Good thing I did, or you'd probably be dead."

So that's how the Motes got equipment and weapons for the strike on Targite. I'll bet Jati gave them strategic advice that they ignored. They were the Patent War connection.

"Yeah, well lucky for me I'm an ambassador with negotiation skills," Keen said.

"I knew you'd be alright. But I'm curious how you managed it. You'll have to tell me all about it."

"But Jati, how did the Motes know about my travel plans?"

"You got me, Draden. Did you set it up under the table?"

"Yes, it's personal."

"Well, all I know is you were in the cube-mark database. They said you'd just been added."

Ghost traders, always selling lives to the highest bidder. I should've waited to discuss financial business in person on Heroon.

"Come on, Draden. Let's get this poor fellow to the morgue and find your partner. Then I'll get you a drink to make up for the one you let go to waste on the wall and we'll catch up."

Jati lifted Crest on their own and made for the pod stairs.

"She's not my partner," Keen said, following Jati down the steps of the pod.

"Whatever you say."

The ship trembled.

"Did we just jump?"

Jati raised one hand with a thumb's up while carrying Crest as they crossed the docking bay to the elevator.

"Where are we going?"

"Taking a stroll around the galaxy. I need to make a pick-up at the moon base on Tarkassi 9."

"Tarkassi 9. Picking up what?"

Jati hit the transport tube button and the capsule opened.

"Let's drink. Then talk shop." Jati winked.

RAZOR ENTERED the ship's mess where Keen and Jati sat working on a bottle of kartan. Worked was more like it. Jati poured out the last bit into Keen's glass. Finally, some decent drink. He hadn't sipped kartan in a decade. It was impossible to come by, distilled from the secretion of the rare karta plant that thrived in the atmosphere of one uninhabitable planet near the end of the Arm. The decoction was so prized that the world was left unshaped to preserve a supply of the ingredient. Two minor wars and a handful of attempted coups in the system were preserved in the Third Age annals over the lure of the extraordinary plant. To get their hands on a supplement Jati must have been doing some serious jumping through systems. Not to mention greasing the right palms.

"Where've you been?" Keen asked as she joined them at the table.

"Resting," Razor said. "What's that?" She gestured at the slender flute in Jati's hand. Ten inches high with a narrow sinuous curve from rim to base, the elegant kartan flute matched the sophistication of the elixir.

"Kartan," Keen said.

"Never heard of it."

"How about it?" Jati offered Razor their glass between index finger and thumb. Razor went to grab it. Jati pulled it back.

"Like this." They demonstrated how to hold it with the two digits. "It's a tradition, ages old."

"You drink?" Keen asked.

Razor took the glass between finger and thumb and took a sip.

"That's not your crass Mote juice," Keen said.

Razor ignored him. "It's good." She smiled at Jati in thanks. "I'll have some."

"Excellent!" Jati slammed both hands on the table. "Grab that bottle Draden and fill us all up."

You've got to be kidding...

Everything hurt. Even rising from his seat was enough to make him want to...

"Ouch!" Keen bolted a few steps as Jati slapped him on the ass. "What the heck, Jati?" He rubbed his butt to still the pain and walked to the counter.

Jati laughed and motioned to Razor.

"See how he moves?" They pointed a thumb back at Keen. "Just checking to be sure you still could, old tot." The same happy-go-lucky teasing expression was on their face as back on Heroon in the Legion.

"Shall we make sure you're keeping up with your dailies? How many push-ups can you do?"

Razor chuckled. Keen snapped his neck toward her with a glare.

"Come on, how many?" Jati asked. "Why don't you drop and show us?"

"In your dreams." This had a limit. Time to end it before he morphed into a total fool. The growing amusement on Razor's face wasn't helping.

"What? Something funny, Razor?"

She didn't respond. Instead, her grin widened.

Keen grabbed a glass and another bottle off the shelf.

"I just realized something," Razor said. "They outrank you, don't they?"

"That I do." Jati whistled a smug swirling note and rested their arms below the tail of their mohawk.

"Cut the crap, Jati."

"Chunks or slices?" They winked at Razor, who burst out a laugh. It was the first time she'd lowered her guard since they'd been thrown together. So, she did have a sense of humor beyond sarcasm.

"I'm guessing toilet jokes are popular in Mote culture?" Keen said. "You two are having so much fun, aren't you?"

"You're blushing, Draden," Jati said, pointing at him and winking.

"I'll still drink you under the table any time, you back planet Gor hunter."

"Hah! That's the spirit," Jati rose and put their arm around Keen, buddy style. "That's the Draden I know." They hugged Keen. The strength and solidity of Jati's muscled frame was palpable against his flab. They'd kept themselves fit. He was glad for them. Jati'd been through their own world of horror in the war. But they were always a survivor, even from their earliest days raised on the cold and bleak planet of Ortor by Garassian ex-pat parents. You could use them on a promotional for the Legion and they'd pull in a dozen recruits each day with their warrior grin.

"You always bragged you could drink anyone under the table," Jati said, and sat back down, "but I remember that time at Parshoo marsh."

"Parshoo marsh? Really? How many times have we been over this? You and Lexar didn't stay until the end. She told everyone I passed out, but Reardon..." Keen paused.

Jati's grin went limp. Razor, aware of the tension, lowered her gaze in the silence.

"Come on," Jati said to both of them. "Let's get this mission rolling. Sit down, buddy."

Keen put the glass and bottle on the table and sat. Jati poured some kartan for Razor.

"Now, get me up to speed. What's all this about and why am I taking you to Heroon?"

IT WAS LATE. The three still sat at the table, on the fourth bottle of kartan.

Keen was fading. The early start. The ambush. Pox. The slaughter and trauma. The kartan. Ah, the kartan. No more pain but his mental will was on overtime and ready to clock out. His eyelids gave notice, but his mind refused to accept their resignation. The two battled, revealing and veiling the view of the table and his companions.

"So, let me get this straight," Jati said and pointed a finger.

"Haven't we gone over this three times?" Keen slurred.

Jati ignored him. "The Targitians need you dead or else they've got a political mess on their hands. And they brought *her* in to stop you."

"A pox on Pox," Keen slugged back more kartan to steel himself against the memory of the bounty hunter.

"A pox on Pox," Jati echoed his words and slammed their drink.

"We took her out," Razor said. "She's not a problem now."

"No, no, no, Razor." Keen shook his head. "That monster has a way of surviving."

"She went down. You saw it."

"Tell her, Jati." Keen gestured and knocked over his glass, spilling kartan.

Jati picked it up and refilled it. "Unless you have the body, assume she's alive," they told Razor. "That killer has a way of reappearing like a ghost. I tell you it's uncanny and a real nuisance." Keen watched Jati gaze at Razor's hand on the kartan flute. "May I see your hands?" Jati reached for her fingers. She extended her arms towards them. "These are beautiful markings. I've heard of the Dunemarks but I've never seen them."

"Thank you."

"Get on with it," Keen said, breaking up the interlude.

Jati released her hands.

Did they linger? Or am I drunk and seeing things?

"And Razor," Jati said, "you say Keen is going to organize military support for your coup attempt to take Targite, to seize control of the city and their energy production? In short, total revolution. If you get him to Heroon."

Razor nodded, sipping her drink. "My people are in a do-or-die situation. We either overcome our oppressors or we're wiped out forever. It's time for us to rise."

"And Draden," Jati leaned towards him, wobbling from the booze, their steel green eyes hinting at the heavy intake of kartan. "You need to get Razor weapons and a sizable militia? You say you're going to get the Council to fund this to remove the Targitian competition?"

"That's the plan." Keen slammed back another shot.

Which means speaking with my parent on Council. I can't wait.

"It better work, *Ambassador*," Razor said.

"Fuck you, Razor."

"Fuck you, Keen! You Dreck. You think…"

"Hey, hey!" Jati held up their hands.

"Stop it, both of you. Keen, what's in this for you?"

"What does that mean?" he asked.

"It means why are you doing this?"

"Made a deal," Keen cast a salty eye at Razor. "That's how I got off that pile of sand."

Jati raised a polite hand to stay Razor's retort.

"I mean, why are we taking you to Heroon?"

"That's private," Keen slurred.

"I know why," Razor whispered, staring into her glass.

"You don't know anything, Razor."

"Easy buddy." Keen felt Jati's giant paw on his arm.

"I do," Razor said. "You have a child."

"How the…?"

The mess room started spinning and his head grew woozy.

"A child?" Jati asked.

"Yeah, Jati. I have a child."

"On Heroon?"

"Yes." With regret, he watched Jati's face through the kartan haze. It went soft with confusion at the implications during the war.

"I found out when you were juiced. The medallion opened when you laid down in the cavern. It was there in front of me," Razor said. "I needed information for leverage. I'm sure, being a politician, you understand."

It doesn't matter. Nothing matters.

"On Heroon?" Jati repeated.

"Yes, she's on Heroon… leading some futile cause and stirring up trouble."

"Not *the* cause?"

"I don't know, Jati."

"Keen." Even through the drunken haze, Keen picked up on Jati's shift in tone. And their unusual use of his first name. Razor's eyes perked up from behind her kartan glass.

"What?"

"Is her name Reynaria?"

Keen slammed back the rest of the kartan. "What is it with you two? Now you're mind readers?"

"Keen, is it?"

"Yes, it is... Reynaria. How'd you know?"

"Everyone on Heroon involved in the resistance knows Reynaria. Her name is getting attention in tenuous systems around the Arm." Jati poured themself another glass and topped off Razor's as well. "I think both of your problems are no longer separate."

"Is that good?" Razor asked.

"I'd say it's... complicated."

"You know her, Jati?" Keen asked.

"Everyone on Heroon knows *of* Reynaria. But I know her more personally. I mean, professionally."

"How?"

"She's the leader of the Resistance."

"The Resistance?" Razor interjected. "That means she's aligned with Targite."

"Like I said," Jati took a sip of kartan, "it's complicated."

The leader of the Resistance? Jati had to be kidding. The irony was growing at an exponential rate. *That* required more kartan. Keen reached for his glass. He couldn't get it. Two appeared in front of him and he kept choosing the wrong one.

Jati slid it into his hand. "You're about done, old tot."

Keen moved his mouth to the glass rather than the other way around, sipping, an old drunkard's trick. "You mean, 'personally'?" he asked Jati.

"I'm in the arms business now," they winked. "Used to move ice from the outer planets but that went sour when the Targitians challenged Garassian territory. Can't compete with those wind energy prices even on the edges of the Arm."

"You're supplying my oppressors with weapons?" Razor eyes were on fire.

Hope this stuff doesn't have the ignition of Mote juice.

Jati raised both hands in their defense. "I'm freelance. But I'm for the exploited, no matter what 'side' they're on. My heart is Legion, even if I no longer wear the uniform. If someone's getting screwed by big business or a monopoly, I'll help them push back."

"And what about the Hamut Alliance?" Razor asked.

"What about them? They're enforcers. What choice did they have after the war? The Hamuts lost everything, even their home planet was destroyed." Their head bobbed to Keen. "As far as I'm concerned, both sides are at fault. Sorry buddy, no offense to your profession or your parent on Council but I won't forgive what they did after the war. It's wrong to enforce a non-proliferation act. Because you had something first doesn't give you a right to keep others from it as well. Worse is to deny people from producing energy with the means their planet provides. Sanctions hurt no one but the common people. I'm for humanity. For self-reliance. For dignity."

"And what about the dignity of my people?" Razor asked. "How are they served when you're arming a Resistance supported by a monopoly that kills its own kind?"

"Reynaria wants Heroon released from sanctions, freed from the abuses of the Garassian colonial chokehold. She needs the Targitians to do it. Aiding her cause is a thorn in the Council's side. It pushes back against Targite's rival, so they give her funding. Do they want an independent Heroon? Of course not. But helping them resist is better than the planet staying in the hands of their rivals."

"Isn't going to happen. It's all screwed up," Keen said. "We're all biting our asses."

"What does that mean?" Razor asked.

"It means it's all about money and power," Keen said. "Always is."

"And your child is in the middle of it," Jati said. "Like parent like…"

Keen whipped the bottle off the table with a swat of his hand. "Take that back, Jati! And as for you," he pointed a finger at Razor. "You don't know anything." He rose and stumbled over his chair, slamming down on the cold tile.

"Whoa, old tot." Keen levitated. Razor appeared upside down at the table. "You're done. I'm putting you to bed."

"You don't get it. Either of you," Keen slurred. "You don't know what happened."

"But I do, buddy," Jati said. "I do."

Keen watched the floor pass as blood rushed to his head. The upside-down room blurred. It was the pleasure of the fade, drink's beautiful way of making it all disappear.

His world went dark. A repetitious up and down bouncing of footfalls rocked him into a stuporous lullaby. His mind switched into low power mode.

"Hey, Draden."

Keen re-emerged from his kartan-induced stupor but his eyes didn't open. He was prone. That much he knew, with his back on a soft, cushy surface.

"I'm sorry, Jati."

"It's alright, old tot. Nothing to be sorry about. We're Legion, you and I. To the End."

Keen let out a sob that echoed through the darkness.

"Shhh…"

Jati's powerful hand rested on his forehead.

"How do you do it, Jati?"

"Do what?" Jati's voice was low, only a whisper.

"Forget? How do you go on like it's all ok?"

The hand stroked his hair.

"You think it's easy?"

"You're fine," Keen said. "How are you fine?"

"I'm far from it, old tot. I've learned to make peace with it. But it comes and goes. I might appear all together on the outside but every day's a struggle."

"Is it worth it?"

Jati sighed.

"Jati?"

"You have to find something to make it worth it. That's why I do what I do. I tell myself I'm stopping what happened to us from happening to others."

Keen's mouth trembled as he held back sobs.

"Hey, it's ok. You can let it out. It's just us. I know… believe me, I know."

"The dreams, Jati… the dreams. They're too much."

"I know."
"I was holding it together. But she's back… Pox."
"Shh…" Jati's hand stroked his head.
"You have something now. Something to make all this worth it."
"What?"
"A child."

FIFTEEN

With Crest gone, it was all on me. The weight of the new responsibility sunk into my chest. But it also gave water to a dormant seed. I'd wanted this for as long as I could remember: to be the one at the front of the line, the one to whom others would defer at the Throat Pool and the one to take the chances and bring home the reward. I didn't want Crest dead. Yet I didn't mourn him the way I did Gushet, or Hoti, or those who weren't my blood. This was different. We were siblings of a different kind. Our people were our children. When someone's time was up the next in line stepped in to ensure the Two Eyes. That's how I felt when Keen shook his head over Crest's body. It was my turn.

That, more than anger or lament, was what I had to face when I stormed out of the pod. In the safety of the ship, once we jumped, fear of that reality looked back at me in my reflection.

And then there was Jati. They were just a weapons smuggler we'd hired before the failed abduction, all business on our first encounter on neutral ground in some dingy watering hole at the Kol 2 jump hub. Intriguing? Yes, but under those conditions, the cold boundary of commerce and politics stood between us. Jati was just another drifter living on the edges of the Arm until I walked into the ship's mess to find the two of them drinking.

They were like two bookends from the war. Both had survived (or had they?) by finding their way to places where they could cope. They stood on opposite ends of the shelf, using separate coping mechanisms that worked just enough for each to bear the next breath, the next day, the next jump. The one who gave in to anger, resentment, and self-importance ended up an ambassador. The other found a tolerable form of acceptance in neutrality masquerading as moral nomadism (maybe it was it guilt?). Embers of bravery still burned inside Jati. A low heat fueled a course that focused on the needs of others. Was either of them more right than the other? Each had a heart cut and chipped by war to a small life pulse, desperate to go on beating despite the persistence of memory.

The letter was a moment of pettiness. Death, anger, fear... that day was filled with insidious beasts clawing and tearing me to pieces. It ended with me drinking at a table with someone I wanted to thank but still considered an enemy. That reveal was my way to take a small nick out of Keen's heart. It might have given me a brief, fleeting satisfaction, but he'd forgotten it the next day. That was the drink doing what it did best for Keen, as it did for Gushet and so many others who suffer unspeakable personal horrors. I was relieved he didn't remember. I was able to take something back that might have made it more difficult between us.

Jati was like a referee between two prizefighters in a ring around the kartan bottle. Despite our tensions, it was a brief respite and distraction from the stress of that day to witness Jati turn Keen's arrogance and privilege dial down to a low hum. It drew up a different song, in the same key as the one I witnessed when he engaged Pox and aided our escape. The Legion soldier cast its light and pushed the ambassador into shadow, albeit briefly. But if you remember, a broken person emerged in that ambush. Since the first day in the pod when I pointed a blaster at Keen, the support systems around him fell away. He was returning to a former self while slipping into the abyss of personal trauma that came with it.

I didn't stay at the table that night, sipping kartan like a parent relishing the silence as their partner carried a misbehaving child up to bed. No, I followed them. It wasn't voyeuristic on my part. It was diplomatic. Keen's life kept rubbing off on me as he shed it. When Keen was drunk, his inner light shined bright. I got to know him most then, as immoral as it was to make myself privy to such intimate things. I crossed an unspoken boundary and regretted it. The honest words that reached my ears outside his room weren't meant for anyone but Jati. I violated Keen's privacy and the guilt lingers still, years later.

I did lay down with Jati that night. But all we did was sleep, embraced. They knew what I needed and respected an unspoken threshold. At the table drinking kartan, Jati didn't ask me what my Dunemarks said, as Keen had. They requested to view them, to hold the hands of my people and scrutinize them with close eyes and tender touches. Whether they knew their meaning or not, it mattered to me that they took the time to enter into a relationship with an intimate respect for my privacy, my culture, and my self-expression (how ironic that only minutes later I'd violate that very principle).

Jati followed the same ethic in how they handled Keen. It didn't matter that we were now on opposite political sides; they would help if he needed it. Jati's soliloquy while we poured kartan down our throats stung. The apolitical gesture of support against hegemonic regimes, regardless of the particulars, was the first new test for me with Crest gone. Could I stretch beyond my circumstances and ego, and place things within a larger picture? What responsibility did I have to others in similar situations to my own? Old Urtani came to my mind, a new sympathy for her choices and actions rising in a swell of guilt and self-reproach that crashed as I lay in Jati's strong arms. She and I were now the Eyes, but the vision of our people was fractured and beset by distortions of distance. And generations.

As the night wore on, and we passed through time and space at immeasurable speed, it all faded into background noise. For a brief few hours, I found solace and respite from it all.

SIXTEEN

"Well, if it isn't my dead child back from the grave. So, the Targitians didn't get you after all."

"Hello, parent." Keen sat in the *Carmora's* com station, the holographic transmitter connecting two humans over a distance greater than 3,000 light-years. Ceron was inside the edge of the ship's transmission range, edging a belt of star clusters that otherwise blocked communications through high radiation emissions. Jati managed to shoot the needle and get him a brief window while they made the pick-up at the moon base.

Keen felt like he'd been smeared with a festering pile of detritus, which was perfect for a conversation with his parent. Bones and muscles moaned and wailed in full trauma reaction from his injuries and Pox's abuse. His innards were in shock from the amount of kartan he'd consumed the previous night. Together they made for one hell of a wake-up party.

Keen was as uncomfortable talking to his parent, Aradus Draden-ti, in virtual form halfway across the Sag-Arm as he was in person. The legendary Ambassador never failed to stir his insecurities into a frenzy. Didn't all parents? It was what Aradus didn't say that did it. He'd drop a pause in a conversation that would fester inside the psyche for weeks. That same talent made him a brilliant diplomat and political negotiator. The best thing you could do, he always told Keen, was to make sure whomever you speak with leaves without being able to leave you behind. And speaking of not being able to leave Aradus behind, his parent ate, breathed, and slept diplomacy. Retirement wasn't in his vocabulary. At 81, he was the oldest and most senior Council member and still spoke words of lightning that electrified listeners.

Keen, as his parent reminded him often, never lived up to expectations in their profession. Even before he and his sibling joined the Legion, Aradus marked Reardon as the one with the potential for a career in diplomacy. His first child's future held the promise of the family legacy and its prestige. Reardon demonstrated a scholarly aptitude from an early age, combined with a brave heart and infectious good-natured kindness. It was a hard act to follow for a second child who was less inclined to books and history and more interested in physical activities and challenges of a competitive nature.

Reardon's shadow loomed large in the Draden household and Keen never did quite escape it. Despite the amicable friendship between the siblings, a dynamic of favoritism was ever-present with Aradus. The lack of attention and mentoring their parent gave to his younger child only added fuel to the fire of disappointment surrounding Keen.

"I assume you have an explanation for your failure? You always do." Aradus's dusty brown hair was thinning and pushed back, with identical patches of white running above his ears. His features were narrower and sharper than Keen's and gave off the intensity of a bird of prey.

Failure? Does he mean Targite or in general? Because if it's in general we'll be a while.

Levity. The only cure Keen ever found for the parental dynamic. But it was always unspoken. Inner monologue was such a good therapist. That and drink. The latter worked for all failures in his life. Ah yes, drink; panacea for the world.

"I survived an attempted abduction turned assassination attempt."

"Clearly." Aradus directed his gaze off-frame and ran his finger across a tablet held by someone who needed his signature. "You always do seem to survive the most trying of circumstances, even when others more capable, and heroic, fail to do so."

Keen pushed down the guilt. His parent's not-so-implicit reference to the loss of his older sibling in the war had come up earlier than usual this time. If Aradus knew the truth about Reardon's death, would he still chastise him so? The specifics of Reardon's end, and by whose hands, was locked deep in a closet. It was too painful and too complicated, to share with anyone. So far as Aradus was concerned, Reardon fell during their escape from the Hamut prison, heroically sacrificing himself so his younger sibling could survive.

"Alright, Keen. How much is it going to cost this time?"

"Actually, I've got an opportunity…"

"I'm sure you do," Aradus said.

"No, parent…"

"How much, Keen?"

"It's complicated."

"It always is," Aradus said.

"No, let me explain."

Aradus rolled his eyes and leaned back in his chair, gesturing for his child to proceed with predictable theatrics.

"The Targitians are in a bind. Now that I'm off Kol 2, they have a problem… a big one. They can't defend their attempt to play the Mote ambush as an opportunity to sway the Council by killing me and making it look like I was a casualty of the abduction."

Aradus's aged eyes perked up.

Keen continued while he had his parent's ear.

"I'm on my way to Heroon."

"Heroon?"

"Parent, please. Let me finish."

Aradus gestured his hand in a roll. Keen knew the signal well. His parent used it both at home and on Council. It meant 'proceed but get to the point.'

"I've got one of the Motes with me. She's leading a last push. Their people are prepared to make a coup attempt on Targite. If we provide them with the weapons and militia support they need, they can take the city."

Keen watched Aradus's demeanor. One thing he'd learned from his parent was how to entice.

"I have a connection," he said, continuing. "With Council funding, I can set up a clandestine force."

"The Council can't fund this."

"Not openly, but…"

"It's too risky." Aradus shook his head.

"We can shift the balance of power in the Sag-Arm, while also helping the Motes in a just cause."

Aradus laughed. "Don't tell me you're growing a heart again?"

Keen ignored the snide remark. "It doesn't matter. This is a way to take out the Targitians obliquely."

"And if it fails and we're exposed? What then?"

Failure? The possibility hadn't crossed his mind. He'd been so wrapped up with the Motes and the escape he hadn't stepped back to reflect on the full picture. He needed the Council to bite on this, otherwise, he wouldn't be able to follow through on his word to Razor and he needed to get to Heroon.

"Keen, Keen, Keen," Aradus shook his head. "Always pursuing an easy win and never thinking things through. This isn't worth the risk. Forget those sand savages." Aradus waved a flippant hand. "We can use your escape to wring a slew of political dealings out of the Targitians through the backdoor. The Council can bleed them slowly. And quietly." He sighed. "At least your trip wasn't a complete failure."

What the heck does that mean?

"Better yet," Aradus raised an eyebrow, "dump the Mote off at the orbit port in the Ortor system. I'll have the Embassy liaison take her into custody. We can use her to strengthen our position. The Targitians would love to get their hands on one of these rebels now that they're free of the Diasporic Clause. I'm sure their population is thirsting for a religious spectacle. You know how hard it is for them to come by a justifiable excuse for public humiliation."

Keen's insides went hollow, both from the suggested course of action and a reminder of his parent's sadistic streak. Too many times he'd been ashamed by how much enjoyment Aradus got from executions. And he'd heard the gossip. While never a soldier, Aradus's hands-on approach to the "punishment" of criminals of the Garassian state over the decades passed in whispers through the Council. Rumors of his penchant for the cut of steel on flesh spread by word of mouth. A liking for poison, especially when its effects could be witnessed firsthand, ran as murmurs among fellow diplomats. Such implicit immoralities in the family line drove both him and Reardon to join the Legion.

"Yes, this is the correct course of action," Aradus said, nodding.

This was heading in the opposite direction. How was he going to get out of this now?

"It'd be easier on my end if we let her walk away."

Aradus shook his head. "No, it's a gem of a gift. We'll use her at the right time."

"Parent, I..."

"Just get back to Ceron. Make a layover at the Ortor port to surrender the Mote." Aradus gestured to his assistant outside the holo-screen. A hand with a tablet appeared and he signed another document.

"I need to stop on Heroon first," Keen said.

"Absolutely not. That place is getting worse. And more dangerous. Damn rebels have thrown the planet into chaos. We're losing ground."

Reynaria...

"You're to return to Ceron directly. That's an order."

"But..."

Aradus raised his hand, indicating the discussion was over.

"I'll have an envoy from the embassy on Ortor sent up to orbit. They'll be more than happy for the opportunity to get off the planet for a few days. That place is so cold and dismal it's vying for the least attractive system in the Arm. The envoy will have your arrangements ready for departure at the jump hub," Aradus continued. Keen read the usual patronizing disgust on his face. "Do what you do best. Drink yourself into a stupor on the way back to Garassit."

Aradus cut the transmission.

Keen stared at the blank holo-screen. How perfect. He couldn't explain to his parent why he needed to get to Heroon. That alone would take hours. And now with his child involved in the Resistance winning back portions of the planet against Council territory? Trying to get that across would only further the trench of wrongs he'd dug over the years. At this point, it was already deep enough to throw himself in.

I wonder who'd sprinkle the first handful of dirt? It'd probably be…

"Draden."

It was Jati, via com-link, from down on the moon base.

"Yeah, Jati."

"Good morning, old tot. I could use a hand. I'm heading up to orbit now. Can you meet me at the loading bay?"

Sake of the Arm… I'm working now?

"Where's Razor?"

"Still asleep, I'd guess. She was when I left."

A vague memory of last night, in the form of suspicion, entered Keen's mind. What was it? Something about hands…

"Draden?"

"Yeah, alright. I'll be down."

"Roger that. It's only a ten-minute shot up to the ship. So, move your lazy ambassador rear end."

The light on the panel went red as Jati cut the line. Keen rose, gingerly. His whole body hurt. The last thing he needed was to do some heavy lifting and hauling.

He took the tube down the two decks to the docking bay. The portal opened to a flurry of activity. A team of people unloaded and hauled away large units of unidentified cargo.

"Hail, Ambassador." It was Jati emerging through the workers. They had on an orange jumper zipped up the front and heavy boots. The lavender mohawk wasn't in bloom. They'd slicked it back with some kind of hair product. "How're we feeling, old tot? I need you to do an EVA on a rotating com-sphere with me."

"You're kidding me, right?"

Jati slapped him on the shoulder and smiled. "Joking. Come on. I want to show you something." They turned and walked back through the workers.

Keen followed and caught up, walking next to them. They passed a team opening one of the cargo containers. A red caution icon for explosives blinked on its sides.

"Where are these going, Jati?"

"Better you don't know, for both of our sakes." They put a hand on his shoulder. "If something happens and you end up having to answer questions, it's best for everyone involved if you don't know." Jati winked. "Get in," they motioned to a transfer shuttle docked in the bay.

"Where are we going?" Keen hobbled up the ramp, wincing and groaning.

"Down to the moon base. Put on one of those jumpers." Jati pointed to a rack in the aft section. "Your boots are fine, but you look like a floating lake ready to ambush someone in those fatigues. We're going for subtle and nondescript. You'll stick out like a sore thumb. Already do with that salt and pepper mess on your head and face."

"Orange is subtle?"

Jati held up a hand from the pilot's seat with a can of booster juice. Keen's world went from miserable to joyous. "Thought you might like this. Should get you back up to sub-par."

He grabbed it and slugged it down.

"You want to ride up here?" Jati motioned to the co-pilot spot.

Keen joined him.

"Ever been to the outer-rim?" They fired up the pod. Workers scattered and made for the exits before the bay doors opened for departure.

"Once. Settled a small trade dispute on Bolaris."

"Bolaris? You call that outer-rim?" Jati pulled back on the stick, lifting the ship off the tarmac as the *Carmora's* outer doors retracted. "My friend, you haven't seen a thing." They hit the thrusters and Keen's stomach sucked into his seat.

Jati grinned as they shot out of the ship. "Turbo boosters. Got em' custom from a client."

"Yeah, unfortunately, I'm familiar." The moon was dead ahead. Half the sphere was dull clay as if someone had run a hand through shallow water, disturbing a layer of silt. The other portion lay in shadow. A settlement in the form of concentrated speckles of lights broke the pitch on the dark side. Tarkassi 9 orbited an uninhabitable gas giant. The moon was as far as you could go before leaving the Arm. Keen had to admit, walking away was appealing. Living at the farthest outpost of human civilization and flipping the bird to everyone and everything? He could do it if it wasn't for Scarpa and the letter.

He had to face Reynaria and make things right. He owed it to Scarpa. He owed it to himself. She was his child too, even if she was technically the 'enemy.' And what did that even mean? He was on that side too, once. He didn't care about the Council. Regardless, he had to confront her. Otherwise, he could be as far off into the Arm as he wanted, and the hurt would linger. And he'd still be carrying his baggage. Pain and memory didn't fade with distance. It required confrontation to absolve.

Jati did a flyby of the settlement. Dilapidated structures passed in the dim, artificial light. The interconnected buildings, worn and old, were out of date to the point of being dangerous habitations on a world without an atmosphere.

As if reading his mind, Jati spoke. "They're squeezed on two sides out here. Too far for the Garassians to bother with them and the Targitians demand too high a price for the distance."

"You mean they live without cells?"

"They get them rationed," Jati said, "per the Humane Act."

"The Humane Act? You're kidding me? That's an antiquated law. You can't get by on that amount of energy these days."

Jati banked hard to port. The central cluster of buildings entered the pod's cockpit window. "They do." Jati swung the ship around to head back to the landing station. "The Motes don't even have that. They're left to scavenge. And rob. Think about that."

The Motes. With each passing light-year from Kol 2, the less obliged he felt to help and the less Razor's struggles and losses held a grip on his memory and conscience. In fact, the further he was from Razor, the better he felt overall. Maybe his parent was right.

"I can't imagine having to persevere like that," Jati said. "And to think the entire Arm knows it and lets it happen. Out of sight, out of mind."

"I know what you're trying to do, Jati."

"Huh?" They glanced towards Keen. "I don't know what you mean."

"Yeah, you do. It doesn't matter. My parent didn't go for it. He said it was too risky."

"Well, let's put this thing together on our own," Jati said.

"Why bother?"

"Why *not* bother? What else are you going to do, 'ambassador' things?" Jati released their hands from the controls as they spoke, making air quotations to emphasize the superficiality.

"It gets worse," Keen said. "He wants me to surrender Razor at the Ortor jump hub."

"Ortor?"

"It's halfway between Kol 2 and Ceron. That's where they perform under-the-table 'deals.' My parent intends to use her as prey to bait the Targitians with a political bribe. I'm to go directly back to Ceron afterward, so I'm safe from their reach. That way he's got all the cards."

Jati banked a hard right, away from the lights of Tarkassi 9.

"Where are we going?"

"Round the bend, old tot." The empty, shadowed arc of the moonscape filled the window. Keen watched the craggy, desolate surface pass in the darkness. A few minutes later they cleared the satellite into space.

The edge of the Arm; the farthest fingertip of humanity's reach. It reminded Keen of the Lorassian Sea on Ceron. As a child, he and Reardon spent countless hours gazing at the endless, unbroken waters to the horizon. Adventure and curiosity stirred them to wonder in front of that sea. Reardon, always the braver one, ventured out in the deep water. Keen was more hesitant, never going farther than his knees, his bare feet rooted and visible on the small pebbles in the clear water. Reardon splashed and played while Keen stared at the horizon. It was the same now except the scale rose to encompass all of humanity – an entire species gazing over the edge and peering beyond the pale of history.

"I love it out here," Jati whispered.

"You think there's anything out there?" Keen reveled in the emptiness of space and myriad of distant, twinkling stars.

"Has to be," Jati said.

They'd had precious moments like this in the war. Brief interludes of beauty and sublimity that awoke the mind like flint to spark. The present was put into its place. It offered personal escape and bonding of a kind unique to those who trusted one another each day as they faced death. Why was it that tragedy bore such passionate fruit? Scarpa's pain and suffering brought Reynaria. Inhumane dismissal seeded the Motes' sense of honor and hard justice. And Jati. They emerged from a war of horror to fight for the ones who can't fight for themselves, no matter what 'side' they were on. Where did that leave him? His life was a tragedy. Was he responsible for it or was the war? Where was his fruit?

"You know, last night when I put you to bed... you asked me something," Jati said, interrupting the silent philosophy.

"What're you talking about?"

"I wasn't sure you'd remember."

Keen fidgeted. Nothing was worse than a reminder of something you did when drunk that you couldn't recall.

"It's fine," Jati said. "No reason to revisit it."

Finally, someone spares me the embarrassment.

"It's just..."

Oh, for the sake of the Arm.

"Alright Jati, I apologize for whatever it was I said that offended you. But you were pouring kartan like a..."

"No, it wasn't like that. Listen to me." Jati flipped on the autopilot and turned to Keen. They cruised away from Tarkassi 9 into oblivion. "You can go this way," Jati pointed ahead. "Believe me, I've gone that way. It's a safe place. No self-reproach, no blame, no responsibility. It's a damn paradise." They switched off the autopilot and veered back towards the moon and the *Carmora* in orbit. "Or you can go this way," they pointed back past Tarkassi 9 into the Arm. "It's as scary as facing down a swamp boar. You have to take a real hard look in the mirror. And you have to work. Not just sweat. Tears." Jati's green eyes welled up. Against their chiseled features, they were two glistening gems wedged between slabs of golden marble. "It'll break your soul apart."

"Then why should I do it?"

Jati flipped on the autopilot and placed a hand on his shoulder.

"Because when you pick up the pieces and put them back together, your life and your world are bearable. You're whole again. I'm not saying it doesn't come back. It does. It always comes back. But it's in pieces, shards that you've glued back together. You'll be broken then reassembled, like a vessel after it's shattered, preserved through patient and determined hands. It'll always show in the mirror. But you'll know what each of those shards is, where they come from, and what they do to you. You'll know how to hold them together to keep you whole. You'll always be that vessel made of shards, but you'll be whole again. Wounded, but whole."

"I can't, Jati. I just can't..." Keen's hands covered his eyes. He hadn't been prepared for this when they got in the pod. In the darkness of his blind shelter, he felt Jati's hand on his own. Jati slid Keen's palm down to his chest, resting it on top of the bump where the medallion lay under the jumper.

"It's not that you can't. You're Legion. You can do anything."

Keen sobbed once, embarrassed.

"I'm not that person anymore."

"You'll always be that person. And you have a reason right there, over your heart, to find your way back. Your sibling would want you to do this."

Keen shoved Jati's arm away. He screwed his eyes tighter shut to further shield himself in darkness.

Screw all of this. I just want a drink. I need to forget.

"Stop hiding behind the ambassador," Jati said. "That life takes you the other way, out and away from the Arm. You wind your way around and through problems, so things always work out and you avoid confrontation, except when all else fails. And your parent leads you by a chain. Start being a soldier again, Draden. Confront the enemy, directly and with your chin high."

Keen opened his eyes and gazed ahead. Over the lip of Tarkassi 9, a blanket of stellar bodies glimmered. The Arm. Billions of people living varied lives. All his problems lay scattered through star systems in a long trail of pain. It meant opening up the suitcase of memory, turning it upside down, and dumping out the contents. Could he spill all that baggage out onto the floor of his conscience? He didn't even know where to begin.

"But who's the enemy, Jati?"

His old war comrade's face shifted; their mouth opened, but they paused in dubious hesitation.

"Jati? Who is it?"

"It's you."

KEEN MADE a list of what he hated about Tarkassi 9 as he walked its main avenue. So far, he had the following: it was dirty. It was cold, literally and figuratively. And the air was thin, set to the lowest O2 levels possible. He and Jati had been in the facility less than 10 minutes and they both sounded like they'd run a race.

As best as he could tell, everyone here was in the red. Not a single person they'd passed was doing well. No, scratch that. Not a single person was even getting by. Tarkassi 9 was like a pauper's convention.

"Jati, this place is awful."

"This is the nice part of town," they said.

"That's a joke, right?"

"I wish it was."

Keen watched several pedestrians stroll by and added one more thing to the list: orange jumpers. Everyone was wearing them. He hated it. Something about forced conformity rattled his innards. Not to mention it was the worst color possible against the dreary architecture and grime. So, on top of everything else, his eyes hurt too. Between that and the headache from the low O2, Tarkassi 9 was making a great first impression.

"What's with the jumpers?"

"Goodwill gesture from a philanthropic organization that works to support the needy in the outer-rim."

Keen's eyes went from pitiful person to person on the street.

"Don't stare, Draden."

"Why are we wearing them?"

"Do I need to answer that?"

Keen imagined the two of them walking around in their usual attire. Not a good idea when you're trying to be discreet. Jati needed to keep a low profile for business reasons. They didn't want to draw attention to themselves. And who knew if someone in the paid service of Targite was on watch for an aging, pathetic ambassador who looked like he'd just escaped death on a desert planet. Without having any certainty that Pox was out of the picture, he decided he liked orange jumpers.

They rounded a corner onto a side street and Keen shivered.

"Is it me or is it getting colder?"

"Temps are kept at a max minimum in the non-commercial sectors. We're transitioning between neighborhoods."

A resident, her identity mark a cool blue on her neck, sat on a step to a bunkhouse fiddling with a folded piece of paper. She ran it across her lips, lapping up the morsels left on the wrapper.

Keen hadn't seen an identity mark in over a decade. They were used for citizens, often war veterans, with vocal and/or physical disabilities who could not speak or sign their gender identity.

"I need to make a pit stop, old tot. It'll take me about thirty minutes. You'll want to head there," Jati pointed down the street to the next corner. "That's the bar. Tip of the Beyond."

"Great name," Keen said. A darkened window next to the portal cast a dim violet glow.

"Solazi-tu owns the place. They're good people. We go way back. They were in the war. Not Legion but fought on our side against the Patents on Heeglio and Yaqit."

"Yaqit? At the end?"

Jati nodded in earnest. "Left a lung. Brought home the Cough."

Yaqit. Keen had heard stories about the terrible conditions and brutal combat. The Reaper gas shifted the tide against the Patent forces and their allies on the planet. It was an egregious human rights violation, a first in the Sag-Arm. The Hamuts dumped the noxious fumes onto soldiers unprepared for the invisible and deadly chemical. It wasn't enough and the Hamuts still lost the war, but it did turn the tide, against them. The backlash of that action saw the destruction of all human life on their home planet Xerteej by a biological counterstrike. A mutating, human-specific virus bred in a weapons laboratory on the edge of the Arm was brought against them. The organism was a rampaging, voracious, and unstoppable entity that had spread once before during the Second Span with near-devastating results. To this day, Xerteej is an uninhabitable sphere orbiting its star. Their own unethical choice bit back, forcing them to live as diasporic refugees spread across the Arm.

Those who made it out from Yaqit alive lived with permanent lung damage, portions of which had to be removed. It was called 'the Cough' because your lungs were forever stuck in trauma response, seeping constant fluid to protect the remaining alveoli. It was a vicious condition. Like memories in the psyche, it existed in a perpetual state of recurrence, a physical reminder of the traumas of war.

Keen looked around. Why would someone with the Cough choose to live in this low O2 dump?

"Or, if you're inclined to change direction in your life," Jati winked, making light of their earlier conversation, "a groomer is right around the bend. That's where I had this done." They ran a hand through the slicked-back lavender mohawk. "Latest styles in the Outer Rim, Draden. Don't let the outside of the shop fool you. They keep pace with fashions in the center of the Arm. Would clean you right up."

"Thanks for the tip, but I'll be in the Beyond."

"Clever diplomats, always with the wordplay. Here," Jati flipped on a callback disk and tossed it to Keen. "I'll find you when I'm done. And use these." Jati slipped something into his palm.

A stack of Rim wedges, the illegal underground currency used in areas resistant to the monopolies, lay in his hand. The self-regulating exchange bypassed taxes from monopoly pricing. The money thrived where Hamut dissension loosened enforcement of the patents, putting pressure on the Council for better salaries and fairer treatment under their post-war punitive conditions. In Tarkassi 9's case, the moon outpost was so distant and without lucrative potential that the quasi-anarchic economy was allowed to thrive, regardless.

Keen couldn't blame the Hamuts for their apathy. With thirty-odd years left on the terms of service outlined in the Peace Treaty, they still had three decades of enforcing the Patents for the Council. With no agency to develop an independent government until it expired, you couldn't knock them for their unmotivated work ethic.

"I can't use these, are you…"

Jati raised a hand to silence him.

"Trust me. You don't want to go strolling into the Beyond and paying with Garassian money. That should be more than enough for you to catch a good buzz." They turned and walked away. "And try the Tarkassi Tail," they said, swinging around and walking away backward. "Solazi makes a great one."

Keen squeezed the wedges in his hand. Something tugged on the sleeve of his jumper. A grimy and ragged child, barely reaching his hip, held out a hand.

"Spare a wedge?"

"Beat it, kid."

Keen walked away. He glanced back.

The child stood, palm open.

Sake of the Arm. This place is one giant guilt trip.

The interior of the Tip was about as exciting as one could get on Tarkassi 9. Inside a low and dimly lit room of violets and reds were scattered tables, a few gambling stations, and a long bar at the back. Oh, and one patron.

How cliché. You couldn't script this.

Keen heard a cough.

Solazi. But where?

Another cough.

The joint was empty but for one lone customer at the corner of the bar. Keen sat down towards the other end, far enough to not have to talk but not far enough to make it obvious he didn't want to talk.

"Morning." A head popped up from under the bar. He almost jumped out of his seat.

"Fuck!"

"No thanks, too much hair on top, and too much salt in the pepper. Plus, I like them younger." The person smiled and coughed into a rag that Keen knew was assigned that one responsibility. He could only imagine what that thing must be like at the end of the shift.

"Good one." So Solazi was a razzer too. They and Jati probably verbally jousted for hours.

The bartender was gaunt, with a kind of beige skin that had been stretched too far and then released only to find the frame it covered shrunken, leaving sections of flab and ripply space. He guessed by the way they carried themselves that they had been through some serious action and didn't scare easily. The eyes were like his – emerald green. Something about them spoke of hardship, but not just war; a long history of pain shone through small cracks in a persistent, yet tired, facade of strength and endurance.

Keen could not find an icon anywhere on the proprietor's loose-fitting top so he waited for them to self-identify. He wasn't surprised. This was the Outer Rim and regulations were lax, but he knew from Jati's use of "tu" that they identified as bigender.

"What'll it... *(cough)* be?" Solazi hand-signed "tu-té," indicating that she was presenting as "té."

Keen reciprocated, signing "ti," enacting the standard social etiquette for casual and crowded social interactions such as a bar. When quick or mass social exchanges occurred throughout the Arm, especially those that were consumer-based where people did not introduce themselves, hand-signing was ideal.

"I'll try a Tarkassi Tail."

Solazi put both lanky arms on the bar and leaned towards Keen. He reared back as she eyed him.

"You messing with me?"

"What?"

"Are you *(cough)* messing with me? Who told you to say that?"

Keen opened his mouth to speak but Solazi raised a bony hand to silence him. That gesture was becoming too common in his day-to-day life.

"Was it Jati?"

He nodded.

"Hah!" She slammed the hand down on the counter. "They're here and didn't come in? I'll *(cough)* kill 'em." Solazi's brows furled. "So, who are you?"

"I'm just a nobody who wants a drink. What is it with this place?"

"Don't get me started," she smiled and reached down to get something. "You'll be *(cough)* here all day."

"If a drink's in my hand, I don't mind."

She pointed at him. "I like you 'friend of Jati's'. What's your *(cough)* name?"

"Keen Draden-ti."

"Well, Keen, you look like an asshole."

What?

She slapped him on the shoulder. "I'm messing with you!"

What is it with everyone slapping everyone out here? Enough already.

"I'm Solazi-tu-té, but you probably know that already if Jati sent you in." She put an empty glass in front of him.

"What's this?"

"The closest you'll get to a fuck in the Tip." She poured an amber liquid into the cylinder. "But unlike most of 'em, it comes in twos *(cough)*. Knock that one back and then I'll pour the other. You have to drink them both within 2 minutes."

"Why?"

"Because that's how we do it in the Tip," she said.

"This place is weird."

"You got that *(cough)* right, Keen Draden."

Keen reached for the glass and his jumper sleeve caught, exposing his forearm.

Solazi grabbed it.

He froze with the drink halfway to his mouth.

She rotated his arm so the Legion tattoo was facing upward.

"Heroon?"

"That's right," he said.

"With Jati?"

Keen nodded.

"Been a long time since I've *(cough)* seen anyone from the war out here. Other than Jati, who comes and goes now and then."

Solazi seemed to relax. Her body loosened if that was possible in her physical condition.

She released her grip and Keen took a sip of the drink in his hand. It went down rough, with a nutty sting that reminded him of an illegal bracer he'd had as a teen in low-end bars in the Garassian capitol. Solazi's palm rose, gesturing that he should finish the entire thing.

She grabbed a bottle from underneath the counter and poured a red liquid into his empty glass. A vapor trail snaked its way up into the air over the bar as the remains of the first elixir interacted on contact with the second.

"Your Tarkassi Tail, Legion soldier. This first round's *(cough)* on the house. One vet to another."

Maybe this place wasn't so bad after all.

He knocked back the shot and fireworks went off inside his mouth. A crackling sensation traveled down his throat and into his stomach. It was odd, but... interesting.

"Now that's different."

"Like it?"

He nodded.

"Good." She grabbed a second glass and poured another round, this time with the two liquids next to each other. "This one first, always," she pointed at the amber liquor and moved down the bar to the regular at the end to refill their drink.

He felt a tug on his jumper. It was the kid again.

What is it with this place?

It was like any chance of happiness or contentment had to be interrupted before someone had a positive respite in their life.

"Spare a wedge?" They held up a palm. Two fingers were missing. Their extremities were ruddy. Dark splotches formed a patchwork on elbows and wrists.

"For what, little one?"

"Heat cell. And food."

"Where are your parents?"

They shook their head, swinging messy cherry-red hair back and forth.

"No parents?"

"They took her."

"Who took her?" Keen asked.

The kid looked at the floor. He guessed they were probably six or seven, and still had a few years before declaring a gender identity or lack thereof. Not that it mattered officially what you selected to be input in the Arm registrar. No one strictly followed what they listed, nor was it enforced, but you did have to orient yourself by the age of twelve for bureaucratic reasons. Planetary nation-states and their star system colonies and territories utilized the information as census data. Interstellar demographic profiles were manufactured and often exploited, to argue for the allocation of budgetary resources for various Arm-wide social services, as well as to drive the marketing of consumer goods, entertainment, and style trends.

"You got anyone else?" Keen asked.

"No."

"Another parent?"

"You're annoying." They raised two fingers and thumb a bit higher, pleading.

Keen laughed. "Heard that before. You better work on your tactics, kid. Insulting someone when you want something from them isn't a great approach."

They rolled their eyes.

He couldn't help but laugh a second time. "You're a tough one. Attitude too, I like it. So, no parents, huh?"

"Gerib says she isn't coming back."

"Who's Gerib?"

"My friend. In my head. He makes me feel okay when I'm alone and scared."

Keen was mid-sip on the first of the two shots.

The words hit him like an arrow through his core. The child's plight hadn't made a damn bit of difference to him before now. They were just another unfortunate person born in the wrong place at the wrong time. Unfortunate but unfortunately not uncommon. The unfortunate were here, on the Outer Rim. They were on Heroon and other planets at the mercy of the monopoly. Even the Motes fit the bill. And here stood a little kid, alone and scared. With a damn imaginary friend to cope and make things okay, or at least bearable until the next day when they hoped their parent would return. That was personal. Heck, this could be Reynaria.

The wall that shielded Keen from caring crumbled. He glanced at Solazi down the bar. Was she ok out here, on the edge with no one else to talk to about the war? Did she need to be here to make it bearable?

The world is broken. Forget my body and its shards, the whole Arm is shattered.

He put down his drink and pushed it away. "Here," he gave the youth all the wedges but two. He closed their hand around them. "Do you know how to keep those safe?"

They nodded, floored at the amount of money in their hand.

Keen winked. "You take that and use it to keep warm and eat, ok?"

Bright red hair and head went up and down with gusto.

"What's your name?"

"Ailo. What's yours?"

"Keen Draden-ti."

"With a 'K'?"

Keen nodded. "Well Ailo, you're lucky to have Gerib."

"I know. He's the best."

"Get along now."

The youngster dashed out through the tables and chairs so fast that Keen did a double-take.

Kid's got some moves.

"Solazi." The old war vet-turned-bartender raised her head from down at the end of the bar. He held up a wedge. "Does this cover it?"

"And some, let me get your change."

"Don't bother. One ex-soldier to another." He flicked the coin on the countertop and headed towards the door.

"Hey, you left your Tail. Are you *(cough)* finished?" Solazi asked, confused by the half and full glasses he'd left on the bar.

Keen stopped but didn't turn around. "I am," he said.

Finally.

He turned back and gestured to her. "Farewell, Solazi. And thank you." He made for the door and exited the Beyond. His legs moved without guidance. He rounded the corner and walked through the portal into the groomer's shop.

"Greetings," the person inside said. "Want me to take a bit off the ends of those curly locks and that beard? Could take ten years off you at least."

"Cut it all off."

———

"I DON'T WANT to talk about it."

"Sure thing, old tot." Jati fired up the pod.

"Get going." Keen burned a hole through the cockpit window. The edges of his ears felt like they'd been on ice. A draft tingled the small passages alongside his head. It was like a bad dream where you're standing naked in front of a room full of people.

"We were a bit long here," Jati said. "Cutting it close now."

Keen glared at them.

And I get hassled for diplomatic wordplay?

How long would this go on? And he still had Razor to deal with. He hoped that she'd stick to her usual Mote rhetoric. The less she said, the better.

Jati fiddled with the edges of their slicked-back mohawk, eyeing Keen's forehead.

"What are you doing?"

"Fixing my hair. It's so shiny. I can see my reflection."

"Oh, screw off, Jati. Let's go."

"Hah!" Jati slapped him on the shoulder. "I'm messing with you. I'm glad you did it, Draden. But sake of the Arm, that's a close cut." They tried to run their hand over the top of Keen's bald head. He swatted it away.

"I told him to cut it all off. Hair and beard. I wanted it tight, Legion style. He shaved my damn head."

Momentary revelation followed by a dose of humiliation. It was becoming an all too familiar routine in his life.

"Well, at least you still have the mustache."

Keen ran his fingers over the thick brown handlebars dropping to each side of his lips. They fell to his chin, following a gestural ritual almost two decades old. All he grabbed was empty air where once a long goatee and ruby pendant resided.

"It's weird," Jati said, "but you kind of have a good look going with the jumper now. You want to keep it, you can."

Keen folded his arms and ignored them.

"I've got some leaky pipes on the ship that could use fixing."

Jati the joker. They were going to ride him for days.

The pod cruised up and out of the landing area. Keen watched Tarkassi 9 fall away. The moon was a barren and craggy landscape of milky ochre and rust-colored rock and dust. A world of undisturbed silence, the remote base lurked in darkness, shy of the sun line.

There goes the Beyond.

He was both relieved and terrified. He'd had his last drink and hadn't even finished it. Maybe that was for the best. What mattered now was getting to Heroon and figuring out how to deal with Razor and the Motes.

"Jati, on a more serious note. How invested in all this are you?"

"What do you mean?" They veered the pod up and away towards the waiting ship.

"This is crazy, Jati. Mustering up a militia? Funding a coup attempt behind my parent's back? I gave Razor my word I'd get her military support in exchange for getting me off that planet. I didn't care all that much when I did it. It was only to save myself. But now…"

Now if he didn't do it, he'd be failing himself as much as Razor and the Motes, and that little kid.

"I can't do it. Not without the Council. I'm way over my head." He ran a hand over his bald head. "I screwed this all up."

Jati laughed.

"What?"

"You're switched on, Draden. It's good to have problems."

"I'm serious, Jati."

"So am I," Jati said. "Listen, I'll take the lead on the militia. A group of mercenaries for hire I know are desperate for a job."

"On Heroon?"

"No, but easily contacted. Let's just say some tough fighters are tired of being low-paid enforcers. They're seeking more amenable partners and an investment in their future. I hear their numbers are growing. Operators are picking up lots of chatter on the pirate frequencies."

Enforcers? That sounds like Hamuts...

"Who are they?"

"Better to wait on that, Draden. We need to sit down and talk through one or two things after we make the jump to Heroon. I've got a way to do this so it works out for everyone. Just trust me. And I've got you covered on the weapons and equipment. I can get that set up. The issue is money."

"It's not an issue," Keen said.

"But you can't use Garassian funds without permission from the Council. Or do you mean to abscond?"

"Not abscond. That'd bring a whole new layer of problems to the table." They weren't understanding. He wouldn't either. It wasn't worth getting into now. "Money isn't an issue, Jati. Just get me to Heroon."

"We'll get you there, old tot," Jati said and veered the pod into the ship's docking bay.

"You're not anxious when you return to Heroon? I mean, it's... a lot, you know?"

Jati didn't answer. Or, by not answering they had.

Keen shifted in the co-pilot seat.

"You focus on finding your child and making things right," Jati said. "As for Heroon, we'll be together. It'll make it easier. And I've been back enough times that I'm getting numb to it. But you have to talk when you need to, alright?"

"Yeah."

The pod dropped onto the floor of the docking bay

Keen exhaled. This wasn't going to be easy, but he had to do it. It was the only way, either that or go back to the Tip of the Beyond and drink himself to death.

"You want me to put everything where you can't get it?" Jati asked, shutting down all systems.

Keen knew what they meant. "Thanks, but no. That's not the way to do it. Chin up and head on, right?"

"Right." Jati slapped him on the shoulder. "Welcome back, old tot."

"Thanks, Jati, you made all the…"

A ship alarm interrupted Keen.

"Jati, what is that?"

They held up a hand, quieting him. "Go ahead."

"We've got a problem," an edgy voice said. "Vessel approaching on intercept. Came out of a jump on the far side of the moon."

"Profile?"

"Hamut. Type A-Class. Twin Needle. Armed to the teeth."

Jati's eyes confirmed it.

Pox.

SEVENTEEN

There was a rat in the wiring. Somehow, Pox knew where we were headed. She couldn't jump across the Arm in so short a time unless she knew our jump track before we departed Kol 2. But it made no sense. It couldn't be one of my people. None of them would work with the Targitians. Or would they? Could it have been someone with Crest when we first negotiated the bounty cube with Jati, before the setup for the ambush? That didn't add up logistically. How could someone still on the planet know we jumped to a moon base on Tarkassi 9? I didn't even know that was our destination until we broke the space/time barrier.

The only answer left was Jati. But Keen's old war pal? What about all their talk and pride about justice for the oppressed, *all* of the oppressed, regardless of circumstance? Something didn't add up.

Time to process all of this never came. And I didn't know what was happening until the first shots hit the shields and bounced me from Jati's bed. I'd never been on a ship in combat. Alarms sounded and the lights went dim, calling the crew to battle stations. My instinct, born on solid ground and familiar with land travel on cutters and sails, told me we'd slammed into something. That we'd experienced the near impossible and had a collision in space.

As I made my way down the corridor outside the cabin, I remember being bumped and banged against the wall by crew members darting past me. They yelled at me that I was going the wrong way. That was when I ran into Keen. Or, rather, I plowed into a bald person in an orange jumper who I mistook for the ship's mechanic. My confusion as I worked to re-connect the links of his identity chain was lost on him. One thing shone in his green eyes: fear. That's when I knew it wasn't a collision but an attack. She was alive. Pox was back.

The ship accelerated, banking hard in what I assumed was an effort by Jati's crew to engage or buy enough time to set jump parameters and attempt an escape. I knew that much by the pull on my insides. My organs were drawn to one side of my body as if by an invisible magnet. That's when the second round of detonations hit. The shield did its work for the first few shots. But the fourth or fifth impact was different. It wasn't like being pushed; it was more a sensation of being stabbed. The whole corridor shook in response, like the tremors of an aftershock on Kol 2. I knew the feeling. I'd had a knife in my side once, on my second cell raid at a Turbine Field. I would have been dead if it wasn't for Crest, who came to the aid of a rookie about to be overrun by a more experienced Targitian.

How to describe it? Not so much injurious as a violation, something thrust into my body without warning. What followed was the horror of realization, of comprehending that your side had been pierced, uncertain of the severity. You can't know the extent of the injury when you're stabbed. You only see the cut and the bleed. My side was turning red. At that point, your mind switches from the wound to your overall survival.

I did the same thing on Jati's ship. Somewhere deep inside, I'd built a crude interpretation of misaligned and tenuous parts, stacked up into a dubious structure – a 'surprise' attack by a bounty hunter I'd assumed dead, a lurking suspicion about Jati, doubt about Keen's pledge to aid my people. But the crux of the situation was immediate triage: get off the ship and have time to work through all those unstable pillars one by one, exposing the corrupt parts and reaching a sound conclusion. So, I pushed Keen back the way he came and we made for a pod.

Keen ranted about a child on the moon base as we ran to the docking bay. I wasn't listening. Back when Crest dragged me onto the cutter, bleeding, and raced me back to the caves, I remember nothing other than being mute with fear until I opened my eyes. With my twin hovering over me, euphoria took me. She smiled and touched my cheek. I knew I could go back to worrying about the injury and begin work to heal it. That's all I wanted now. I wanted off the ship. I wanted to reach a point far enough into safety that I could let go of the ship's bleeding and focus on the wound of betrayal.

I never made it.

EIGHTEEN

Keen grabbed Razor's arm. "Wait!" Her lean figure flashed in and out of view as the lights flickered and alarms blared. "Razor." He tugged and she lost her footing and lurched back. The Mote caught herself against the wall of the ship's corridor. "This is wrong."

"Wrong how? We need to get out of here."

"No, I won't go." He released his grip. "I'm not leaving Jati and the ship."

Razor's blue eyes narrowed. "They've sold us out, Keen. It's the only explanation."

He shook his bald head, refusing to agree. It wasn't logical. Jati wouldn't turn on him. They were Legion. And the two of them had just…

"I'm going," she said. "Stay if you want. You'll never reach Heroon if you do."

"Go where, Tarkassi 9? Then what?"

"I'll figure that out after I get out of here, alive."

She started towards the hangar.

"Razor, no. It's not right."

She turned back, her eyes fierce with frustration. "When did you ever care about that?"

Keen's organs surged into his spine as the ship straightened out and accelerated. They were making a run for it. Jati was trying to reach a jump track.

"Well?" She said with arms outstretched.

He didn't have time to explain what happened on Tarkassi 9 or over the two decades leading up to it.

"I do now, ok?"

In two strides she had a fistful of his jumper in her hand. "What did you two do on the moon base?"

Why was she so angry?

"It's complicated."

"Oh, forget this!" She released her grip and pushed him away. "It always is. It's never simple with you."

She was right. He sounded like his parent. But it *was* complicated. Too complicated for the circumstance.

Let her go. It's her choice.

"Fine, go if you want. I'm staying. But if you do our deal is off."

Her face went fierce. The same intensity that pierced her eyes and spiky red hair during their pugilistic debate in the ruined pod after the crash on Kol 2 rekindled into white fire. Keen stood firm. It was fair. He knew it. He was pretty sure she did too.

"We're making for an open track, Razor… to jump. That was the second turn and acceleration. It shouldn't be more than a minute. Jati's got top defenses on this bird. Trust me, we'll make it."

"We're hit, Keen. I felt it."

"Yes, but it's not that bad. It was aft in a non-vital section of the hull. They've shut down the area. The vacuum's solid."

"How do you know this?"

They bounced against the walls as another round from Pox's guns pounded the *Carmora*. The shields were up and working. Sake of the Arm, he'd thank Jati later for being the arms dealer they were. "It was on the com, over the whole ship. Didn't you hear?"

Razor's face went blank. Keen knew it well. It happened in combat.

The world around you shuts down and you go mute. It was a game of internal chess, the body and mind clicking into survival mode.

Razor shook her head, admitting she hadn't.

"Draden." A crew member stepped down the corridor and handed him a remote com. "Jati, for you."

Keen triggered the device.

"Draden, old tot. You ok? Razor with you?"

"We're both here. Can we jump?"

Razor's eyes watched, uncertain, and suspicious.

"Ten seconds. A track is open ahead, but…"

Keen didn't like the sound of Jati's voice as the sentence trailed off. The floor bumped. They'd jumped.

Razor looked to the crew member for confirmation. They nodded. She slid down the wall to the floor in relief. The crew person headed back the way they came in haste.

"Where are we heading, Jati?" Keen asked.

"Had no choice, old tot. Better change into something more diplomatic."

"Where, Jati?"

"Heroon," they said.

"That's good, isn't it?" Razor asked.

"It would be, if our exit point wasn't the jump hub station, inside the Council-controlled grid."

"Sake of the Arm," Keen said.

"Sorry, old tot. It was the only available track. Normally we'd come in on the far side where I've got peeps that'll turn a blind eye. For the right price."

"What's the problem?" Razor asked Keen.

"You want to tell her, or should I?" Jati said.

"Tell me what?"

Keen sighed. Why was his life so complicated? "I need to get you up to speed on some things."

"Clearly." She eyed him, referring to both his words and his appearance.

Razor snatched the com out of his hand. "We need to talk, Jati." She glared at Keen. "I have questions that need answers."

She had to let her suspicion go. They had bigger problems now. It didn't matter how Pox found them, not in the short term.

"Agreed," Jati said. "Give me thirty minutes and meet me in the mess."

"I'm sure we could all use a drink," Razor said.

Sake of the Arm. As if it wasn't bad enough already.

"Not all of us," Jati said.

Keen felt Razor's gaze on him, seeking an explanation for Jati's remark. He stayed silent.

"Hold off on the kartan until I arrive," they added.

You could cut the awkward silence with a knife.

"Razor?" Jati asked over the com. "Just wait, ok?"

"Sure." Razor glared at him.

Keen glanced at the floor. She'd figured it out.

"So much for today starting well," Keen said and plopped down next to Razor. "At least you got to sleep through most of this."

"Tell me about it," Jati said over the com. "On top of everything else, I'm about to arrive in a Council-controlled port of entry without proper registration in a damaged ship, with a cargo hold full of contraband explosives destined for the rebels fighting to take back the planet."

"SO THAT'S IT?" Razor folded her arms.

"That's it." Keen slid his chair closer to the table and rested his elbows on top. The ship's mess was small, more utilitarian than social in function.

"And, now what?"

"Not sure. Not that you would've made it if you'd tried to leave. Before we jumped, I mean."

The portal opened. Jati barreled in and collapsed into a chair at the table. Their stout frame dropped like a chunk of rock. They wiped some sweat off their forehead and ran a hand through their mohawk. "Damage isn't too bad. We had to shut down one of the sleeper cabins. I've got half the crew in double bunks in another section to bow. The sewer lines on that side are blasted so all bathroom activity needs to be to port."

Razor gestured with a hand, requesting clarification.

"That's the left side of the ship," they said. "Don't worry about it. Anything off-limits is blocked. It does strike me as odd, though."

"What does?" she asked.

"The Needle had a clear shot on us. It could've gotten the reactors farther back or the bridge up front to take us down."

"What're you suggesting? That they didn't want us dead?"

Jati shrugged. "If you made me write up a report, that'd be my strategic assessment. I'd call it a 'cautious strike,' focused on disabling the ship rather than destroying it. Pox wanted us alive, or at least some of us."

A long silence passed as the three pondered Jati's statement.

"I was explaining to Razor what happened in the conversation with my parent," Keen said, breaking the quiet. "And about my personal decision after visiting the moon base."

Jati nodded.

"And you can get the kartan bottle. I know you want it." Relief washed over Jati's face. They rose and went to the cabinet. Jati gestured to Razor, holding a glass. She made a 'yes' with her eyes and they brought two over, sat, and poured.

"And?" Jati's eyes homed in on the tabletop in front of Keen. They got back up and grabbed another kartan glass, filled it with water, then placed it in front of Keen.

"And I intend to resign my ambassadorship."

"What?" Jati pushed back their seat. "Are you sure? Why not use that to work for change... for influence?"

Keen shook his head. "I was never cut out for it. It's done nothing but corrupt me. And I have to do it to release my parent's grip."

"I'm not so sure about either of those conclusions, old tot. Plus, you've got an art for words and people." Jati gestured with their glass to Razor and Keen, winking. "To escape. Never mind the circumstances. Savor the fact we're alive." They took a swig.

"This is about people, not economics," Keen said, sipping on his water. It wasn't that bad. At least it was festive in the kartan glass.

"Can't separate the two in the Arm, old tot," Jati said.

Keen nodded. "But economics always trumps humanity. And the state always usurps the individual."

"Not when you have no state," Jati winked.

"I'm not talking about anarchy. I'm talking about ethics." Keen turned his chair towards Jati. "In the Legion, fighting against the Hamuts, that wasn't an ethical war. It was an economic war about the philosophy of commerce and power."

"But it affected the lives of millions," Jati pointed a finger.

"Agreed. That's the big picture. The Hamuts had no right to run around 'taking' planets to build an energy production empire. We fought for peoples' right to live in states of independence."

"But it's not the same thing," Jati said.

"It *is* the same thing," Razor said.

"I see this from a political standpoint, in the literal sense of the word," Keen said. "I've been a diplomat for over twenty years. I've become blind to the individual. Diplomacy sees 'citizens.' It's distant and dehumanizing. I'm talking about people's well-being. Politics is blind to empathy when it goes to bed with economics. It focuses on masses with 'needs'." He looked at Razor. "You view the world more ethically than I do because that's been your life. You've watched how a hegemonic, and in your case, extreme political disparity impacts individuals in a direct way... felt, and experienced. Me?" He pointed at himself. "I only saw that in the war."

Jati nodded agreement, raising their glass.

"You don't know anything about the way I see the world, Keen," Razor said. "So, don't even begin to assume or patronize me."

"He's experienced war firsthand," Jati said, "and has the tattoo to prove it." Jati raised their arm displaying the Legion branding.

"It's not the same thing."

"You're right," Keen said, lowering Jati's arm down to the table. "It's not the same thing. I saw it affect others. I didn't live it."

"You saw it from *your* perspective," Razor pointed an accusatory finger at him. "You have no clue what it is to be where I am."

Keen held up a hand. "Not saying I do. But as a diplomat, I've traveled the Arm. And I can say this: violence is everywhere, happening every day to a great many people. It's lived through lack. Through discrimination and denial, whether that be one's actual existence and rights, heritage, or culture. It bears the fruit of privilege, at the expense of others."

"Here, here," Jati said and drank kartan.

Keen ran a hand through his mustache. "'Out of sight, out of mind,' works."

"One little kid on a backstar moon base did this to you?" Razor asked. "The arrogant ambassador who didn't give a Hamut's ass about anyone or anything other than themselves? Only where they'd find the next bottle?"

Keen was silent. What could he say other than to confirm it?

"We all have our triggers," Jati whispered. Golden skin creased around the edges of their eyes as they drifted into personal memory.

Was Jati's retort meant to still a brewing argument or anesthetize the hurt of Razor's words?

"I'm sure you have yours too," Jati said. Their tone was a tiptoe dance as if they'd put their hulking body between him and Razor without either noticing.

The Mote eyed her glass of kartan, fingering it delicately. "I've used them all up." She took a sip. "I'm numb."

"I doubt that," Jati said.

So much for the celebration. You could cut this tension with a knife.

"And what happens," Razor asked, shifting her gaze from Jati to Keen, "when you need to choose between your family and the state?"

"That," Jati pointed at Razor, "is the most difficult of all." They tipped their glass and drank.

Keen had to admit, that very dilemma was germinating within him. Not yet ready to sprout, it edged closer to the surface with every light year as they hurtled towards Heroon.

"Can we dispense with the philosophical musings and self-awaking session for the time being?" Razor interjected. "We have an immediate problem on our hands, one with my life on the line, which means the future of my people is in jeopardy." She aimed her gaze at Jati. "Not to mention the unanswered question of how Pox found us at Tarkassi 9."

"Let's get Pox out of the way first," Jati said. "Until we do that, we're not going to trust one another enough to figure out how to deal with our arrival at Heroon. Agreed?" They refilled Razor's glass.

A memory flashed in Keen's mind. Parshoo marsh. The outdoor canteen along the riverbank. Jati doing the same thing to an ornery soldier from another platoon who thought he'd been wronged, disrespected during a friendly bar competition. The recruit wasn't more than a month in and thought he was tough enough to go the distance with Lexar on the swamp box. She pushed it a bit at the end, got him pretty bruised and muddy, but his arrogance made it deserving.

Stupid rituals, now that Keen thought back on it. Barbaric games that reinforced hierarchy and submission in the ranks. Regardless, Jati was more the diplomat than he. They knew how to diffuse a situation without resorting to violence. Ironic, when they were the one who could pretty much knock anyone to the ground.

Razor nodded. Although reticent, patience and calm rolled over her like a blanket of clouds blocking a sun. It wasn't Jati. She'd cooled herself off. One thing he'd give her, she was fierce, but she also had wits of ice. That was why she was such a good pilot. She would've been an ace in the Legion Air Brigade.

"What?" Razor asked.

"Huh?"

"You're staring at me like I've got two heads."

"Sorry, was somewhere else," Keen said.

The Motes could be a brilliant force, maybe even unstoppable with the right equipment and support.

"So, we're agreed?" Jati repeated.

Razor and Keen nodded.

Jati gestured to Razor to open the discussion.

"How do you explain Pox's 'surprise' attack on the ship?"

"I can't," they said. "I was as shocked as you were."

Razor turned to Keen.

"Don't look at me. I've got no explanation. I told you already, but I'll say it again. Jati wasn't involved. It makes no sense. Their ship's damaged. We almost bought it, all of us."

"How much time would she need to jump to Tarkassi 9?"

"Depends on when she found out our location," Jati answered.

"Let's say, within the time you two went down to the moon base," Razor snarked.

"The only track in range would've been the Alliance outpost near Tellar. But she'd need to be at their orbital port, waiting for word. It's possible if she was refueling or seeking information from the Alliance."

"And she could get here how soon?"

Jati rolled their head back and forth, considering. "Thirty minutes, give or take."

"So, it could've been while you two were at the moon base?"

"What exactly are you accusing me of, Razor?" Jati asked.

"I want to know how she found us! No explanation is possible other than that you got word to her. How else would she know we came here? Neither of us knew," Razor gestured at Keen.

Keen held his hands up, indicating he wasn't complicit in her accusation.

"What?" Razor barked at him. "You have a different theory?"

"We were down there for a brief time. Jati went to meet someone…" Keen trailed off.

"My arms dealer," Jati said, jumping in. "The one delivering the explosives we took on board."

"And you trust them?" Razor asked.

"Not really."

"What does that mean?"

"Listen," Jati said, "it wouldn't make any sense for them to rat on me, or you two."

"Why not?"

"Because they're Hamut."

"What?" Razor rose from her seat. "Are you kidding me?"

"Sit down, Razor," Keen said, trying to calm her.

"Shut up, Keen. Same as that bitch who killed my sibling. What is this?"

Jati flung their chair out from under them and sent it crashing into the wall. "Now you listen to me. That Hamut's skimming weapons off the top from the Alliance. He's *stealing* from the ones you're fighting, sending arms off to be used against the Targitians and the Council. He's on *your* side."

"My side? You mean he's on the side of making money."

"No, he's on the side of liberty. Don't lump an entire culture under one politic. Not all the Hamuts want, or like, being enforcers. They'd just as soon be left out of this mess, as hard as that might be to believe. Like you, they've been pushed down and cornered, their will forged by the iron and fire of abusive post-war enterprise. They're tough as steel by circumstance, not by choice. Don't forget they lost their home in the Patent War. And now they're victims of economics as well."

"Everyone lost in the Patent War," Keen said. "Targite was the only winner and that's because they sat it out. Spent their time well too, inventing unrivaled energy technology." Keen sipped his water. "But the Hamuts did start it, Jati. They invaded the Cardon Twon system."

"We could point the finger the other way before that." Jati folded their arms. "And so, the circle turns in the Arm."

A long silence passed.

Razor broke it. "Your arms dealer still could've done it."

Jati shook their head. "If they out me, and you two, they out themselves. Plus, they don't even know you two are with me."

That was true, Keen realized. Unless Jati offered it up, no one would know. Except…

"Oh no," he said.

"What?" Both Razor and Jati said in unison.

"The Tip of the Beyond," Keen said to Jati. "I didn't even consider…"

"The Tip of what?" Razor said.

"Sit down, both of you," Keen said. They both obliged. He rose. "I was in the bar, talking to Solazi. She saw my Legion tattoo."

"It's not Solazi, Keen," Jati said, shaking their head.

"Who the heck is Solazi?" Razor asked.

"Let me finish. I agree, it's not her." He looked at Razor. "She's an old war vet. Runs a watering hole, The Tip of the Beyond. It's where I waited for Jati. Another patron sat at the end of the bar the whole time, for the entire conversation, including my exchange with Solazi about the war. I even introduced myself by name."

"You think this person contacted someone?" Razor asked.

"It's possible," Jati said. "Nobody ends up at the edge of the Arm except for dubious business or because they've given up on life."

"Did you see their face?" Razor asked.

Keen's mind ran backward. He was so focused on the little kid. "I can't remember."

"Try, Draden. Run it through in your head," Jati said.

Solazi moved down the bar after pouring my second Tail. She refilled the person's glass. They took a sip.

"I did." Keen hung his head in his hands. "A Hamut. Galangi ring on their drink hand. Sorry, I think this one's on me."

"Could've been any of us, old tot." Jati put a hand on his shoulder. "But it does make sense."

Keen raised his head and caught Jati nodding towards Razor, encouraging her.

"It does make sense." She nodded a reluctant apology to Jati.

"Likewise," Jati nodded back, mimicking the gesture. "I lost my temper. I would've suspected me too if I were in your shoes."

"Thank you both for understanding," Keen said.

"Don't look now, Draden, but I think you're being diplomatic." Jati raised their glass in an elegant gesture and took a sip of kartan for dramatic effect.

Razor smirked. "Although you have to work on the look. The jumper isn't cutting it."

Jati laughed and knocked back their kartan. They slammed the delicate flute down just hard enough not to break it. "Now, since we all agree we're screwed, courtesy of Ambassador Draden's lack of undercover skills, let's move on to our next problem. How are we going to get out of this jump port mess?"

KEEN LAY IN BED, staring at the star program projected onto the concave ceiling of the small bulkhead. He'd set it to the view from Heroon's southern hemisphere at night. The stars of high summer glimmered with all too familiar memories.

Three more hours passed in the mess, working through a plan for their arrival at the Heroon jump port. Lots of kartan flowed, but none from the bottle to his glass.

Engaging with intoxicated people sober was interesting. For about five minutes. After that, it was annoying beyond belief. Being on the 'other side' of the table was only adding weight to his guilt. He couldn't even imagine how many people he'd tortured over the years under the reverse circumstance.

As for the plan, of course, Razor and Jati outvoted him as to the 'best option.' Best option... if you could even call it that. More like a *drunk and stupidly daring* option. Only ten hours to go until they'd start preparations. Another seven after that and the *Carmora* would come out of the jump and it would all begin.

He needed to sleep. But of course, he was wide-awake and felt awful. Weren't you supposed to get healthier when you stopped drinking? And damn if it wasn't hotter than Kol 2 on this ship. His body was like a toxic waste facility that sprang a leak. He was sweaty, agitated, and annoyed. His skin was oily and disgusting to boot.

Close your eyes, imagine you're back on Heroon with Scarpa under the stars.

He clasped the medallion on his chest and shut his eyes. It wasn't working. All he could think about was how many people had endured his drunken banter over the years.

"Damn." He threw off the sheets and rose.

I might be in custody, or dead, in twelve hours. Or worse than both of those, on my way back to my parent in Garassit. I'm having a drink. If we make it out of this intoxicated-driven plan, then I'll call it quits. If we don't and I'm detained, then I'll have no choice. I'll have to quit. Either way, that's... logical.

He threw on the jumper (why? Jati had stocked his closet with several less ridiculous outfits) and left the cabin.

Thankfully, the mess was empty at this late hour. That was one small gift, at least. He went to the cabinet with the kartan. He'd violate protocol. Forget the glassware. Straight from the bottle. To heck with bogus rituals and longstanding traditions.

He opened the door. No kartan. Only a small note.

"*Sorry, old tot. One step ahead of you. There's some delicious chlorella algae booster in the cooler behind you.*"

Jati... he told them not to put the bottles away. What was with them? It was like they were a mind reader on the side, when not running arms to rebels. *They're probably awake in some secret compartment on the ship right now, wearing a flamboyant headdress and stirring a cauldron, watching a play-by-play through a spell that conjured my reflection and cackling at my expense.*

That's a very weird thought. Snap out of it and get your head together.

He popped open the cooler and slugged back the algae booster. It was filthy stuff, tasted 'healthy.'

What the hell was he supposed to do now? He damn well wasn't going back to the sleeping cabin.

"I shall locate the Officer of the Watch," he mocked official proclamation to the dead air of the mess. "Do I hear any objections from the floor?" His head went around the room to the pretend assembly gathered in the stands. "No? Then I will proceed with haste." He swirled his hand like a stage performer and exited. Whoever they were, if they worked for Jati they'd have a stash of something. Heck, he'd even take Mote juice... anything to cut through this sobriety nightmare.

The halls passed like a winding labyrinth. He went down a deck level to access the Bridge. Rounding a corner, he confronted a wooden sign outside a portal. Its anachronistic and worn timber was out of place in the ship's aesthetic, but to Keen, it was all too familiar. Laser-carved words in a unique font, elegant and sophisticated, stood in marked contrast to the standard military didactics on the rest of the ship.

Leave your shit outside. It's more dangerous than the enemy.

The corners of Keen's mouth edged upward. Jati had a training room. Keen's belly stirred and sparked, like a hand striking flint. The kindling ignited. Did he want to move? To sweat?

He opened the portal. The hum of the ship's FTL drive vanished. Beyond a small entry area, a raised wooden platform took up the majority of the room. The Legion crest colored one wall and a single black wall-high cabinet stood in a corner. The spartan room held an eerie silence.

Keen took a tentative step inside, crossing an invisible threshold. He wasn't ready, but he wanted to be up on the wood floor. His body pulled him like a ship under acceleration. He removed his night sandals and placed them aside. Even with no one present, he did what he'd always done. What one always did before entering the sacred space of a training session. He bowed. It was the Way.

Something stirred. As he raised his head, he spoke the Legion creed.

"'Treat me as I would treat myself. Be my shadow. Lead me to Stillness so I may become Empty. Self-defeat is my enemy.'"

His bare feet touched the platform. The wood was cold, but his feet smiled. It had been a long time. He sized himself up in the mirror.

You're not the person you used to be.

His mind shot back twenty-five years. The figure in the mirror transformed into a young, muscled youth – fit, lean, and ready to conquer the world.

He jumped into a fighting stance. His reflection grinned back at him.

"You still got it?"

His feet shuffled as he released a three-round fist burst. A jab, double-counter followed by a foot sweep takedown.

Hips are still behind it like they should be. I'll be damned if it hasn't been programmed in me for life.

He moved again, ducking in a feint and coming up with an uppercut elbow, spiraling around behind an imaginary opponent to form a rear-naked chokehold in the air. Sweat marks dappled his armpits and chest on the orange jumper. His chest heaved up and down.

"You're out of shape, old tot."

He walked off the exertion, hands on his hips. The cabinet in the corner caught his eye. Was it locked? He tried it and the door swung open. And so did his mouth.

A Talon Caster.

It rested vertically, fastened by two pressure pinch clips as if suspended in time. The Legion soldier's weapon of choice, an original from the days of the Patent War. A long staff with a three-pronged tip like the claws of a bird of prey on one end and a laser saw extension on the other. The height of a tall adult, it was a three-barreled gun, a fighting staff, trident, and a cutting blade all rolled into one weapon.

"Jati…you crafty old Legioneer."

So, they were keeping up with their practice. He wasn't surprised.

Keen's hand went to the center of the pole and pulled it from its clamp, releasing it. He eased it out and gripped both hands in a fighting position.

One run-through. For old time's sake. Nothing fancy.

He switched on the cutting blade and set it to practice. A glowing red laser grew to three feet at the bottom of the staff. Any contact with that portion of the weapon would send a small shockwave through the superficial layers of skin and muscle. Just enough to let you know you messed up and got cut. If switched to combat mode, it'd melt through anything except sophisticated metals and solid rock.

His arms thrust the Talon Caster out in front of his body. It stood in a vertical line running from head to toe. The three-pointed forked barrels rested in front of his vision. He grinned in the mirror from behind the talons. With great concentration, he moved through the practice form. His mind emptied. A dormant memory bank opened. His moves flowed without thought or effort. He'd done them too many times as a Legion soldier for them to be erased. He'd been one of the best.

The attempt was clumsy after a quarter decade, but the body mechanics were still sound. His breathing synchronized with the expansion and contraction of the weapon's movements, but nuances needed work. Like sandpaper, he'd need to smooth out rough edges.

"You move like a wounded Swamp Boar."

Keen didn't flinch. He finished the lunge and reverse head cut and spun around. Jati stood smirking at the edge of the platform. Keen squeezed his eyes closed and open, halting the sting of sweat running down his forehead. With no hair on top, it ran like a river over his olive skin, beading off his nose and chin.

"I haven't seen anyone run the Grey Bone form in years."

Keen relaxed, shut off the cutting blade and rested the bottom post of the Talon Caster on the floor.

"You always liked that one, didn't you?"

Keen nodded. "Fit my body type well."

"Not anymore, old tot. Even in that jumper."

Keen laughed. "True."

"No offense meant. Fit or not, we aren't the same Legion bodies we used to be. You should work on something more grounded now, like… the Stone Fall series. Now give me that."

Jati held out his hand. Keen threw him the Talon Caster. They hopped up onto the platform.

"Grab the other one from the cabinet. Let's have some fun."

"How did you know I was here?" Keen went to retrieve the weapon.

"Got a call from the Officer of the Watch, something about a wino wandering the halls."

"Couldn't sleep."

Jati's eyes went to Keen's sandals and the empty algae booster by the room's entrance. "Oh good, you got my note?"

Keen switched on the cutter blade to the practice setting, aware of the loaded comment. "Yep. Thanks, I needed that. Although, at the time I wanted to rip your living soul apart."

"And now?"

Keen waved a hand. "Left my shit outside."

"Well, well, well… a Legion soldier is on the floor. Come on, let's run some drills for old time's sake. If nothing else, I'll wipe that childish grin off your face and knock you on your butt enough times that you'll finally get some sleep."

NINETEEN

Waiting. All it did was raise doubt. I was hundreds of light-years from Kol 2. This was a fool's errand. Was I expecting to round up an army and return triumphantly to save my people?

I'd never traveled with FTL. Just processing the technology overwhelmed my life of sunrises and sunsets, of distances measured by human footsteps and the tack of a sail. Without faster-than-light speed, an entire age of the Arm would pass in the time it'd take to return home. It made all of this – my plight, Keen's agenda, Jati's dubious actions – seem so insignificant.

The only other time I'd left the atmosphere was the one run up to orbit to bring Keen down to the surface of Kol 2. That, and the quick ride to Jati's ship after the escape from Pox and the Tide Wave. And that wasn't flying; the auto-dock algorithm sequence did almost everything once we were exo. I'd learned to be a pilot in the transfer pods we'd stolen from the Targitians, but it was always in-atmosphere. Like the rare Dune Eagle, I could fly at speed, hugging the rise and fall of the sand, or climb to soaring heights that made Kol 2 appear as an endless ocean, only to dive with precision to take out my prey. My wings were bound to air and wind, thermals, and open sky. Space was a foreign void.

A thrill to this kind of travel couldn't be denied. But now that I was in limbo without the wonder of scale and cosmic beauty out the porthole or the distraction of a chase and life-threatening danger, the void revealed its hidden secret. It was an alluring and seductive temptress that cast a fog over the home I left behind. I hurtled through a hole in space and time, not knowing if my people were safe or even alive and growing more suspicious with every passing minute.

I couldn't understand Keen. An intelligent person spoke, a sober one, in the mess. But he was arrogant, more so than when he was drunk. Or, to be more specific, his selfishness transformed into an implicit self-righteousness that edged into authoritative prejudice.

Why was I surprised? He was the enemy. We'd taken him hostage because he was part of the problem. Somehow that shimmer had dulled since we left Kol 2. But it shone again in the mess.

Keen was attempting sobriety and had a personal revelatory experience on the moon base. He had confronted a tragic scene, unsheltered from his post-war ambassador social circle. It wasn't so much revelation as forced exposure to an uncensored version of the Real. Not war, but the vernacular Real that was the everyday norm for so many of us. And what? Now he was going to become a crusader for all those who live in oppression. An ally? That doesn't change the system. It perpetuates it through pity.

I'd made up my mind as I lay in bed (alone). As soon as I had an opportunity to find a safe route back to Kol 2, I'd take it. If I returned with an armed force, by some miracle, so be it. If Keen was heading further into a trench of self-pity and guilt, or worse, leading me along until he found his child, I'd leave and do whatever it took to get out alive. Forget them both.

It was a mistake and it was on me. I can admit it now. Keen's diatribe only reinforced my growing anxiety about my worldview. The more time I spent with Keen and Jati, the more I understood the complicated nature of our world. Of how one small isolated planet's problems couldn't be separated from the rest of the Arm. I know I cursed at Keen for that exact problem, for being 'complicated.' I can't help but see things in earnest, with strict precision. I'm from an arid land of extremes. My world is either dry or wet. There is no damp. My culture is either alive or dead. There is no hybridity. Our politics are either ethical or unethical. There is no compromise. It's life or death. Right or wrong. Would that same world exist when I returned? Could I live in it again, at peace? Or, had I become complicated?

TWENTY

"O.K., here we go," Jati said.

Keen stood with Razor at the back of the Bridge, watching as the jump terminus approached. Dressed as his old self, he shifted a layer of the expensive fabric wrapped around his shoulder. He was dressed as his old self. Jati had pulled together a mashup of fashionable extras from his crew's wardrobes. The idea was to look important and not to be questioned. He'd retired the orange jumper. Something about moving past it made him sad. He'd taken the first step to sobriety and turned his back on the Beyond in that thing. Plus, it made him feel more like everyone else. Now that he was costumed in extravagance, his insides felt imprisoned by a fraudulent veneer. Razor was in her blue sand fatigues, blaster holstered on her thigh. Militant and intimidating; that was the idea.

An important heir to a fortune from the Patents and their bodyguard, heading to Heroon's capital to meet with developers about a possible investment in the planet's future enviro-synchronization (once the rebel resistance was eradicated, of course). Since Heroon was under Garassian control, Razor could be Razor: a rogue Mote turned bodyguard with as little love for the Targitians as those governing Heroon.

They'd utilize Keen's new hairstyle (or lack thereof) as a further disguise and take the bold approach. Chin up and head-on.

If a request to go through customs before descending to the planet came over the board, they'd accept and taxi into the hub, with performed annoyance for the time-consuming nuisance. The heir was in a hurry, the delay made more convincing by the performed annoyance from a self-important person. Razor and Jati agreed Keen would have no problems with the dramatic role. They'd laughed at his expense over their kartan on that one. Drunks.

Once on station, it was time to undo his disguise. Keen would use his diplomatic credentials to bypass the usual chip scans in the public entrance. And he was certain someone in the diplomatic area could be persuaded by his status to send him back out to the ship without being bothered with time-wasting (and "insulting") procedurals. It was good to be an ambassador, sometimes. Keen planned to taunt any underlings working the initial checkpoints with well-practiced pomposity. Threats, done subtly and with enough arrogance, can work wonders. It was a serpentine political lesson he'd learned from watching his parent.

If all went well with what they called 'Plan B' ('A' was they never leave the ship, pass through the entry point without incident, and are granted permission to enter Heroon's atmosphere), and they were sent back (with apologies), then it was right back to a taxi out to the *Carmora*.

As for Jati and their ship, it'd be impossible to dump Keen and Razor off and jump away before dealing with the orbit port authorities. Within the Council sector grid, FTL was disabled through a jamming frequency and so long as they avoided a boarding party, they'd pull this off.

Jati intended to include a damage report in the Port of Entry log, requesting repairs on the planet. It would state that they'd taken a travel commission to deliver the heir to Heroon but were ambushed by space pirates while leaving the heir's homeworld of Urollo. Unable to hold off the marauders, and taking a beating, their ship was forced to make a quick jump to the edge of Arm. Waylaid on Tarkassi 9 for a few days to make repairs, they reached their intended destination but were late, much to the frustration of their paying client, and in need of haste.

Once they cleared the port, they'd ride a course through the atmosphere towards the capital. At 10,000 ft Jati would deviate from the approved flight plan and steer them into the continental interior where the rebels held sway. They said the *Carmora* could handle anything the Council had on the planet that came after them. Once they crossed into rebel territory, they'd be safe (according to Jati). The Garassian-controlled government on Heroon didn't cross that line to chase a single ship. Not these days. The Resistance was too strong.

The whole thing was ridiculous and simple, which according to Razor and Jati was the best way. They both agreed that people always defaulted to more elaborate and evasive techniques that led to mistakes and problems. Keen called foul, or to be more accurate kartan excess.

The worst-case scenario, they were boarded and that meant Plan C. By the time they got to that one drinking in the mess, Jati and Razor were three bottles in and decided they'd make a desperate run for the edge of the FTL jamming grid or "improvise something."

That last phrase would have sounded fine to him too if he were drunk with them. But sober, it didn't sit well. Keen thought it was worth reminding them both about his old friend. But Mr. Irony kept his mouth shut.

At least he got some sleep. Jati did their job well. Keen was humbled into realizing how much he'd slipped since his prime. He'd gotten about four hours of shuteye and a shower. He'd be a Swamp Boar, but he felt good. He was sore, the good kind of hurt. His body was saying, 'Hey, thanks for taking notice of me.' The hot water washed away the toxic emissions he'd purged through his pores. A subtle irritation gnawed at him. His physical appetite, mind's usual routine, and expectation of going numb daily were dealing with his abstinence by getting agitated. So far, he was holding them at bay. It was early for them which made it easier. But this evening? After what today might hold? That'd be another story.

"Coming out now," the navigator announced.

The blue stream of light cut short. Keen's mind lurched forward but his body stayed put. A battle the length of a nanosecond ensued before his brain emerged victorious. He took a step to catch himself from falling. Razor did the same. The synchronized action mimicked the involuntary jolt of surprise to someone descending steps who assumed another stair was left at the bottom. Although no side effects of coming out of an FTL jump existed, it still jarred the psyche. The eyes took in a scene that brought back the torturously slow reality of traditional human space-time.

There it was, out the Bridge window: Heroon. The planet, deep emerald with flowing blue rivers and wide deltas that opened into a sea, waited to starboard. It loomed large, its arcing sphere engulfing the viewing pane.

Keen's eyes glazed over as the planet's spell took hold. Fear broke the surface of his subconscious. This wasn't going to be a memory to be pushed back down. It was real. He pulled his gaze from the planet and turned his back on Razor and the others. He closed his eyes and steeled himself.

Chin up, Draden.

He turned back around.

"You alright?" Razor asked.

He nodded. A hand went to his chest feeling underneath the wrapped sash and tunic top to touch the medallion like a talisman.

Heroon wasn't just Keen's problem. It'd been a continual thorn in the Council's side since the end of the war. Technically a Garassian territory, its political security was tenuous. Every year or two, another coup brought unrest and instability and another wave of Council sanctions. The planet had been lost to the Hamuts and it was only the resolution of the Arm-wide conflict that gave it back. Why the Heroonese sided with the Hamuts during the war always surprised him. Even Scarpa was sympathetic, to a degree. He assumed it had something to do with a shared culture of worship and potent belief systems.

"Something doesn't look right," Jati said from the command seat.

An array of ships, some battered and damaged, hovered at arbitrary positions off the orbit port. A flurry of smaller vessels patrolled the sector. It was too much activity, from Keen's familiarity with space travel.

"Independent Vessel #479, identify and state business." The hub station controller's voice sent everyone's head on the Bridge bobbing around in confusion.

"Sake of...!" Jati said. "Don't send that entry data," they told a crew member.

That voice. Keen's diplomatic years made him well-versed in accents.

"What is it?" Razor asked.

"It's a Hamut."

"What?"

"Independent Vessel #479, identify now."

"Heroon hub, #479 here," Jati responded. "This is the *Carmora*. Requesting entry to Council Territory."

"Negative, #479. This is no longer Council Territory. You're within the sector grid of New Heroon," the controller said.

"New Heroon?" Keen muttered to himself.

"What the heck is going on, Jati?" Razor asked and walked forward. Keen followed her.

"I can only think of one thing," Jati said.

"Revolution," Keen said.

"What?" Razor asked, eyes wide.

"The Council's lost its grip on the planet. The rebels are in control," Keen said.

"Then why are Hamuts running the hub?"

"Remember that militia for hire I mentioned?" Jati asked Keen.

"The one that was going to help the Motes take Targite?"

"They're no longer available."

Keen read a hint of worry on Jati's face. The chiseled features softened in a way he'd not seen before. Razor's face had the, 'I knew this was going to happen,' expression.

"#479 halt and cut engine power."

"Hub, this is the cargo ship *Carmora*. We're bringing a delivery to Arshoo Mareet. We should have clearance to the surface. Check with her liaison." Jati held up a hand and crossed their fingers.

"Negative. By authority of the Heroon Liberation Front, now the Territory of New Heroon, your crew, passengers, and ship is under house arrest pending inspection and interrogation. Two passengers on your vessel are wanted by the authorities and will be taken into custody."

"Not the answer I was hoping for," Jati said.

"Your ship's been flagged, #479. Cut your engines now and prepare for boarding."

"Get to the pod, you two," Jati said.

"Is this Plan C?" Razor said.

"Just do it!"

"We'll never get anywhere," Razor said. "They'll blow us to bits as soon as we're in open space. And there's no more militia now." She turned to Keen. "Garassit has no more control here. And your parent won't help my people."

There it was. Mr. Irony, making an appearance. Always a show-stopper.

"Forget this. All of it," she said. "You want to make a run for it in a pod? Because I'm not staying."

Would the Hamuts take him to New Heroon? If so, he'd reach his destination. Or at least get close enough to persuade his captors to give him an audience with his child. Reynaria was now running the entire government. Unless her hatred for him was so severe she'd hand him to the Targitians? She wouldn't do that. Would she?

"Well?"

"Sake of the Arm," Jati said, interrupting them.

Pox's Twin Needle ship stood a few miles to port. It had blipped out of a jump.

"We make a run for it, yes," Keen said.

Jati gestured to a crew person on deck. "Get them down to the bay and fired up, ready to go." They nodded and motioned them off the Bridge. "Keep the line open and be prepared for my instructions."

"What're you going to do?" Keen asked.

"I know these thugs. Plus, these explosives are going to the rebels. I mean, the new government forces. We can't let them get their hands on either of you. I'll be fine once they realize who I am and what I have to deliver."

"You're not coming to Heroon?" Keen asked. He was counting on Jati being with him. He *needed* them with him.

"And how are we supposed to get past them with Pox sitting in waiting?" Razor asked. "I'm not letting anyone haul me off to a Targite prison."

"Would an explosion help?" Jati smiled and raised their hands. "It's all I've got. Unless you two have any better ideas?"

"And where are we going if we make it to the planet?" Razor added. "We can't just land in the capital and ask for an audience with your child, who is now the leader of an independent territory and an entire damn planet."

"Make for Erront," Jati said. "It's a small outpost south of Parshoo marsh in the interior. A counterinsurgency should be still holding out in the backcountry. Ask for Hirok-ti at the local canteen. Use my name and try to speak with the proprietor, Scorpi-ti. You'll recognize him. Old and tan, with no shirt. You can trust him."

"And then what?" Razor asked.

"If I'm not in a stinking cell on this orbit port, I'll meet you in a short time. Give me a week. If I don't show by then, add breaking me out of prison to your list of things to do."

"Hirok? From the Legion?" Keen asked. "As in the Fourth Battalion?"

"The same."

"Boarding vessel and three Vilo escorts left the hub," the navigator said.

Jati waved them off the Bridge. "Welcome to the Revolution."

"WHEN THAT POD leaves the bay, give a ten count, and hit those boosters to full." Jati's voice was calm but earnest over the com system. "Don't worry about the afterburn damage, just get out of here."

"Got it," Razor said. She flipped a switch above Keen's head. "Can you count to ten?"

"Very funny. Should I respond with an obscenity or just use a smile?"

"Admit it, you're enjoying these life or death pod flights with me." Razor smirked and gripped the controls, her Dunemarks stretching over the rounded steering mechanism.

"You're in a good mood considering we're about to be shot to bits and left to drift for eternity through space."

Razor shrugged. "Maybe you'll get lucky and spiral out of the Arm past the Tip of the Beyond."

Keen scoffed. "With my luck, my arms will be blown off. Solazi will be holding out a drink for me and I'll just drift right by."

"I thought you were done drinking?"

"If I'm dead? Forget that."

The levity passed. A short silence brought the reality of their situation back into sharp focus.

"I've made my peace," she said.

Keen observed Razor's face. Her eyes weren't as hard as usual.

"I'm going home," she said. "If we make it out of this, you'll be free of me."

"What about mustering military support and the coup?"

"I shouldn't have left my people. I'm going back to find them. We'll make our own fight. We always do."

"Well," he said, "for both our sakes I hope you fly today as good as you did in the Tide Wave."

Razor raised an eyebrow. "Never really flown in space."

"What?"

"Other than the quick in-flight with you and the docking run to Jati's ship."

"Are you kidding me?"

She shook her head and drew her lips into a wide grin.

Keen slammed his head on the back of the seat. "Why is my life like this?"

"At least your outfit is vomit-free. For now."

"If I had a bottle of kartan, I'd..." Keen halted mid-sentence as the decoy pod shot out the hangar.

Razor flipped a button, taking them off standby. The turbo booster charged up and hummed.

"You're not counting," she said and whacked him on the arm. "Start on 4."

"5, 6, 7…"

"You forgot 4."

"Sake of the Arm, Mote. What am I supposed to do now?"

Keen's head slammed back into the seat as the pod burst out of the ship, turbo boosters punched to full. Before he could scream an expletive, a massive explosion sent the tranquility of space into chaos. The pod veered right, thrown by the blast of the now vaporized decoy. Everything went yellow and white.

"Ten?" Keen said, gripping the console for dear life. They shot through the plume cloud and debris and out into clear space. It was a clever ruse. Make it appear as if they tried to escape in a pod but were blown to bits by the *Carmora*. Jati's cargo order might be a crate short, but if it was going to the new government did it matter? They'd used it to purpose and demonstrated their 'allegiance' to the authorities. "Improvise something" might have some merit after all.

Razor sent the pod towards Heroon. A world of green and blue, with patches of purple cloud cover, approached.

"You think we made it without being seen?"

A radar alarm dinged.

"Nope," Razor said.

The data board lit up. The two Vilo Darts en route to the *Carmora* veered course to intercept.

"Can they catch us with these boosters?"

"Nope."

Motes.

"So, we're going to make it?"

The alert blipped and a yellow light flashed.

"Nope."

The Vilos couldn't match the pod's pace, but they both spit out pairs of Seeker missiles. Those could keep up and then some.

Razor thrust the controls forward. The pod dove sharply. She held her hands there, obstinately. They were making an upside-down loop. The pair of lead Seekers plunged after them.

"You're smiling," Keen said. "Please tell me you've got a trick up your sleeve?"

She pulled up and yanked the pod's controls left and right. They spiraled up through the path they'd followed. The second set of Seekers hadn't traveled far enough to track their inverted loop. They were now heading straight at them from the left. The impact alarm went off.

"Sake of the Arm, Mote. You've killed us," Keen said.

Razor's eyes closed. Small crinkles on her forehead evidenced what Keen took to be calculations on an internal virtual grid.

"Nope," she said. Her face relaxed as she pushed the turbo booster throttle. It edged a little farther.

Crafty Mote. She'd left a bit of juice.

Razor yanked the controls into her stomach. They hurtled upside down. In a fraction of a second, it unfolded in his mind as if it were in slow motion.

She maneuvered us and baited the missiles.

Keen watched the board, inverted, as the two sets of missiles collided with one another underneath them. The explosion sent turbulence upward. The pod spiraled out of control, spinning rapidly. Heroon's green and blue orb crossed the front window like a looping holo-feed. Keen was struggling to hold himself together. Between the gees and the dizziness, he was losing his ability to keep his equilibrium and guts in check.

Not again. Not on this outfit. It's already offensive.

"I don't know what to do. I can't stop it," Razor said.

"Try," Keen said through gritted teeth. "You have to use the... stabilizers."

"The what?"

"Side thrusters," he grunted. "Not the controls."

The pod slowed its rotation and stabilized.

"Nice work," he said, eyes closed and struggling to regroup. He'd managed not to hurl. So that was a small victory.

"It wasn't me."

"What?" He opened his eyes. The Twin Needle ship stared at him through the cockpit window, its two pincers casting subtle beams of yellow triangular light that cut through the void of space.

"Oh no," Keen said. "This is a living nightmare."

"What's happening?" Razor was trying all the controls, attempting to fly the ship.

Keen felt his insides seize as he gazed at the golden rays cutting through space.

"You can stop," he said.

Razor worked the controls with no response. The pod drifted towards the Twin Needle.

"It's a gamma capture."

"Gamma what?" She stopped and stared out the cockpit window.

"A gamma capture. In layperson's terms: tractor beam."

A docking bay opened between the pincers. Razor reached for her blaster.

"Don't bother. That won't work either."

"So now what?"

"You get to meet Pox."

―――

THE POD SELF-DOCKED in the bay of the Twin Needle and the door to space shut behind them. Air rushed in as the vacuum was expunged, replaced with breathable oxygen. The hissing subsided. Stillness overtook the room.

No welcoming party. No Pox waiting with a death smile on her face. For that, Keen was thankful. But as the minutes passed the limbo wrought anxiety of the unknown.

"What's happening?" Razor asked.

"Apparently nothing."

"I'm getting out." She tried the door to the pod. It wouldn't budge.

"Try yours."

"I doubt it'll open."

"Try it"

Keen did. It was locked tight. A subtle sense of motion tingled through his body.

"We're moving," Razor said.

"Thank you, I hadn't noticed." He raised an eyebrow to drive the nail of sarcasm home.

Razor ignored him and pulled her blaster from its holster.

"Don't even think about it,"

"Why not?" She aimed it at the door.

"First of all, it's not going to work. I've told you that. Second, if it does, you'll burn yourself like a Tide Wave and probably me too. Thirdly, what's your plan if it does open? After I might add, I retrieve the medkit and attend to your severe burns and my own. Go and find Pox? Tell her thanks for pulling us out of an uncontrollable spin that we were in because we'd never flown in space before and didn't know you had to have a grasp of stabilizers?"

"I'm not staying in this damn pod!" She kicked at the door, trying to smash it open.

"Would you please stop? We might still need this thing."

Razor pulled the trigger on the blaster. Nothing happened.

"I told you."

"Why are you so calm?"

The docking bay rattled. A faint but palpable resistance pushed against the ship.

"That's why," Keen said, referring to the vibration. "We're going down to Heroon."

He closed his eyes. Now the looming reality was unavoidable. His feet were going to be back on the planet, stepping in mud and dirt. He would breathe humid air. His skin would feel the stifling heat. A cornucopia of voices from the animal life in the dense and lush tropical forest would resonate through his ears. Memories would swirl around him, recalling love and war. Two forms of trauma like night and day, forming a whole that was his life.

"Why?" Razor asked.

"It can only be one thing. Pox can't kill us outright. We're now the property of New Heroon, at least for the present."

"What does that mean?"

"It means," Keen spoke with his eyes shut and hands folded over his chest, "that I'm going to get to meet my child."

"So, we're prisoners, for the time being?"

"That'd be my guess, yes."

"And Jati?"

Keen shrugged. "Not sure. They've got their own explaining to do with the Hamuts for hire. If they don't end up in a cell next to us, you'd be wise to lean your personal feelings towards the positive. Jati may be able to influence what happens to us, or better yet, get us out of this."

Razor scoffed. "Yeah, right."

Keen remained calm and didn't move. "You still don't trust them?"

"Did I ever?"

"Did you?"

"No," she whispered. "I wanted to, but I can't. They have no side."

Keen opened his eyes and sat up, addressing her in earnest. "They have a side, Razor. The side of what they believe is right and just. It's your side too. If anyone shares your values, it's them. Yours is specific and one-dimensional. Jati's is universal. It might appear like ambiguity to you through the narrow lens you use to view the world."

"Don't lecture me, Keen."

"I'm not lecturing you. But for the Sake of the Arm, you have to understand others have problems, too. You're not the only one. And it's not easy living in the wider world of the Arm. Things don't work simply. There's negotiation. And compromise."

"So now you're the ambassador again?"

"That's how you engage with people. You can't fight everyone who stands for something different."

He leaned back and closed his eyes, both to avoid Razor's expression and to shut out where he was and what was coming. Memories festered, laughing with sinister anticipation. He knew when he got to the planet they'd be back. In its own ironic way, the longer he maintained the limbo of confined travel inside a craft piloted by the person he most feared in the Arm, the better off he'd be.

A trigger clicked as Razor tried the blaster again. He guessed she'd aimed it at the front window.

"Put that thing away. Let's hope you didn't damage the door with your foot. Sit back and tell me a story of your people."

He heard her sigh and return the blaster to its holster.

"Why?" she whispered.

"Because I'm interested. And it may be of help if I need to negotiate… or compromise."

And I need to be taken away from here, or I'll scream with horror.

TWENTY-ONE

My decision to flee was laughed at by fate. Like the backdraft of a Tide Wave, I was pulled against my will to face the choice I'd made when I left Kol 2.

Was this one of Crest's ripples across the glow pool? Or was this the price I paid for overconfidence? I could fly with the best of them in the atmosphere. That was clear when we evaded Pox through the Wave. Space was liberation, like throwing off the shackles of an epoch as a new one introduced more advanced technology. A grueling effort to do a task became simple through human innovation, removing an insurmountable obstacle. I soared without the pull of gravity, turning and moving at speed. And I showed the Hamuts, and Keen, what it meant to give chase to a Dune Eagle set free from terrestrial bonds.

But then there was the spin. It was like a metaphor for my life. Bold, daring, escaping death again and again until I found myself in circumstances beyond my abilities and my knowledge. At that point, someone else was in control. I hated it. I was supposed to be here, far from the desert wind, to take control of my people and their future. A last hope, graced with good luck and fortune, to return a savior. Instead, I'd given up on that dream almost before it had begun. Why?

Was it because I doubted Keen's commitment and sincerity, or my suspicions about Jati's allegiance? Or was it about me?

Keen's words as we sat, impotent in Pox's ship, punctured the armor of my weathered desert skin. My panic and frustration weren't so much claustrophobia as realization. If I wanted something from the world, I had to give to it in return.

I was riding a high in Jati's hangar, waiting to fly. But inside of the Twin Needle, I crashed into a landscape of doleful ennui. I didn't mind facing death. I would've preferred it then, which is why I wanted out of that pod. I was boiling with vengeance for Gushet, Hoti, Crest, Keltek, and the others. But I was also anxious about Heroon. I'd be on another planet for the first time in my life, a stranger on solid ground. I was scared more about that than being thrown in a cell or returned to Targite as a prize. I was going to be in Keen's shoes now.

And so, we sat for the duration. No communication from the ship came during the entire descent to the planet. I told Keen about the fracture of our people at the time of the eco-shaping, of what we preserved that was forsaken by our kin who joined the world. As I spun the tale, it became clear that they gave to receive. Before we got far enough along for that to become uncomfortably obvious the Twin Needle landed, and my unwanted future stared me in the face.

When the *Carmora's* bay opened behind us, we had no choice but to wait for whatever welcoming party walked into the ship. When they appeared, two worlds collided. The culture I'd be facing wasn't entirely new. And although Heroon was light-years from Kol 2, it looked a lot like home.

TWENTY-TWO

Keen stared at the three robed figures standing in front of the pod.
"Is this what Jati meant by 'complicated'?"
"Maybe," Razor said.
"Are they…?"
"Helleuan priests," she answered.
"So, we're under Targitian authority? This isn't good, for either of us."

Razor's eyes narrowed, scrutinizing the figures. "Not quite. Something's different. The insignia… look, it's been altered."

She was right. They passed for Targitian elders but with a distinction. A simple triangle, the signature of the Targitian regime and its religious Apex, contained an unfamiliar icon in its center. It meant only one thing. New Heroon, like its political backer, was a theocracy. That meant that Reynaria was…

"Place the blaster on the dashboard where we can see it," a voice announced over the com. It wasn't Pox. And it wasn't one of the three robed figures either. The accent was Heroonese.

Razor did as instructed.

"Now remove the charger and toss it aft."

She slid the bar out of the blaster's handle and tossed it over her shoulder.

The pod's power flipped back on. The control board in front of them came to life. "Step out, both of you. Slowly."

A pair of soldiers, battle-worn and with the same altered insignia on their fatigues approached the cockpit door on Razor's side. They had Talon Casters in their hands.

What the...?

Keen peered over Razor's shoulder, out the window of the door. They were originals. How did old Legion weapons come to be in their hands?

"Open it and step out," the omniscient Heroonese voice instructed.

Razor tried the door. It wouldn't budge.

"We can't open it," Keen announced to the omniscient voice on the com. "It's damaged."

"Tell the Mote to move away."

"Tell me yourself," Razor snapped. "I don't take orders from…"

"Quiet, Mote. Ambassador Draden, have her move back."

"How dare you?" Razor said.

No response.

"Just do it," Keen said. This wasn't the time to prove anything.

Razor's eyes shot to his own, fierce with rage.

"Negotiation and compromise," he whispered.

The Mote glanced at the blaster charger in the aft section of the pod.

Keen shook his head. "Don't. Follow me on this." He held out his hand.

She hesitated, shifting in her seat.

Keen encouraged her with a hand. "This is diplomacy time. It's not the time to fight."

She took it. Her skin was dry and calloused. Bony fingers wrapped around his thick flesh. An odd tension passed between them. It was the first time they'd willingly touched one another. Up until now, it was one or the other forcibly grabbing, pulling, or pushing, usually Razor doing it to him. Keen pulled her back from the damaged door and made room for her on the seat, sliding over towards the pod's wall. He nodded to the three robed figures.

A soldier stepped forward and fired up the cutting blade of the Caster. It sliced through the door. The soldier kicked it open.

"Down now, slowly."

They both exited into the ship's bay.

"Bind her," one of the robed priests said.

Keen noted the use of Razor's pronoun. *So they know us already.*

A soldier went for Razor's arm. She pulled it away and sent a back fist slamming into the soldier's cheek. Blood splattered from her victim's mouth. The other soldier thrust the cutting blade up at her throat. "Enough," the robed figure nodded to the soldier holding the Caster. The victim of Razor's blow got up from the floor, her face flush with pent-up self-restraint. The two soldiers bound Razor's hands behind her back.

Keen put his arms behind him for his pair of cuffs.

"That's not necessary, Ambassador," the priest said. "I trust you'll behave in a manner appropriate to your office."

"What is this?" Razor asked. "Who are you?"

The robed figure ignored her and went to Keen.

"By the authority vested in me as a keeper of the Ascendency, with the backing of Helleuan as it is foretold, you are now in the custody of the Sacred Seer, Governor, and ruler of New Heroon."

"Custody?" Keen asked.

"You are both prisoners of war, Ambassador. Per the rules of diplomacy in the Arm, you will please follow us."

"What about my partner?" Keen asked.

The priest raised their head, revealing a face. Old and sage, it radiated authority despite the wear of years. Lines and wrinkles descended in earnest, pulled by the gravity of time. Something was familiar about them.

"The Mote will come as well, but without the privileges accorded to you."

"Unacceptable," Keen said.

"You have no authority here, Ambassador."

"It's not my authority to which I'm referring. She is a representative of her people, accorded the same status I have with mine. Uncuff her."

"Absolutely not. The Mote is not on Council. She's a rebel and has no political legitimacy."

"And were you not the same until a few days ago?"

The face smiled. The old priest stepped to within a foot of Keen. Earnest brown eyes burned with a low but steady life glow. The features, despite the wear of years, were familiar.

I know this person.

"I will not mince words with you. She's an enemy of Targite and therefore an enemy of New Heroon."

"For a Liberation Front turned Independent Territory you seem to be short on autonomy, and quick to forget your history." Keen adjusted his sash for dramatic effect. He felt foolish doing it as if it was an old trick that had lost its charm.

The priest looked him in the eye. A flicker of inner strength ignited on their features.

Yes, I know you from somewhere.

"Don't push your luck, Ambassador."

"Never had any. Doesn't seem to work for me."

"Indeed. That's well known to us."

And my reputation proceeds me.

"And it's 'ti' when you or the Mote speak to, or of, me."

But we don't get a name.

This was the opening move. The tone had to be set now, at the outset. Keen stared back into the old one's eyes.

"Shall we bind you too, then?"

Out of the corner of his eye, Keen saw Razor turn. He kept his gaze on the robed individual. This was so much easier now, with nothing to lose. The usual pressure of an expected political result under orders from his parent and the Council was lifted. He had both the diplomatic negotiation and the desired result in his control.

"If you won't take hers off, yes."

"Fine." He nodded to a soldier who locked Keen's wrists behind him. His mind pushed down the fear of the restraints. This was the second time he'd been shackled on Heroon. The memory of the first was pushing, fighting to break the surface of his consciousness.

"Better?"

"Equitable," Keen snarked.

The robed figure gestured to companions who led the procession out of the ship. Keen descended the ramp between the ship's needles and took his first step back onto Heroon.

His shoes settled into heavy dirt; the weight of his body embraced by the planet's skin. And he remembered. A strange, unknown and deeply rooted force lay at Heroon's core. You sensed a soul under your feet. An energy lurked here that wasn't present on any other world.

A solitary, crude but pious structure stood a short way off amidst a lush forest along a wide, running river. Its water was deep and strong, moving at a steady rate, consistent and with determination. It didn't rush but wasn't slow-moving. The water wouldn't be stopped. It reminded him of Jati.

Where were they and how were they faring?

Flocks of white birds swooped over its waters. Nushaba's rays shimmered off the swirling current on its surface. Peaks of towering purple clouds loomed on the horizon. Nothing but endless tropical rainforest lay in all directions. The geography didn't register with his topographic inventory from the war. Where was the capital? Gontook, Heroon's most populated city and the center of culture and politics, lay along the coast of the planet's single continent. He should be smelling the salty air of the ocean.

"Move," the priest said.

They walked, emerging from between the ship's massive needles. Ahead, Pox stood with her two AI droids.

"You!" Razor screamed and lurched towards her. The soldiers restrained her. "I'll rip your Hamut head off!"

Pox grinned but didn't flinch, nor address Razor. Her eyes were fixed on Keen. Icy fingers stroked the handle of the Spineblade secured by the combat belt around her waist. She blew him a fake kiss with dramatic flair.

Keen broke eye contact and stared at the ground.

A Hamut kiss. The classic trademark of the bounty hunter class after a most prized trophy. It signified merciless pursuit that could only end one way: your still heart in their bloodied hands.

"Draden," she called after him as they passed.

He didn't turn.

"Welcome back," she said. "I'll be seeing you soon."

He'd been right. The bounty hunter was at the mercy of New Heroon politics. So, there was some form of independence to the Territory.

One of the robed figures veered from their party and walked towards Pox. The two exchanged words.

"Keep moving, Ambassador," the priest said.

Why weren't they in the capital? Judging by the empty wilderness around them, they had to be deep into the continent's interior.

Keen walked the cobbled pathway down to the river. The trees edging the road were trimmed back so no shade sheltered the single-file procession. Nushaba's rays beat down on Keen's naked crown.

Razor was ahead of him, the two soldiers in front and behind her held their Talon Casters at the ready, cutting blades on and glowing.

They rounded a bend and approached the river's edge. A wooden barge was moored to a crude dock. Several soldiers prepped it for departure. The boat was sleek yet stable; a wooden runner designed for the unique currents of Heroon's rivers. Quick and frequent turning was not in its vocabulary. The craft worked as a long-distance cutter, running either down or upstream. Its front section was open to the air. The back half contained a covered interior with ornate carvings on the doors and walls and a raised platform at the rear. Keen recognized the wood as the prized cantinool tree, deep violet with grains the color of wheat. A silent engine idled at the stern, churning river water in bubbling rhythms. Its sleek design pointed to Targitian eco-technology.

"Where are we going?" he asked while stepping onto the boat. Nothing but pristine rainforest ran up and down the river's banks in both directions.

Their captor gestured to a row of seats carved into the barge in the bow.

"Sit, Ambassador."

The guards motioned Razor forward and shoved her into another seat further up.

"To our new capital," he said.

"New capital?"

"The Temple of the Coming Wind." He raised a hand, motioning them off and away from the dock. "The Governor wishes to meet you."

Reynaria...

All the pieces fell in place, but the game board wasn't the one Keen expected.

Razor gazed out over the river, taking in the foreign scenery. A subtle breeze drifted across the boat, warm and heavy with humid air. It spoke of moist, fresh earth and memories of war.

"You feel that, Ambassador?" The priest lowered his hood, exposing his head. A faint band of grey hair ran around the back from ear to ear. It was wispy and thin, almost imperceptible. The heavy folds and wrinkles of his face continued down his olive-skinned neck, disappearing underneath the collar of his robe. He closed his eyes relishing the gentle, wafting breeze. His stubbled chin rose, a smile drawing on his face. "Do you know what that is?"

Keen didn't answer. He knew what it was to him. Potent memory. Did his captor know about his past? About what happened to him on this planet during the war?

The old one's eyes opened and rolled to meet his own. "That's the future."

KEEN PUT ASIDE the bowl of half-eaten fruit and stared at the ripples of water shimmering in the sunset.

"The waters move differently here," Razor said, staring at the passing river.

Keen peered over the side of the barge. It was as he remembered: rich in color, verdant green in its deepest portions, and leaning more toward amber at the surface. Long tendrils of the strangler plant, black and shadowy in the waning light, ran horizontally in the depths, pulled by the current.

The sun lingered above the tree line. As if refusing to set, golden rays streamed at them as they drifted downriver. A large bird, elegant and slow-moving, flew gracefully across the water ahead of the barge.

"That's a Ribbed Garkin," Keen said, pointing. "There's only one pair for every hundred or so miles." Razor was silent, watching the pair pass. Their wings rose and fell with languid confidence. Keen followed them until they vanished into the hanging trees on the far riverbank.

After the boat cleared the shoreline and rounded the first bend beyond the outpost, a soldier removed their cuffs without so much as a word. Keen knew why. There was nowhere to go. You didn't want to jump ship out here, not with the Strangler plant infesting the waters. You'd be lucky to make it to shore. If you did, without proper supplies and provisions you'd never last in the tropical wilderness.

They'd been fed well, handed bowls of fruit and steamed river fish with leafy greens by the soldiers manning the ship. Keen's mouth came alive with memory at the first bite. It was prepared with marmish, the distinct spice that defined Heroon's cuisine. Sweet, tangy, and spicy – the nectar was everywhere. The cantinool trees produced it year-round from their large yellow and orange cupped blossoms. In the rainforest, especially at night, the nectar's idiosyncratic aroma lingered in the air like a planetary perfume.

Keen had seen no sign of the robed trio since his brief exchange when they first left the dock. The mysterious veiled figures remained cloistered inside the cabin to aft.

Mile after mile of tropical forest drifted by them. Dusk surrendered to the dark. Strange noises rang out from the riverbanks. Animals, some unfamiliar to his ears, called out in song.

Heroon's night was a paradox, both a terror and comfort, a world where he'd been exposed and vulnerable on night missions but also sheltered in Scarpa's loving embrace away from the horrors of war. It pulled him between repression and nostalgia.

No cure for either was within his reach. Drinking wasn't even an option now. He doubted his captors were the kind to indulge. And so far, he'd seen no sign of a bottle being passed among the crew.

Maybe that was for the best. He didn't have to fight on two fronts. It was only the physical withdrawal now. The psychological decision of whether or not to abstain was off the table. The purging lessened as the days passed. His skin was no longer a surface for internal toxic residue. And he wasn't as agitated as he'd been the first few days.

Ran, the vanguard of Heroon's three moons, rose ahead to their left shining bright pink. As if triggered by its warm lunar light, needle flies emerged off the water's surface, hatching into winged form and flashing their mating signals. The river burst alive with intermittent, flickering crimson.

Razor broke the silence. "What are they?"

"Needle flies. Beautiful but deadly." *Like this planet.*

One fluttered about the bow of the boat.

"It won't sting unless provoked," he added, finding the statement apropos to the planet's temperament. The view from the boat was akin to a canopy of stars set ablaze by a fire's reflection.

"There's a spot for you to aft. To sleep," a soldier said behind him. Keen turned. They were holding a small infrared ball to light their way. Their face was cold in the warm glow, stoic and unsympathetic. It made clear the offer was one of courtesy for his status, not one of hospitality.

"And my companion?"

The soldier eyed Razor with malice. They shook their head. "She sleeps up here. On the floor."

"Then so do I," Keen said.

"Go back, Keen," Razor whispered, staring ahead at the river and the needle flies.

"No, I'm staying."

The soldier withdrew aft.

"You don't need to do this," Razor said.

Keen didn't respond. It was as much for his well-being as hers. The nightmares were sure to come. He didn't want to be back near the others when they did. It would be an embarrassment and a weakening of his position in the subtle power play.

"Look," Razor pointed to their right over the tree line.

Heroon's twin moons, Harmon and Karpel, rose. Cold as ice, they constituted two halves of a previous single moon shattered eons ago. Caught in an endless rotation around one another, the cosmic anomaly defined the Heroon night.

"Harmon and Karpel," Keen said. "Harmon is on the right now. Every hour they switch as the night passes."

"Were they one moon?"

"Yes, long ago. Now they're known as..." Keen realized the pain inherent in the next word.

"Twins," Razor whispered, gazing upward.

Keen opened his mouth, but no words came out. Razor didn't seem to mind letting their exchange dangle, unresolved.

"Is Altiron visible from here?" she asked, head up, looking at the stars.

Again, he'd have to disappoint her. "No," he said. "Somewhere there," he pointed back behind them to the left, below the horizon.

Razor's head didn't follow. Her eyes remained forward towards the twin moons. "Keen, why are there no ships? No air traffic?"

She was right. Utter stillness reigned in the skies above them.

"I'm not sure."

Shuffling and movement at the back of the barge interrupted their exchange. Keen peered back. At the far stern, behind the covered cabin, three silhouettes appeared on the elevated dais. Ghostly shadows in the moonlight, the human forms stood with arms raised to the sky. A low and guttural chant reached Keen. The mantra repeated over and over as if the trio were in a trance.

The speech was ancient. Keen's ears recognized the distinct phonetics: early Contex, a now-dead language from the Second Age of the Arm. His linguistic tutors had read aloud portions of the extinct speech to his cohort during his diplomatic training. It was the root from which all languages in the Arm sprung.

"They're calling to Helleuan," Razor said in a hushed voice. "The Ancients on Kol 2 performed the same ritual. I've seen it on the walls of ruined caverns of old. And heard it told by the Lore Masters."

"Do you understand it?"

Razor nodded. "The basic meaning, yes. Our indigenous language is old, a direct descendent that grows from the same root."

"Why are they worshipping a wind god?"

"I don't know," Razor said, staring at the crimson starred lights of needle flies on the river.

So, they worshipped Helleuan? The wind god of Targite. They were priests... Keen's mind whispered the old one's words.

The future.

RAN'S MOONLIGHT cast a subtle glow on the thick vegetation under the towering trunks of the cantinools. The air was dense with moisture and heat, so heavy it paralyzed the forest. The only thing moving was Keen's chest. It was as if a god-like hand had paused the world and only he'd been left breathing. The weather, the growth, and death of plant or animal life, the rotation of the planets around their stars, all of it halted. Other than his inhalations and exhalations, utter stillness and silence reigned.

He peered through a small break in the leaves, one knee sunken in the damp and muddy soil and the other leg bent to support the Talon Caster.

Lexar-té was fifty paces back, to his left, huddled behind a fallen cantinool. She'd have her back to the trunk, ready to rise, turn and let loose with the Spirex Displacer. Once Keen retreated past the ambush line, she'd cut down as many bodies as she could that followed his retreat. With a Spirex in her hands, it would be a massacre. Jati was off to his right, a hundred paces back with the rest of the platoon, waiting to take care of whoever made it through the spewing fireworks of the Spirex's rapid firing death rounds.

Only an hour remained. After that, Heroon's twin moons would rise and transition the tropical rainforest into a world of light and shadows, too bright to hold the position. He'd be spotted by the approaching platoon's remote flyers passing under the canopy. And that wasn't the plan. This was their night raid to rescue Reardon and two others abducted on the night Keen was supposed to be on patrol.

Thanks to the strategic data pulled from the hands of a dead Hamut two days earlier in a tunnel system a few miles upriver, they now knew the direction the enemy was taking the Legion prisoners. If they'd calculated right, Reardon and the other captives should pass straight through this stretch of the rainforest as part of a supply train, following the stream bed to rendezvous with the rest of their forces for a big push to take back the entire sector. If they did, it would secure a road for three Hamut battalions further back to move up for a killing blow to the Legion struggling to hold the territory.

If Keen's platoon didn't stop them now, a crack in the Patent Force dam would burst and end in their defeat and the loss of the planet.

But a cloud of personal guilt now overshadowed that big picture. Keen alone knew that he was supposed to be out the night Reardon was captured. He'd been so stupid, so selfish. Self-reproach and shame festered in his psyche. While he was lying with a lover, a Heroonese woman no less, his sibling was taken by the enemy. Perhaps tortured or even dead.

This might be about saving the war, but for Keen, it was also about saving his sibling and saving face.

It all trickled down to him. From the hackers and espionage groups who first got rumor of the enemy's movements, to the Legion birds who scanned the sector and located the underground command center, to the Wormers, the squad that moved in and slid down muddy tunnels through a dark unknown to kill and grab strategic plans, to the general who set up the counter-strike, it was now Keen's eyes watching and waiting. He had to get the scouts to bite and give chase from the right distance, with the right idea that they were in for an easy kill, or too many would get through and it could turn from surprise to a deadly mistake.

The hair rose on the back of his neck. Had the frozen image in front of him glitched or was it a drop of nectar from a cantinool falling to the understory? He leaned to his left, as slow and imperceptible as a star's motion across a night sky. He was like the tropical night, lungs halted mid-breath. The edge of the leaf moved, revealing a faint image of glistening brush and branches in Ran's gentle light. The rainforest was nothing more than a series of black shapes of varying degrees of opacity.

The Hamut scouting party should be slinking up the creek bed. If that blip was the movement of the lead scout, they'd emerge about a hundred feet ahead. Keen needed to lean a bit farther from the security of the leaf shielding his face. He moved a fraction closer to its edge, the plant's veins and skin passing over his vision like the palm lines of a hand. Another eternity of movement to the left and he'd know if someone approached. The side of the leaf drew back and...

A face was in front of him!

"Keen, wake up."

A hand on his shoulder.

"You were having a nightmare," Razor said.

Keen wiped the sweat from his brow.

"Keen?"

"Yeah, thanks. Was I loud?"

The question's significance dawned on Razor's face. "No." Her eyes went aft towards the cabin. "I don't think anyone else heard."

"Good." He rose onto an elbow. His body ached. The cantinool planks were hard and unforgiving. The sun was yet to rise, but its imminent arrival was foretold by the glow pushing back the night sky. The twin moons had set but Ran remained. It had shifted further to their right and was growing faint in the pre-dawn light.

"I think we're here," Razor said and pointed ahead.

In the crepuscular dawn, the outline of a structure alike to the one at the settlement loomed at a bend in the river. The barge veered towards the shore.

"Eat."

Keen turned. The soldier from the previous night held two bowls. Keen took them both, knowing she wouldn't hand the other to Razor. He passed it to her.

"We dock in a few minutes," the soldier said.

"And then what?" Keen asked.

"We walk."

TWENTY-THREE

Heroon seduced me. I was caught in its perverse grip. Even in my bondage and humiliation pleasures reached me, denied as I was my freedom.

My homeworld was arid and barren. Life flourished in the desert, but only those with a trained eye could find it. But Heroon? It flooded the senses with its fecundity. To live on a world such as this… was this Kol 2 before the eco-shaping?

Thanks to its verdant abundance, my fear and anger were balanced with marvel and wonder. Heroon was a paradox. Keen said it many times. He was right. It was beautiful but deadly.

I knew nothing of the land and sky on Heroon, but it turned out I knew something of the culture. I'd traveled hundreds of light-years only to walk into the same oppression I'd left on Kol 2.

Keen stuck to his newfound ethic during those early days on the planet. He held fast defending me. In a short time, it became clear it was as much for political maneuvering and his self-protection as it was about my right to be treated as an equal. It didn't matter. I'd decided to return to Kol 2 and once that happened everything pulled me farther away. My chance to flee showed its face in the reflection of a kartan glass on Jati's ship. And then, like a cave eel retreating into its underwater rock-dwelling, it withdrew out of sight.

By the time we pushed off from the shore on the barge, I'd accepted it. No going back without first going forward. A path was laid for me. If I made it back home would it be alive or dead? And what did that mean? I could be dead but still breathing. That scared me more than returning without a pulse.

Time moved with haste as we traveled on the river, and flew even faster as we trekked through the rainforest. Days bled into weeks. Keen's nightmares worsened. And it wasn't just Heroon. The more lucid he became in sobriety, the more functional his mind grew during his sleeping hours. His world flipped on its head. Without drink to lull him into a state of oblivion, he was coming alive and finding he'd awoken a beast.

I knew it. By the time we were deep into the journey, he knew I knew it too. When we walked during daylight, he shed the layers, an older version of himself regenerating after decades underneath physical and psychological armor. It was visible in his physique and audible in our conversations, brief though they were.

The Keen walking under the cantinools in the humidity and heat was getting stronger and would be a powerful political weapon in good physical condition when we arrived. But the one that had awoken in the night? That nocturnal creature knew how to conceal its presence in the dark. Only when it couldn't resist pushing its victim past its limit did you catch a glimpse of the power it held over its host. Every time Keen woke his eyes spoke of what he'd been made to endure within the realm of sleep.

We were three weeks on foot. The days passed with ironic ease. I had no agency, no role to play other than to walk. Keen was allowed to engage in short conversations with our captors. The three robed figures didn't speak, but the soldiers grew more comfortable around him. The ambassador was working the relationship. I noticed what others didn't in my state of non-existence. I wasn't interested in any of them, not until we arrived at whatever destination was ahead. Until then, I was in limbo. And so, I gave myself over to the flora and fauna around me.

Each passing day, I took note of the characteristics of the shifting terrain as it repeated, understanding how it ebbed and flowed like Kol 2's wind and sand, but with water and dirt. I made friends with the cycle of the moons. Ran was my reward. At night when we halted our march, I'd relish the rest under its watchful light. Until the Twins rose to challenge its solitary lunar presence, no nocturnal ritual interrupted my meditation. No singing and worship pulled me back to my world and its inescapable, tormented reality.

As if to push the blade further into the wound, Heroon's nightly symbolic call to prayer was a reminder of my fracture. Harmon and Karpel swirled in an endless orbit, as I had with my sibling. And so not only one, but two agonizing memories of home returned every night as if to deny me the preservation of awe and beauty I'd consumed each day under the heat and sun.

When we reached the outskirts of the new capital, the sense of what was before me overtook whatever respite I'd found on the long trek. If I thought the natural wonders of Heroon were sublime, the new civilization taking shape through Targite's support was a harsh reminder of how much seduction was at work on the planet. I'd been taken by Heroon's sweet caress. My captors knew the land and sky, and while our path was arduous whatever dangers lurked in waiting around us were known to them and avoided. With our entry back into the world of humanity (if you could call it that) a different kind of danger was palpable and all too visible. The new government had gone to bed with the very core of the planet. Heroon whispered its darkest secrets in its ear and they used it with terrifying effectiveness on their people.

Minutes after we arrived, Keen and I parted ways. I cannot speak with any certainty about his circumstances or actions after our separation other than what I learned later. Much of what transpired is lost. And what I was told came from sources more dubious than trustful. Then again, as I told you at the outset, Keen's story is filled with lies. Both those told by him and those told about him. And also, those I told myself.

TWENTY-FOUR

"Where are they taking her?" Keen watched the soldiers lead Razor away.

He and the three cloaked figures remained on the stone walkway. The appearance of the cobbled road several miles back was the first sign that the long trek was nearing an end.

"To the labor camp," the priest said. "She'll do her penitence with the rest of the heathens. Her sweat and blood will be preserved in the foundation of New Targite."

"New Targite?"

"It will soon be finished. And then it will be time. Come," the hooded figure gestured for Keen to follow him on the stone way. Keen's eyes stayed fixed on the narrow dirt path winding away into the dense forest. Razor's spiky red hair and lean figure followed the soldiers as they disappeared into the bush.

"Don't bother, Ambassador. Her fate is sealed. It's yours you should be concerned with now."

Again, the priest gestured Keen forward. One thing was becoming clear. The only way he'd influence the situation was through Reynaria. And as of now, that was a tabula rasa. She wanted 'to see him.' But what did that mean? No matter. He wasn't going to get anywhere right now. These New Heroon priests were unwavering in their commitment to their so-called religion.

They walked the road in silence. Birds sang in the nearby greenery. The hot midday sun shone down on Keen's crown. Without the shade of the cantinools the heat was almost unbearable.

Sweat drenched his clothes. He ran a hand over his head and wiped the moisture away. Fingers grazed the fuzz of new growth. A stubbled, crude beard covered his jaw and cheeks. He looked at his arm. The red laser lines of his Delta Sagittarii tattoo looked more intense against his darkened olive skin, tanned under Nushaba's merciless rays.

The tropical rainforest retreated further from the processional pathway as if wanting to disassociate itself with the nearing destination. Razed and scorched earth lay on either side of the stone road. Keen walked with his head down, avoiding the blazing light of the sun. In the haze of the searing monotony, he recalled a similar walk when he first arrived on the planet, heading from the safety of Patent Forces central command into the wilderness. A Legion newbie, he was curious to view the foreign landscape. But it was the same as now – too hot to keep his head up against the sun's rays. Back then, once they entered the canopy that changed. And so did…

"Welcome, Ambassador. You're fortunate. A strong spirit runs in you."

Keen lifted his head. A massive fortification lay in a mile-wide clearing in the pristine rainforest: The Temple of the Coming Wind. A three-tiered stack of hexagons rose skyward, unadorned save for one gleaming insignia on a single post on the top tier. The icon shone blood-red, rotating as if it were a panopticon. Keen recognized it; the same Targitian triangle with the unusual New Heroon symbol inside made all the more potent against the charred and green landscape around the perimeter of the fortress.

Keen couldn't forget the striated rock slabs used in the temple's construction, either. Streaks of black, blue, and green crystals ran like reflective rivers over its walls. He knew those colors. The material was all too familiar: jeekoo stone. Juxtaposed with the verdant emeralds, yellows, and oranges of the nearby forest, the tri-colored crystal streams in the sedimentary rock cast a dark beauty over the site. The aesthetic hovered somewhere between regal and macabre. Light, yet impenetrable by almost any material, the Heroonese treasured the unique indigenous resource. Jeekoo was the ingredient of choice for all important structures, including prison cells during the war.

The old priest directed Keen up the long ramp to the first tier. Step by step they climbed. A subtle breeze caressed Keen's overheated cheeks. Cool air fluttered through the openings in his garments, intermingling with the perspiration on his skin. Despite the unknown ahead, Keen relished the physical relief with the increase in elevation.

Once on the open level of the first rise, the priest led him around two corners of the six-sided structure. At even this lowest tier Keen could see far into the distance. Endless green tropical forest ran to the horizon. Shielding his eyes against Nushaba's rays, he scrutinized the highest level and guessed it must be almost 1,000 feet off the ground. Was Reynaria up there?

"Come." The priest gestured to a small viewing balcony projecting over the open air. Keen approached the edge and hesitated before resting his hands on the jeekoo stone. His skin met rock and the soul of Heroon shuddered, sending chills to his heart. It was mocking him, thanking his foolish pride for returning to its alluring abominations.

A distant object pulled his eyes further from the direction they had come to reach the temple. His mind glitched. A replica of the Fins stood half-completed a few miles off in a long, flat portion of the rainforest.

The future. They're going to eco-shape the planet. Into a desert. For wind.

"Helleuan," Keen said, without realizing it.

The structure rivaled the original on Kol 2. A shantytown around it stretched for at least two miles. Smoke rose from random districts. The plumes caught the breeze high in the air and ran for miles before dissipating into the atmosphere. Keen guessed a million people, perhaps more, fit in those labor camps. Where was the rest of the planet's population? Almost four million people lived scattered around Heroon, most in its capital Gontook, wherever that was from here.

"The wind spirit travels outside of time and space, Ambassador. It's awaited our awakening with endless patience. Those who have the strength of body and mind have made the journey. They work to build the city in which they will live. And prosper."

Keen understood the implicit meaning in the old priest's words. "And those who didn't?"

Like the Motes on Kol 2.

The priest gazed over the vista with brown eyes empty of emotion. "They leave their corrupt spirit to seep back into the core of this heathen ecology. They, along with all the life you now see before you, will die and allow for a new age to rise."

"A new age?" Keen spoke to the priest's hooded profile. "This isn't a historical transformation. It's mass murder. Of both humanity and a planet. And for what? Profit."

The priest turned his cold stare to Keen. "Speak not of commerce and profit to me, Ambassador. Such things are how power is wielded in the Arm. But this is not why Heroon is being shaped. It is…" The priest closed his eyes and breathed in, his chest rising. "Prophecy," he said and exhaled.

Something about the way he spoke the last word told Keen to be on guard. An inherent spirit saturated the priest's words and his reference to Helleuan. New Heroon's religious zeal was their most dangerous weapon.

"What the Arm lacks is piety… humility before the forces at work around us. New Heroon will achieve independence from the stranglehold on its freedom."

Freedom? More like a transfer of authority.

Keen did his best to hold his expression neutral.

A wry smile grew on the priest's face. "Your disbelief and lack of faith can't be hidden, Ambassador. But hope for you remains, perhaps." His old eyes gazed at the half-raised sleek architectural Fins in the distance.

"And your leader? When will I meet with her?" Keen knew better than to personalize this and so used diplomatic rhetoric.

"She summons those with whom she wishes to speak."

"And I was summoned, was I not?"

"You were brought here by request. Whether or not she summons you is another matter."

"Then why am I here?" Was his presence less about a reunion with his child and more about a political negotiation? Did this have nothing to do with family, with shared blood?

"That," the priest lowered his hood to take in the sun's rays, "is up to you." He raised a gaunt hand and gestured to a set of guards. They approached and cuffed Keen's hands behind him. "You need time to think," the priest said, gazing off the balcony. "And to clear your... mind."

He knows.

The priest walked away. "Take him to the Purging Pits," he said.

KEEN SAT with his back against the jeekoo stone, running his hand through the small beam of sunlight filtering through the slit on the adjacent wall. Five shadowy fingers danced on the dirt floor of the cell. Two days. He'd been thrown into the rock square and left with no contact other than brief stops by an attendant with food and water.

He guessed he was on the outer edge of the lowest side of the Temple. That would explain the exposed ground. How many sides were free-standing was uncertain, but at least one offered a sliver of exterior light.

It was cool, thankfully. But other than that, it was torture. Except for the window, the cell was alike to the one he'd been thrown in during the war. The one in that Hamut lockup only had second-hand illumination from a small opening in his cell door. It didn't matter. The past was creeping back. The longer he sat, idle and without purpose, the closer it got. The beast within fed off inertia like a parasite to its host.

Time ran backward. His mind played tricks on him. He kept anticipating the patter of footsteps approaching in the corridor, signaling the imminent arrival of another torture session under Pox's skillful hands. So far, he'd heard no sign of anyone coming or going. The only intrusion on his solitary silence was the nightly ritual under the Twin Moons. He guessed by the resonant voices echoing through the slit in his cell that they were at least a thousand strong, most likely gathered on the steps of the Temple's higher tiers. One voice called on high, above the others, leading the ceremony. The tone was young, determined, and earnest. It held a strange authority. Something told him it was Reynaria.

Was she testing him or trying to break him? If it was the latter, she was wasting her time. He might appear put together on the outside, but he was already broken. This 'new Keen' was nothing more than a hoax, a vain attempt to remake himself. What was he thinking? He wasn't even sure if he got any of the shards of his life glued back in place yet. If Reynaria stomped on them she'd just break them into smaller bits. The soberer he became, the more his world filled with awareness of suffering. And the more fraudulent he felt. Instead of pain, sobriety administered lucid jolts making him conscious of the errors of his ways.

It was all a mistake. On reflection, it was all Razor's fault. If it weren't for her meddling in his life, he'd be back in Garassit, drunk and his normal miserable self after an unsuccessful visit to Targite. The trip would've disappointed his parent but excuses could always be made. Business as usual… that is, if the Mote hadn't hijacked that pod.

No, that's not quite true.

Heroon was on his itinerary. If everything went as planned on Kol 2 he still would've ended up here. Back then he'd intended to drop a large sum of money into a shadow account for Reynaria, meet her for what he'd hoped would be no more than a few hours, and flee back to a burden-free life of self-destruction. The Motes didn't start this war or win out against the Council. Razor or no Razor, all paths led here.

His hand stopped playing in the light and reached for his chest. He pulled the medallion out from under his tunic and opened the pendant. Scarpa's words projected into the cell. He stared at them for a long while, focusing on one passage near the end.

You must make her understand the cause she fights for is beyond the pale of justice. It will lead to nothing but death at the expense of honor.

Why was Reynaria seduced by this spiritual cause? Had she bought into all of this mythological nonsense? Into a cultural exodus and 'purging?' An eco-shaping and so-called 'future'… a prophecy?

The memory of his journey from the balcony to the cell two days earlier returned. They'd escorted him through temple corridors. Narrow rays of light cast from slits in the stone walls illuminated the passageways. Infrared balls rested on sconces unlit, to be used only during the night. The technology was state of the art, no doubt supplied by the Targitians, but the environment was spartan. Why? If they intended to inhabit the Fins and live in abundance inside a sheltered oasis post-shaping, why this ominous structure and harsh asceticism?

He stared at Scarpa's signature floating in the air of the cell. Did she predict Reynaria's rise as a religious zealot, blinded to compassion by an ancient prophecy?

A slow, languid creaking like an old priest's bones broke the silence. The cantinool door at the end of the cellblock opened. Pattering feet, several of them, made their way down the corridor towards his cell. He closed the projection, hastily putting away the medallion, and rose. The door was solid wood, with no opening. He leaned his ear against the small seam by its hinges. The walkers reached his position and moved on. The lock on the cell next door clanged and the door groaned open. Someone entered, harshly thrown inside. The door slammed shut and was re-locked. Footsteps passed back down the hall. The cantinool door to the cell block creaked closed. A final turn of the lock echoed down the hallway. Silence returned.

Keen leaned his back on the door and studied the slit of sunlight on the adjacent wall. Who was it they had brought in? It wouldn't be Razor. Unless she'd resisted, which was possible knowing her track record. But if she had, they'd most likely kill her.

"Is that you, old tot?"

Keen smiled and sunk to the floor. "Jati."

"I take it this time you're not covered in a drink?"

Keen laughed. "Not this time."

"How's the head? Still reflecting light?"

Keen ran a hand over his crown. "More to Legion standards, although I haven't looked in a mirror for weeks." His fingers went to his mustache.

I can't imagine what this looks like by now…

"Bet you miss that orange jumper, though."

Keen laughed. "What happened at the jump port, Jati? Why are you in here?"

"Seems your Reynaria decided I needed some re-education. My little ruse to get you two off the ship didn't go over well."

"Re-education?"

"Yes, old tot. It's not going to be pleasant either, I fear. These New Heroon folks are taking themselves far too seriously."

"What's going to happen now?"

"To me, old tot? I'll probably sit in here a few days and then go before the priests. They'll make me pretend to be humbled and aware of my mistakes… might go so far as to make me pledge to their god and their cause. But I doubt that."

"Then what?"

"I may be working on a new city for a while."

"New Targite?"

"Can you believe it? It's so unreal."

"No." Keen couldn't comprehend it either. "And me, Jati?"

Long silence from the adjacent cell.

"Jati?"

"I don't know, old tot."

He knew Jati too well. They weren't telling him something. His gut told him it could only be one thing.

"Jati is she…?"

"Yes, old tot. She's here. I saw the ship."

Keen's soul became a void, a pit with no bottom.

"But there's no air traffic? And they made us walk for weeks over land."

"They've banned on all flights. Only with special approval from the leadership can someone move in-atmosphere."

"Why make us walk? Why not have 'her' fly us here?"

"These are strange times, old tot. My guess is you were being tested. Or, maybe being made to understand their cause. More refugees, 'pilgrims' they're calling them, are arriving each day."

"They put Razor in the labor camp to work on the Fins."

"Makes sense. I fear that might be the end for her."

Keen closed his eyes. The world was going to pieces all around him.

"Where's the Council's retaliation? Why aren't they pushing back to re-take the planet?"

"They've lost Heroon. It's over as far as the greater Arm is concerned. On the planet, it's not finished yet. It will be, in good time. Pockets of resistance are holding on against the new government. Independent militias, break-off counterinsurgency factions from New Heroon's Liberation Front who don't agree with this new 'ideology.' They're refusing to surrender and accept the Targitian-aligned theocracy. Last I heard Erront was still putting up a strong fight."

Erront. The botched rendezvous and hook up with Hirok.

"And by the way, our little stunt with the pod backfired in more ways than one. Everyone assumes you're dead."

"What?"

"Yes, your parent knows as well, I'm sure. You and Razor are dead to the Arm. It's only these New Heroon priests and *her* who know the truth."

That meant no accountability. They could do whatever they wanted to him, for as long as they wanted, and no one would ever know. A bead of sweat ran down the bridge of his nose. His heart pushed on his chest like a fist slamming on a door. His throat tightened. Air wasn't reaching his lungs.

"I have to get out of here, Jati."

"Relax, old tot. Take some breaths, slowly."

"I can't," Keen squeezed his eyes shut, pushing away the reality before him.

"Shhhh... Deep breaths. Look at the light."

Keen forced his eyes open, panting. He gazed up at the slit of sun.

"On the floor. Not the window," Jati instructed.

Keen lowered his gaze. The square patch of light had moved with the passing hour.

"Focus on it."

Keen stared at the yellow glow. "I have to get out of here."

"And go where? Into the rainforest? Old tot, you're better off here, even with Pox waiting in the wings. Reynaria is testing you. Don't let her or the priests into your weaknesses."

"The dreams, Jati, they're back worse than ever. It's Heroon. I can't take it. I'm barely sleeping."

"Me too."

Keen detected palpable suffering in Jati's words.

"It's pulling us, old tot. I knew one day we'd have to face it again. That we'd end up back here. It comes sooner than you always expect. But you and I are here. You're not alone. And we're Legion. If we die, we die. But we don't cower."

Was Jati crying? That last sentence… their voice was trembling.

"We don't cower, Keen. You hear me?"

Thank the Arm for Jati.

"Yes." Keen stood. He stared down the jeekoo stone wall across the cell.

His eyes caught something. He walked over and furtively, as if others watched him, leaned in and scrutinized the surface. It was faint. Was his mind playing tricks on him? He ran his hand over the streams of colored rock. No, it was real. In the faintest of relief, scratched into the nearly impenetrable stone was the Legion insignia. The one he'd carved in his cell twenty-five years ago.

Keen lurched back from the wall as if it held a contagion.

"Jati, where are we?"

No response.

"Jati?"

"I thought you knew, old tot."

The cantinool door creaked down the hall.

Footsteps approached and stopped in front of his cell. The door opened. Two guards with Talon Casters and the old priest stood before him.

"It's time, Ambassador."

The soldiers grabbed him and dragged him from the cell. The old priest led the way out of the cellblock. Everywhere, it came back. His gaze pierced the renovations and revisions to the architecture. The original structure revealed itself in all its naked horror.

"No!" He screamed, yanking his arms. He flailed about, resisting. He wouldn't go. He *couldn't* go. Not again.

"Legion, old tot. To the end," Jati yelled through the crack in his door.

"No!" Keen struggled against his captors.

The priest halted.

"Bind him."

A soldier took out Keen's knees with the staff of their Caster. They cuffed his hands behind his back. The old priest smiled. "You remember, don't you?"

Keen was panting, saliva drooling from his mouth. He lowered his head, staring at the floor to shut out the memories closing in on the walls around him.

"Show them how it's done, old tot," Jati yelled from their cell. "Aim true."

Jati's words drowned in the rising waters of Keen's soul. The beast within rose from the depths and broke the surface.

Keen's scream of horror echoed down the corridor. The jeekoo stones smiled. It had been too long since they'd heard that voice.

THE WORLD RETURNED FIRST. The memories waited. They always did. The body arrived, allowing the senses to communicate how much damage was done. A slight turn of the neck, the shift of a leg or arm sent small jolts of anguishing awareness through the psyche that brought you back from the realm of non-existence. It wasn't until a full sense of the body returned that the mind entered the room. But when it did, the real pain began.

Keen shifted, tucking his legs into his chest. Pain. The first jolt. Enough to bring him back. His body responded with a sharp inhalation. More pain. Like a call and response, he winced and grit his teeth. More pain. The mind was called to the stage. It told him to stop moving.

He lay in a fetal position. On dirt. The air was cool, the room silent.

Keen knew where he was without opening his eyes: back in the cell. *His* cell. The temple was a cage for his own new horror.

He recalled bits and pieces of the journey through the corridors, those too familiar corridors to the small room. *That* room. The torturer, standing in front of the chair. The *same* chair. This time it wasn't Pox, but a hooded figure with eyes of equal vengeful delight and anticipation. And watchers again, behind the screen. Keen sensed it even through the chaos of the unleashed beast. The guards strapped him in. The hooded figure went to the table and made a selection. It began.

"So, you're Keen Draden-ti?"

That wasn't the hooded figure's voice. And it wasn't in his head.

"I know you can hear me."

Keen opened a swollen eye, head still on the ground. A blurry, sideways image of a young woman sitting in a chair across the cell registered. *Reynaria*. He went to speak but his voice failed him. All he did was exhale.

"They tell me you fared well on the journey here. The priest noticed something of the old you coming back alive."

"Old me?" Keen whispered.

"You don't remember him, then?"

The jeekoo walls laughed.

Keen's mind struggled to push through the traumatic haze, seeking a connection. That face… he knew it.

"Reynaria, I…"

"Don't call me that. You have no right."

"I'm your parent," Keen whispered.

"You're no parent to me."

His vision cleared. It was as if Scarpa sat before him, back from the dead. The same young Scarpa he knew, with long violet hair and a face that drew you in like a magnet. Scarpa was typical Heroonese, her complexion a rich russet not unlike the planet's ever-wet clay soil. Reynaria's skin fell somewhere between her two parents as if in compromise, cast in deep tawny. But the eyes were green, his gift to her. They burned brighter and more fiercely than his own.

She wore bereese, the same traditional fabric Keen remembered on Scarpa. An indigenous fashion of pride for the Heroonese, it hung loose on her frame, with washed-out yellow and red tiered fabric woven from the staple animal source of textiles on the planet. Scarpa… and him, their child.

Keen's hand went to his chest, defying the pain to reach the medallion. It was gone.

"I've read it," Reynaria said.

He groaned.

"Lies. From a caretaker desperate to make amends before her death."

Keen shifted, trying to sit up. He couldn't do it.

She stared without remorse. There was something hard about her presence. No, not hard… arrogant. Yes, that had been his dubious gift, bestowed as an inherited shortcoming. Unlike his conceit, hers projected outward. It pushed against him like an invisible aura of hubris mixed with self-aggrandizement. No wonder she'd captivated millions into rebellion.

"No," Keen shook his head, accepting the pain. It was nothing compared to the anguish of his child's misperception. "Scarpa did nothing wrong. It was me… all me."

Reynaria rose from her seat. "Do not speak to me of fault and blame. I know it well. You carry that burden as both a lost parent to a child made to suffer by your absence and abandonment." She took a step towards him. "And as a parent to the Arm. You were once a Legion soldier? What did you do other than turn against liberty for personal pleasure and gain… for future comfort and security?" Her eyes burned into him. "You're a traitor to your family and your culture. You've bathed in excess and privilege while those of even your own blood were left naked and exposed to suffering."

"I didn't know… about you."

"This isn't about me. It never was. If you came here to make amends with what you assume is your offspring you've wasted your time… and your pain."

"Why are you doing this?" Keen grunted. "Why are you destroying your people and your planet?"

She knelt in front of him. Keen flinched. She only mocked him with a terrible pity.

"You still live in the mirror's reflection. Liberty and transcendence allure you. But the mirror distorts and bends them into submission." She rose and walked to the door of the cell and opened it. "We will free you of its chains," she said without turning. "Two paths exist to that end."

The door shut.

The jeekoo eyed him with malice.

"Jati," Keen called in a raspy voice. "Are you there?"

No answer came.

"Jati?"

The walls relished the newfound silence.

They're gone, the jeekoo stones whispered. *Quiet now, or you'll wake the beast.*

TWENTY-FIVE

I was put to work. Not on the Fins. That privilege was reserved for those who made the long pilgrimage to join in the new world that lay ahead. I was sent to the outskirts of the camp, to portage cargo and materials as it arrived on the river. I was a grunt, surrounded by those unfortunate enough to be rounded up by the new regime. They were heathens, whether because of their affluence and allegiance to the colonial occupation or because their intellectual beliefs and criticism of Heroon's new religion displeased whatever utopian illusion drove the new 'liberated' government.

To me, they were all the same. They were like me. The only difference was that this labor was their 'opportunity' to change. The new regime offered a chance to repent, to come to realize the ideology of 'right' through hard work and religious education. That fact was made explicit and reinforced through programming and word of mouth. Unlike Kol 2, those who resisted weren't ignored and left to fend for themselves.

I wouldn't tell them, but their situation was worse.

I had no intention of staying and sought every possible way to escape. The guards at the street corners and gateways looked second-rate. My guess was they'd been assigned duty in the camp for punitive reasons. I was confident I could disarm and overpower a pair of them. But unless I befriended someone with knowledge of Heroon's wilds and the planet's geography, I wouldn't get far. Freedom was out of reach.

I was captive in a confined space. But more than that, I was trapped in an illusory time machine. Kol 2 of old was Heroon in the present and I was going to witness its transition. My planet's past unfolded in real-time as I toiled against my will. And so, day in, day out, I woke in the sleeping room with hundreds of others. I walked the food line, ate my simple fare, and labored under Heroon's hot sun. I returned at dusk and consumed my meal with feigned attention to the speakers spewing ideological nonsense.

By the light of Ran, I made my way to the staging area with thousands of others to await the nightly ritual. After gazing at the Twin Moons and going through the motions of a religion for which I had no faith, I passed through the depressing doors of the sleeping room, found my bunk, and closed my eyes. I shut out the world around me and called up Kol 2's wide expanse of dunes, the feeling of a blue sea of sand and hot wind. Of home.

Why was I longing for a world soon to be under my feet, one that meant the death of a planet? When it arrived what would become of me? I was here without an exit like the others marked as Unacceptables. No chance of redemption for us. We were exceptional and shared a common fashion in our work suits that distinguished us among the thousands. No one with the potential to transition to the Fins spoke to us for fear of how it affected their chances. The double eyes of guilt and accusation were ever watchful. Piety and faith were now sharp-edged blades. I took note of how powerful a force was wielded when spiritual psychology tangled with commerce.

But it happened. How could it not? We became a community, refusing the title given to us by the forces of ignorance and alienation. We accepted one other, those of us without hope of release from our labor shared our stories. Around the table at mealtime, or as we waited for the Twins to rise, each shared their past and the wrongs that were done.

All but me; I never spoke. You didn't have to share to be among our subaltern community, and I remained silent. I was torn between the past, the present, and the future. I had experience tied to each as a Mote from Kol 2. I was the lone outsider from off-planet. To speak was an intrusion on the expected course of events, like a traveler going back in time, making one small adjustment that echoed through the ages with unimaginable resonance and disturbance. I was Kol 2's past and their future.

So, I sat and listened. And I learned about the oppressed world beyond Kol 2 from people who lived it, not from those who spoke of it from their comfortable and privileged balconies. These were words of experience. Authentic words that carried perseverance, determination, and endless faith in triumph over adversity. Words that wouldn't let those who oppressed deny them of joys, of the things that make us human.

These were not lies. Amidst an ideological ocean, deep in the tropical rainforest, a current ran under the planet's surface. Those at the shallowest levels were superficial and fleeting. They shifted, ebbed and flowed and dazzled with dramatic movements visible to the watching eye, and grew from temporary regimes vying for power and domination. But they were mere accents, embellishments of interpretation to the nature and spirit of Heroon and its people. This was the one that made the water move. It was where the truth lay hidden.

As I carried boxes of unknown items off the barges, it dawned on me. This was the army. *Our* army; the one I had come to Heroon seeking. Not guns and a militia for hire. I had come to find the others, the ones who, like me, were ready to give everything for the chance at a just world. They'd fight because it was *their* fight.

Heroon was where the battle would be brought to those responsible. A misleading deal from Keen had produced strange and unexpected fruit. This was the ripple in the pool. Not the finger that disturbed it, but the rising wave in response to the disturbance. How far would it travel? And where would it break?

From then on, my time in the camp shifted. It was no longer a cage where I relived the past as a witness. It was a present where a second chance at the future lay in waiting. And I seized it in my ravenous grip.

TWENTY-SIX

Keen blew a trail of dust out of the shallow recess in the jeekoo stone. He ran his finger along the arcing line. It was crude and faint but if you looked with care, two fingers clasping a single feather were legible on the surface of the speckled rock. It had taken him all day to scratch the Legion insignia into the cragged, irregular surface of the wall. His arm ached, but it was nothing compared to the beatings. And it had given him something to do today when he was reaching the end of his tether.

Jati's cell was empty. Pox's cronies took them yesterday morning. Keen was doing everything possible to convince himself they weren't dead. If it were so, then his only lifeline to the realm of sanity was cut.

Ten days in a jeekoo stone prison, transported from the ambush site via Rough Terrain Vehicles. He couldn't remember how long a journey it was, and neither could Jati. Both lapsed in and out of consciousness from their wounds and whatever they'd been given to sedate them on the ride.

What he wouldn't give for some of that stuff now. Forget the physical pain, that was bearable. But the haunting hours spent thinking about what he'd wrought, and imagining what was still to come, was far worse.

It had all gone so wrong. From the moment he convinced Reardon to cover for him that final night with Scarpa, to the surprise counter-ambush while on point, the last three weeks were a cataclysm for his soul. Now he and Jati existed as prisoners of war along with his sibling.

Reardon was here, somewhere. The Hamut thugs dragged Keen past his sibling's cell on the way to his own. Pox couldn't resist telling him. It was a mind game and it had worked. He wanted to scream but under sedation his vision rolled and pitched like a boat on heavy seas and his tongue wouldn't work.

Everything had gone wrong. Lexar and the others were all dead. Only he and Jati survived the counterstrike. How the Hamut forces knew their plan was a mystery. It didn't matter now. Everything spiraled back to him. His foolish heart had caused a chain of events leading to where he was now. He'd probably…

A noise outside broke the jeekoo stone silence.

Was that blaster fire?

Keen's ears perked up. Another round of muffled bursts resonated through the stone walls.

No doubt about it, that's blaster fire.

Voices erupted above and around him. More muffled bursts rang out, but closer. Chaotic and desperate cries punctuated the shooting.

The cantinool door creaked at the end of the cellblock. Rapid shots whizzed by on the other side of his door, the distinct discharges unmistakable to his Legion ears. A Spirex Displacer; Legion soldiers were inside the complex!

"Get these open now," a voice boomed down the corridor. "Living and dead, all come with us."

"Yes, General."

The skirmish continued outside. Keen rose gingerly from his knees in front of the incised insignia. His field of vision alighted with stars. He steadied himself with hand to stone and waited for it to pass. Equilibrium returned. He turned and leaned back against the wall across from the cell door. If the Hamut guards killed him before the Legion soldiers broke him out, he'd fall with his back against the Legion symbol.

The next sound would be the latch sliding and the key turning the lock. Would fate smile or laugh at him?

An explosion swung the door open.

"Got one here!" a Legion soldier yelled. Two blaster shots whizzed by their head. They pivoted into the room and returned fire. "Aji, cover!" A series of shots passed by the cell from the left as their Legion comrade kept the guards at bay.

They strode over to Keen and signed with their fingers 'té'. "Can you walk?"

She grabbed his shoulder sleeve and pulled him off the wall. Keen teetered and hobbled towards the door.

"I'll carry you," the soldier said.

"No," he yanked away. "I'm alright."

She raised the com on her arm to her mouth. "Smoke em' Aji. We're coming out."

The familiar plunk rang out as the canister shot down the hall. Chimera gas hissed from the can. The guards returning fire stopped. With the noxious fumes pouring into the air they had no choice but to retreat from the cantinool door. Chimera gas was so atmospherically heavy it stayed put without dispersing, creating a deadly opaque wall with a half-life of minutes.

"Let's go," she said. Keen limped out of the room, one hand on her shoulder for support. They made their way down the corridor.

Jati's cell was open. Keen leaned against the entrance and peered inside.

"We're on it. They moved them." She pulled him away down the hallway.

"My sibling… Captain Draden-ti."

"He's next. Come on."

Aji was at the corner, Spirex Displacer smoking from its barrels. Keen recognized the orange patch on their shoulder. The soldier who rescued him had it too. Legion Search and Rescue. Aji signed "ti" and reset the Spirex with a well-practiced sequence of hand actions to the weapon's receiver and magazine casing.

Blaster fire emerged through the Chimera smoke. A shot almost clipped Keen's backside. Aji pushed him around the corner. "I'll hold em', you two go," he said.

Keen hobbled down the corridor behind the soldier. She led him to a series of steps spiraling down to a lower level. Everything inside of him wanted to break out of this suffocating jeekoo stone dungeon. But if Reardon was downstairs, he'd go all the way to the core of Heroon's dark soul to save him.

The soldier's eyes focused on a holo architectural plan projecting off her forearm. Her nametag below the orange shoulder patch read, "Derelli-té."

"This way. Two lefts after the stairs," she said.

"Clear behind you," Aji said over the com to Derelli. "On my way."

"I'm going ahead to secure the passage," she told Keen. "Meet me at the bottom."

Keen used the wall to stabilize himself and stumbled his way down the spiral staircase. Blaster fire erupted below. Derelli was ripping off rounds and someone was returning shots. Aji flew past Keen on the staircase and almost knocked him over with the Spirex Displacer.

Derelli shouted somewhere below. Aji's Spirex unloaded and rapid fire echoed up the spiral stairs. Keen reached the bottom. The Displacer's firestorm held off a cluster of guards who had Derelli pinned against a door halfway down the cellblock. Keen kneeled behind his fellow Legion soldier.

"Your sibling's cell!" Aji yelled to Keen over the rattling of the Spirex, indicating the doorway where Derelli was trapped. "We have to get up and out. Birds leave in…"

Aji's head exploded. Blood and fractured pieces of skull and brain littered Keen face and body. The Legion soldier's hands still held the Displacer as their body slumped back. Keen contemplated the decapitated body in his lap, dumbly. After ten days of trauma and torture he was numb, so far gone that his mind shut down that portion of his brain affected by carnage. But it was still recording. And it would remember.

Keen's left arm shot up in the air as a blaster round hit his bicep. He reared back into the shelter of the staircase. Pain rang through his upper arm and shoulder, reminding him he had a beating heart that could stop, and somewhere deep within him, a soul that could still suffer. His arm didn't respond to his demands to move up and down, but at least the hit missed the veins and went through the muscle.

He edged up to the corner and peeked around. Someone was sending in rounds through a smashed window at the top of a high wall.

"I left you a present, Draden," a voice said through the opening. He knew its grisly tone.

Pox.

Keen reached for the Spirex with his good hand, expecting it to be blown off. Pox didn't take the shot.

Derelli knelt in the doorway taking fire from the guards down the hall. If he didn't get the Spirex working they'd get to her. And Reardon.

"Bounty hunter bugged out," a voice said from the com on Aji's lifeless arm. "She's pulling back until reinforcements arrive. Eight minutes out. General says we fly in five."

"I'm coming to you." The voice came from Aji's com. It was Derelli.

"No!" Keen yelled back over the fire from the guards. "Stay there!"

Derelli clipped off a few rounds and bolted towards Keen. He fumbled with the Spirex to cover her retreat. She opened her mouth to speak as she ran. "You can't…" Before he could fire her voice halted. Her back arched and blood spewed out of her chest onto Keen's face. She collapsed in front of him on Aji, a three-burst round in her back.

"Aji, Derelli, get out of there now! We're calling it. Time to fly."

"This is Draden," Keen said holding Aji's arm with the com. "Derelli and Aji are down. Two prisoners still here. Need backup. Second level."

Keen wasn't leaving. Not without Reardon.

Let's do this.

He forced his wounded limb against his stomach and rested the Spirex Displacer across it. He cocked the weapon to full and stepped into the corridor. His finger squeezed the trigger. Rounds littered the hallway like an explosion in a fireworks factory. He sent a canister of Chimera gas off the far wall. It bounced around the corner, spewing gas and buying him a few precious minutes.

He veered into the cell. Reardon lay face down in the dirt. Keen tossed the Spirex aside and rolled him over with his good arm. "Reardon?" He cradled his sibling between his legs on the floor of the cell. He tapped on his cheek. "Reardon?"

Shallow gasps came from Reardon's mouth. His shirt was soaked with blood. Keen tracked down the chest and located the source: a stab wound between his second and third rib. The knife had found his liver.

"Keen…"

"I'm here Reardon…. I'm so sorry." Keen rocked his sibling in his arms, clutching him. He couldn't lose him. Not this way. "It's all my fault."

"War, sibling," Reardon whispered and coughed up blood. "Not you… war."

"Hurry up!" Keen screamed at the ceiling. "Someone! Help me!"

Reardon raised a bloody hand and patted Keen's shoulder. "Don't carry this… no better reason…"

"I'm so sorry, Reardon." Tears ran down Keen's face.

"Love… too often the victim," Reardon whispered. His head slumped.

"No, please no…. Reardon?" He tapped his sibling's cheek. "Reardon!"

Keen's psychological anesthesia fled his system. He burst out in raging despair and collapsed on his side, embracing his sibling. His weeping echoed off the jeekoo walls.

Through the blurry vision of tears, an indistinct object on the floor caught his eye. He wept, using the shape to anchor him. In the rocking lullaby of woeful grief his eyes cleared, and it came into focus: a scrap of cantinool paper… on the ground where Reardon had lain face down. Did he write something knowing he was going to die?

Keen set Reardon down, stroking his cheek between sobs. Even in his emaciated and tortured state after weeks in prison, his sibling's expression was peaceful. He looked like a child again, possessed of nothing other than the optimism of youthful promise as if the blood that spilled from his body exorcised the malignant spirit of war.

Keen dragged himself on all fours. His fingers walked across the dirt to the frayed edge of the scrap of paper. He pulled it towards him and turned it over. Two words were scratched, sloppy and in haste, in blood.

"No Quarter."

He screamed and shot upright in the cot, sweating and gasping for breath. In the liminal light of Heroon's moons, his eyes took in the jeekoo stone chamber. The insignia, hidden in shadow on the wall, remained. Choral incantations on high floated through the cell window. The past and the present spun in a whirlpool of suffering. He was a prisoner of both the waking and sleeping world.

DAY AFTER DAY, line after line from the same text: *In Praise of the New Legion*. Each time the old priest finished, the large codex was closed and latched shut. He'd call for a guard and rise, place the hood over his head and exit the cell.

Why was the old priest reading to him of martial philosophy? The roots of the aphorisms the priest recited were familiar. They grew from the stems of the original Legion Manual. But that dormant philosophy sprouted anew through a backbone of divine guidance. Heroon's new dogma infused its battle cries, flavored its routes to mindful presence, and stoic combative tactics.

Keen listened discriminately, extracting familiar martial thought from the veneer of religious dogma. But with time and reflection in his long hours of isolation, he understood the two were stronger as one. Like twins. Or siblings bound together in war.

The daily readings became his nourishment. He grew eager, waiting with anticipation for the creak of the cantinool door and the old priest's feet shuffling down the corridor. Each day the priest read to him, another year of wasted time in his life was bled from his veins. The bucket of immoral excess and decadent distraction emptied into a drain of regret.

On the tenth day, Keen rose in earnest. He moved through the Talon forms. Like a shadow, he danced in and out of the diagonal beam of sunlight cast from the window in the cell. He didn't need the Caster, it stood gripped in the hands of his mind.

He started at the beginning. To do otherwise was both arrogant and disrespectful; one form only each day. He'd wasted ten days in idleness. It would take ten more to complete the full cycle: Winged Lantern I and II, Shadow major and Shadow minor, Stone Fall I and II, and the Grey Bone series, I-III.

On waking on the eleventh day, with the cycle completed, he added his dailies. Sweat poured from his skin. He ached by evening, but awoke stronger each morning, the blood of New Legion philosophy streamed fresh oxygen through his veins. The world of the cell grew vivid. Lucidity bred regret for lost time, its offspring urgency for existence in the *now*. The future was unimportant, and the past was fading.

By the third week, Keen spoke the verses aloud with the old priest. Huddled in the corner, he'd stare at the floor or speak it to the walls. The more he absorbed the words and their meaning, the less the jeekoo stone snarled back.

On week four, he was a beat ahead of the recitation. He proactively enunciated each word, pulling the reading forward. No exegesis. He had all the time he needed in the long hours alone in the cell for that hermeneutic exercise. After every session came the conversation with himself, a familiar routine. He'd argue, debate, and ponder the verses as he paced the room. Many times they were played out in imaginary scenarios and confrontations.

On occasion, he'd grown angry at the skeptic inside. It remained a constant nuisance. But the more the days and weeks passed, the more he learned to snub its advances. After a time, it fled. Not from aggression or intimidation, but from the undeniable assail of logic and reason. It no longer had a justification for its presence.

At first, he'd ignored the nightly ritual outside his window. But after a time, his ears picked up a similarity in the timing, the rhythm, and timbre of the chanting and singing and the verses gifted by the old priest. The words were spoken in another tongue, the ancient language of the Arm bouncing in call and answer.

He'd stand, head raised to the slit where the outside world stood out of reach. The Twin Moons cast silver light onto his face as he took in the beautiful song. He wanted out, to be above ground on high with Reynaria, to protect her and the future.

The jeekoo walls told him it could be so, but the skeptic was forbidden from leaving the cell.

Halfway through the text during the sixth week, the priest closed the codex and halted his reading. Keen finished it in his raspy voice, his recitation precise and filled with anticipation of praise. He wanted to speak it well. He believed what it spoke and wanted to know he was making progress. That day, the old priest stayed seated after Keen completed the recitation. He closed the codex but did not call for the guard.

"Where is the Legion soldier?" the old priest asked.

"In my heart. I'm the freedom of those without liberty." The words emerged from Keen's lips after more than two decades of hibernation. The priest lured them from the dark cave of moral sleep.

"Whom does he serve?"

"The new world."

"How will he achieve it?"

Keen stood up and declared the new code of honor with pride: "On The Wind, our wings will reach those in need of liberation. Our talons will strike down those who oppose us."

"And who is the enemy?" the old priest asked.

Keen hesitated.

"Speak!"

"Myself."

"You failed your sibling in the war," the old priest said. "Will you fail your child now?"

How he knew about Reardon, Keen didn't know. It mattered not. The old priest was right. He'd failed his sibling. He wouldn't do it again. Not to another of his blood. *She's all I have left. Without her, there's nothing.*

"I will not," Keen said.

The hanging, wrinkled skin around the priest's mouth curved into a smile. "Now speak it. Repent and clear your spirit of the ill that has caused the world to suffer."

Keen pulled up the past. Heroon. The war. Scarpa. He'd done such a wrong. Too much shame.

The old priest's eyes were kind, inviting him to open himself and bare his soul.

"It will give you freedom, too. It is the weight that keeps you from soaring." He raised a palm, motioning Keen to speak. "Come, free your burden."

He wanted to say it. He'd wanted to scream it for years.

"It's one final step forward."

Keen's face was a dam, but fissures and cracks around his eyes revealed tears.

"Yes, it is a heavy burden." The old priest nodded in earnest. "A great wrong that you've done."

His expression was stern. Keen wouldn't be allowed to back out.

"Come now, tot. The road to forgiveness is before you."

"I chose love over honor. I chose family over state," Keen glanced furtively at the priest, his mind cowering in anticipation of punishment.

"And this is wrong?"

Yes, he is wise. I must be the punisher.

Keen nodded. "Without honor, there can be no love." It was true. He realized it now. "Without state there is no family."

And why is that?"

"The state is the family. Honor is love."

The old priest nodded.

"No one knows that better than those of the Legion." The priest pulled up the sleeve of his robe. On his forearm, faded by aging and weathered skin, stood the Delta Sagittarii. Above it was the single star of Nunki, the mark of a general.

"Our cause is renewed, sibling."

It was he; the Patent Force General. The one who got him out before the Legion's hold on Heroon collapsed... out of *this* cell.

His mind flashed to the last-minute evacuation. From the gurney, he remembered watching two Search and Rescue soldiers place Reardon's body into one of the other birds.

"The planet's lost," a voice said as Keen was placed onto a transport flyer. "The place is a mess. Just be glad you're getting out in time. Everyone else is evacuated. The general insisted on this op… wouldn't leave you behind."

Keen rolled his head in the direction of the voice. A soldier spoke to Jati, who lay next to him. A person approached and peeked into the craft's hold. He wore a general's helmet and nodded at Keen and then moved on. It was the same person in front of him now.

That was the face.

"The Heroonese will have a mess on their hands for decades. It's going to get a lot worse before it gets better. Take care. Aim True." The soldier saluted and hurried off.

Jati's facial fortress rolled towards Keen, their cheeks battered ramparts, bruised, and broken. They managed a smile and reached out a hand.

Keen clasped it. He felt Jati's squeeze. Even amidst all the pain and torment, their inner strength persevered. Jati's core was solid and unbreakable. The keep within the fortress was secure.

Keen tried to speak. Words wouldn't come. Something inside had shattered. His mouth opened in silence.

"Don't carry the weight of the dead, old tot," Jati whispered. "You'll end up a living corpse."

Keen thought back on the last two decades. How prophetic Jati's words had become.

But no more.

I've ridden full circle. The destination leads back to the beginning.

Keen rose to his feet before the old priest. He crossed his fists over his heart, saluting.

"Time for you to prove yourself and redeem what was lost when your sibling and the others fell on the field of struggle," the general said.

Renewed purpose ran through Keen's veins. He'd shed the decadence, the excess, the arrogance. The booze. And now the guilt that came with misperception. He'd demonstrate his worthiness. He'd do whatever it takes to make up for what he'd sowed.

The beast shattered the gates of his soul with a mighty blow of its fist. It raged in a battle song within him. But it was his now. His heart gripped its reigns. It lurched against his restraint.

When I say.

Keen's eyes were alight with the fire of justice.

The cantinool door groaned. A corner of the general's mouth rose in restrained amusement and anticipation. Keen stood at attention as the cell door swung open, relishing the pride of discipline. The beast lurched, but the hand of the Legion soldier was at the helm and held it fast. It could only snarl and drool.

A guard saluted and accepted something from another soldier in the corridor. They approached the two men in the cell.

Keen's eyes went to the guard's hands. Legion Reds, folded across one arm and a pair of heavy standard issue fighting boots in the other, were held out to him.

"Well done," the general said to Keen. "These should fit you now."

Keen accepted the uniform and boots from the guard. Over the heart was a new insignia formed from the original Legion design: the Delta Sagittarii inside a triangle.

"Come," the general rose. "Someone wishes to see you."

TWENTY-SEVEN

I never liked cantinool. It was too cloying and piquant for my palette. As much as Heroon's natural fecundity seduced me, I preferred spice of a weathered and brittle kind. Roots and leaves that stood stoic for a desert age, hardened by the dry passing of time. The blood of Kol 2's scant plant life steeped a simple, uncomplicated brew to match the soul of its people.

The morning I walked the food line and the lanky old Heroonese cook, Lena-ta-té, handed me a cup of cantinool tea, I politely refused. She insisted I try it. I was raised to accept things offered to you a second time, so I took it. Lena smiled and winked, insisting I drink to the bottom. I remember nodding to be polite. Her expression made you feel like one of her children, as if everyone in the camp eating her food were family. Tall and wiry, with skin of deep russet from Nushaba's rays and a burst of wavy violet hair on top, it was as if she never saved any of the food for herself.

Yet, as I sat with the small band I'd recruited and we chattered back and forth about hope and the promise of life beyond our confines, I found myself sipping the tea. Between nods of agreement about how we'd expand the reach of our recruitment, I tipped the cup of warm Heroon blood to my lips. The liquid transfusion ushered the essence of the planet into my soul. The savory and rich complexity of Heroon filled my desert veins.

We'd made good progress in mustering enthusiasm for our revolt. The news that morning around the table was encouraging. Not only were those in our district supportive of the effort but the underground communication network brought auspicious word from the Fins. A wave of support rose even among those with a chance to live inside the new city, post-shaping. I couldn't believe my ears. What had sparked the willingness to put lives on the line to save the planet's ecosystem and deny foreign hegemonic rule? Regardless of the explanation, this was the best news we'd had in weeks. Maybe that's why the tea went down with ease.

Before I knew it, the last of it slid down my throat. I surprised myself by having drunk it all and glanced at Lena on the service line. Her warm smile communicated satisfaction. She gestured with an open palm, thin long arm outstretched, as if I should drink more. I smiled, indicating I'd finished. But she repeated the gesture, insistently. So, I picked up the cup and performed the act of taking another sip. When I put it to my lips and peered inside, my smile grew into a wide grin. I got my answer. Jati was in the camp.

TWENTY-EIGHT

Cantinool essence. Keen never tired of its aroma. It was the one thing about Heroon he'd always missed besides Scarpa. Over two decades traveling the Arm, he'd often wondered why no one captured its aromatics in liquor for distribution. Now he was glad no one had. To do so would have corrupted its intoxicating and distinct olfactory effect. Cantinool was meant for the nose, like the dampness of summer rain. It tingled and soothed the nostrils, cleansing the mind's tongue in preparation for a taste of knowledge unique to Heroon – visceral and experiential. Cantinool was an empirical elixir, site-specific, and effective only within its indigenous environs. Jeekoo stone, cantinool, the strangler plant, Karpel and Harmon… Heroon had a way of making its cosmology tangible.

His nostrils flared, savoring the tantalizing fragrance wafting in the air of the corridor. The guards leading him acted oblivious to its presence. To them, perhaps, it had become the standard by which they lived in the tropical wilderness.

Thin stone walls lined the passage on the highest level of the Temple. Ascending from the tiers below lifted an architectural burden from the body, akin to removing heavy layers of clothing down to a single shirt. Windows ran along the exterior wall, chiseled from jeekoo with more attention from delicate hands than those that had shaped the lower levels. With nothing above but the towering sculptural insignia, the walls shed the burden of supporting others and stood on their own. They rested atop the shoulders of the stone masses below them, like their leader.

The guards halted at a large cantinool door. One of them rapped their knuckles on the wood.

"Come," a voice inside responded.

Keen walked through and found the source of the cantinool essence. An open suite, lined by an arcade with a balcony beyond, was alive with sound and smell. Bulbous, rough-fired ceramic containers, low lying and wide-rimmed, lay scattered on the stone floor. Each vessel bubbled from some internal mechanism, the orange and red cantinool flowers on the water's surface rocking to and fro, encouraging the release of the petals' oils. Keen's eyes went from one wall to the other, peering into what appeared to be a sleeping room and a bath. In the central room, amidst the bubbling cantinool vessels, stood a large meeting table.

Bereese curtains, woven thin to be translucent, billowed along the arcade. The afternoon light of Nushaba hit the fabric, softening the intensity of its rays. Even late in the day, Heroon's sun worked with full concentration. It wasn't until it was forced over the horizon by the planet's orbit and spin, and the persistent urging of its three moons to move on, that its power diminished, and temperatures cooled.

Reynaria stood on the balcony, a silhouette behind the flowing drapery, her back to Keen. She turned and walked back into the suite.

"Thank you, you may wait outside," she told the guards.

The cantinool door creaked shut.

"Are you ready to speak to me plainly?" she asked gesturing at him to follow her across the room and out onto the balcony.

Keen's eyes took in everything. After so much time in the cell, his senses were like a dry sponge wrung free, waiting to be saturated. The overall design was spartan, matching the rest of the Temple. But the meeting table evidenced the chaos of a project in the throes of execution. Maps and various holo architectural plans on deactivated tablets lay scattered over its surface. One was still on. A portion of the Fins and an expanse of rolling dunes hovered over the wooden cantinool planks of the table as if someone had cut a three-dimensional slice of Kol 2 out and carried it hundreds of light-years to a world of complete opposition.

Keen followed Reynaria through a slit in the bereese fabric out to the balcony.

"Do you understand now what is happening on Heroon?" Reynaria asked the question without looking at him. Instead, she rested her forearms on the jeekoo stone ledge and gazed out over the rainforest.

Far off, to the North, low thunder rumbled from a line of purple and violet clouds, as if the planet answered for itself.

"I grasp the intention," he said. "But do I understand why? No, I don't."

"I'm certain you see the economics and politics of it?"

"Indeed."

Keen went to the ledge but hesitated to place his arms on the jeekoo stone. Instead, he folded them on his chest. They came to rest below his broad and now toned, pectoral muscles. He was sturdy again, even in the midst of turmoil and uncertainty. His body reunited with its old partner, his mind. Like Heroon, the philosophy of the soldier was made manifest in the physical portion of his being. That power saturated the psyche, buttressing the diplomatic intellect that stood lucid and unshackled from the burden of indulgent anesthesia.

"And you agree with the mission of liberation from monopolies?" she asked.

"By what means, exactly?"

The side of her mouth rose in a subtle smirk.

"So, it is the methods that are suspect?"

Keen let the statement hang in the humid, cantinool tinged air. It was open enough to be left as a rhetorical question or answered. He chose to let it linger, like the cantinool.

"I often thought about what you'd be like," she said, "despite my resentment for you and your choices."

"Is that your way of making a compliment?"

Still in profile, she scoffed but kept her gaze on the rainforest.

At least she shared something of his levity. He'd hate to think that her entire life to this point had been nothing but earnest struggle and determined vengeance.

"How do you find solace?" she asked.

"I used to do it with the bottle. It worked wonderfully for decades."

"Yes," Reynaria whispered. "For her too."

Scarpa? The words soaked his conscience with guilt and remorse. For how long? What had it done to her life and the life of their child?

"Was she free of it before the end?"

"No." Reynaria turned away.

What have I done?

As if in response, a low rumble of thunder echoed like a chorus confirming his responsibility.

"I seek solace." Reynaria spoke the words in a whisper. "I fight against an endless parade of counterfeit and suspect peddlers that offer it." Her voice grew louder, matching the emotion behind them. "But for now, I shelter myself in the embrace of myth." She turned around, her gaze meeting his own for the first time since he arrived. Her violet hair and emerald eyes were alive with the fire of her soul.

"So, you don't believe it?" He knew it. No way was his child blinded by religious zeal and false prophecy.

She returned to the balcony and leaned on its stone ledge.

"What does it mean to believe?" she asked. "To put your trust in those who interpret and corrupt faith? If that's the question, then no, I do not. But if you're asking if I believe in a larger force guiding my hand to do right, then yes. I do believe." She turned to view the Fins off in the distance. "Look around you. A vista of power and its potential grows each day, more effective than brutish force and violence."

Keen was torn between pride for her artful rhetoric and lament for the seductive appetite its application wrought on the ears of those on Heroon. Now he wasn't so sure of her insight and ability to discern reason from fallacy.

"And more humane than sanctions," she added, "that hurt without war, injuring those with no responsibility and no role in the conflict. My parent and I suffered for decades, victims of a political stranglehold. So many succumbed to death after long suffering."

Keen shook his head. This wasn't the same dogma the general

touted. Honor and fidelity did not equal the exploitation of power through prophecy. Such 'reasoning' was how tyranny was bred. "This is political persuasion, nothing more. It cloaks itself as a form of civil disobedience to outside oppression. What you're encouraging is a soothing and manipulative practice of ruinous force. A graceful lie, wielded by a theocracy with more lasting damage than war."

"It *is* war, she whispered, "of another kind."

Keen had expected open arms, or at least a congratulatory remark at the outset of their discourse. Not disillusionment. This couldn't stand. It was nothing more than self-inflicted aggrandizement, and that never ended well.

"This type of weapon is wielded with worse effect on the hand that strikes with it than the ear and heart that consumes it," he said. "I know, I'm a veteran and victim of both."

"Until another way presents itself," she said, "We must meet the enemy on the field of battle, whether that is as a war of belief or a war of the iron fist."

This was the ugly side of his arrogance. It was his fault it had blossomed into a dangerous and alluring weapon. If he'd been there while she was growing up, maybe he could've kept it in check.

His internal hypocritical meter rang an alarm.

Who am I kidding? I was worse than her.

He'd worn the badge of arrogance smugly for over two decades, slashing and hacking his way through a socio-political landscape with nothing more than self-interest and a desperate need to please a resentful parent as motivation.

That's the past.

He thought of Jati, pointing back towards the Arm from the cockpit of the pod over Tarkassi 9. What had they said about it breaking your soul apart? About having to take a hard look in the mirror?

Did that mean accepting a degree of compromise? Wasn't that what he'd admonished Razor for?

Razor.

"And my companion, the Mote?" *Use her name.* "Razor," he added in haste. Their battle on that first day after the pod crash on Kol 2 flashed in his mind. She'd put his arrogance into check, opening a semblance of mutual respect and etiquette between them. It was Razor, bold, confident, and self-righteous to a fault, who'd done it. That was how she and her people survived.

"I need her as leverage."

Keen detected hesitation in Reynaria's tone. "She doesn't deserve to be…"

"You've done the same for decades and called it 'diplomacy'."

"I have and I regret it now." Keen took a step towards her. "She's not of this world. This isn't her fight."

"The wheel is turning. Her people have a place in politics at work in the Arm. At least her sacrifice will help free those that the Council… that you and your parent…"

"*Your* grandparent."

"He's nothing to me! We're as far apart as two spans of the Arm."

You're more like him than you know.

Reynaria wiped sweat from her brow and tied her hair back. "I will free those that you and *your* parent used to purpose for the benefit of family *and* state. It'll be done through subservience to faith. That's what the Arm lacks. Piety is discipline, a humbling means of worship that casts a cloak over blatant and willful greed."

It's as if my parent is lecturing me, or seducing his rivals with words.

Had she found solace in religion? Or was it a cunning weapon she'd wielded to survive and vanquish the burden of her life circumstances? Her gift for rhetoric was even more alluring, more deadly than he'd first realized. That was her most dangerous poison. It had won her the high seat of New Heroon.

"The more time passes," she continued, "the more it can diminish to a perfunctory role. But this must be the course of action at the start."

She's convincing herself as much as me.

"And the general? He buys into this 'piety'?"

"Like all of us, his faith is guided by prior defeat. For him, it offers the backbone for a second chance at victory. A means to redeem lost face and the discipline to rebuild an army of true warriors of freedom."

Reynaria's finger traced across the ledge of jeekoo stone. How much she moved like Scarpa! The subtle gesture reappeared like a language unspoken for decades, a jumble of vocabulary forming into the syntax of a lost companion. Reynaria's body betrayed her. His child was conflicted.

"But I sense that in the general, somewhere underneath his priestly shell," she continued, "he too understands it is a weapon of convenience." Her eyes darted from the view and caught Keen's own, scrutinizing her in earnest.

A tinge of guilt spiked his conscience and he shifted his eyes away. But more than that, he was seduced by the traces of a lost intimate companion. What had been erotic love with Scarpa transformed into platonic marvel and admiration for a partner's spirit running through a child's veins.

"Are you not a soldier again, in your heart?" she asked.

Her words pulled him back from the bosom of rapture.

"Have you not benefited from its ability to reshape an undisciplined veteran?"

"I don't know that I would call physical abuse 'beneficial'."

"That was punishment of another kind. The general needed to be sure the soldier still lived…" Her words trailed off into a whisper. She turned to him. "This is not a choice I have the privilege of stepping away from. We're already at war."

There it was, even clearer and brighter; Scarpa's fire burned in Reynaria's eyes. "I choose it because it offers… life. It offers a new future for the Arm."

Keen gazed out at the Fins. Soon the exterior would be completed. He guessed only a few weeks more and preparations would begin for the eco-shaping.

Nushaba's daily journey across the sky neared its end. Parallel rays of golden light skimmed the top of the rainforest's canopy and bounced off the Fins' mirrored surfaces. The five sleek buildings glimmered like precious gems in pageantry on an undulating green and verdant blanket.

"This is a step towards freedom for the people of Heroon," she said. "And from there, to all the systems under monopoly tyranny. Along the way, all those who suffer from sanctions, distance from production sources, and restrictions on planetary manufacture will be liberated. None will be ignored."

He kept his gaze on the Fins.

"And we are not alone," she continued. "Others are ready to walk a new road. They wait only for a demonstration of our earnest success. In a short time, a tide across the Arm will turn. To the shock of all."

Jati's talk of Hamut dissension returned. Was this what she was referring to?

"The road to autonomy lies before us."

Us?

He could almost see Scarpa's arms resting on her shoulders, her head peering at him from behind his child. "Will you walk it with us?" Reynaria asked. "With the second-coming of your Legion brethren? With those fighting for their planet? With… your family?"

With his family? Was this acceptance of his apology? A path to redemption?

War. The bombs, the carnage. He wished it on no one. Yet, Razor's people suffered from the 'other' war. The weapon wielded against them was ideological. At least they lived. At least they had a means to resist and survive, even if the road was paved with stones of perdition.

What choice did he have? If this shifted the balance of power and loosened the monopolies, what resonance could it carry through the rest of the Arm? Could it reach a poor, parentless child on the most remote outpost of human civilization? Was it wrong to exploit belief as a form of discipline? Hadn't he been raised in the Legion by that very model?

A fang-mouthed ethical serpent snaking its way across the Arm. Would its farthest tail reach out as a lifeline to that little kid on Tarkassi 9? Or would it curl around and bite its tail, as humanity had done in the two previous ages of the Arm, only to start the cycle of greed and division once more.

But that was why the Legion was here. To ensure honorable practices are enforced, even while fighting for this new rising belief system. Where was the breaking point, the threshold of compromise touted to Razor as a requisite aspect of diplomacy and civilization? As it crossed the Arm, would the serpent's skin shed and forge a path to the Fourth Span?

Family and state, they each sat on both sides of the decision. Yet, the New Legion made no distinction between them. His parent stood on one end, Reynaria (and Scarpa's memory) on the other – a hegemonic monopoly and a liberation movement spreading religious ideology as a cause of right. How different was his family from the state?

What had Aradus done other than encourage him to exploit others through a veil of political competition and economic gain? As a parent, he'd never once asked him about anything personal after the war. He put him to work with a tone of regret and disappointment while mourning Reardon's death. Ignoring the reality of his living child's trauma, a lens of hubris exposed only embarrassment and shame to his professional reputation. That was no family.

Reynaria was troubled, young, and bitten by pride like her grandparent. But an undercurrent of morality was at work in her that could be brought forth with staggering potential. He'd help her peel away the layers of arrogance and misguided ideology and open the dam. The New Legion was here to be the compass needle. Together, they'd wash away the past.

His eyes took in the tropical expanse. Two Ribbed Garkins made their way west over the distant canopy, gliding towards the snaking river beyond the Fins. Their wings moved as one, synchronized in elegant harmony. The motion was visual poetry. It spoke of the ease and grace of life free of the struggle and gall of ruin.

"Yes, Reynaria. I'm with you." What else could he say or do?

"Thank you, parent." Reynaria reached out her hand to him. Keen grasped it. Her fingers squeezed his own. The exposed seams between the cracked shards of his life filled with light. His child's touch, this was the reward of turning back towards the Arm. Of accepting the challenge Jati laid out before him. It wasn't the way he expected or the way he wanted it to happen. But it was done. For Scarpa. Anything for her. The letter could go now. The request would be fulfilled. Reynaria had it in her possession and she should keep it.

The door to the suite creaked open. Footsteps shuffled across the floor. The general passed a large bowl of cantinool water and bent over to run a finger across the surface. Small ripples bobbed the flowers and splashed the edges of the ceramic lip. He approached them on the balcony.

Reynaria released her hand, the softened features on her face withdrawing into an earnest expression. Determination and an eagerness to move forward radiated from her eyes.

The general lowered his hood and smiled.

"And now, parent," Reynaria said, "the Wind will rise."

TWENTY-NINE

I'd developed a fondness for cantinool tea. Jati's messages kept arriving, scratched in crude handwriting on the bottom of the cups. My guess is Lena scrawled the words before handing me the tea. The idea that she was a link in the network's chain made so much sense. This was her kitchen, even if it was an official New Heroon facility. Lena had access to supplies and oversight of deliveries and the ordering of inventory. That made her a perfect point person for the clandestine resistance. Plus, I just plain liked her. Lena fed us and enjoyed watching everyone consume her fare. Coming to the line at dawn and dusk each day was a way of decontaminating my daily exposure to the harsh realities of labor and an indeterminate future. It washed away the political anxiety and ideological exhaustion, like the thermal baths in the rock hills of my home.

Ironically, the confines and restrictions of the camp weren't that different from those of my Mote lifestyle. We didn't have the privilege of abundant accessories or superfluous pleasures and so relished the unpretentious joys of modest communal hospitality. Whether eating or drinking around a fire, debating at a glow pool, or sitting in silent communion in the baths, we passed what we had to others with grace and humility.

More layers were shed from my armored skin. As my myopic shell peeled away, I understood that all of us, allies and enemies alike, are cut from the same cloth. It was the world and our choices of how to navigate through it that made us complicated.

The news Lena scrawled into my cups renewed my moral spirit. For the first time since I'd arrived at the camp, the prospect of revolt and liberation for Heroon's people shifted from an idealized dream to a tangible and very real possible future. It instilled hope and perseverance into the malnourished will of a Mote a thousand light-years from rolling sands, cragged rock bluffs, and Tidal Winds.

Jati's one-way communication evolved to a two-way channel. In the morning, Lena would hand me tea. At the evening meal, I'd whisper my missive to her on the food line. By the next day, another response was forthcoming. No trail of evidence remained. The cups, made of thinned cantinool bark and disposable, were torn up after use and tossed into a collective bin, dumped in the camp's latrines. I never mentioned it to Jati, but if they'd known where they ended up a snarky joke would've issued from their mouth. Our surreptitious exchange went like this:

JATI: *Miss me? Working on the city. Heavy lifting. Not good on my back.*

Me: *You're here too? How long? Heard from Keen?*

Jati: *Just arrived, don't intend to stay. Keen in Temple cell. Not good. What's population like?*

Me: *Desperate. But inspired. Have group who want to organize/revolt.*

Jati: *Music to my ears. Can you muster them to action?*

Me: *Yes, but no means to resist.*

Jati: *Heading for Erront soon. Have the arms. Need the army.*

Me: *You'll have it. When leaving for Erront? How?*

Jati: *Tomorrow. Midnight. Want to take a river ride? Still don't trust me?*

Me: *Yes to ride. No choice (trust). Hearing of your speaking ability around camp. Hope spreading.*

Jati: *Parents said I should've been a lawyer. Try the soup at breakfast (guess I have a side after all).*

. . .

THE FOLLOWING morning Lena served soup. At the bottom of my bowl was a crude map of where to meet Jati. I'd be ushered through my district unseen by the network. They'd get me to the camp boundary near the river. A checkpoint gate for deliveries remained open through the night as cargo arrived. I wasn't told how but I was assured they'd get me through and out.

Hirok's rebels were heading upriver with a huge cache of arms. Jati and I would rendezvous with them down from the Fins. Hirok's counterinsurgents planned to hit the Fins hard from the South, as far from the Temple as possible. From what I'd gathered through my brief exchanges with Jati via the cups, an explosion would draw off a large portion of the central New Heroon troops from the Temple. Once the melee ensued, the city and cargo camp districts would rise and riot, with the hope of overrunning the security forces to open channels for Hirok's rebels arriving on the river.

Jati and I would supervise the arming of the masses in our respective districts. While Hirok's counterinsurgency did their best to destroy the Fins and pull the New Heroon troops away from the Temple, the people's army (led by myself and Jati) would take the Temple by storm.

If successful, we'd take back New Heroon and rescue Keen. That was, assuming he was still in the cell. A part of me hoped he wouldn't be. To think of the dreadful condition he'd be in after all this time imprisoned in the Temple, by his child, made for a haunting image. Whether he was in prison, or elsewhere, we'd find him, both because it was the right thing to do and because we needed him as our diplomatic liaison. It'd be complicated with Reynaria (if she lived through the siege), but Jati assured me he'd oversee a judicious process rather than mob violence.

After all, if it wasn't for Reynaria's revolutionary fervor (despite her egregious and unforgivable actions against her people) the Garassians would still run the planet. A misled revolution was better than no revolution at all, or so I decided at the time. I reasoned that it opened the door for a result with the potential to become *bona fide* political independence, that Reynaria's misguided politic nevertheless played a role in the dialectic of revolution on Heroon.

Perhaps I was changing more than I realized. That compass needle that never strayed from its laser line, where was it now? Had I become morally malleable?

On that last day in the camp, I was excited, filled with anticipation for what lay ahead. Both the freedom of escape and the culmination of my desire to lead that I'd spoken of when Crest died had arrived. It dressed differently than I'd expected but if all went as planned, we'd have the Temple and the planet within twenty-four hours. Jati and I decided to default to Plan C again: 'improvise something.' You'd think we would have learned our lesson the first time.

THIRTY

Keen gazed over the rainforest as Nushaba broke the horizon, his arms resting on the jeekoo stone balcony. The beast snarled, but he ignored it. The fear it instilled was held at bay by renewed discipline and the promise of a revolutionary future with his child. He'd run through his dailies and the Grey Bones Series and finished a light breakfast before the planet's first light.

The Temple's second tier commanded an expansive view of the landscape and the Fins, but with more intimacy than the highest tier. Unlike the omniscient perspective from Reynaria's private quarters, this level maintained a visceral connection with the flora and fauna of Heroon.

The sun's first rays tinged the mists over the rainforest's canopy in deep orange. A Wailer, one of the more nimble tree-dwelling primates, called forth, announcing the dawn. Nushaba's early light brought back the memory of the Turbine Field raid on Kol 2. How changed he was now. No longer fumbling along at the heels of a Mote renegade, not even respected enough to be given a weapon. Out of shape, lost in the arrogance of his post, and consumed by addiction, that person was now a shameful ghost. How could he have been so different only a few months ago?

At the horizon beyond the Fins, a line of purple storm clouds lurked. They'd been waiting since he arrived, interjecting distant rumbles of thunder as if to gnaw at his mind amidst the unfolding changes to his life. They were shifting position each day, riding the horizon's rim from West to East. Keen guessed that tomorrow would dawn without Nushaba's usual bold and dramatic entrance.

Another Wailer, more distant, cried out. The long, descending howl carried the mournful tone that gave the species its name. A knock on the door of his quarters broke into the tropical aria.

Keen crossed the suite and opened the cantinool door. A guard saluted.

"The general needs you."

"Give me a moment." Keen went back out to the balcony. Something about the weather unsettled him. It wasn't just the coming storm; a darker energy lurked. Waiting.

He inhaled, his chest bulging as it filled with Heroon's dubious air.

Scarpa. I never expected all of this.

He let out a long breath and crossed the suite. In the hallway, he nodded to the guard to take him to the general. They made their way down the corridor and the flight of steps to the ground level.

At the bottom of the Temple, Keen stepped out into the early morning light. He greeted the general.

"You cleaned up," the old priest said.

"Yes, General." Keen ran a hand over his neatly-trimmed beard. It fit close on his jawline, brown throughout except for two grey sections straddling his chin. His hair was now a few inches in length and combed back with a subtle wave. To a Legion cadet, he'd look like a senior officer who'd retired from the field; to the civilian population, he'd be described as distinguished.

"How're you feeling today?"

A low rumble of thunder reached their ears.

"Fine, General. Rain is close," Keen said. A clear sky persisted overhead but thunderheads approached Nushaba's rising track near the horizon. Sun and shade swapped intermittently like Harmon and Karpel.

"Indeed. No more than a day or two away," the general said. "Something's happened. You're required."

Keen wanted to ask what it was but knew better.

"Come, let's walk to the river. It will loosen our minds and warm our bodies."

The mists clinging to the rainforest canopy were losing their battle to maintain the cool night's trace. Nushaba bore into them, the moisture evaporating and making the air heavy and humid.

"I remember hearing of your ability with a Caster," the general said, breaking the silence as they strolled the winding path through the rainforest. "Your sibling was also adept, was he not?"

The mention of Reardon made Keen's constitution tremble.

"He was." Keen watched a flock of small, colorful birds migrate from the branches of one cantinool to another. Rays of light peeked through the forest, dappling the verdant floor with yellow radiance. "We both had an affinity for the Grey Bone Series. Although he always bested me when cornered."

"Older siblings will do that," the general said, keeping his gaze ahead on the trail through the greenery. The end of the path where the open landing field and river station stood approached. A slice of the river, visible through the opening at the path's end, gleamed with morning light.

Keen's diplomatic intuition rose within him. He sensed a didactic edge to the general's response. Something more was forthcoming.

"So, he was more skillful, then?"

There it was. This was either a test or a lesson.

"Indeed, General. But he had two years on me and so was longer trained."

"I see." The old one's tone carried an edge of dissatisfaction.

Keen fought to find his words to continue. His mind raced through a shadowy labyrinth of implicit references hiding beneath the general's words, seeking the clarity of the exit back to the light. He couldn't find the way out of the maze.

The general gave him a quick, furtive glance as they walked in awkward silence.

Before Keen could regroup the path ended and they emerged from the rainforest.

"Was it experience or intimidation?" The general asked.

Before Keen could respond, his attention shifted to the ship resting on the landing field: Pox's Twin Needle. The ramp between the pincers was open and New Heroon soldiers scurried in and out of the spacecraft.

"Good morning, parent."

Keen turned toward the voice. Reynaria stood with an attendant and four New Legion bodyguards. Her violet hair wafted in the subtle breeze. Without the trees and greenery of the tropical forest, Heroon's thermal current, usually a clandestine presence, revealed itself. The river flowed by behind her at a short distance. Keen's eyes went further to the right, tracing the river's edge. At least a hundred New Legion troops stood in strict formation along the banks.

"What's this?" Keen asked. The general's remark about intimidation swirled in his mind.

"We've discovered a traitor in our midst," she said.

Traitor?

Reynaria nodded to the general. He gestured to a line of five soldiers by the ship. They moved aside, revealing a kneeling figure with arms bound to ankles.

Pox.

"A copy of the full tech data on Targitian Turbines, as well as the pattern layouts for their installation, was found copied to her ship's drive," he said. "It was linked to a com-line with codes to a destination on Ceron."

"Ceron?" Keen asked. "But she's working for Targite." What was Pox doing with a com-link to Ceron?

"Officially, she's in the employ of Targite, yes. And she desperately wants you as her bounty."

Keen looked at Pox. That was personal as much as it was professional. She caught his eye and bared her teeth, orange eyes glowing with rage amidst her restraints.

Sake of the Arm she's fierce. A monster even when captive and restrained.

He held her stare. Was it newfound bravery, or was it that she was shackled?

"She can't get to you because I haven't let her," Reynaria said.

Keen pulled his eyes from his nemesis.

The general took a step forward. "She's a traitor, working both sides."

A double agent...

"So, she was going to sell the plans to the Garassians?"

"We tracked the code to a shadow account. Someone in the Garassian government was hoping to get those layouts. And was willing to pay an exorbitant price," Reynaria said. "She was attempting to leave without permission. I grounded her ship after you and the Mote were delivered."

Keen smiled; of course, she did. It was a crafty diplomatic move. Pox couldn't transmit anything unless she got out of the orbit grid beyond the jump port. Until any craft was outside the FTL jamming zone all transmission signals were impotent. While grounded, without permission to kill him, she couldn't take Keen back to Targite in a body bag. Jati was right. Being in that cell had been the safest place on Heroon.

"She almost made it under cover of darkness. Her AI droids gave her away. Their com-links auto-connected to the airfield's network when they were heading to her ship."

Human technology creates artificial intelligence. And it comes back to bite us. My old friend, Mr. Irony... with impeccable timing, as always. I get the feeling this is going to be one of those days...

At least he wouldn't have to worry about Pox. Was this the end? No more tracking and tormenting him in real-time? No more having to look over his shoulder?

Will they put her in a cell to rot or will they kill her outright? If the latter, I wonder how they'll do it.

"This is your final test. A demonstration of both your commitment and your skill," Reynaria said. She gestured back towards the waiting regiments of New Legion soldiers. "The general believes in you. As do I. But you need to prove yourself to our army. They will follow you, a

Legion soldier and veteran of the Patent War. But they cannot be expected to trust you and risk their lives on words alone."

So, this was what the old one was getting at on their walk.

"I'm eager to observe you with a Caster in your hands," the general said. "It'll be done the traditional way, as in days of old. One to one. Weapon of choice. Hand to hand. No projectiles."

"Are you ready to make the final leap?" Reynaria's tone was that of a revolutionary leader, not a child.

The beast bounced off the walls of its internal cage. In a frantic panic, it rattled the bars and slammed itself from wall to wall, bloodying itself in an attempt to burst free. Keen did his best to hold it back, but the noise and impacts resounded through his body. His heart thumped in his chest.

He descended the psychic rope into the darkness and stared the beast down. Its eyes locked on his own, pushing back.

Keen stood his ground. The creature within lashed out. He didn't flinch. A forge ignited. He took the hot iron. His will blazed and he drove the fiend into the corner of the cage with his stare.

I am your master now. You will serve me.

The creature rose. It approached the front of the cage with furtive steps. He stroked its snout.

I will need you before the end.

Keen's gaze went from the general to Reynaria.

"I'm ready."

It's time. Long past time.

"If you succeed, our Apex is complete. The three points of the Triangle..." Reynaria gestured at the general. "Faith." Her hand went to her chest. "Politics." She pointed at Keen. "And the Iron Fist."

So, this was how they'd get rid of Pox. Or him. Either way, New Heroon won. If Pox was gone, they moved forward as a tripartite. If he failed, they'd deliver him to Targite and use his corpse as leverage for their independence.

Yes, it was going to be one of those days.

A LONG ARROW in silver ran along the length of the Talon Caster's shaft. Elegant prongs topped the barbed stems of its three talons, a signature of pre-Patent War design.

"This was mine," the general said, resting it across both palms. "It's seen its fair share of death." He offered it to Keen. "Made on Sarkuna by the legendary smithies before the planet was destroyed at the end of the Gamma Quadrant Conflict. A lost relic from a different age." Keen accepted the weapon and swirled it a few times. It was well balanced and light yet contained enough mass in the core for effective damage in hand-to-hand combat.

"Yours are the fourth pair of hands to wield this weapon," the general added, wiping sweat from his bald crown with a cloth. "Are you sure you don't want armor plates?" The old priest looked over to Pox. "She's wearing light armor. I can get you a set from those standing by."

"No." Keen stopped swirling the Caster. He took off his red Legion top and handed it to the general. He'd fight bare-chested, in pants and boots.

"Old school." The general nodded. "The troops will admire that."

"It's not for them." He ran a hand over the tattoo on his forearm. "This is how I train. So, it's how I fight."

The general looked back at Pox. "She's Hamut by blood only," he said. "A drifter, with no side."

"You know her background?"

"Only the basics, but she was raised on Yaqit in a refugee camp. Those people felt the sharpest edge of the blade before the Patent War." The general glanced over at Pox, who was kneeling in the open staging area by the river. Still bound, two guards stood to either side of her hunched form. "Certainly explains the rage and vengeance streak."

Why was the general telling him this now? If he was trying to evoke pity, it was a hard sell.

"Balance." The general's tone was earnest and drew Keen's gaze. "An even keel in the sea of thought. Don't let your desire for revenge stir thoughts to a raging storm. Find the place of No Mind."

The general was helping him. The old priest recognized the anger and bloodlust that festered underneath the fear of his nemesis. He'd been present at the end and knew the truth. The commander's remarks about Pox's past humanized her, opening a space for empathy to counter the imbalance in his subconscious.

Keen exhaled in earnest, blowing out everything about her other than her physical presence.

She's nobody. A body moving in space. Respond accordingly.

He'd been running for over two decades. From trauma. Guilt. Regret. Pushed forward by denial and fear. So be it. It all led up to this moment. When Pox first returned to his life on Kol 2, he was terrified, wishing only that she'd shown up a year or more before Scarpa sent the letter. It would have been quick. He would have given her the opening to hasten it. He didn't give a damn then. But now? He wasn't only driven to live; he was determined to expel this life-parasite no matter the cost.

"Where's your shit?" the general asked.

Keen smirked. "Left it back there." He pointed a thumb over his shoulder.

The general nodded and led Keen forward to his opponent.

Keen took in his immediate surroundings, as much to locate Reynaria as to get the lay of the land. His child was to his left with her bodyguards. She stood a few feet in front of the lines of New Legion troops. Straight ahead, behind Pox, was the river, about a hundred feet back. Beyond a stretch of open flat ground behind the bounty hunter, a short edge of grasses lined the shore. A narrow dock extended into the water further upstream. A ways back behind him was the Twin Needle ship.

The general signaled him to stop twenty paces from Pox. Keen rested the deactivated Caster's blade side on the dirt, the shaft gripped in his right hand, leaning on his shoulder. The three-pronged talon, empty of projectiles but still a sharp and deadly weapon, stood a head above his own.

Thunder rumbled in the distance, louder than the day before. Nushaba blazed down with late morning intensity, unblocked by the clouds looming near the horizon.

"You both know the rules and have agreed, yes?"

Keen nodded.

Pox spat at the general's feet.

"To the death. If the victor lives, they'll be treated by the medics to the best of our ability. If victorious, the accused will be released, per the rules of old." The general turned to Pox. "Without stolen property and with full disclosure of your activities given to all involved parties, of course."

Keen's mind wandered at the ramification of Pox being set free and the news of her double-dealing reaching the Targitians and his parent. Then it dawned on him: if that happened, he'd be dead so it wouldn't be an issue, at least for him.

Focus.

"A Talon Caster has been chosen by this side." The general motioned at Keen. The old priest turned to Pox. "Do you request your Spineblade?"

She raised her head and shot her orange eyes at Keen. "Caster."

Keen's psyche hiccupped. *Caster?* She'd fight him with a Legion weapon?

"Bring forth a Caster!" The general's bark to the line of troops brought forward a soldier with a Talon Caster. She handed it to one of the guards.

"Should you turn your attention from your opponent towards anyone else, you will be riddled with kill shots by the line," the general gestured at the troops. "Understood?"

"Oh yes, *General*," Pox said. "Understood. I'd much rather walk to my ship and depart this swamp hole after he's dead." The bounty hunter glared at Keen. "With his heart in my hands."

The memory of her abuses cut through his psychic armor. His chest pounded. Doubt rose to challenge newfound confidence.

"Understood?" The general asked Keen.

Keen's mind swirled with distraction. Like a rising sand devil's winds, it pushed his courage to the edges of his internal sight.

"Understood?" The general repeated.

The old one's voice broke the spell. He nodded. Pox's resting state was anger and violent aggression. She had no beast chained inside. She *was* the beast.

This was a mistake.

The general nodded to the guards. One of them deactivated Pox's binds. She curled forward into a ball, releasing the tension from being bound. Everyone waited. This was the Old Way. The duel was carried out with both sides ready to engage, not before.

A low, guttural hum resonated from inside her tucked body. She unfurled and the voice rose to a raging pitch, the veins of her throat bulging. She stared down Keen and screamed a battle cry, her face red with fury. The bounty hunter jumped up to her feet and held out her hand for the Caster. The guard gave it to her and stepped aside. Pox swirled it in front and over her head with ease.

She knows how to use this weapon.

"Await the horn." The general announced and walked by Keen. "You never answered my question about your sibling," he whispered.

And so they stood twenty paces apart, the killer and the avenger. But who was who?

A memory flashed into his mind of gazing out the pod above Kol 2 before the abduction. He'd wanted this then and fate delivered.

Embrace it. You've no other choice.

The fragrance of cantinool wafted into Keen's nostrils. He bent down and grabbed a handful of dirt, running it between his hands while cradling the Caster at his elbow. He put a finger to his tongue, tasting the rich soil of the planet.

So it was on Heroon that his life's course was to be decided. Not during the Patent War, but over twenty years later. Pox was at the center of the trial. So be it.

Keen's eyes stared down his opponent. He initiated the Elemental Breath Cycle. Three-second inhalations and six-second exhalations, the somatic action sending calming signals to his firing neurons. He closed his eyes and entered the visual world of his mind, seeking the Place of No Place. A breeze stirred the still water of a lake with no shore. Just a trace, a buffing of watered glass, evidence of the potent energy circulating inside him.

The horn blared. He opened his eyes and set his stance. He'd fight with Grey Bone; fast and fleeting strikes with spirals of the staff and quick diagonal footwork. He raised the Caster into position, trident forward, and ignited the cutting blade at the shaft's bottom.

"No quarter, lesser sibling," Pox said and sparked the blade on her caster. Her taunting words were loud enough for all to hear. "Your parent will be disappointed when he hears I had to kill you."

Ignore her words.

Pox charged. Keen danced the Grey Bone, shifting and sliding. She moved left, and the cutting blade seared his ankle. Talons swirled at his face. He ducked and lunged the Caster at her knees, nicking the armor of her left leg. Pox spun and recovered, standing in Shadow Stance. Keen's expression of surprise at her fluency with the Caster forms couldn't be hidden from those in the crowd.

"Like a shadow, Draden, I've haunted your steps for over two decades."

Keen's eyes were on the center of her sternum, his peripheral vision in heightened attention towards her feet. If she moved from the body center first, it meant she'd fight in Shadow minor. If her feet initiated the attack, then it was Shadow major. He had to decide whether to wait and respond or strike first and make her shift to the respective Shadow form.

Patience. She'll make a mistake.

Keen felt the trickle of warm blood inside his boot where she'd grazed his lower leg.

They edged closer. Sweaty skin tingled as the energy between them compressed. The slow, sliding, and scraping of their feet resounded in his ears. Tension tried his patience. Keen pounced, giving in, directing a series of strikes with the talons at her legs. He was working her low to open her neck and head. Pox shifted back, her defense sequence one of the most basic. Keen wanted to take advantage of its rudimentary limitations but knew it must be a feint to bait him in.

Don't.

He let her go without pursuit.

The bounty hunter lashed out with the cutting blade in the Infinity Spiral. She was shifting forms, now in Winged Lantern II.

Keen's reflexes took charge. He drove the talons of his Caster through the nexus and twirled the staff. Pox's weapon was ripped from her hands. It spun wildly, missing Keen who had to duck. A boot cracked into his shoulder, sending him back into the dirt. He rolled, shutting the cutting blade instinctually for safety. Keen recovered only to find the Caster back in her hands. She drove him back with a series of lunges from Grey Bone II. She was all over the place with the forms! He had no choice but to retreat to gain time and regroup.

Rabble rose from the ranks along the sideline, concerned with the turn of events.

Keen's sixth sense told him he was close to the river's edge. The distance between them was now right for him to counter. The cutting blade ignited with red light and he struck, driving Pox left with a series of quick swirling attacks. The soldiers raised their voices in cheers. He had her, the end sequence of Grey Bone II would finish her with a low-to-high combination with the blade and talon. His stroke swept up, but his torso didn't twist with the full extension needed for the technique. It fell shy and his strike cut through Pox's thigh plate but was too shallow to penetrate her flesh. His talon strike to the face was wide by as much as a fist's distance.

Damn!

Pox swirled low. Keen managed to jump over her weapon. He landed and stumbled, leaving him no choice but to retreat further.

You're too tense. Relax your movements or you're doomed!

Again, he tried a favorite strike sequence from Grey Bone II, and again he came up short. His flexibility wasn't there.

Pox drove him back, smiling.

"You're too old for your weapon, Draden!" Pox returned to Winged Lantern I and the cutting blade crossed Keen's side, slicing into his flesh.

His body winced against his orders, interrupting his flow of motion. Pox came around and swatted him in the face with the side of a talon, sending him tumbling.

Gasps rose from the soldiers around Reynaria and the general. The crowd followed, breaking ranks and moving towards the dueling fighters.

Keen knelt, gasping for breath, eyes watering from the impact. Blood poured from his nostrils.

"Your blood is worth more to me than all the money in the Arm, Draden."

His mind rattled. He'd lost his hold. The beast bouncing off the walls of the cage usurped the still water of the lake of No-Mind. It burst forth.

Pox charged. Keen retreated in desperation, swinging the Talon Caster wildly about in hasty defense.

I need time!

He was no longer fighting. All his movements were buying time against the inevitable. Each swing and strike from Pox drove him further back on his heels. The river's edge approached. Only the dock remained a short way off to his left. Further retreat was impossible.

Pox's battle cry screamed out. She had him where she wanted him and was relishing the torture of victory. It was only a matter of time before he tired, and she penetrated his remaining defense.

Grey Bone, his form, had failed him. He fought in desperation; the beast unleashed.

I'm too old!

Pox's cutting blade clipped his ribs on the other side, the price of thought tearing his flesh and spilling blood.

Keen glanced left. Could he make it to the dock? It was either that or fall here and now.

You can't get past her. Unless...

One leg lunged towards his foe. He struck the pronged head of the Caster into the ground. His hands gripped the weapon with as much strength as he could muster and he vaulted. His body surged up and over his enemy. Pox managed to strike his Caster as he came down on the other side but not hard enough to knock it from his hands.

Keen ran onto the dock. The wooden planks teetered left and right with each bold stride, disturbing the river's smooth current with intrusive splashes. His ears picked up the shouts of disappointment from the soldiers. He didn't worry about them. This was tactics.

"*Too old for Grey Bone, old tot.*"

Jati's words on the training floor of the *Carmora* filled the ears of his mind.

He turned and set his feet. They were in Grey Bone, which was also the same opening position as Stone Fall II.

I don't think she knows it.

"So, you choose to die in Grey Bone?" Pox swirled the Talon Caster. "Say hello to your sibling for me."

She went for a killing blow to the chest with the talon. Keen's body instinctually responded with the Stone Fall defense. He struck into her attack. It required a full understanding of timing and years of working the lighter, more open forms to develop the reductive mechanics for proper execution. So he too had become the wise warrior.

Pox's weapon flew from her hands as Keen's Caster went into her defense. The talons drove into her breastplate, stopping her attack and throwing her back. If she hadn't had the armor on, she'd be dead with a three-pronged talon in her chest. The crowd around the shoreline erupted in hushed gasps.

Keen stood, blood dripping from his ribs and sweat beading down his chest through streaks of Heroon dirt. He looked at the crowd on the shoreline. Reynaria's eyes were wide with awe. The general's stoic face spoke volumes.

A gust of wind rushed through the trees and along the river, interrupting the humid silence. All those gathered on the shoreline took notice. Heroon's temper could no longer be held back. The weather shift had begun.

He looked at Pox.

Why is she smiling?

The bounty hunter's hand slid into the seam of her thigh plate, the motion like a snake entering the den of its prey.

"Oh, the secrets we keep," she said and pulled out a gleaming, silver spiral.

A galaxy star.

His fate was sealed. He couldn't stop the weapon and hold off Pox's physical attack. The galaxy star responded to its target like a seeker missile. When thrown in advance of an opponent's attack it left the defender in a strategic paradox. To move and fight against it opened you to the aggressor's strikes, yet to address their attacks left one vulnerable to the star's poisoned edges.

"Just your luck, Draden. I've got the angle and the distance."

She was right. No one else could see her hidden devilry from their position on the dock. She could retrieve and toss the assassin's clandestine weapon in the river before anyone arrived.

Rage streamed from Pox's eyes. She flung the star and charged.

A current of energy dappled the surface of the endless lake, whispering a secret to Keen's inner mind.

Give in. Invite it to take you.

Keen stepped forward, the Talon's prongs held only inches above the wooden planks of the dock. The galaxy spiral slowed, its internal drive ensuring it kept the appropriate distance from its wielder to allow for the tactical advantage when it reached its intended target.

Keen knelt and lifted the trident head as soon as it was underneath the galaxy star, spiraling it upwards. The lethal object tracked the movement, following the pronged head of his weapon overhead. Pox's hands went for his exposed neck.

Keen released the Talon Caster. It twirled and he acrobatically regripped it with reversed hands. The laser end came up and tore into Pox's chest, penetrating through the plate armor and emerging out her backside. He moved left in a subtle slide that carried the weight of a mountain shifting in an earthquake. His Caster sent the bounty hunter head-over-heels overhead. Keen surged the Caster in an arc and shut the laser blade off in one motion. The galaxy star, sensing the approaching surface of the water slowed. Pox's forehead collided with its poisoned spikes and she plunged into the river.

Keen rose and turned, peering over the edge of the dock. Pox struggled under the water no more than a body's length down, tangled in the Strangler plant. Its black tendrils entwined around her limbs, forming complicated knots and binds. Her eyes were open, a lifetime of hate glowing like two suns on the brink of going nova. She screamed, sending bubbles of fury upward. The poison took hold and her arms and legs slacked. The exclamation reached the surface and broke, releasing her final words into the humid air of Heroon. The light in her eyes extinguished.

Keen stared at her lifeless face. Pox's anger and hate and his fear, guilt, and self-loathing… a part of himself lay dead under that water.

The dock swayed and rattled under his feet. The steps of several figures creaked the timbers.

"The Wind of Helleuan does not lie idle when the sail of Justice is unfurled." It was the general's voice.

"Heroon has called you home, parent. Well done," Reynaria's voice added. "The Apex is complete."

"Both," Keen said and turned around.

The old priest cocked his head, a single eyebrow rising.

"The answer to your question. Intimidation *and* experience."

The General nodded.

"What question?" Reynaria asked.

"About my sibling, Reardon," Keen said, eyes darting to the water where Pox lay submerged. He knew the answer applied equally well to his former nemesis.

And my parent too.

THIRTY-ONE

Some days in your life never fade. Deep in the desert on Kol 2, remote sand belts exist where only the Dune Eagle flies. Undulating blue hills pass in unbroken rhythm under its sharp eyes, except for the occasional shadow cast by an unmoving desert hermit. Lone and defiant against the harsh winds and hands of time, the Recluse tree's roots grasp the planet's inner rock fast and defy the world above ground. It appears no more than a bony skeleton under Altiron's blazing light. But deep in the subterranean silence, its roots inhabit cracks and fissures in the dark, coveting the paltry moisture that sustains it.

Those final twenty-four hours on Heroon are a Recluse tree in the desert of my mind. That day stands ever-present while the rest of my life's memories are blown into smooth rolling blue sands in a blurry stream of lost experience. Everything in my life led up to that moment. Everything since was fated by my choices and those imposed on me by others that day, none more so than Keen. It began when I went to meet Jati.

Lena's network escorted me to the edge of the compound without incident. But after that things fell apart. The usual gatehouse attendant on duty was absent. To make matters worse, five soldiers stood guard in front of the roadway. They didn't have Casters, but they did have blasters.

Jati would be waiting at the riverbank, ready to push off in a makeshift raft in mere minutes. Unless I was the gullible victim of another ruse and they were gliding downstream. I remember how easily my trust in them fell away when we hit the roadblock in our plan. It was like I was back on the *Carmora* all over again.

Under the cloak of darkness, I lifted my terrestrial eyes to the night sky and shot through space, light years passing in an instant. I was back in orbit off Tarkassi 9, waiting to get stabbed a second time. But this time it wouldn't be the ship's hull. A knife would slide deep into my pride.

I remember the scent of cantinool wafting by on the wings of Heroon's warm night breeze. The planet politely reminded me that it, and all living things under its roof, were also under threat and deserved to be defended. Heroon's diverse ecosystem shouldn't fall under the sword of human avarice and competition. The voice of Heroon, spoken through the cantinool's breath, punctuated my awareness of the big picture and my small, but important role in its proceedings.

Even with the cantinool in my nostrils I still doubted. With all I'd been through could you blame me? You'd assume someone of my ilk would know better, that the moral fortitude people muster in the face of oppression shouldn't have surprised me. But it did.

So many selfless acts go undocumented in the cause of freedom. Choices and sacrifices essential in a line of evolutionary progress culminate in various forms of human victories and defeats. Yet names and faces are washed over by the spectacle of collective history. If only I knew those who helped me that night, I'd recite a eulogy in their honor and carve their initials in stone to outlast all life in the Arm. But like the wind, they pass and diminish into a fading memory. And others always step up to take their place.

That's the thing I've learned about justice. It's doesn't abate. It might ebb and flow, but like water caught by the tide it keeps moving, and so did we.

In the brief sacrificial mayhem, I got out. Surreptitiously, I made my way through the grass towards the river's edge. Jati was nowhere to be seen. My lingering suspicion gnawed at the resoluteness of my inner-conscience. Kneeling in the tall reeds, Gushet's memory came to me. My eyes again went to the stars. The clarity of my situation and how far I'd come hit me like the shift of the Wind's Tide. What would my sibling do?

Never fight the Tide.

That's what she'd always said. Yet, hadn't she done that her whole life? How I missed my dear twin, then. I pined for the protective shield that those few minutes of additional time in the world gifted her. If she were here, she'd decide for me, right or wrong. For us.

Not this time. I'd wanted leadership and I'd received it. Even though I was a thousand light-years from Kol 2, the weight of my people pushed down on my shoulders.

Which way was the tide running? My body pulled me back to the gate. But my heart remained stubborn. Where had following that gotten me? It was a chipped and scarred mess. Maybe it was time to relieve it of the constant burden of driving my life. Yes, I remember that moment well.

It was time to accept the unthinkable and turn back.

Someone grabbed my arm and I nearly killed them. Good thing Jati was strong as jeekoo stone. I wanted to speak but their hand was over my mouth. They cautioned me to be quiet and directed my attention to the river. That was when I saw the body. On the end of a dock, under the light of infrared balls, New Heroon soldiers pulled a corpse from the water. I couldn't make out details at our distance, but the river resisted giving up its prey.

"Strangler plant," Jati whispered. I watched as soldiers hacked at long tendrils attached to the cadaver, working it free.

The idea of drifting on the river wasn't as appealing to me.

But we had more pressing problems. Word reached the soldiers along the shore of the confrontation at the gate. They rallied to aid their fellow troops. Jati and I watched, low in the grass, as they spread out from the shoreline to the walls of the compound.

"They're sweeping the area," Jati whispered in my ear.

A line of New Heroon troops strode towards us along the river, infrared lights illuminating long-stemmed reeds and knee-high grass. A flock of birds squawked and took flight as the line of soldiers encroached on their nighttime refuge.

I'll never forget the sound of legs swishing in the tall grass. My heart was pounding in my chest. I wasn't used to a landscape with visible cover. The tension of hiding in plain sight was foreign to me. I was alive with jitters. If we didn't move, they'd run right over us.

"We'll never make it to the raft now," Jati whispered. "Plan C got here sooner than I expected."

And so, we improvised, or at least I did. I decided on my own without discussion. I wouldn't even call it a decision. It was more an impulsive gut response formed of necessity.

I don't know why I did it. Maybe it was because what others had done for me was fresh in my mind and I didn't want their sacrifices to be for nothing.

I told Jati to go. It was my turn. Without them, we wouldn't have the arms we needed. It had to be me. Now I understood why the others did what they had for me minutes earlier.

I doubt Jati would have acknowledged that it was the right decision had I asked. They were the type of person to go down with you rather than present an option that involved self-preservation at another's expense. All this time I'd had the sense that was the case with Jati and Keen. Now I knew it.

I remember the last words they spoke to me before scurrying off to the raft. "Just don't get yourself killed," they said and clasped my hands. Strong, calloused fingers ran over my Dunemarks. Then, my hand was free. And so was Jati.

THIRTY-TWO

Keen straightened the sleeves of his Legion reds as the guard unlocked the cantinool door. The latch slid back, and it creaked open. He hesitated.

You're not the prisoner now.

The jeekoo walls still intimidated. The square stone mausoleum forever held the inventory of his horrors. Even with his transformation to the new Legion warrior as part of its history, the air inside the jeekoo cauldron was still suffocating. Keen made a personal vow. This would be the last time he'd step foot into the cell.

In the shadowy light cast by the rising Twin Moons through the slit in the wall, Razor sat ghostlike on the cell's narrow bed.

"Finally." She rose. "So, you got them to release me. Are we leaving?"

"Not quite."

Her expression shifted to confusion as Harmon and Karpel revealed his uniform.

"Pox is dead," he said. "She was a double agent, attempting to sell information to Garassia."

"What? How?"

"I killed her. In a duel."

Did he hear a whisper from the jeekoo stone?

"She's dead?" Razor asked.

Keen nodded. "Very dead. Strangler plant finished her off."

Razor's eyes went wide. "At the river?"

"Obviously. Why do you ask?"

"Nothing." She broke eye contact and looked at his outfit. "Why are you wearing a uniform? You look… younger."

Finally…

"Keen?"

"You've complicated things by aiding Jati's escape."

Razor's head cocked to the side at the blunt accusation.

He was trying to make this work and be delicate at the same time.

"There's more going on than you understand, Razor. But for now, as 'wrong' as it sounds, I need to know where Jati went and what they're intending to do."

Razor took a step back. Her widening eyes made clear she grasped a turn of politics between them.

That wasn't the right approach.

He'd messed that up. Maybe playing along to have her tell him in false trust, assuming he was ready to flee with her, would have been wiser? No, that was the old Draden. This was the only way. She'd made her own choices and they stood across from one another because of them. Honor and discipline, that was the side on which he now stood. He was in the general's shoes. She was where he'd been. There wasn't much time, but he'd get her to understand. And it would help her too. It was a good solution, considering how complicated things had become.

"What's happened, Keen?"

"Many things. But most importantly, we're on the edge of turning the tide in the Arm. New Heroon is now ready to lead a charge against…"

"New Heroon? What're you talking about? Why are you in Legion reds?"

"I command New Heroon's army now."

"What?" Razor reared back from him.

"Listen to me," he said in a hushed tone, holding out a palm to gesture for her to relax. "I've got a solution that can get you out of here."

She didn't respond so he went on.

"Reynaria is willing…"

"Reynaria? So, you've made amends?"

"Yes. But more than that, I've come to understand that she's on our side. This is the cause of freedom."

"What are you talking about, Keen? I've been in a labor camp, with thousands of others, for months because of her tyranny and abuse of power."

"It's part of the future."

"Have you lost your mind?"

"Listen to me, we have to stop Jati. They're not helping. Their resistance is hurting our ability to take down the monopolies."

"You want me to sell them out?"

"No, I…"

"Jati's the closest thing you have to a friend. Someone who legitimately cares for you despite all your faults." She paced the cell. "Who lived through the war with you and still carries your burden."

"I can get your children out of Targite prison."

She halted. The Mote fire in her eyes was earnest.

"And get you and them safe passage to a colony in line for shaping. You can start a new life. The Targitians don't want New Heroon to fall. They're willing to forget about you to have that."

"And if not?"

"Then I can't help. You'll go to the Targitians. Most likely they'll put you in prison and use you to purpose. You've got a lot of symbolic capital, especially with the Motes still unaccounted for."

Razor turned at the mention of her kin.

"And my children?"

This was the unknown. He hoped it wasn't as bad as it sounded. "Reynaria said they'll be 'sanded'. That was the Targitian's term. I don't know what that means."

Razor's face quivered. It was the same seismic tremor as back on Kol 2, riding the River Hidden

"I do," she whispered. Her shadowy form walked to the window and illuminated under the light of the Twin Moons. Her head tilted up toward the slit in the jeekoo stone. "How can you ask me this, Keen? How dare you come here like this, after all that's happened?"

"You'll be helping us do what's right. This is what I'm trying to make you understand. Jati too, if I can find them before it's too late."

"We can still leave," she said. "We can go now. There's still time. With Jati... we can do what's right."

"No, Razor, that's not what's 'right'."

She faced him. "Then I can't help you."

"You're putting your trust in Jati? Since when did you stop suspecting them of moral neutrality?'

"Since I shared time with them in a labor camp as prisoners of war."

"I've also spent time with Jati under similar circumstances."

"And since then you've done nothing but tell me Jati has a side. And they do. Where's yours, Keen?"

Why was this so difficult? They were on the same side. All she needed to do was understand that he wanted the same thing.

"I can spare Jati, even though they've gotten themselves wrapped up in this mess. That cause is futile. It's only a matter of time before the counterinsurgents are brought down. What you two don't seem to understand is we're fighting the same enemy."

"We are?"

"Yes, why is it so hard for you to see? We're breaking free of oppression. It's built on the back of worlds without Wind."

"I'm not fighting for that change, not for the people of Heroon."

"You don't want a better future for them?"

"It's about more than people and economics."

Keen frowned

Razor's face shifted. Her gesture reminded him of a parent growing frustrated, about to regroup and offer a didactic lesson rather than a scolding.

"This is a beautiful planet," Razor said. "With a thriving culture. Kol 2 was once like this before outsiders intervened. All the inhabited systems can make their energy if they're allowed to do so. There's harmony to each planetary ecosystem. It's only because of monopoly patents and their enforcers that shaping needs to occur."

The power in her eyes wasn't the one he'd come to know during their time together. Instead of repressed fury, they shone with emotionally charged lament. "And it comes at the expense of nature, culture, and social autonomy. All for what? Power, greed, and ego run rampant."

She walked back to the corner of the cell. The cool light cast her silhouette with a silvery edge.

"You want to stop the rise of my kind, Keen?" She swung around and faced him. "Or the persistence of resentful, angry, embittered folk out for vengeance and the satisfaction of right over wrong through violent and destructive retaliation?" She paused and folded her arms.

Does she mean Reynaria?

"Then stop the cycle. You're simply taking control away from one dominant group and putting it into the hands of another." She turned back to the light of the moons. "That's not freedom. It's a transfer of power. It doesn't change the world, except to further ruin and exploit it."

"But it *is* a transfer of power," Keen said. She wasn't grasping the destination at the end of the road. "It takes time, Razor. And trust."

"Trust?" She approached him in earnest.

Keen almost stepped back, unsure of her intention.

Razor stopped an arm's length from him. She shook her head in disappointment.

Or was it frustration? What had happened to her? It was like she was defeated yet stronger in her commitment to what she considered just and right.

"You can't let the world fall to save one child, Keen. Even if it is your own."

"Don't tell me what I can and can't do!"

He'd never let the tragedy of Reardon happen a second time. Never. He wouldn't abandon Reynaria no matter the cost.

"You're more delusional now, without your crutches of excess than you were as an ambassador. You're blinded to guilt, trauma, and your resentment... and what's your way of 'coping'? You find a 'cause' and seek 'justice' but it's revenge veiled through a false notion of righteousness. You blindly support your blood kin while they are unjust. Your choices will lead to nothing but the same... just an ebb and flow of the tide. Nothing changes. It only shifts."

"The world is changing, Razor. You either change with it or die." Who was she to lecture him? He was standing on his own two feet as a free person, clean of his past corruption. "You ended up in a cell, defending a lost cause."

"Nothing is lost!" She paced the room, furious. "Where were you a few weeks ago?" She pointed at him, her anger rising. "Right here." Her arm waved around the room. "In this same cell. But unlike you, I won't cave to delusion."

"You don't get it, do you?"

"You've changed, Keen. You think you're on the path of redemption, but you're blinded by familial love and an idealistic vision of the future. It will lead to nothing but ruin."

"Hasn't it already?" He was losing patience and growing frustrated. "Wake up and look around you, Razor! What's the alternative? I'm offering a compromise that will allow you to survive."

"You offer my selfish survival at the expense of an entire people."

"This isn't your culture!"

She stared at him, eyes ablaze. "That's what you still don't understand. These *are* my people. The struggle isn't just on Kol 2. It's all across the Arm. I was alone until I came here, with only a small band of my kin. But now I'm one of hundreds of thousands. Maybe more. You're trying to stop the cause that you so desperately want to emerge victorious."

"So, you're a martyr now?"

"Fuck you!" Her eyes went wide with rage.

This was going nowhere. They were on opposite banks of a philosophical river. "So you refuse?" he asked.

"I don't even grace your question with an answer."

"I'm sorry it has to be this way, Razor. I've offered what I can to help you."

"Don't do it, Keen. I don't know how to make you understand, but you're being led by desperation and pride. Trust me, I've seen it before. Gushet suffered from it."

"What would you have me do?"

"Fight for freedom. You're a soldier of liberty, aren't you? Let people live independently, without outside oversight. That's how to aid your fellow human beings in the Arm."

"We are! It'll take time. They don't have the knowledge; they'll fail without oversight."

"You arrogant fool!" She spun around and stepped back to the corner under the light of Harmon and Karpel. "Leave. I'm better off talking to the stone walls than to you."

"Your children will die, Razor."

She didn't turn. "They're already dead," she whispered. "You killed them the moment you opened the door to this cell."

"This isn't my fault."

"No, it never is."

It was like everyone in his life was so thickheaded they couldn't grasp the struggle he was dealing with and how he had to navigate the turbulent, ironic waters of his life.

"You can live without them?" Now that Reynaria was by his side, the thought of moving on and leaving her felt impossible. He couldn't imagine having two children, raising them only to have them taken from him.

"Take back that question," she whispered. "It should never be asked of anyone."

"But that's what will happen if you won't…"

"When thousands of others will die for it?" Her head tilted back to absorb the cool moonlight entering the cell, her back to him still. "The weight of that selfish burden would destroy anyone with a conscience."

How dare she? The reason she wasn't dead was because of him.

"Why do you think I made my choice?" he asked. "I did it because as a parent, I had a responsibility to my child."

Razor's exhalation echoed off the jeekoo stone. Her hand went to her mouth, the fingers circling in slow motion. Even with her back to him, Keen knew the gesture.

Why was she doing that now? A flood of memories returned to him: the underground ride on the River Hidden; Gushet's lamentation at the dock when they arrived; the flickering light of glow rings; Razor accepting her sibling's command to live at the Turbine Field.

"The Targitian delegation arrives in the morning."

Razor didn't shift a muscle.

I tried.

Had he? Of course, he had, to the extent possible. His needs were important, too. It was about balance. Negotiation. *Compromise.* That was the way the Arm worked. It didn't matter if you were a soldier or a diplomat. So, she's understood the Arm is a big place with others like her; she still can't understand that the world works through giving as well as taking. He wouldn't carry the weight of her guilt. She'd give up her children, and her family, for a larger political cause that was sure to fail? Three Spans of the Arm… the same fight every time, it never became an untainted reality. Always it played out in degrees of compromise. To believe otherwise was pure naiveté.

"Razor, please. This isn't how it should end."

She didn't respond.

"Razor."

In the cool light of the Twin Moons, her backlit form was almost otherworldly. Keen watched as her hands tightened into balled fists. The veins on her forearms bulged, casting faint shadows like rivers running down her skin.

"A child-bearer can make choices that others, even their partners, cannot understand." Her fists unclenched and she dropped to her knees.

"Goodbye Keen."

THIRTY-THREE

How do I convey the internal anguish writhing within me in that cell? My heart, what was left of it, was like a wet rope. The merciless hands of sorrow twisted it with miserable force, the liquid, my lifeblood, leached to the last drying thread. It bled out in streams of despair. For my children. My choices. My foolishness. When those pitiless hands released their grip on my heart, I could do nothing but gasp for breath. Insufferable wailing and soft lamentation moved in continuous rhythm between the rope's wrenching. With each new twist, I broke and shattered. On it went through the night until my heart was empty.

As if hearing my anguish, Heroon's atmosphere took pity on me. The sky rumbled in anger; it cloaked the Twin Moons with a cover of clouds in the growing night, acknowledging the need to shelter me from their sight. To recall the metaphorical relevance was too poetically cruel.

What hope remained for Jati's rebellion and revolution now? Could the subaltern people, my people, follow without their leader? And why was Keen's betrayal more painful and damaging than the collective abuses I'd suffered as one of the oppressed? Was it because of my children? How dare he walk into the cell and ask that of me, when his lost child pulled him halfway across the Arm and into the face of his worst nightmare. I should have left him for dead after that first crash in the dunes. Or shot him in that pathetic state, as he asked.

Other than a desperate hope that Jati might still take the Temple and break me out, what could I hold on to? The fate of my children was decided. I wouldn't set foot on Kol 2 ever again. Even with my heart drained and empty, their lost screams would echo through its vacant chambers as soon as my feet touched blue sand.

That night was the longest of my life. I was trapped in the slack water of a jeekoo cell, mired in Heroon's standing ideological tide.

I rode out the long night while thunder rattled the surrounding rainforest. But not the jeekoo stone; it held fast, unaffected. Nothing moved or passed through its hallowed walls. How many others had withered in this cell because of their moral secrets? How ironic that what the prisoner knew and believed, more than their physical presence, bound them inside stone walls. That was the potent threat to the world of the corrupt and tyrannical. The cowards and the fools. The deceivers and traitors. Death was forced upon others like me by their own tragedies of right.

At the first light of morning, a solitary certitude crept into the cell and stood before me. Had this moral ghost eluded the wringing hands of fate that gutted my heart? Or did it germinate from the ashes of my burned soul during the dark night? Either way, the jeekoo stone smiled at my newfound epigram: If the dead whispered secrets from the grave, the weight of their truths would bury the living.

THIRTY-FOUR

The view at dawn from Reynaria's balcony left Keen unsettled. Purple and violet clouds swirled above him. Gusts of wind swept over the rainforest canopy, swaying the cantinool trees. Without the light of Nushaba, the weather felt like an ill-placed intrusion. Storms were common on Heroon and they provided steady rain to feed the tropical climate. But most passed in the night, fleeting and scattered cloudbursts that nourished the rainforest's endless thirst for moisture. Ones like this were rare. Keen had experienced another storm of this intensity when he arrived on Heroon during the Patent War. After it receded something was different about his surroundings, as if one age ended and another had begun.

In a way, it was true. The new one was war.

He looked at his Legion uniform. It glowed an eerie magenta in the ominous light.

"Did she talk?" Reynaria appeared at the balcony's ledge next to him. She held back her violet hair as it blew in the wind.

Keen shook his head. "She's too stubborn with pride."

"Then she goes to the Targitians," she said and gazed out over the rainforest. "It's better this way. We can take care of your former Legion renegade on our own. Handing her off to Targite will make them think we're doting on them and groveling at their feet with gratitude." She looked up at the sky. "This is going to be a big one. Everything will come to a halt while Heroon reminds us who's in charge."

Keen's nostrils drew in the moisture-laden air. It smelled of imminent rain. No cantinool aroma spiced the breeze. Without Nushaba the flowers wouldn't grace the day with their presence.

"I remember a storm like this during the war. We had to…" Keen turned at the sound of the general's voice from Reynaria's quarters. The old priest passed through the billowing bereese fabric to the balcony. He lowered his hood.

"The delegation may delay their arrival due to weather. Not surprising." He looked up at the sky. "If they do, they'll hold at the jump port a day or two before descending."

Reynaria nodded. "And our on-planet nuisance?"

The general raised an eyebrow at Keen. He shook his head, indicating Razor wouldn't talk.

"Their attack on the Fins started before dawn. What we expected. A last gasp, more a show of pride than a real threat. I've sent the central force to put a quick end to it. My patience has run out." His eyes rose to the clouds. "I think Heroon's has as well."

"Maybe I should go?" Keen said. "In case it's more than we think. This may be a ruse for something larger."

"No," Reynaria said. "You stay here."

"It'd be good for him to lead the troops on this," the general said, giving Keen a covert nod. "An easy victory to start his tenure."

"No. I don't want to risk any word of your presence getting to the Targitians. Having you 'dead' is one of our most valuable hidden cards. You'll have plenty of time to lead our army once we begin our secession from Targitian authority."

Thunder clapped. All three heads turned. Muscular clouds towered in the atmosphere to the East. At the storm line, the rainforest disappeared in a lavender mist, accented by sporadic flashes of lightning.

A resounding boom from the west turned their eyes. Keen watched a plume of orange rise on the far side of the Fins. It reminded him of Razor and the Mote assault on Kol 2.

"Human thunder. Mere rumblings," Reynaria said. "We smashed

the Garassians with ease and drove them off the planet. They retreated on the heels of our righteous might like petulant cowards. These 'rebels' are but a fly to be swept off our arm."

"And the Fins?" Keen asked.

"We can make repairs and stay on schedule."

"Our other 'friends' are ready," the old priest said to Reynaria. "They await only a demonstration of our power."

What other friends?

"General?" A guard called through the curtains. The old priest walked inside, spoke with the guard, and returned to the balcony.

"It looks like the Targitians decided to arrive early and beat the storm. They're coming into the atmosphere now and should make it before the weather turns. I'll meet you at the gate."

Reynaria nodded.

So, Razor's fate was sealed. It had been a long road with her since she took him hostage in that pod. She'd be out of that cell if she had agreed to help him.

"What is it?"

"I was just thinking about Razor. At least she'll have the chance to see her children, even if it's behind bars."

"Her children were executed after the Motes attacked Targite. They were dead before you were off Kol 2." Reynaria strode through the curtains.

Keen stood transfixed.

How could that be if I offered…

He turned, mouth open to call her back, but Reynaria had exited the suite.

She'd lied to him, and put him in a situation where his offer to Razor proved dishonorable and deadly. Her tone was so candid, so unsympathetic. The remark rattled him. It wouldn't settle. He ran a hand over his face.

He'd just sent Razor to Targite. What would have been the alternative had she agreed to give up Jati?

Scarpa, things have gotten so complicated and messy.

His hand went to his chest. The medallion. He needed to read it, to remind him of his charge and why this was all worth the effort.

It has to be here.

The wind picked up and drizzle speckled the jeekoo railing. All the more reason to move inside. He passed through the bereese curtains into the suite and scanned the main chamber, eyeing anything that might hang or hold the chain. Save for the main planning table littered with plans and designs, the room was spartan. No sign of the necklace and no drawers or other compartments that might contain it were to be seen.

He leaned his head through the doorway of the bedroom. Clothing and other items were thrown haphazardly on the bed and surrounding furniture.

It was a breach of trust, but he crossed the threshold into her private quarters.

I feel like a snooping parent. Exactly what I always said I'd never become when I was a child.

On top of a dresser, a series of images sat displayed on small stands: a young Reynaria with classmates, no more than five or six years old. Another depicted her graduation. She was dressed in blue, looking like Scarpa. The largest was of a group of rebels, including Reynaria, kneeling pridefully (yet quite dirty) in front of an assault vehicle. It was a Carpati Runner, hard-won from the Garassian colonialist forces.

The last was of Scarpa. She stood outside a hospital in the capital. It couldn't be far from the end. The bereese dress hung like a billowing sheet over her gaunt frame. Her face had lost its strength but not her eyes. Her soul was still afire with that familiar flame that kindled Keen's love and desire. His tanned finger went to the image's surface and dragged down her cheek. It must have been taken no more than a year or two ago. Despite being ill she'd aged well and looked younger than he expected.

Keen could sense her presence lingering in the air.

Why didn't you write to me sooner?

He bent over to examine the scene, his green eyes on the edge of pooling with sorrow. On the other side of the street, he recognized the courthouse. The date should be displayed inside the pediment running in numbers on an eccentric machine ages old; a well-known historic landmark on Heroon. It read '3039'.

That's ten years ago?

Thunder clapped. Keen jumped. His arm knocked the picture and sent it falling off the dresser's ledge. It smashed on something and hit the floor.

"Sake of the Arm." He knelt and gasped: Scarpa's childhood chest. He recognized it by its distinctive cantinool exterior and child-like initials scratched into the wood. He removed shards of the broken picture and lifted the lid.

The medallion rested on a bed of pink bereese.

How could that be ten years ago? She said the illness was sudden.

He lay the medallion around his neck, tucking the pendant under his Legion top, and pulled aside the fabric. Below were more letter chips.

They were addressed to him.

And they were unsent.

Keen's heart screamed from behind a wall of denial. His rational mind, what was left of it, held its hands over its ears, refusing to listen.

"The dates," he sifted through the chips. "3040, 3038, 3039...."

He opened one.

I'm writing again, Keenie. I beg you, please respond.

Another:

Bedridden. Our daughter is sending these for me, for us. Please respond.

The most recent, eight years ago:

I fear it is now too late, for both of us. Our daughter has become blinded by...

He tossed the chip back in the pile and sorted them by date, frantic with growing horror. "Please don't let it be here. It can't... she wouldn't."

The oldest one in the pile lay at the bottom. The date read '3038'.

Don't do it.

The beast awoke from its impotent slumber and growled.

Don't do it. Walk away.

"I have to." He flipped on the chip.

Dearest Keenie, I've thought for years about writing this letter to you.

Every time I convinced myself to do it, the reality of what might happen to you stayed my hand...

"No." The word came out so faint that even the jeekoo stone walls couldn't hear it. If they had, they would have refrained from mocking him.

Reynaria hadn't posted any of the letters. Not until after Scarpa was long dead. And then she only sent a copy of the first one. He'd been reeled in across the entire Arm with the bait of love and guilt. Guided by deception, he'd been living a false dream of love and a self-made promise to do right by it.

All for naught... too late by a decade.

And Reynaria? She'd been a teenager when Scarpa died, left to fend for herself. It was no wonder she gravitated to the Heroonese rebels. This was born of spite, anger, and resentment over the war's impact on her life, and matured into opportunistic political gain. Keen's stomach turned. She'd punished Scarpa, watching her suffer in physical pain *and* emotional grief as she lay dying, hoping in vain for a response from the one she'd loved.

I could've seen her again. We would've had ten years. We could've raised our child together.

The beast inside lashed out and bit him. It told him he was a fool and whipped him with his irony. Why did he need her to call him? He could have gone on his own.

No, not after Reardon. I couldn't return. And I didn't know I had a child.

It didn't matter. Reynaria won her revenge and secured a military leader and diplomat for her cause, all in one sleight of hand. Would she have turned into this person had he not been broken and unable to function at the end of the war? Would she have grown into a loving, honest person under the care of parents who loved one another and raised her together?

Rage surged through his body. He hurled the chest across the room, smashing it against the far wall, and ran out. He burst through the bereese curtains onto the balcony into the rain and wind.

"Scarpa!" He yelled with a force that sent an emotional echo through the soul of the planet. Even the jeekoo stone flinched.

The hum of a transfer pod's engine broke into the thunderclaps and gusts of wind. Keen raised his head from its slunk position on the ledge of the railing. The Targitians.

Reynaria and the general, mere specks in the open plain below, hurried towards the landing platform through miserable weather. The pod passed overhead, fighting turbulent air and struggling to maintain stability. Its rudder and flap system wasn't built for high winds.

Keen watched it bucking as it descended. His breath froze mid-inhale.

That's not a Targitian pod.

He shielded his eyes from the pelting rain and looked at the rear engine. Carpati pinwheel exhaust.

It's from Garassit. It's disguised...

It was a trap.

KEEN GALLOPED across the open plain. His voice cried out in the swirling storm. Reynaria couldn't hear him. Heroon's spiteful soul sucked the pleading cries from his mouth and cast them into the angry wind. They swirled and rose into the purple tempest, swept away unheard except by he who called out; a siblingless, widowed, absent parent with nothing left but a child.

Three robed figures descended the pod's ramp. They greeted their hosts. Keen's panting echoed in his ears. Rain pelted his face. He wiped his eyes clear with an arm and ran faster. The storm's gales pushed back as if fate's sardonic gatekeeper refused to let him pass through the torrent.

The world slowed as it had in the pod before the crash with Razor. He fought it, straining to keep pace with time. It was futile.

The robed figure in front of Reynaria raised an arm. It fell. She hunched forward and collapsed onto the tarmac.

"No!" Keen's anguished cry attacked the wind and rain. It battered Heroon's malicious spirit, striking blows in rage against merciless fate. His voice pushed through the wind and rain but came up short of the finish line. His entire life flashed in front of him. Always falling short... with Reardon. Scarpa. And now Reynaria.

The general dropped to a knee. The old priest raised his arms to block a second blow. It broke through his guard. He collapsed to the ground. Two robed figures dragged him up the ship's ramp.

"No!" This time his scream reached the lone, remaining figure. The assassin stepped back from the body and tracked Keen's haste up onto the tarmac.

"Reynaria!" Keen dropped to his knees and cradled his child in his arms. The tempestuous storm struck. Rain blanketed the tarmac.

The bereese fabric on her stomach ran red. Reynaria lifted a bloody hand in awe. Diluted streams of crimson tracked down her arm.

Her eyes went to the chain on his neck.

"The letters…"

"Shhh… it's alright."

Keen ran a hand over her face. He pushed back her soaking violet hair.

"I was so angry," she said.

"It's not your fault. I'm to blame for all of this."

Reynaria shook her head, defiant. "She was right… the words in the letter. War is at fault."

Keen cradled her head. The storm blew sheets of drenching rain over them. Reynaria pulled back and teetered, her strength waning. Her face lost its maturity and filled with a child's fear.

"I didn't…" Her eyes widened in panic. She gasped, trying to speak between gulping breaths. "I…" Her eyes darted about in fear of facing the unknown.

He grabbed her face with both hands. "Reynaria, it doesn't matter now."

She gasped for breath, gulping. Her hands dug into his shoulders.

And fell.

The House of Keen Draden collapsed.

Keen raged in pleading sorrow. He wanted to rise and erupt in violent anger, but he had nothing left. Only the power of acquiescent lament remained. Rocking his child in his arms, he turned to the robed figure. "What have you done?"

Despite the storm's fury, the person lowered their hood and approached.

"Keen?"

The face registered and Keen's mind faltered in its attempt to succumb to delusion.

"Parent?"

"Child?"

"No!" The world split open under his feet. Heroon's core rose in the fissure and shot molten cruelty up into the storm.

"My lost child. Is that you? You look... I thought you were dead?"

"You killed my child!" He rocked Reynaria in his arms. "Your grandchild!"

"You're not well. Come." Aradus reached for Keen's arm but he pulled it away.

"Get away from me!"

Aradus withdrew his hand. The wind and rain swirled about, his parent's disguise billowing and flapping.

"She's my child." Keen clutched Reynaria to his chest, cradling her head. "My partner was from Heroon."

Keen's eyes were shut, but he knew the look on his parent's face: shock turning to understanding. And from it would breed only scorn.

"This can't be," Aradus said, rain pelting his exposed, aged face.

"It is. Are you shamed?" Keen lashed out, glaring at his parent with newfound rising anger. "Can you accept your family now?"

"This is no grandchild of mine. She's a product of a foolish, misguided urge. A bastard of enemy blood."

"She's *my* child."

"She's a traitor of the state. Nothing more."

"Have you no honor, parent? Even for your own family?"

"Do not lecture me about honor, child," Aradus's tone grew impatient and spiteful. He wiped water from his aged face. "Your life as a soldier and an ambassador are tainted by your selfishness and foolhardy weaknesses."

Keen met his parent's gaze. Malicious regret burned within the patriarch's eyes.

"A foolish and impulsive mistake made during war."

"What do you know of war? Nothing! You sit high on your chair and send others to do your bidding. You don't know what it's like to face down the barrel of an enemy's weapon, to hold a dying comrade in your arms. To feel the bitter sting of sanctions, watching as a sibling or parent dies of starvation."

Aradus shook his head. "You never came back from that war. I lost two children that fateful day."

"I came back. I returned, broken and ashamed. You took advantage and wooed me into an immoral service, feeding me with extravagance and indulgence to avoid seeing a reality you didn't want to face. You fed me anesthesia to keep your embarrassment at bay. You wanted a hero to return, but war isn't made of ideal dreams. Heroes return, broken, and shattered."

"My hero didn't return!" Aradus's eyes welled up as he screamed. "He fell on this beastly planet! Saving a lesser child!"

Keen nodded, holding Reynaria tight. "Yes," he whispered. Finally, the truth from a lifetime of living lies.

"You defied me, Keen. You defied your post."

"I defied nothing. I came to the support of my family."

"You fool of a child! You know nothing of what's happened here. Even in death, you've wreaked disaster." Aradus bent down and shoved his raptor-like face close to Keen's.

He could get as close as he wanted. Nothing mattered anymore.

Go ahead, yell at the child.

"We gave her the planet. It was a feint. You never learned how to wield the power of deceit. You bumbled with it over and over. The Council lowered her guard. We were ready to pounce and smash this so-called coup and seize Targite's technology. But you defied my orders with your meddling. Your new 'morality' sent it all spinning."

"My morality caused your political crisis? Your murder?"

"Not murder. The end of rebellion and treason. I bought that, for a hefty sum."

"Bought it?"

"The bounty hunter's weakness was power. It always is with mercenaries. Rather than spilled blood, I gave it to her in currency. She sold the information that this false prophet you claim as your offspring planned to break away from Targite. Many ears are listening in the Alliance."

"You knew and did nothing?" Keen looked at Reynaria's lifeless body. "You didn't help them push back against Targite?"

"Oh no," Aradus shook his head. "I did my job and weighed the options. I exploited diplomacy and made a deal."

"With the Targitians?"

"Who else?" Aradus splayed his arms wide. The gesture was all too familiar to Keen.

Like child, like parent.

"We agreed to work together to destroy her. They had little choice with you out of their reach. The sooner I had you safe the stronger our position in the negotiation. But you made a mess of it by jumping to Heroon instead of following my instructions to proceed to the Ortor jump hub. You *defied* me."

He told Pox our position.

"You know why you survived that run from Tarkassi 9?" Aradus raised an eyebrow.

Keen thought back on the argument and accusations between him, Razor, and Jati and the *Carmora* fleeing the attack by Pox.

"I paid the bounty hunter to push you towards home. I worried the Targitians might find you first and we'd lose leverage on our deal."

"But not worried about me."

"Keen, please. That's why I insisted she drive you like hounds to the hunters. Even with her bloodlust for you she, like everyone, has a price. I was keeping you safe."

My sibling's killer, hired by my parent to keep me safe. Irony in its most brutal and deadly costume.

"Pox is dead. By my hands."

Aradus sighed and wiped his face clean of rain. "You never cease to complicate things. The Targitians were promised the Mote. Does she live?"

"No."

Aradus scrutinized Keen's face like only a parent could. Keen held fast and stared him down.

He knows I'm lying.

"Still you defy me." Aradus's scorn pushed through his wrinkled and gaunt features. Keen knew the look all too well. The shell might be ragged and old, but the soul underneath shone with the same rigor it had since his childhood. "We'll find her in good time. Dead or alive she goes to the Targitians. We must honor our side of the bargain."

"Bargain?"

"My proposal to the Targitians proved too enticing to pass up. It was mutually beneficial and beautiful in design. They keep the patents on their tech. Garassit provides the planet. Profit is split down the middle. Council Territory and Targitian technology, each solving a shared rebel nuisance."

"An alliance with Targite?"

"A path to the future of the Arm. A true monopoly. The first of eleven systems to be shaped together. Think of the potential." Aradus's wearied eyes turned youthful at the future prospect on the horizon.

"All the power in the world won't turn back time, parent."

Aradus scoffed. "Except in your case. You look twenty years younger, my child. Not to mention you managed to come back from the dead. It's brilliant. Your life and death antics have been a game of cat and mouse between the Targitians and us. They'd won after you 'died' trying to escape from your comrade turned gunrunner. Targite backed out. With you gone, we lost our hold over them. They decided to wait until the time was right and deal with New Heroon on their own. So, we pounced first."

Keen clenched Reynaria tighter against him. He wanted to shield her dead ears.

"But *she*," Aradus pointed at Reynaria's body, "this bastard child inherited the diplomatic skills you lack. What a shame. She wouldn't let the Targitians have you. She knew holding you alive was a chip over them that could cause their downfall against the Council – their failed assassination attempt would wreak havoc on their political allies across the Arm. You were the strong-arm that would twist New Heroon free of Targite's grip."

Pox had to die so she couldn't report back to Targite that I lived. The plans going to Garassit were secondary.

He looked down at Reynaria. Why did she inherit so much deceptive blood? Or was it the fault of circumstance?

"The technology would've been ours had you not killed the Bounty Hunter. The planet could've been sacrificed."

What have I wrought?

"And now?" Keen asked.

"I think you know." Aradus eyes glowered with disgust. Keen clenched Reynaria tighter in his arms. He wasn't leaving. He wiped a tear with his shoulder. His lips trembled. He wanted to wail but wouldn't give his parent the satisfaction.

"Once again, I will bail you out. But your career is over. You'll retire and live out the rest of your days in some backwater town on our planet and drink yourself slowly to death. You'll take this… 'child' to your grave. But first, you'll be paraded in front of the Council to rub it in the Targitian's faces. We'll seize their territories in our grip as their allies flee from exposed corruption. It'll make for a quick war."

"I won't do this. I'm not leaving."

"Oh, you *are* leaving. The only other option is to be tried for treason, disgraced along with the general. You'd join him willingly at the gallows?"

"I'm already dead, parent. You've been too blinded by ego to see it." Keen looked down at Reynaria. "I've been a living corpse for years."

"Have you no honor left, Keen?"

Had he ever had any? Both his parent and child were riddled with cracks of immorality in their political shells. Honor twisted into mere patriotism for the state, equated with economic might and the wielding of domination at the expense of other's subservience. Where had it left his family? One lay dead in his lap, another died in his arms. Scarpa withered from a broken, lonely heart. And his parent called on him to muster up honor? He had none of the kind being asked of him.

"Honor, *Aradus*, is to be found in those who are traitors to injustice."

"You're a fool, child." Aradus shook his head in frustration. "Always have been. Immature and intent on drawing attention to yourself because you were a lesser child. You'll do as I say, given time. You'll come to your senses on the return to Garassit."

"I'm not…"

An explosion drowned out Keen's words. Aradus's mouth dropped open. Keen lay Reynaria's body down, stood, and turned. The red triangular spike atop the Temple crashed into the lower tiers of jeekoo stone, shattering into a dangling and twisted mess.

Figures emerged on the three levels of the Temple, yelling and cheering. A line of New Legion guards walked out from the gate at the lowest level led by armed civilians, their heads lowered in disgrace.

The rains slowed. The wind swirled, alternating between gusts and brief periods of respite. The storm front marched on to ravage the rainforest beyond the Temple. Armed masses made their way towards the tarmac. At the head of the group Keen recognized the unmistakable lavender mohawk fighting to stay upright in the rain and wind.

Jati.

"YOU'RE TOO LATE FOR REVOLUTION," Aradus snarked as Jati and the crowd of armed rebels approached.

"I'm afraid not, old tot. We have the Temple and the Fins. They're being destroyed as we speak. The people's army runs New Heroon now." Jati cracked a smile. "You sure look like a Targitian to me, despite your expression. It's the robe and hood." They cocked the Spirex Displacer in their hefty arms. "Their kind is no longer welcome here."

"You cannot stand against us alone," Aradus said.

"But we're not alone, are we?" Jati turned to the crowd assembled. They shouted cheers.

A sea of violet hair ran across the plain like a lake reflecting Heroon's storm clouds in the sky.

"Three battalion fleets are in orbit. This mini-drama is over," Aradus declared. "The planet is in the hands of Garassit. And that's where it'll stay."

"*Were* in orbit." Jati rested the Spirex Displacer over their boulder-like shoulder. They looked at Keen and winked.

"Excuse me?" Aradus said.

"Your Garassian force to retake the planet is under siege. In fact, they've surrendered and called for a pause to escort you and leave. The planet is ours."

"Ours?" Aradus scoffed. "You have no side, gunrunner."

"But I do, old tot. It's the one I've always fought for... never stopped fighting for it. It's just neither of your sides. It's the side of free people. The side of a liberated Arm. The Alliance is collapsing. Actually, it's already crumbled. The Hamuts are tired of being enforcers and not having a world of their own. That's what happens when you punish rather than showing mercy as victors in war. This harvest was sowed over two decades by you and the Council."

Jati... you crafty Gor Hunter.

"They're releasing control of the ten other star systems. Your hold over the Arm is dissolving. You've no more thugs, Councilman. Hamut reinforcements from the hub, the ones who ran off your 'three little battalions' are on their way down as we speak, now that the storm's passed."

"You lie."

"No, you do enough of that for all of us." Jati nodded to Keen. "Apologies, old tot. But it's the truth."

Keen cracked a smile of satisfaction. *It sure is.*

"Your monopolies will fall. We're stopping the shapings. All other energy systems will be renewed. You and the Targitians better get used to being content with sources from your own planets. Or," Jati did a little shuffle, "you could always buy some surplus cells if any of us 'liberated' folks have some to spare."

The crowd erupted in laughter at their humiliating razz.

Jati. No wonder you mustered a people's army.

"You think an empire built over two decades falls with one counter-stroke?" Aradus spoke with the passion and confidence of a person long in power. "The Arm isn't made up of these backwater outposts that barely qualify as civil and habitable planets. Heroon can't even be tallied as a legitimate victory. Your minor rebel ruse is nothing more than a pathetic nuisance of 'justice.' You're rebellion is *nothing*."

Keen read the familiar recipe of arrogance and vengeful desire on his parent's face.

"Our reach and power extend much farther than you realize,

gunrunner." Aradus turned his back on the crowd and made his way towards the ramp of the pod.

As much as Keen didn't want to admit it, Aradus was right. The Garassian Council would remain a powerful force despite losing their monopolies and territories. Even if all else fell, his home planet of Ceron was near impossible to breach, no less conquer. This was going to be a long and bloody conflict.

"Bring it on, old tot," Jati said to the Aradus's back. "If it's a war you want, it's a war you'll get."

Aradus stopped.

"And this time The Legion won't end up fighting for justice only to have their allies turn on them and descend into ill-used power and greed," Jati said.

Keen knew what was coming. His parent's fists clenched whenever mocked in a challenge.

Aradus turned, his bony cheeks flush in anger. "I will crush your so-called Legion and see you paraded dead in front of my city before the end."

Jati took a step forward and rose to their full height and girth. "This is New Heroon, Councilman Draden. It's time for you to leave." They rested the Spirex next to them. "As for all of you," they shouted at the New Legion soldiers returning and lingering without purpose after their defeat at the Fins. "Is this not what you've fought for?" Jati turned and waved their arms around at the crowd behind them. "To defend liberty? Care to join the cause?"

New Legion soldiers crossed to the rebel side.

"It's over," Jati yelled. The hordes cheered.

"Come, Keen," Aradus said. "It's time for us to depart."

Jati swung around and looked at him. "Come now, old tot. You're staying here, aren't you? Your army needs you."

"Keen?" Aradus's tone was earnest. "The Council awaits your appearance."

Keen stood frozen, staring at the crowd. A distant rumble of thunder broke the silence. It shook the chaos of despair within his soul. Heroon... how long had he been deaf to its planetary chorus?

"I'm sorry, Jati," Keen said.

His old Legion comrade's head cocked in confusion.

"I'm coming parent," Keen barked, loud enough so all could hear. "I'll tell everything to the Council. We'll take down Targite and return to conquer this heathen outpost. We'll win a quick victory. Garassia will rise as the new, solitary power in the Arm."

Aradus smiled in smug satisfaction.

How does the irony taste, parent? Bitter?

"Keen, your side is with us, old tot," Jati said. "We're Legion. To the end."

Yes, dear friend. To the very end.

To the East, flower cups opened as Nushaba returned on the heels of the passing storm. Cantinool wafted into Keen's nose. Clarity revealed itself, naked of all uncertainty.

Razor must be here somewhere. She'll do it this time.

He turned to face the rising smoke of the demolished Fins.

Scarpa... I finally know what's right, after it's too late.

"I offer you a gift, parent," he announced. Aradus stopped halfway up the pod's ramp.

The gift you're always giving.

"From your 'lesser' child."

Aradus's turned.

"I know where to find the Motes."

His parent's greedy smile beamed with smug satisfaction. The face saturated with a self-righteous and manipulative victory.

Keen closed his eyes. He drew in a breath.

"They took the..."

The blaster shot hit his back and blew through his chest. The pain was joyous. Keen dropped to his knees.

"No!" It was his parent's voice.

Keen smiled with smug satisfaction.

He swayed and reared back. Arms caught him before he fell. Strong arms. The anvil arms of Jati.

"Old tot, what've you done?"

Keen reached to his neck, his hand groping to clutch the medallion.

"Here," Jati unlatched the chain and handed it to him.

Keen grasped the pendant to his heart and smiled through the pain.

From under the medallion, warm blood pumped out and down his chest.

I'm coming Scarpa.

"Razor?" Keen whispered.

"Yes, old tot. It was her."

Keen looked up at Jati. The fortress stood, eyes saddened but proud.

A clamor erupted nearby

Jati looked away and back at Keen. "I hope this brings her the peace she deserves."

Keen let his head drop to the side. Two cloaked Garassians led Razor up the pod's ramp. She turned and, for a brief moment, their eyes met.

"She'll be sent back to Targite to face trial," Jati said. "You're still a Notos Ambassador so it's an interstellar crime. Justice can't be blind, old tot, even when reflected in a mirror. It'll be life in prison, I fear."

"My fault," Keen muttered and coughed. Blood ran down his chin.

"No, old tot. She made her choice. You gave her an offer worth accepting. Now the Arm is safer and so are her people." Jati's crow's feet crinkled tight as their eyes watered. "You two have an odd way of working together to fight for justice."

Keen managed a smile, fighting the pain. "Aradus?"

"Leaving." Jati's eyes met his own. "I'm sorry."

"He left me decades ago." Keen winced as his body fought the inevitable.

"Well, he's got no evidence now. Your typical bumbling heroics have secured the Council's downfall."

"It won't be easy, Jati."

"No, old tot. But I think I've got one more war left in me," they winked. "Curious to try this 'general' thing on for size."

"Garassit won't fall…"

"Don't be too sure, old tot. Even the strongest tide must ebb."

"Reynaria?"

"She's right here."

Keen felt a lifeless hand placed into his own. He squeezed it with his remaining strength. "Jati, what have I done?" A final burst of sobbing life broke through the wall of imminent death.

"Relax, old tot. I'm here." They smiled. "I'm always here."

"No more dreams, Jati?"

"No more dreams, old tot." Jati stroked his head. "You'll be at peace now."

Keen lifted his eyes skyward. In his dimming vision, soft lavender clouds from the waning storm parted. Nushaba's warm rays burst onto his face and thawed his growing chill. His nostrils caught the humid scent of hot air rising.

"Summer rain," he whispered.

"Yes, old tot. The storm is past."

"The smell of..."

"Shhh. Rest, Keen. You've done your work."

The light of Nushaba flickered. The clouds receded.

He wanted to say more, but his lips wouldn't move.

"Relax," Jati said. "Let go now."

Keen's vision narrowed. Heroon vanished.

Out of the darkness came splashing and laughter.

Clear water dappled white pebbles around his bare feet.

"Come on, Keen!" Reardon waved his lanky, adolescent arms from out in the water.

Keen looked back. Scarpa sat on the sand, supporting a toddling Reynaria who was just getting her walking legs. Scarpa laughed and looked at him. Her lips rose into a smile.

He smiled back.

"Come on, sibling!"

Scarpa encouraged him to go with a wave.

Behind Reardon, the Lorassian Sea went on forever. The fear its depths held in life was blown away on a fleeting breeze. Now the water sang of only freedom and forgiveness.

Reardon reached out his hand. "Trust me, little sibling."

THIRTY-FIVE

And so, I rest. Alone and unattended, at the end of our tale. On Heroon, justice is meted out. Lives are saved. An oppressed planet is renewed.

Light years away, my people are kept safe.

But while the future looks brighter for those who've suffered under hegemonic regimes in the Arm, Jati still had a long fight in front of them.

My cloistered life denies me access to outcomes. Perhaps my efforts were for nothing and greed squashed the promise of justice. Or, it could be that I pass silent hours on the last remaining outpost of an older, more unforgiving world. I've played out both conclusions in my long years alone in this cell.

Only one thing is certain.

Keen is gone.

But not forgotten.

Coming to terms with all that happened along the way during our time together is easier now. I've made friends with the dignity of humility. I'm still angry at him despite what transpired between us at the end. Leaving, as he did, without giving me the opportunity to take back things I said and did. But then again, I know it would sour the tragedy. Our tragedy. At least we have that. We built it together.

Keen made his choice and it worked. I hope he did it because it was the right thing to do, regardless of what was looming over him. I'd like to believe that. I need to believe it.

Can the gravity of sacrifice ever be weighed? Tainted by imminent demise, can such a selfless gesture still equal one performed by someone without the baggage of shortcomings and earlier wrongs? Does it even matter?

That was Keen. Complicated to a fault. His life's story an irreconcilable contradiction bogged down somewhere between right and wrong.

In the end, his wall crumbled. At least it gave him the strength to finally accept himself. If that was enough for him then that makes it enough for me. Everything else is a guessing game anyway. Leave it for the chroniclers after our time fades into story. For now, Keen deserves to rest where he fell. That's the finale he chose. Rather than drag him to the resolution, I'll leave him where he belongs. Laying still and I hope, content.

In the third act.

Just before the end.

As for me, I'm back home. Confined in a cave of my own making, I abide by the sparse accommodations of my prison cell without regret. An ostensible silence reigns, save for the occasional drip of moisture to remind me of the abundant world above. But I'm no fool. My sober ears hear the unjust wailing, the isolation of suffering that hums from these hallowed halls.

This is where I belong. Not only for my choices. As I said, I'm home. My blood runs blue, you remember. These rock walls are familiar. They speak my language. We've come to understand one another again, the sand and me. It took only a short time to get reacquainted. Like old friends, we reminisce with shared pride of hardship, endurance, and refusal to alter course. But eventually, the conversation between us goes silent. We both know the time of my people is over.

Nevermore did word from Urtani and the others emerge. They ran the River Hidden into oblivion. Five decades of idle silence reigns below my planet's surface.

But Kol 2's stoic walls embrace me with the assurance of our place in their legacy. Lost to a future of the living, our memories will live on embedded for the ages in their compacted geology. They'll hold us fast, bound by a weight of time beyond human measure. One thin layer of blue sand to stand for a life age of humanity.

And with that promise, I release my grip on survival. The aged skin on my fingers is tired. Red words, my lifeline, are stretched and blurred with wear and endless effort. With mercy, I let the letters dissolve knowing that when they go so goes my heart. That chipped, carved, and cut core of my soul has honored its kin beyond expectation.

There is no shame. I surrender with ease, the last to return to a world that will always be ours. A land of blue sand and endless dunes, of wind and currents that blow warm on hardened skin… one grain crashing with the final wave. In its wake, I come to rest and fall into the ground, joining the myriad of others who sink into history. Gushet, Hoti, Crest, my children…

The walls smile at my elegiac revelation, nodding approvingly. They know it's time. I may be the last, but I carry a wisdom gifted by all those who come before me.

The Tide ebbs and shifts. The final drawback approaches.

Arid words are all I have left.

My body will not be laid to rest or mourned by other eyes. I prefer it this way. To vanish, blown back into an ocean of dust. Let me pass quietly and unnoticed, one small ripple whispering the struggle of hard rock, dry sand, and grit.

ACKNOWLEDGMENTS

As an avid gardener, I can't help but think of a book's journey to publication like a growing season. You raise and care for a plant with the support of others until it yields crops at harvest time. Many people nurtured, trimmed, and pruned this book until it reached maturity and bore literary fruit. First and foremost, I want to thank my wife, Mallary, and my mother, Nancy. Both of you were there whenever I needed your eyes and ears, no matter the hour or mood, and helped me plant the seed that started this story. Much love and gratitude to you both.

Beta readers are the unsung heroes for a writer, reading half-baked versions of a manuscript and offering invaluable feedback. Thank you to Heath Mensher, Sharon and Vince Burke, Mark Milone, and Stephen Wood for your constructive comments. And to my critique partners, Lindsay and Michael Wells - fellow writers whose insights on world building and plot, and empathy for an author's fragile ego and love for their characters, improved my craft. You have my gratitude. Early editing by Jonathan Oliver and a subsequent sensitivity reading by Catarina Nabais turned a wobbly and imprecise first draft into a stable and more thoughtful manuscript.

I owe thanks to Susan Floyd, who pulled out the voice in my writing and gave strength to Razor and Keen. To Jessica Moon and Mandy Russell, founders and directors of Shadow Spark Publishing: your support for, and dedication to, authors who take risks and walk with one foot outside the literary boundaries of the expected, the ordinary, and the traditional is admirable. Thank you for seeing the series potential in the Wind Tide universe and for being the first to bring this manuscript to book form.

ABOUT THE AUTHOR

Jonathan Nevair is a science fiction writer and, as Dr. Jonathan Wallis, an art historian and Professor of Art History at Moore College of Art & Design, Philadelphia. After two decades of academic teaching and publishing, he finally got up the nerve to write fiction. Jonathan grew up on Long Island, NY but now resides in southeast Pennsylvania with his wife and rambunctious mountain feist, Cricket.

You can find him online at www.jonathannevair.com and on Twitter as @JNevair.

Lightning Source UK Ltd.
Milton Keynes UK
UKHW020611201022
410791UK00011B/520